Daughte

Daughters of Lac

Georgina Hutchison

This edition published 2014 by Belgarun
Typesetting by Gatecutter
Belgarun is an imprint of BGU Limited

BELGARUN
THE NEW FACE OF PUBLISHING

Belgarun, Huddersfield, England
www.belgarun.com
ISBN-13: 978-1-84846-001-0

Belgarun is a trademark of BGU Limited.

A Note for the Reader...

Before the Western reader dips into this story, it may be of benefit for me to clarify one or two cultural issues. In Vietnam, people are known by their family name, followed by a middle name, followed by a given name. The given name is mostly used. To illustrate, we may meet a Ho Van Danh. We would call him Danh. If we wished to be formal we would use some kind of prefix, equivalent to Mr Danh. His wife would retain her own family name, so would not adopt the name Ho on marriage, but would adopt a prefix equivalent to 'Mrs' and use this with her given name. I have striven for clarity and simplicity within the novel and a list of character names (including information on which characters actually exist in the historic record) appears at the back of the book.

I have selected the names of my fictitious characters from a list of names in current usage. However, some of the family names are authentically archaic and there are of course many historical characters within the novel whose names appear as recorded in various ancient sources. Both Han and Lac characters in the novel are predominantly referred to by the Vietnamese, rather than by the Chinese rendering of their names.

China and Vietnam are not referred to by these modern names throughout the story. China is mostly referred to as the 'Middle Kingdom' or the place of the Yellow River, and its people as the 'Han'. Vietnam is known in the novel by many names, as will become apparent, but for the period of history herein, modern-day northern and central Vietnam along with southernmost parts of China was known as the Giao Chi Circuit. Giao Chi Circuit contained nine commanderies, one of which was also called Giao Chi (centred around modern day Hanoi). Where I have used place names, for villages, towns, commanderies and provinces, these are based on historical information and so, just as iron-age names are no longer in common use in Britain, neither are these generally used in modern-day Vietnam. There are, however, occasions when I have used a modern-day place name, where the Trung-era equivalent is unknown (or inaccessible to me) - I have referred to Cat Ba Island, for example, even though the name 'Cat Ba' comes from a later legend. A list of placenames appears at the back of the book for easy reference.

To simplify life for most of my readers, and indeed for my printers, I have omitted all the accent marks that should accompany the Vietnamese words. To the reader of Quoc Ngu, these marks represent a complicated, tonal language, very different to English. It is to this latter group of readers that I must apologise, for being unable to render place names and character names precisely.

There were numerous occasions in the writing of this novel where I had to balance the knowledge of modern cultural norms in Vietnam with the imagining of the Trung period of history. Very little is known about early Vietnamese cultural identity, and centuries of Sinicization (the process of influence of China upon Vietnam) have obscured what may have been a very different cultural character than today's society would suggest. We know that the ancient Lac people had animistic spiritual beliefs, well-developed agricultural ability and locally-developed metal-work skills. They were not backward, undeveloped or wild, as compared to the Han, but sources suggest they may not necessarily have bothered with shoes or even clothes, and that they tattooed their skin and blackened their teeth. By the time of the Trungs, the region had been struggling to adapt under direct Han rule for over one hundred years, and Confucianism, Taoism, Legalism and Animism probably clashed and evolved in fascinating ways in this distant outpost of the empire. This is the nature of what I have tried to depict and I apologise for any errors in my understanding of the period of history herein. My thanks are due to Professor Keith Weller Taylor of Cornell

University who was able to answer many of my questions and who is entirely innocent of blame for my mistakes.

My aim in writing this novel was to bring a dramatic part of Vietnamese history to life for an English readership. The beauty and heritage of this incredibly bio-diverse sliver of South East Asia has been obscured for centuries by warfare and exploitation, not least the war of the twentieth century which entirely dominates the image most of us carry about this exotic land. Scrape the surface and a magical past emerges, where legend and reality blend together in majesty equal to any great civilisation. The Hung Kings, for example, are part-mythology, but the bronze drums of the corresponding Dong Son era, found by archaeologists to have spread throughout South East Asia, are a vivid reality that attest to the possible existence of an established, organised power base in northern Vietnam in the mists of prehistory. Vietnam's past is complicated and messy, the relationship with China both turbulent and symbiotic, but the spirit of national identity, patriotism and pride has always existed and the story of the Trung Sisters is central to this. Their legend has served as part of political ideology and national sentiment for centuries. As with 'Cartimandua', I hope this novel brings a more intimate and human dimension to Trung Trac and Trung Nhi, two women of monumental achievement and martial skill.

It remains only for me to thank my loyal readers, whose eager anticipation of, and questions about this novel have added to the pleasure of writing it.

Georgina Hutchison

November 2013

For Emma Barker
and all those who miss her

The greatness of the two women from Me Linh, and of all the brave people of the year 40, was in their realization that thousands of ancient customs and habits carried the soul of the nation; they thereupon arrived at a time when a question fraught with responsibility was placed before all the people and before history; was this life of the people, together with independence and freedom, worth defending with flesh and blood? People of the four directions, from the territories of the old Hung kings, seizing their weapons and standing up as one, answered - answered for themselves and for all later generations.

Pham Huy Thong, 1975
(Director of the Archaeological Institute in Hanoi)

★★★★★

You've no doubt heard of those who are good at holding on to life:
When walking through hills, they don't avoid rhinos and tigers;
When they go into battle, they don't put on armour or shields;
The rhino has no place to probe with its horn;
The tiger finds no place to put its claws
And weapons find no place to hold their blades.
Now, why is this so?
Because there is no place for death in them.

Lao-Tzu, Chapter 50 of Book One (Te) of the Way,
6th Century BCE

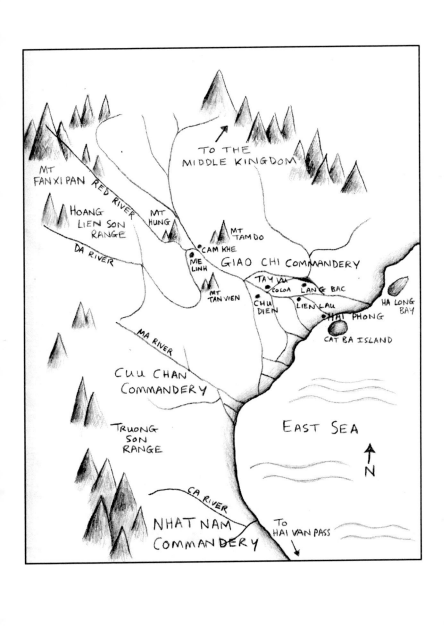

1

In war, as in all things, one must have discipline. When a wild cat stalks her prey, she controls every muscle of her body and even her eyes are unflinching. Even the frogs in the trees fear the poise of her shoulders, even the nuthatches up high dread the tread of her silent feet. Do the dowitchers, the gulls and the egrets ever preen on the mudflats past their season? No. When they feel the winter recede, they unfold rested wings and lift away, in tune with the world, yet soaring to the beat of their own hearts. Posture, control and rigour will free your bodies

★

How will it? We're fixed, like statues!

★

First comes stillness, then comes knowledge and only then comes movement. In stillness, great leaders dream the victories of tomorrow. In knowledge, they prepare to conquer and finally in movement, they draw blood. These are the lessons you must learn. Listen while you train and I will tell you of all the great rulers of Giao Chi

★

Giao Chi is ruled by the Middle Kingdom. Was it not always so?

★

Our land has not always been Giao Chi. Once, Giao Chi was Nam Viet and before that it was Van Lang and before that, in the most ancient of times, it was Xich Quy - the land of the red devils. Xich Quy was the name that covered the northern mountains well beyond the Passes. It was the name that covered the Red River delta and all the land down to the Ca River. The Middle Kingdom clan was not so strong then - they clustered in the far north, around their Yellow River while Xich Quy was strong and proud in the south.

★

People lived in our beautiful lands for many countless hundreds of generations, hunting, fishing and living well amidst the tropical bounty of the great, green forests, wide rivers, high mountains and east sea, until Xich Quy became Van Lang. In the Middle Kingdom, emperors began to rule and one of these was the great Than Nong, who now watches over the crops from his heavenly palace. Than Nong was the great-grandfather to King De Minh, who ruled Van Lang with his wife, an immortal creature he had met and married whilst traversing the high mountains. King De Minh's wife carried in her soul the spirit of the ancient ancestors and she bore a son. This son was Loc Duc, who became Duong Vuong, changing his name as our great leaders do when they assume the highest position. Duong Vuong was a giant of a man, filled with mortal ambition and pride and imbued with the unnatural longings that sprang from his immortal heritage. He took the fiercest lady he could find for his wife - Than Long Nu, the much feared and skilled daughter of the Dragon Lord of the Sea. And so the son of a mountain immortal had married the daughter of a sea dragon. The Middle Kingdom were afraid of this great alliance and of the power now spawning in the south

★

Duong Vuong and Long Nu lived passionately and violently, cleaving their growing country into a place to be reckoned with. After only a short time, their volatile love brought forth a precious son. This son was Dragon Lord Lac Long Quan. Lac Long Quan was a golden child, strong and shining and full of vitality. As he grew, he tempered his father's heavy tread and eased his mother's fiery rhetoric and, under his guidance, Van Lang became a place of stability and strength. People were always well fed - they had learned all the skills of wet rice-growing whilst the Middle Kingdom still relied upon yellow millet. But a happy, strong state is often considered dangerous to equally powerful neighbours, and while the people to the west presented little threat to Van Lang, the people of the Middle Kingdom in the north were increasingly uneasy and covetous. They wanted the rich produce of the Red River people for themselves. The Emperor of the Middle Kingdom suggested his own daughter as a match for the great Dragon Lord, and broke apart her existing marriage. The Emperor's daughter was Au Co, an immortal fairy queen who carried the blood of the Middle Kingdom but also a thread of life more ancient. Like King De Minh's mountain wife, Au Co had the spirit of the high places in her bones and she carried a potent

2

magical ability

★

When Au Co arrived in Van Lang, a great black spirit bird saw her power and swooped down in anger on this new arrival. Au Co shimmered into a beautiful white bird and attempted to lift free of her predator, but the black bird gripped her tightly in its claws. Lac Long Quan, who had been riding out to meet his new queen, saw the birds locked in violent struggle on the grassy plain and searched on the ground for a sharp stone. When he found one that would fit in his palm, he lifted it and took aim, sending the blunt weapon direct to the breast of the large black-winged spectre. The black bird fell down, its wings folding in a heartbeat. The white bird fluttered free and towards him, hovering in mid air, where it shook out the snow-white feathers and transformed into the pale-skinned, black-haired Au Co. Lac Long Quan fell in love immediately and was therefore most relieved to find that this strange girl was his intended

★

Au Co and Lac Long Quan were wonderfully happy with each other and he eagerly showed her the sights of Van Lang, which she admired. Yet she never quite felt fulfilled. She wanted to live nearer the mountains, he by the sea, and though they settled halfway in between, it was not enough for either of them. For many years they lived well enough. Au Co gave birth to a pouch of one hundred eggs and the pair nurtured these fine young infants into strong children who were loyal and intelligent. When the girls and boys came of independent age, Au Co and Lac Long Quan decided they would part and return to the places their hearts longed for. They embraced and wept, for they did truly love, but then they turned away from each other without regret. Half of the children followed their mother, excited to be travelling to the mountains. The other half flocked towards the sea with their father - all except one. When this young man stood apart, both parents looked back and named him Hung Vuong, the first of the Hung Kings to rule Van Lang. His brothers and sisters, the other children of Lac Long Quan and Au Co, would keep loyal and bow down to him, governing all things in his name

★

Were they Lac Lords, like father was?

★

Oh, mother, will I be one when I grow up?

★

They were the very first of the Lac Lords. But you, my girls, will be something different. Your path is lit by the eye of the jade tiger. The day will come when you will bow to no one

2 Nhi

Everything glows very bright and clear today. The grass is blooming vermilion and the sharp mountain ridges grin against a white glass sky. I can hear someone calling to me, a faint howl through many people, blocked by clamour, but friend or foe I can't tell. I'm staggering along, just making for the trees. The field abuts the forest, low and broad-leaved with a welcoming shade. I think I could make it, if only I were strong enough. This burden I carry is so heavy but I can't put it down.

I'm in the throng. Around me, swords flash and short daggers whip. There are sticks and shovels too, axes and clubs, splitting air and head with indifference. It seems incredible to me that I am making progress – surely the Han soldiers know who I am? I expect at any moment to be seized and ripped by my hair, back across the plain towards Ma Vien, for my wrists and ankles to be bound, for my head to be neatly removed from my shoulders. I'm not scared. I'm too tired to be scared. I just keep on moving, towards the rhododendrons and the last of their white blossom, spattered with scarlet tears. If Mother was here she would say that being tired is no excuse. But Mother is at the front. Now I must be like Mother, though I am the youngest daughter.

There is a head in the way. I nearly trip over it as my upper body drags my unwilling feet along. The surprised eyes stare at me from the ground, as if I've committed some offence against etiquette, the eyebrows raised at my impropriety. A warrior shoves past me and for a moment I imagine a headless woman, searching for her missing piece, until the warrior shouts and pinches my arm hard. Go that way, screams the face that does exist after all, the cheeks and forehead covered in sweat and dirt, the hair black and tangled. She is pointing me towards a cluster of Trac's rearguard, who have pushed the enemy back on the south end of the field and who are hastening my escape along that route. It will be further to the trees, but I have more chance of reaching them in that direction. I arch my encumbered back and stumble on, my spine slick with sweat and blood. Around my neck, the carved jade tiger swings relentlessly, padding against my chest in time with my steps. I must look just like the warrior who pinched me - dirty, straggly; more animal than woman, though I was always the prettiest one, with a round face and almond eyes quite wide apart. My lips are plumper than Trac's. She has a small mouth, slimmer eyes, more like our mother. When I was very young, I used to infuriate her by saying that she had the Man looks of our maternal ancestors, whilst I had the fairy eyes and the dragon lips of the ancient Lac.

My pace has quickened. It helps to get lost inside my own thoughts, though it carries a risk, on the battlefield. Mother always said, it's what you think that counts. What you do flows from what you believe. If you are cold, she said, you must imagine the heat of the summer sun on your skin. If you are too warm, think of the mountain dew and the breeze of winter drawing near. I'm hurting now, so I'll think about being fit and strong. I'll imagine my skin as it once was before all these random cuts were made by Han blades. I can summon a vision of my long dark hair, brushed straight and black with a tortoiseshell comb and left loose over my shoulders, before the days when I tied it in a wrap. I can skip, golden-limbed, to a time of strength when my breath was even and calm. There. The trees don't look so far away now. Even the shouts around me are merely the cries of water birds and monkeys. A lifetime of training has paid off. My four-year-old self would laugh in delight. I never did see the point when I was young.

★★★★★

It was hard for me to appreciate what Mother expected of us, because I had no gentle introduction to life like Trac did. I entered their lives when Trac was five, and my squalling baby years are a mystery to me. My first memory is of Mother, cradling me close and whispering things to me, late at night when I couldn't sleep. I would wake up drenched in sweat and crying, though I couldn't say why and Mother would soothe me until I drifted back into sweeter dreams. Father was concerned. I have precious few clear memories of him, but I do recall him asking me about my dreams and whether there were animals in them, or anything else notable that I could report. I would shake my head in silence. Father thought I was plagued by a bad spirit or that a spirit was sending a message that something was left undone, but if it was indeed a message then the spirits should really have made it clearer. I never knew what had woken me up and Father was left disturbed and unsatisfied. He was a stout man, with hair that laid very straight down his back when he released his bun, and eyes that were large and framed with eyebrows that were thick on the upturn and sharpened to a fine point on their shallow descent towards his ears. At mealtimes, he would pass me bones to gnaw on, laughing at the way I nibbled shreds from pork ribs, or he would hold my small bowl of soup for me, so I wouldn't spill while I drank the sour broth. He liked to cuddle me but sometimes he would be very serious and liked to sit still to think.

I was three when he died. Trac was eight but may as well have been Mother's age, she seemed so old and wise to me. She went everywhere with a serious expression on her face, even more so when Father was returned home from the Red River on a stretcher. He had caught a fever whilst inspecting the canals and coordinating the dyke-work for the coming season with the Prefects of the other districts within the Commandery. General Lac, as he was known, controlled all of Me Linh, just as the other Lac Lords controlled their own pockets of the Red River Delta. He sang from up high and the lesser men danced to his tune. Way up on the canopy were the Han administrators to whom all the graceful Lac Lords answered and the chirruping masses bowed.

With his death, our household changed. Trac had always

done some martial arts training, but never so prescribed and mandatory as Mother then insisted. You must remember, I was only three and the memories I had accumulated by that age were ephemeral and disjointed, so the structure of my childhood was built after Father's death. I was thrust into daily instruction by Mother, in all things she considered important. Trac had enjoyed eight years of peaceful family life, whereas I had only just emerged from my baby time. At first, I was excited by our new routine. Mother purchased small training weapons, to add to her own collection of fighting implements and she arranged these along the wall of the main living space in our huge wooden, stilted home in Cam Khe. We were allowed to handle the training weapons, but not those with sharp edges. I remember being four, playing in the dirt outside, poking a stick in the wet ground and hearing her voice cry out, 'Trac, Nhi, come inside now,' Trac hurrying past me, head down as usual. I dropped my stick and followed. My hands were muddy and Mother shook her head and pointed to the bowl of water that the servant girl had left on the floor. I rinsed my palms and dried them down the front of my deep blue *ao tu than*. Then I lined up with Trac, facing Mother.

'Good girls,' she said, 'Now, first position.'

That always meant the start of a long training session. In my infantile illusions, whole days passed frozen in those forms, but to be fair to Mother, it was usually perhaps an hour or two. I screwed up my face and held the pose, wobbling on my bony legs and biting my fat bottom lip in bored determination. I preferred to be outside, to run wild as Mother would say. On a morning, I would pull on a rough skirt, fasten my *ao yem*, the square of material that covered my undeveloped chest and tied with string across my back, and throw on my outer dress, the hemp edges frayed and dirty with dust from the previous day, and hurtle down the wooden steps at the front of the house, out onto the plain. Bao would be over by his house, chasing chickens around or feeding their exceedingly ugly old pig and I would run across the grass, waving, with my tunic-style dress lifted to my knees and my sash still clutched in a hand, waiting to be tied at my waist, around my *ao tu than*.

Bao was older than me, but not as old as Trac. We played together, first outside our houses and then venturing further as Mother became more resigned to my independence of spirit. Bao had a long face, with thin eyes that disappeared into long-lashed creases when the sun shone brightly. His mouth was always open in a smile, fighting against the melancholic shape of his face. He wore plain hemp tunics more ragged than mine and his fingernails were rammed with muck, the result of all the chores he performed for his plump little mother who ran this way and that, from market to home and back again. They were a busy family, with a grandmother and grandfather living in the back of the house, but Bao's own father was rarely seen. He travelled all the time, fishing and hunting and searching out goods to sell. Bao never seemed to mind and treated his father's occasional short returns as celebratory incidents in a generally pleasant life. It was comforting to have such happy neighbours, especially when my own household was so sombre. I would shout, 'Hello Auntie Chau,' as I ran across and Bao's mother would pause in the midst of her frenetic activities, squint and grin before raising her arm and shouting back, 'Hello little Nhi.'

When Bao and I felt like having an adventure, we would set off walking, past the cluster of stilt houses and along the worn track, down towards the river. At the start, we always went that way, never towards the hills and karst outcrops. The water drew us, with its whispered promise of life and refreshment, of cool wet feet and maybe a fish if we were lucky. Bao always carried his net, sometimes strung on a stick, sometimes rolled up and carried in a fold of his tunic. We would walk down to the bank of the Red River, find the place we liked best and then sit on the flat grassy knoll that allowed us to dip our feet and swing the net into a shallow overflow from the river's main artery. As I got older, my preferred trick was to wade along the edge, upstream of Bao and then venture out just a little into the fast flow, where I would raise up stones and send the hiding fish streaming down towards his nets. It sometimes worked, but we only caught tiddlers, which would make Mrs Chau laugh when he proudly presented them. In the rainy seasons I couldn't do this of course – the river became a thrashing, twisting serpent, lashing through the valley and rising out on the plain at either side of its normal course, leaving no safe, shallow threads. At those times we stayed well back from the waters. The broad plain of the lower reaches of the Red River was no place for children to take chances in the rainy season, when the water could surge, flooding out over the surrounding land. The canals and dykes controlled it to some extent, and our own home was relatively safe from the threat, but houses closer to the river frequently flooded, their floors awash with silt, babies bundled into cribs on top of tables while parents and siblings got on with daily work.

We didn't have to worry about such minor crises – Father's irrigation and canal system kept the backwash well away from us, a lasting legacy of protection after he had died. Mother was as famous as General Lac had been in our area. She came from a grand family herself and was known as a good lady, who ruled the local populace with a strong and benevolent hand in Father's absence. Mrs Chau called round every week or so, depositing herself in the living area and enjoying a half-cup of rice wine with Mother whilst they gossiped about neighbours, miscreants, traders, the Middle Kingdom people and whatever else had occurred of interest. Mrs Chau was Mother's informant on the world beneath her and the knowledge she imparted allowed Mother to strut like an all-knowing pheasant through the streets of Me Linh and to dispense her profound knowledge and judgements with confidence. Bao and I sat on the steps on one occasion, covertly listening to them discuss rhinoceros horn values.

'Tell me, Chau, why have these values risen so?'

'They want so much! These Yellow River traders and bureaucrats alike are always asking, have you rhinoceros horn? And I tell them that there is just so little available and that we could procure it but it will cost us to transport it from the southern jungles. And they say, what price? And I tell them and they agree.'

'They don't haggle?'

'Sometimes, Thien, but they don't like to. Haggling with us would mean they were *trading* properly with us and they don't like to think of it like that.'

'All these many years, Chau, and they cannot get used to dealing with women.'

'It's to our benefit. We get better prices this way. Especially with rhinoceros horn. They don't like it that we know why they want it.'

'Why do they want it?' I whispered to Bao, out on the steps and he sniggered and leaned close to me to answer. Then he jumped up very suddenly and went running down the steps and out towards the paddies. Inside the house, Mother turned and saw me and flapped an angry hand to send me away. I got up too and chased after Bao. He finally stopped, breathless and panting at the edge of the rough grass, where the ground dropped slightly and became boggy. We were well away from our houses. Neither of us spoke, busy retrieving our breath instead. When I could talk, I said, 'What's a man's thingy?' That's what he'd called it. The powdered horn, he said, made a man's thingy big and hard.

Bao just smiled, infuriatingly, and pointed at the area of his crotch, hidden behind his flat, hemp tunic.

'Is it different from what a woman has?'

'Yes,' he laughed, then in a more serious tone, 'I can show you if you like.'

'All right.' I put my hands on my little hips and watched

11

derisively as he raised up his tunic and revealed the fat silk worm that hung between his legs.

'Now you have to show me your thingy,' he said, tucking his penis away matter-of-factly.

'I don't have one,' I answered.

'Yes you do. Show me.'

I shrugged and lifted up my own tunic. 'See?'

Bao knelt down on the floor and looked. Then he stood back up and I dropped my tunic into place. We looked out towards the rice paddies, where tiny bent figures and bobbing heads planted seedling after seedling. The sun lit the wet land into a mirror, and the hills beyond a blinding, garish green. I pulled at the long grasses that grew all around us. I had questions I wanted to ask Bao - I still didn't really understand about the rhinoceros horn medicine - but there was something peculiar and vulnerable about the little thing that dangled between his soft, pale legs and it made me feel queasy, so I kept quiet.

'Let's walk that way,' said Bao, pointing beyond the bobbing rice-planters towards the low range of sparkling jade hills.

'It's a bit far,' I said, covering my eyes, but he laughed and said, 'I'll look after you.'

We walked for many miles that day, just as we did in days to come. With Bao I learned all about the villages dotted around Me Linh. I saw the huge stretches of rice paddies, washed with rich alluvial waters from the Red River and I learned about how the waters were directed, manipulated by dykes and canals that men like Father had built. I watched the rice grow, saw the stalks turn yellow, learned how the fields were then drained and the sheaves gathered in by sickle. When it was threshing time, we joined in, stamping the grains loose. Up beyond the villages, where the little peaks glowed, our district of influence ended and we dared not go further. You'd think Mother would have been worried, but she passed a blind eye over most of my activities, only becoming irritated when I was out for whole days and missed my training with her. Trac was angry then too, hissing in my ear that I was lazy and selfish and would never learn anything if I roamed the countryside all day long. Her eyes got all mean and tight when she spoke to me that way and I guessed she was annoyed that she'd had to endure endless training forms, moving and balancing her body to Mother's command, whilst I was out having fun. I asked her why she didn't just come along with Bao and I.

'Why would I want to come out with you children?'

'Bao's nearly as old as you,' I said, 'and you'd see all the lovely things – the river and the paddies. We could go fishing. I'll show you where the spoonbills wade.'

'I do not have time for playing. I am too busy helping our mother,' she said, her mouth a tight, closed flower bud. Eventually I caught her in a rare moment of weakness and prised her petals apart a little, just enough to make her come along for that first walk together. After that, she deigned to accompany us more regularly, though usually under the guise of needing to watch over me. Some of my favourite memories of my early years are of Trac, Bao and I, out together walking, shoving each other with the light menace of youth, three children framed in a backdrop of iridescent, emerald fields, the shining river at our feet.

3 TRAC

Nhi persisted and she wore me down. That is Nhi's way - to continue on at length until an opponent succumbs. She has boundless energy and as a child she was a challenge to both my mother and I. The first time I bowed to pressure and went walking with her and Bao, I did so under sufferance, with an attitude of forced benevolence, if there is such a thing. I told her I had no desire to go out, getting dirty and wet, playing their silly games and I quite believed myself. Bao smiled his silly, constant, slitted-eye smile which I ignored and Nhi pranced about like a laughing-thrush, hopping in my way and giggling over nonsense. I allowed them to show me their favourite places and we walked a winding route down to the river where Nhi assured me I would be absolutely thrilled with their fish-catching escapades. I was dubious but settled myself down to watch while Nhi cast her outer dress off onto a rock and went dancing upstream and Bao set up his net level with my viewing position. I watched as Nhi waded through the rushing waters and I admit to a nervousness that she would lose her footing and be swept under, bashing her head on a stone as she went. Then she began expertly lifting great stones and splashing her little legs about, the wet tail-ends of her black hair slicking against dewy shoulders. All of a sudden she cried out, 'Here's one Bao,' and despite myself, I stood up and pointed, calling to Bao, who hovered in the water with his net.

'Bao! It's there, look.' The fish scuppered in a zigzag pattern, coming downstream towards us and Nhi clapped her hands together with great glee, looking at me rather than towards the fish. I sat down immediately, somewhat embarrassed, but when Bao lifted the net and showed a silvery, squirming body inside, I smiled and clapped my hands also.

'You see,' she said, on the way back home, 'you had fun, didn't you?'

'Yes, Nhi, I had fun,' I agreed and she clasped both her thin arms around me. It was perhaps the first time I had been unreservedly glad for her presence. I admit, I was not always the bigger sister she deserved.

When Nhi was born, I was five years old - old enough to watch the growing bump on my mother's front with trepidation. I asked her why her tummy was so fat and she reminded me of the baby growing in there.

'But how will it come out?' I worried, 'You won't die will you?' I could only imagine that the baby inside would grow larger and larger until it burst right out of her.

'No, I won't die. It will slip out easily, like a little fish.'

'But it won't be a little fish, though?'

'No, it will be a little person, just like you. Only smaller. A friend for you.'

I could see the logic of having a playmate nearer my own age. In my dreams, I expected another little girl, who would emerge as fully formed as myself, only a little bit smaller, ready to play with pebbles and stir uncooked rice in play-pots and serve imaginary food to my lumpishly-sewn jute bear. Maybe when this little girl arrived, our father would finally let us have a monkey to look after. I had begged for a long time now and he refused, saying I was not old enough to care for a monkey properly and the servants would end up looking after it, but with two little girls to take care of it, surely the monkey was now a possibility? So I waited happily for the new child to arrive and I watched as the bump grew bigger than I thought was possible. My father gave me a baby doll, carved from golden cypress wood and just the right size to fit in the crook of my arm. She was a bulbous little thing, with a round tummy and grooved hints of fat arms and legs curled against herself. She had carved, sleeping half-moon eyelids and a circular, sucking mouth. I wrapped her in an old piece of cloth and carried her with me, laying her to sleep beside me on a night and telling her all about the real little

15

girl who would soon be joining us.

What a disappointment it was. What emerged from the bump I had so eagerly and nervously watched was not the little girl I had expected, but a scowling mass of stinking wetness. My mother had birthed her with relative ease, though I only understood this later, and brought her to me in the evening, balled up in a cotton wrap.

'This is Nhi, your new sister,' she said, handing her to me to hold and I awkwardly took charge of the bundle and tried to settle it on my small lap. Nhi stared though misted black eyes and began to howl, sucking her cheeks in as she bellowed, and looking nothing at all like my placid, content cypress baby.

'Don't cry,' I instructed, 'we can play together if you keep quiet,' but she went on screaming and my mother reached down to take her back.

'She needs to feed. They want milk all the time when they are newborn. You were the same,' and she sat down and pulled aside her crossed-over dress, latching the tiny, struggling Nhi onto her breast. The awful screaming sound stopped and my father leaned over with a bowl to give my mother a drink while she used both hands to settle and adjust the baby.

'Women get very thirsty when they feed babies,' he told me as I watched my mother gulp the drink and then relax, stroking Nhi's hairy yellow scalp and fat, gobbling cheek.

'She can't play with me, she's too small.'

'She'll grow,' said my father, who had perhaps noticed that I was close to tears, because he came and put an arm round me. 'Here, baby doll wants a cuddle.' He picked up the cypress baby from the floor beside me and nestled her against me.

In the weeks after Nhi was born, my father stayed home, looking after my mother and me while she cared for the baby. We were a rich family. He was a Lac Lord, which made him a noble of Giao Chi, and one of the third generation of Lacs to be harnessed through many layers of bureaucracy to the Han

Emperor. Everyone called him by his title of General Lac, except for my mother, who called him Lanh. My mother was Lady Man Thien and came from a noble family on the northern fringes of the Giao Chi Commandery. The servants we had were quiet Me Linh women, who walked to our home when they were needed, tending the chickens, preparing food or cleaning as required. Like most others, we had a wooden house, erected on stilts, but ours was much larger, having extra room at the back and being decorated with unusual furniture and ornaments. Against the wall in the living area was the lacquered cabinet which my mother adored. Her family had purchased it from a trader in the Hop Pho Commandery, many years before, when Giao Chi was part of Nam Viet and ruled by the Trieus. It was shiny black with strutting peacocks adorning the doors and the edges were inlaid with mother-of-pearl. Inside, she kept aloes-wood for burning in the incense dish, and bottles of medicines acquired from the markets at Lien Lau, deep within the plain where the waters of the Red River - the *Hong Song* - branched out like a hand. There were off-cuts of silk and cotton in the cabinet, a dish of broken treasures - a glass bead necklace come apart, a figurine with one arm missing - and our mother's finest bowls. Fingerprints on the lacquer were an abomination, wiped away daily by my mother with a small piece of silk and an accusing eye. Even though she told me not to, I couldn't help but run my small fingers over the reflective surface, following the mother-of-pearl with my fingertips then shearing away across the blackness to the statuesque peacocks.

It was not the only beautiful piece of furniture. A large piece of polished jade sat on a low table under the window and a raised bamboo frame near the heat of the stove provided a day bed for guests to sit on, as well as being the place where Mother and Father normally slept. I had an area at the back of the house for sleeping in, with a *kang* - a raised bed of clay bricks that the servants heated with fire in cold weather. I had a bamboo table too, where my folded clothes and my comb sat, the latter waiting for my mother to routinely snatch it up and drag it through my long, thick hair. There was a second room at the back, next to mine, with another *kang*.

Now, my parents' bamboo bed in the living area was shared with Nhi, sprawling and screaming and waking all through the night. I laid in my bed clutching onto cypress baby and wondering if it was possible to give Nhi back. But back to whom? She could not go back in my mother, I was certain of that, but where had she come from before she was in my mother's tummy? Perhaps she could go back there, wherever it was, since she did not seem to want to be with us any more than I wanted her. I suggested as much to my father but he was quite stern, refused to answer my questions about where exactly Nhi had come from and gave me a lecture about loving one's family. I had been small and noisy once also, he told me, but that time passed, as it would with Nhi, and in any case, she was my sister and I should be a good and honourable big sister and love her. I cried again and, soft-hearted man that he was, he hugged me and spent some time playing with me, feeding cypress baby from a dish filled with mud and grass and helping me to clean her afterwards. You could do this for Nhi, he said. You could wash and clean her and that would be a help to your mother. I agreed and later on, when Nhi had more strength in her neck and head I was allowed to bathe her, lifting her firmly with both my hands into a big cooking pot of warmed water and rubbing around all the crevices where milk and filth collected. She had learned not to cry so much, and even gurgled when I did this, with a dimpled little smile half-formed on those lips that already looked much plumper than mine. She liked to hold my finger, which made it difficult to wash her properly and I would say with much authority, 'Let go Nhi, big sister needs to wash you,' and she would gurgle even more, blowing spit bubbles as I tutted and shook my head. Then I would lift her out onto a woven blanket spread on the floor and rub her fat little body dry, taking care to get into the creases, just as my mother had taught me.

I helped more in the home after Nhi arrived - it was not just a question of necessity, with my mother so often stopping what she was doing in order to feed Nhi, but an issue of carving out a new role for myself. I was no longer treasured baby daughter. I had become first daughter, eldest child, and with that position came the responsibility of easing the burdens of my mother and father. I became the one to instruct the servants in their tasks for the day. If mother was stirring sticky rice in a cooking pot for Nhi and had to rush away to wash Nhi's dirty bottom, I would take the spoon and keep stirring, dishing up the squishy meal with soft flakes of fish ready for when Nhi was cleaned up. If my father came home and my mother had not already done so, I would pour out a cup of rice wine for him and take his sandals away and bring a bowl of hot water to soak his aching feet. I shook the bed blankets outside daily to air them and I even took over polishing the lacquered cabinet, which the servants were not allowed to touch. If visitors came to the house, I would receive them with my mother's manners, even if it was only Mrs Chau, our closest neighbour, with her chubby little toddler, Bao. It was his fingerprints that I often had to wipe off our precious cabinet and I smacked his hands more than once when he went to touch it.

My mother and Mrs Chau would sit and chat while Nhi rolled about on the floor and Bao sat sucking on a piece of sugar-cane. I preferred to sit in the corner, not one of the children any more. If Nhi needed cleaning or settling to sleep, I would quietly take charge and leave my mother speaking with Mrs Chau or whoever was visiting while I looked after Nhi. I was not quite six years old.

By the time Nhi pulled herself to standing and began to take tentative steps, landing in a troubled heap on her bottom, I had become first daughter in truth and what is more, I was comfortable as well as competent in my role. It would have happened without Nhi's arrival, I am sure. It is just the kind of person I am. Cypress baby sat in the corner of my room, more ornament than toy, now that I was so busy in the daytime. Nhi needed more looking after than ever, now she was capable of moving about and getting into difficulty. I had to spend a lot of time holding her chubby palms as she learned to walk and finding things to entertain her with. Now that she wanted to play with me, I found I had almost forgotten how to do that. I got out pans of grain for her to stir with the big spoon and I gave her a corner of cloth so she could copy me when I cleaned. As she got older, I brought baby doll out for her, which earned me approval from both parents, who had wondered if I could share that most loved possession. I did enjoy playing with Nhi and reminded myself that this was what I had wanted a baby sister for. Yet I no longer possessed that gleeful spontaneity of early childhood and, though I could not have expressed it at the time, I was mournful, as if Nhi and I had missed out on something. We should have been twins.

Yet I cannot complain of those years, because that was the time when I had my father. All that came after was laced with grief at his departure, even now, when there is so much else to grieve for. When he was brought home ill, we were kept away out of fear we would catch the fever but when it became apparent that he would not survive, we saw him once. He was much diminished and we understood that we were to say goodbye. Nhi stood sobbing, holding my hand. Three days later he was buried, dressed in his ceremonial tunic with pieces of jade and haematite placed around him.

★★★★★

I dislike thinking too long upon my childhood because it always comes to that – his sudden, gaping death. I suspect tomorrow will be a day I cannot think long upon either, if I live to remember it. Nhi is sitting across from me, black hair streaming round her shoulders in the firelight as she talks to several of the generals. I have perhaps been staring at the women whilst lost in my thoughts because they are looking back at me oddly. I stand up and walk purposefully a few steps away, with my hands held behind my back and they continue their discussion.

Tomorrow I will face Ma Vien again. We have fought once before at Lang Bac and have fallen back here, to Me Linh, where we've spent a restless few moons, waiting for this next and final battle. Emperor Guang Wu is determined to bring us under direct rule once more and has taken back most of the northern Commanderies. I have seen their army, have already fought them and will do so again tomorrow, but I fear it will not be enough. I can see all the firelight dotted on the plain where my army camps. Singing voices rise occasionally and the crackle of roasting wood sends shimmering red embers into the air. Far away in the night, the cacophony of the forest hums and drifts over the delta. All those animals and birds, moving in their night ways – the civets prowling and the barbets and fairy bluebirds roosting and the pit-vipers sliding through the under-storey.

Nhi is laughing and I move so I can see the profile of her face, beautiful and round just as it was when she was a child. At twenty years of age, she is fearless and proud and she wears an *ao tu than* of golden, growling, embroidered tigers. I wish her life could have been simpler, with all the charm that those early years of fishing and rambling with Bao promised, but life is not a choice, it is a path and this is ours. I tell myself this as I look out at my sister, the baby my mother and I raised, who will fight tomorrow for the freedom of our country.

4 TRAC

After my father died, my mother became very withdrawn. Since Nhi and I were still very young, our mother's brother and his wife came to stay for a while, taking care of the house and of us. Uncle Hien was older than my mother and lived on higher ground to the north in the ancient homestead of their family. He and Linh had three children themselves but they were practically adults and could be left alone to watch over the rice terraces while their parents came to care for us. Auntie Linh was a good woman – quiet and respectful but with a sense of humour that flashed now and then and took us by surprise. Uncle Hien was altogether more serious, pacing about with a slow, exaggerated kind of wariness as if he might accidentally act improperly. He kept his long hair fastened back into a neat little bun and his eyebrows arched and flicked out at the sides over his narrow eyes. He demonstrated a deep respect for my mother, bowing his head low whenever she walked past and refusing to finish any of his own meals whilst she was deep in mourning.

Auntie Linh was different, continuing quietly with life and giving the occasional gentle prods that would eventually displace my mother from her lethargy. She kept Mrs Chau at bay too, rearing up in the doorway when our neighbour came up the steps and subtly manoeuvring her back onto the grass, talking all the while about how Thien needed rest. Auntie Linh knew that if Mrs Chau were to see my mother, she would doubtless chat about her afflicted state to all and sundry. We did not want that. Lady Man Thien had a reputation to uphold, both within her own kind and also with the Middle Kingdom administrators in the big town of Lien Lau. Better that Mrs Chau be sent home with the simple news that Thien was still resting and dealing with her blow.

I watched all these things and understood, roughly, what was going on, but Nhi was clueless. She cried and had tantrums, wailing for her mother and sometimes even railing at her, accusing her of not caring about any of us. She screamed at our mother for having let our father go out and catch a fever, for not being able to make him better, for not being able to bring him back or tell us where he had gone. When she had these outbursts, I folded myself into a corner with my head in my arms. I hated her for distressing us all but I loved her such that her pain increased mine tenfold. Auntie Linh was the one who had to calm Nhi down and she did it well enough, having had three children of her own to raise. She took Nhi outside, away from Uncle Hien and my mother and me. Then later the pair would return, Nhi with red-rimmed eyes, curled up against Auntie Linh who carried my exhausted three-year-old sister.

Auntie Linh and I never spoke about my father. Our exchanges were about household matters and she praised me highly for my help. Uncle Hien was also pleased with me. He had a fondness for philosophy and had taken it upon himself to discuss with me the rather abstract notions he had distilled from the Confucian and Taoist teachings of our Han overlords.

'Confucius said, be what you are, name yourself correctly. What are you?'

'I am a daughter,' I answered, after some thought, 'and a sister.'

'Yes, yes, so be a daughter and a sister and be those things well. When everyone fills their given role, everything is clear and the world works better.'

'But Uncle,' I asked, 'who gives the other roles? We are all sisters, brothers and so on, but who decides who becomes a king or a governor or an emperor?'

'Ah, splendid! And I give this answer - Lao-Tzu said, if you're tranquil, you can become ruler of the world. Now, what do you think that means?'

'I do not know, Uncle,' I said. 'Does it mean that kind people are rewarded?'

'Perhaps, Trac. Or maybe it means that from stillness comes

knowledge, that from being quiet and observing we learn how to take power. Or could it mean that from non-action comes action, as naturally as from dark rises the sun?'

He lost me often, but I concentrated on his questions when I could not sleep at night and I rolled his words around my head to block out grief and sadness. Maybe my mother did the same, because she would often sit silently nearby while we talked. Once I left the pair of them whilst I went outside for something and when I returned they were sat in an embrace, Uncle stroking her hair. I had never seen him touch anyone, not even Auntie Linh, he was ordinarily so contained, but I wept to see him comforting my mother and I wished I had tried to hold her more. Nhi had embraced her often, attaching violent little clutches to her legs as our mother tried to walk by or extracting midnight cuddles when she had awoken from her regular night terrors and slipped into our mother's half-empty bed from the *kang* which she usually shared with me, yet I had held back. I thought if I touched her, I might unleash a flood of anguish.

There came at last a day when my mother arose and dressed in good time. She made food before we awoke and she greeted myself and Nhi properly when we emerged from the back of the house. Nhi giggled and ran full force into her stomach. I smiled and we sat down to eat. Within seven days she sent Uncle Hien and Auntie Linh home. They left gratefully – no one can stomach adopted misery for too long and they were eager to get back to their own offspring and lives. Even so, Auntie Linh had watery eyes as she bade us farewell and she promised to come and visit soon. Uncle Hien asked me to consider our conversations carefully and told me I should seek further insight from my mother, who was equally well educated in philosophical thought. They were relieved that my mother's malady had receded, undoubtedly leaving grief in its wake, but allowing her now to function as was proper. We waved them off in relative happiness.

It was eerily quiet with them gone. I had grown quite used to Auntie Linh tapping and stirring at the stove and Uncle Hien's low-pitched, off-key voice. We sat about oddly, the three of us working out how to be around each other in this new era. That was when Nhi started to spend a lot more time outside. She would burst cheerily out onto the front steps, holding onto the wooden rail for support since she was not yet four years old, and set herself down to play in the dirt and grass, waving and laughing at passing neighbours and servants. I would sit with our mother, sometimes in silence and sometimes talking, in and amongst the daily chores - there was, after all, still a household to run.

'Trac, I would like you and your sister to work more on your movement and defence skills,' she said one day, while we worked at the stove. She was boiling up a beef broth in which to cook a joint of pork and she sliced ginger and bark of magnolia, throwing the pieces into the pan from the edge of her knife. 'You should be training daily.'

'Yes, mother,' I said. I was not averse to the proposal, given that I enjoyed our martial arts education. She had always liked to instruct me, from as early as I can remember, and my father used to teach me also. With Nhi's birth, my martial training, like life in general, had become disrupted and disorganized but I thought my mother was right that we were now both old enough to train with more discipline.

'I have asked Mrs Chau to acquire for us some training weapons of appropriate length and weight. I am not yet ready to visit Lien Lau myself but I am sure she will find the right kind of equipment.' She kept her face turned away from me. It was not easy for her to make any reference to her state of mourning.

'I could go with Mrs Chau, to the markets,' I said, thinking that it might be exciting to see busy Lien Lau again, with its row upon row of rickety shops and market tables, wares open to the air.

'No, Trac. We'll go together soon. Just not yet.'

Mrs Chau brought the training weapons late one afternoon, when the heavy monsoon rains were deluging the boggy ground and battering the roof. My mother was surprised that Chau had made the journey back from Lien Lau that day.

'Oh, don't fuss, the tracks are quite passable,' she said, 'better to travel today than be stuck there a week if the bridge floods. 'Here.' She unwrapped two half-length swords carved from pine, along with two bamboo staffs and handed them to Nhi and myself. Nhi immediately began waving her sword about while I ran my hand along the staff, checking the surface for splinters.

'Be careful, Nhi,' warned my mother, 'these are not toys.'

I picked up my sword. It was light enough for me to handle and a good length. Nhi tapped at it with her own and I swung the *kiem* up and swept it against her wooden blade, knocking the little practice weapon from her hands.

'Not fair, not fair,' she wailed, 'I wasn't ready.' She brought her sword up and thrashed at my own, before our mother stood up and snatched both swords from us.

'A sword is not to be used lightly. These are for real training and you will learn to use them properly.' She put both swords and staffs up on top of the lacquer cabinet where Nhi could not reach.

'Almost forgot,' said Mrs Chau, 'mounts for them.' She passed a small package over to my mother, which contained eight thick and long bronze nails with bulbous heads. 'Just hammer them into the wall, wherever you want them. How will you train the girls, then? It's very exciting, don't you agree, girls? So many would give anything to be in your place, learning from the great Lady Man Thien! Has she told you of when she was young? Oh, a great fighter, so skilled in the Way!' Mrs Chau looked expectantly at my mother, who sat impassively and fingered the bronze nails.

'I shall simply train them as I was trained,' she answered.

'None of us knows when we shall need the martial arts at our disposal and it is well to be prepared. How was Lien Lau? Is the Governor in residence?'

'No, he's out at Ha Long, interfering with the port traders again. There's talk on the streets of new rules for all of Giao Chi. Vo Xuan is pushing for more change.'

'People will not accept it,' said my mother 'Tich Quang did not behave like this.'

'What change? Who is Vo Xuan?' asked Nhi, only half-caring, gazing up at her new toys on top of the lacquer cabinet. They ignored her and kept on talking. Mrs Chau looked tense now, all the playful spirit sucked from her. I kept up with some of their conversation and it helped that I knew that Vo Xuan was the Han governor of all the nine Commanderies of Giao Chi Circuit, from as far north as Nam Hai to as far south as Nhat Nam's boundary at the Hai Van Pass. With Tich Quang returned to the far north, Vo Xuan, his deputy in Giao Chi, had assumed control. I would have heard more of their conversation, but Nhi was restless and to save my mother's temper, I took my sister outside to play.

That was often the way when she was little. I would miss important conversations and visitors to whom I wanted to be introduced because I was out of the way, taking care of Nhi. When Bao began hanging around I was quite happy to leave the two of them playing together while I watched from a distance. Bao had a dependable air about him that came from being the eldest boy in a predominantly fatherless family, so I believed he would take care of her. He was tall for his age, so that perhaps lured me into a false sense of security, but even if he was at heart a child, he was a good-natured one. Stupid, maybe, but kind. It allowed me to cleave closer to our mother. I wanted to be there when Mrs Chau was gossiping, or when men came up from the canals and paddies on business or when minor Han officials from the Me Linh garrison came to discuss administrative and tax issues, because I couldn't bear her to deal with them all alone. If my father was not there at her side, then I believed I should be. Nhi never understood that. She was still young enough to see our mother as an omnipotent grown-up, fully in control of our three lives and head of Me Linh region, but I had glimpsed the darker side of our Giao Chi existence and I knew that all was not well in our province and that our mother, Lady Man Thien, widow of the most supreme Lac Lord in the Giao Chi Commandery, and therefore most elevated native noblewoman in the whole of the delta, was in the very thick of it.

★★★★★

Despite my precocious involvement in politics, I was still a child. At the river, watching Nhi and Bao catch the fish, I felt the carefree excitement of being young, if only for a few moments. The air was fresh and warm, the noise of the water soothing. I never wanted to miss our mother's carefully planned training sessions, but in the mornings I started to go out more with Nhi and Bao. I was eleven, Nhi six and Bao must have been about eight. The natural superiority fell to me and I was able to calm some of their more outrageous plans. Bao wanted, one day, to steal a little dugout canoe, left tethered on the riverside and I gave him a stern talk about theft. In truth, my larger fear was that had I not been there, Bao would have allowed himself and Nhi to be swept away downriver as far as Lien Lau or even further, through the rapids and diverging distributaries that led out through mangrove forest or tidal mudflats to the sea. Neither yet knew how to properly handle a vessel in the water.

Our excursions took on a more purposeful attitude as we learned about what we could trade or what our mother and Mrs Chau could use. We began to take baskets with us and collect from the wild whatever might be useful - rattan grasses, attractive feathers that had floated to the ground from passing birds and betel leaves for chewing with areca nut. Sometimes after the threshing, we begged armfuls of rice stalks that we could dry out and make into brooms, or weave into baskets. My mother once showed me how to make a pair of very serviceable sandals out of rice stalks. Before us lay the vast wealth of the Red River Delta, bathed in warm rain and steady sunshine, suffering only mild winters and tempered summer heat. The crackle of life was all around and I learned, mostly from Nhi, about the frogs, the shrews, the barbets, the snakes and hundreds of other small beasts that shared our grassy plains and low forests. We practised lying low in the dark under-storey of the woodland, watching for pangolin, sniffing along with their pointed muzzles to the ground hunting for ants. Once I saw a loris, hunched snoring in the fork of a pine tree, the furry stomach rising and falling below his slumped, round head. We stayed near the edges of the forests – to go too far in would be dangerous, my mother had forbidden it and in any case, it was dark and intimidating – but even on the fringes, the larger animals stalked and slept. The monkeys were less cautious, and those we saw in abundance. They swung and flashed bright teeth in our direction, screeching like horrified women. Nhi wanted to catch one to take home, but I disallowed it.

'You would need a baby. One of those adults would never tame,' I said.

'I'll find a baby, then,' she said.

'And take it away from its mother? You never would.'

She was downcast about not having a pet, but reminding her of the work needed to look after one usually cured her longings. I no longer wanted a monkey. That desire was long past.

5 NHI

For a smart girl, Trac could be pretty stupid at times. She could
argue a complicated philosophical point but she had no idea
how to catch a catfish and she could sit on a rock right by a frog
and never see it, spotted brown against the ground. I was the one
with an affinity for the outdoors, for the animals and the forests
and the thick, dark swamps. I didn't care if the sun was shining or
the rain pouring, I just needed to be out in the air, breathing the
hot scents of the ten thousand things and seeing new creatures,
new trees, new people.

I talked to others more than Trac did. She looked down
on plump little Chau, even if she spoke to her respectfully.
She couldn't help but notice that Mrs Chau was not nearly so
intellectual as Trac herself was. Yet I could see that Mrs Chau had
a working knowledge of Lien Lau, as well as our own Me Linh
market town, and knew all the important people in the trading
community. She had a kind of intelligence that Trac had not yet
developed – the knack for intuiting peoples needs and finding a
way to fulfil them that would leave her all the richer. Of course,
this meant Mrs Chau had the sensitivity of a water buffalo at
times, charging into the most private topics of conversation. I
never much minded. Sometimes I even preferred her direct way
of speaking. When Bao, Trac and I were out walking, I liked to
chat to people we met – rice-workers in the paddies, women
with children travelling to markets, labourers from the canals.
Even a simple 'hello' could lead to an unexpectedly fruitful
conversation. I think that's why, as we grew up, Trac stopped
treating me quite so much like a naughty child. There came a
time where she realised that on certain subjects, I knew more
than her.

I wonder sometimes how I would have turned out if Auntie
Linh had not stayed with us during those horrible months after
Father died. I was very angry and confused then, although I

don't actually remember feeling that way. What I do recall is Auntie Linh spending time with me, explaining things to me and quietly persuading me of my own importance within our family. I said some terrible things to Mother and I must have thought she would no longer love me, because I have a vivid recollection of Auntie Linh's oval face before my own, saying very clearly that Mother would always love me and would only go on living because of Trac and myself. I missed Auntie Linh when she left – not so Uncle Hien whose thin lips and fat eyebrows made my skin creep. They came back to visit us, over the years and each time, Auntie Linh hugged me with especial affection. It was Auntie Linh who pointed out to Mother that I was spending a lot more time with Bao than was perhaps ideal.

Bao had grown into a lanky and bellicose ten-year-old. We had more arguments when we were together and he began taunting me deliberately as a tactic to keep me in check. This I realised because Trac, with her thirteen years of wisdom, had observed his behaviour and explained it to me.

'Bao is scared now you are growing up,' she said to me, 'and he can see how clever and beautiful you are becoming. He is frightened you will no longer be his friend.'

'But why wouldn't I be friends with him?' I asked, astonished by her compliments.

'Because you might find him inferior and no longer entertaining. Haven't you noticed how he only picks and teases when you've said something he doesn't understand or when you perform a task better than he can? He makes you doubt yourself so you will continue to rely upon him.'

'It doesn't matter to me if Bao is clever or not.'

But it did matter to me that Bao was becoming rude and aggressive. Now, when we were out collecting the betel leaves or catching turtles or whatever we had decided to do, he would jostle me in a way that I did not like, pinching my arms or twisting my wrists in ways that genuinely hurt. He tried to do it when Trac was not looking, because if she saw him behaving that way, she would shout at him and send him home. I was still only eight and not yet fully aware of my status. Trac knew, already, that Bao was lucky to be our friend. She knew she could wield her power over him and he must obey. If he twisted her wrists or hit her, she would be likely, first to floor him with her superior defence skills and second, to report him to Mother, who would insist that Mrs Chau reprimand him severely. In the end, it was Auntie Linh who caught him out.

They had returned for a late summer visit, Uncle Hien his usual serious self, worrying again about whether Sang, their eldest son, would manage the estates alone. Auntie Linh wrapped long, warm arms around me and spoke a loving greeting to Trac over my head. They stayed for eight days, and on the fourth day, Auntie Linh came to fetch me back from Mrs Chau's house. Mother wanted to show Auntie and Uncle how our martial arts skills were progressing but I had gone to Bao's that morning and been there longer than expected. I'd lost track of time, but also, Bao was in a strange mood. His mother was out, his grandmother was napping in the back room and his grandfather was outside with the other children, doing some repair work to the house. Bao should have been out there helping, but had ignored the old man's plea. I wanted to leave. I didn't like the way Bao was rude to his grandfather. Bao had got in the way of the door. When I went to push past him, he fought me, laughing and shoving me off balance. For Bao, I think it was still a game. He was twisting my arm up behind my back while I gasped and cried on the floor, when Auntie Linh stepped inside.

Bao jumped up immediately, horrified and ashamed of himself. He could hardly look at me, but muttered an apology to us both and fled into the back while Auntie Linh swept me up by the unhurt arm and hurried me outside.

'Bao has misbehaved,' she said to his grandfather, as we walked past, 'He has hurt little Nhi by twisting her arm.'

'I will see to him now,' bowed Bao's grandfather in alarm, 'I am very sorry, Mrs Linh.' I turned my head as we left, watching him go up the steps with his head still low in embarrassment. I felt awful for both of them – Bao with his guilt and the ageing man with his shame. Such a silly, childish incident to end in such miserable, adult feelings. Auntie Linh spoke to me as we approached our house.

'Why was Bao fighting with you, little Nhi?'

'I don't know, Auntie Linh. I wanted to leave and he wouldn't let me. Then we fought and he pushed me down.'

'Has he hurt you before?'

'Sometimes. Trac says he is angry that I am growing up. But we're friends, Auntie Linh. I don't want him to get into trouble.'

'I understand,' she said, kneeling at my side for a moment. 'He plays with you the way brothers and sisters play. Yet you are not brother and sister, so it is dangerous. Perhaps you should not spend so much time with Bao, at least until you are a little older and he can learn to be more respectful.'

I stayed silent, feeling that my honesty had gone against me and not entirely understanding the danger she alluded to. Back in our house, Mother was waiting impatiently with Trac so we could begin a demonstration. Uncle Hien squatted on the bamboo day bed, silent and pompous and Auntie Linh pushed me forwards, so I had no time to dwell on the situation but ran to stand next to Trac. Mother said, we will go through the stances first, and went to stand next to her brother, from where she watched us with all the pride of a mother duck. I mirrored Trac, settling into the familiar routine and a peculiar thing happened. As I moved my body into the graceful poses, thinking about the distribution of weight over my feet and the readiness of my arms to fend off an aggressor, I forgot all about what had happened with Bao. When I raised my right arm up before me, left arm tucked, left leg slightly bent and right leg in a shallow lunge, all I thought of was the rightness of the posture.

The distress of seeing Bao's grandfather entering the house to punish him, fled right out of my head. It was a revelation, that training could ease my mind and settle my thoughts. I had only ever found it a hindrance, preventing me from going out to play. I wonder now if Trac enjoyed the training from the beginning because it helped her cope with her grief. And if Mother taught us because teaching eased her pain.

Uncle Hien was full of praise for us. He especially liked our combative demonstration where Trac and I attempted to strike one another's upper body, defending ourselves with rapid, flowing arm movements. It was like a dance and admittedly, Trac was pulling her punches because I was smaller and not as good, but Mother looked on approvingly and Auntie Linh shared a smile with Uncle Hien. When we had finished, they all talked about how skilled we were, then we all settled to eat a meal. Mother had cooked a pheasant with a sour plum sauce and on the side were shreds of lettuce and also mustard greens which I hated. They tasted brackish and musky. Auntie Linh ate quietly, not mentioning Bao until very near the end of the meal. Then she said,

'Nhi and I spoke earlier and we think it would be best if Bao did not spend so much time with her. Nhi wants to concentrate more on her martial arts, don't you Nhi?'

Trac looked over at me in surprise. I shrugged.

'What has brought this change of heart?' asked Mother, picking out a tasty-looking little slice of pheasant on the central platter.

'Bao is still a young boy. He doesn't understand how to play properly with girls of Nhi's age,' said Auntie Linh in a voice barely above a whisper. I stared at my rice, nearly cold in the little bowl. Uncle Hien banged his hand on the table and began breathing too heavily. I wished on the heavenly golden turtle that Auntie Linh had not spoken.

'This conversation does not belong at this mealtime,' he

34

began.

'Husband, he was just a little rough, nothing more than that.'

'How so? Nhi, what did he do?' Mother asked, ignoring her brother's discomfort.

'We were playing and he twisted my arm a little bit. Nothing bad,' I said, looking with anger at Auntie Linh.

'Play fighting? That's not so bad,' said Mother. 'I thought you meant the other.'

'Enough!' said Uncle Hien, standing up. 'We will not have this conversation.' He looked ever so angry and, if I had not been angry myself, I might have giggled.

Mother put the piece of pheasant in her mouth and chewed slowly. Then she said,

'This is my house, this is my land and I control all of Me Linh district so I will speak about what I want, when I want.'

Uncle Hien put his hands behind his back and paced to the door, gazing at the floor as if he was greatly tried.

'Thien, the girls would benefit from learning some propriety,' he said.

'Propriety is the thin edge of loyalty and sincerity which is the beginning of disorder,' she quoted at her brother. 'In my house, the Way is not lost.'

'The Way is as much a Middle Kingdom idea as the other principles you choose to ignore,' Uncle Hien scoffed.

'No Hien, the Way transcends our earthly disputes. It does not belong to the Han.'

Trac was staring so intently at both of them that I kicked her and pulled a face of mock seriousness. She swatted at me with the back of her hand.

'Settle down you two,' Mother said. 'Nhi, I think you have made a good decision to focus more on your training. You may still see Bao, but perhaps he should visit here instead of you going over there.'

I nodded and Uncle Hien lowered himself back down to

the floor by the table, fixing me with a gaze that was no doubt intended to convey his sagacity. Trac had a lot of time for his philosophical meanderings but I didn't. I was the rebel girl, the naughty little sister, the runaway who missed training but I was also the one who listened to and believed everything my Mother ever said. That's the price second children pay – they fix their devotion upon their parents in the desperate attempt to match the cynical, enquiring aptitude of the first born star. Besides, I understood Mother's words. I felt the Way. It was in the pines and the sedges, the clinging orchids and the tumultuous river, the vast delta and the karst outcrops; it was in the people and the rains. I felt it when I was outside, under the wide skies of the Red River delta. I had no time for rules and strange notions of hierarchy and obsessive worship of ancestors dead and gone. Uncle Hien hankered after Confucianism, as did the Han overlords we served, but Mother's heart swung towards the Lao-Tzu teachings and something earlier, something more primeval. Mother, like me, felt the spirit of the wild things.

6

If you are ready, we will begin. Take first position

★

Will you tell us stories today?

★

They are not stories, little sister, they are our history

★

They are legends. I will continue where we left off, if you will both be silent. Lac Long Quan and his fairy queen, Au Co, had given rise to the great Hung Dynasty of Van Lang, which ruled the plains, the mountains and the Red River through the Lac Lords. But no Dynasty lasts forever. When the eighteenth Hung King reigned over Van Lang, a warlord called Thuc Pan dreamed a victory. He ruled Au Viet, high in the northern hills, and from his seat he gazed on Van Lang and dreamed of ruling the Red River delta. The mountains he owned had not the means to raise him to the heights he yearned for. His people lived well, but in the valleys of Van Lang he saw the future, mapped in the veins of our waterways and seeded in the waving paddies. He had heard of the King's beautiful daughter and, though he prepared for war, he planned on marriage. He entered Van Lang, claimed pretty My Nuong and raced her on horseback into the hills

★

Did she scream? Did she bite him and slap him?

★

Who knows? He was handsome and strong so perhaps not, now resume your posture. The lord who had been promised her hand fought for her, chasing after the pair into the mountains, but the higher he went, the higher Thuc Pan rose, until the lord was exhausted and could follow no longer. Shortly after, when the old Hung King died leaving the thread of tomorrow in the hands of his distant daughter, Thuc Pan returned with his Hung princess at his side, to claim their rightful place. They united My Nuong's river people and Thuc Pan's hill dwellers into the kingdom of Au Lac. The Lac Lords kept their seat at Me Linh and Thuc Pan built Co Loa at Tay Vu, from where he ruled

⋆

I am familiar with this story. Thuc Pan is King An Duong, who was himself overthrown

⋆

My arms ache

⋆

Move now into the next stance. Thuc Pan, our revered King An Duong, ruled until he was old and his long hair was white. His Queen, My Nuong, had birthed him a daughter who had grown into adulthood and they were content, but just as King An Duong had once dreamed his fate sitting motionless in the hills of Au Viet, so too did the Qin warlord, Trieu Da, dream a future. Trieu Da was from the Middle Kingdom, sent by his emperor to subdue all the people in the south who dared to flout their supreme leader. Trieu Da was tall and fearless, terrifying like his kinsman, who had been the great Qin emperor. He ruled on behalf of the Middle Kingdom, but when the emperor died, Trieu Da released himself from stillness and took control of his grand southern commanderies. He had seen his son, Trong Thuy, married to King An Duong's daughter, My Chau. Thuy and Chau were another pair designed to unite a nation, but they were also in love and King An Duong believed he and Trieu Da were in peaceful alliance. When Trieu Da descended with terrible speed upon the Au Lac capital at Co Loa, King An Duong was surprised and though he fought hard, Trong Thuy had done him a grevious injury by revealing to his natural father all the weaknesses of the huge Co Loa defences. Poor Thuy, he watched his wife die as she fought in vain for her father's honour. He couldn't bear that death had taken her from him under the banner of his own treachery, and neither could he bear to watch his new home conquered by his own father

⋆

Oh, what did he do? What did he do?

⋆

Why don't you just listen and then you will find out?

⋆

Third stance. He did what an honourable person does in those kinds of circumstances, when all hope is lost and to live on is to shame oneself. He fled to the river and threw himself in to drown. Trieu Da ruled, in great sorrow and humility and the people forgave him and accepted his dynasty. He joined Au Lac with his own lands in the south of the Middle Kingdom and we became part of Nam Viet. Trieu Da asked for thirty thousand women from our lands to marry men from his own, to bind his territory, and he named our area the Giao Chi Commandery, and the land below us became the Cuu Chan Commandery

★

I liked Van Lang better than Nam Viet. Or maybe Au Lac. They both sound nice

★

When, then, did we become simply Giao Chi?

★

When an evil wind brought the Han. The descendants of Trieu Da were executed and the men of the Yellow River took their place, dismantling the kingdom of Nam Viet and reducing us to a mere Commandery of the Middle Kingdom. They have ruled over us all since the time of my grandmothers. Now the fourth stance, remembering to spread your weight across both legs, ready to spring in either direction. Consider, as you hold this form, how your body is prepared for movement. Consider your enemy

7

I didn't see Bao for a few weeks. Mother kept me busy indoors and I didn't argue. At first there was Auntie Linh to play with, and after she and Uncle Hien left I made good on the promise she had extracted from me and concentrated more on my training and on listening to Mother. By the time Mrs Chau came round with Bao miserably tailing her like a beaten gibbon, I'd almost forgotten the whole arm-twisting incident. Even so, Mrs Chau made him apologise to me for it and she apologised to Mother too, who took a forgiving attitude. They allowed Bao and me to sit in the corner while they drank their regular rice wine together and chatted.

Over the months, we settled back into a more familiar routine, but I never went to Bao's house unless his mother was in. We were either out walking or at my home and often, as before, Trac was with us. She kept a close eye on him now and I suspect Uncle Hien of having a quiet word in her ear about the situation, though perhaps she had simply paid attention to the gist of that awkward mealtime argument. I didn't mind, though. I had started to realise that Trac's sometimes overbearing behaviour towards me was how she showed that she loved me. She never said it and rarely showed clear affection, but each imperious glance she threw at Bao reminded me that she was my big sister and protector.

Trac was also becoming more vocally aggressive. She began to argue with Mother more, questioning her on points of politics that I did not always understand, and though they seemed to be in broad agreement, Trac found flaws in Mother's reasoning and blew these into unnecessary disputes. She was at that age, when children begin to quarrel more with their parents, but I couldn't help feeling that if Uncle Hien had been around, she would have earned his disapproval. Yet Mother rarely took offence for long. She would stomp off into the empty room at the back, castigating Trac for being troublesome and not respecting her elders, but then later she would return and pick up the thread of the argument, having meditated her way around Trac's logic. They were as bad as each other. Mrs Chau once said to Mother, 'That girl should be careful. No man will want her if she argues so much,' and Mother said, 'Trac will not want a man who cannot match her in debate.' Trac was outside and though I overheard, I didn't tell her what they had said. Trac was shy about boys and marriage and I thought it might upset her.

When Trac was fifteen, Mother decided she needed new dresses and took us both to Lien Lau. We had been on occasions before and Trac liked it there, though I was less impressed. The busy people and the many voices clouded my brain and there were too many different smells, too many unknown men rushing past, too many Yellow River people. What I did enjoy was the cool and sour river air, the way that the waters of the river thrashed past Lien Lau having spliced apart, further upstream, beyond Chu Dien. Lien Lau lay on the southern side of the main branch. From the first division of the Red River, fingers of water spread out like a peacock's tail, reaching out for the east sea so that all the coastal part of the delta became a fan, the land veined in water that had risen from faraway highlands and pulsed through northerly narrow gorges. The constant flooding had left permanent lakes all around Lien Lau and the other small towns that banked the river. Some of the lakes were beautiful, covered in lilies and duckweed and attracting songbirds who thrashed and cleaned in the still waters. Others were thick with human refuse or silted up and clogged with dying plants, but these were in the minority. One of the benefits of living in the lee of the Red River was that it got washed clean by the monsoon flooding on a regular basis. Equally though, life got stranded in these isolated lakes and pools - giant turtles and catfish, circling each other in their limited new territories. The turtles must have liked it. You saw them sometimes, sunning themselves on the banks before sauntering back to the muddy depths to avoid the avid fishermen.

I had more of an eye for the natural life in Lien Lau, quickly being crowded out by the growing city, than for the tailor's shop Mother had taken us to. Nguyen Tuan and his wife, Dang Chi, ran the business from the front room of their slim house in the centre of Lien Lau's trading district. It was nestled in between a carpenter's workplace and a shop front filled with vessels and artefacts. We entered through a rickety door from the thin, dusty street and Mr Tuan ran forwards and bowed to Mother, thanking her for coming. She looked about her, at the bolts of silk and cotton, the folded piles of hemp and jute, the table with cut pieces laid out and then she gave him one of her radiant business smiles.

'Tailor Tuan, you are keeping busy! These packages here, all for delivery!' She patted a pile of wrapped garments on the edge of a low table by the door.

'Yes, thank you Lady Thien. We are doing quite well. But always time for a valued customer like you. Come in for a drink. Tailor Chi will measure the girls.'

He appraised us both with a cloth-cutter's eye, the drifting gaze impersonal and calculating – this much material for the underskirt, this much for the outer, this much for the trim. From behind him, Chi came running forward.

'Lady Thien, so pleased to see you again.'

'Tailor Chi, these are my daughters, Trac and Nhi.' Mother gestured to each of us in turn. 'Nhi will want two outfits – one must be ceremonial and decorative, the other more durable. Trac will need four outfits. A ceremonial *ao tu than*, two that are becoming and attractive and one that is plain and simple.'

'The best silk, Lady Thien, for the fancy tunics. I have a finely woven jute that will make a good, plain garment.' Chi busied around us, passing a thin length of marked hemp around our bodies. Mother went to the back of the shop with Tuan and

42

sat down, talking quietly. Chi prodded my back into a firmly upright posture.

'Pretty girl,' she said. 'Look like your father. You don't get the "becoming" tunics then? Too young, too young. Out playing, I expect? Or no - learning with your mother, I've heard. She is teaching you the martial arts, yes?'

Chi moved on to Trac. I hadn't answered any of her apparent questions because she spoke so fast, like a spot-breasted parrot-bill, bobbing about with her measuring strip and pushing my arms up, down, turning me side-on, backwards, forwards. She was only a little taller than me, with shiny black hair only visible at the hairline, caught up in a fabric wrap to stop it falling in her way as she worked, but her face was creased and her dark eyes were hardly visible in their tight folds.

'And you, old enough for a husband now, eh? Need pretty clothes for meeting men! Or are you a fighter too, like little sister? Your mother, she trains you both, they say. Lucky girls. Everyone knows Lady Man Thien is expert in the fighting way. There. Done. Slim girls, both of you. But strong shoulders. Very straight.'

'Which silk will you use for my outfits?' Trac asked, cutting through Chi's incessant monologue.

'Which do you think? This one here has a pretty pattern, but the colour, hmm, not good for you, I think. Better for little sister.'

I looked at the bolt of yellowy-orange silk, like the rich stripes of a tiger or a sunset shining in the water, patterned with brown and red leaves, and agreed wholeheartedly that the colour was good for me.

'I think this one for you, eldest girl,' said Chi, pulling out a roll of green silk. She unrolled it a little way and held it up against Trac's face. The rich jade sheen reflected in her black eyes and made her skin luminescent. A pattern of opal-coloured swans lit the surface of the fabric, interspersed with golden trees.

'It's beautiful,' agreed Trac.

'And this one,' said Chi, pulling out a blood-red bolt, 'for your ceremonial dress.'

'Will it suit?'

'Truly, I think so. The orange over there is too bright, but this crimson is good for your skin.'

'When will they be ready, Tailor Chi?' asked Mother, standing up and smoothing down her own sapphire tunic.

'Five days, should be done.'

'Very good. Thank you Tailor Chi, Tailor Tuan.'

We left the shop into bright daylight. Trac was looking a bit smug and I suddenly resented the three pretty outfits, as compared to my one.

'Mother, why does Trac get three silk tunics while I get only one?'

'Because she is older,' said Mother, drawing us along the narrow street and out onto a wider thoroughfare.

'Is it for meeting men? Are you going to find a husband for her, like Chi said?'

Trac flushed and Mother pushed us both across the street, hurrying us in front of a small detachment of Yellow River soldiers heading on horseback towards the Lang Bac road, and a cart that trundled to their left.

'I find that suggestion quite crass. Your sister is not a sow in the marketplace. Come on. My cousin has invited us for lunch. No more talk about men.'

She took us along the rough paths and tracks until we reached a modest courtyard surrounded by a horseshoe of houses. In the left wing, a woman waited for us. Mother greeted her and introduced us.

'Girls, you remember my cousin, Auntie An.'

'Hello, Auntie An,' we chorused. She clasped her hands in admiration.

'Oh, come in, girls, come in.' She took us through to her

44

living area, where we sat down on mats around a wooden bench. Pho An was taller than Mother, and thinly built, like a starved pine, tilting in the wind. She had a long face and wide, flattish nose with sincere, smiling lips.

'We've just been to order clothes,' Mother said, settling herself into a squat by the table.

'Oh, indeed? Where to?'

'Tailor Tuan and Chi's shop. I go there normally.'

'They are very good. Tailor Chi has an eye for the fabrics and the cut.' An went to the back, where a cooking pot stood smoking over a fire. She ladled up stewed fish into a dish and carried it over to the wooden bench. Then she hurried away again and brought back little bowls and a dish of cooked rice.

'There's palm wine to drink,' she said, passing small cups to each of us. I sipped mine, enjoying the coconut flavour. The fish stew had a coconut taste too and I slurped up wet mouthfuls with a bamboo scoop after filling my little bowl with rice and sauce. Mother and Auntie An talked about people they knew, families that had delivered babies or suffered losses, relatives in the hills or on the coast. An spoke a little of her husband and son, who were away sea-fishing. They travelled southwards and made great catches there that they salted and brought home to Lien Lau to sell. An dealt with the selling and knew the other fish and meat traders in the city. She knew Mrs Chau also, and commented that Mrs Chau had brought much news of the three of us during the time Mother had stayed mostly at home. Mother didn't respond to this; she just nodded with a smile.

'I'll tell you who else I saw recently,' An said, sipping her palm wine. 'Thi Hoc, down near the Jade Temple. He asked about you, and about Trac and Nhi. He wishes to call on you sometime and renew your acquaintance.'

'How is Hoc,' Mother asked, indifferently.

'Quite well. Some aches and pains, he says, but if anyone is best-placed to remedy those, it is Hoc himself.'

45

'Does he still practice his medicine?'

'Yes, he was in fact in Lien Lau to purchase medicines. His son was with him too – the eldest child.'

'Mother, who is Thi Hoc?' I asked. I hated not knowing what was being talked about – all the relatives I had never met and couldn't picture.

'He governs Chu Dien district, below the river between here and Me Linh – his land and your father's shared a common border and they were friends. You would not remember, but in days gone by, he was often in Me Linh, or your father was in Chu Dien with him.'

'Is he also a doctor, as well as a Prefect?' asked Trac and Mother nodded.

'I told Hoc you would most enjoy seeing him again. I hope that was correct? He rather caught me unawares and I didn't like to be rude. And since his son is near Trac's age, I thought they might enjoy each other's company.' An smiled at Mother who nodded and said that was possible.

I grinned at Trac, who flushed just like she had earlier. I knew the tunics were all about boys.

★★★★★

They came on a wet, cool day, travelling in from the south on horses. Thi Hoc looked cramped in his saddle, bent at the side as though the ride had been difficult. He had an elongated chin that seemed to drag his bottom lip so that it turned outwards slightly in the manner of a sad child. Yet his eyes were alive, creased and smiling, and in the contours of his face it was clear he'd once been an attractive man. I noticed all this immediately. Trac was hiding in the bedroom.

'They're here,' Mother called, 'I want you out here to greet them, Trac. How will it look if you're hiding in there?'

To which Trac retorted that she was not hiding, merely getting on with something more important – a sure sign that she found this visit all too important and was agitated. She came out as they were dismounting and tying the reins of their horses to the post where the water trough sat. By now, I'd had a good look at the son too, who was glancing politely at us from behind several strands of thick, long, black hair that had escaped from the bun at the back of his head. He wore a tunic in luminous paddy-field green and carried a short, curved sword, girdled at his hip and a longer weapon across his back. He followed his father to the foot of the steps leading up to our house, where Mother greeted them warmly. Trac stood next to me and I clutched at her fingers for a moment and whispered, 'He's very handsome.' She squeezed my hand but then pulled it away. Her face was burning - little spots of amber glowing on her cheeks revealing the loss of her almost constant composure. But Trac's lack of composure was akin to anyone else's best manners and when Mother introduced her, she gave her customary nod and made some bland remark before we all went inside.

Hoc's son, Thi Sach, lowered himself to sit on the thick bearskin while Mother and his father sat on a bamboo bench. Trac hesitated, then busied herself fetching drinks and some food to nibble on that the servant girl had left near the stove. I threw myself down next to Sach. He grinned at me.

'How old are you, little girl?'

'I'm ten. Trac is older than me. She's fifteen. How old are you?'

'Nineteen,' he answered. 'And I have two younger sisters. One is your age. The other is a bit older.'

'Oh, you should have brought them,' I moaned. 'I would have had someone to play with then!'

'Next time,' he laughed.

He was so personable, and Hoc and Mother were so deep in conversation, that I told Sach all about how I didn't have a brother, but instead had a friend called Bao and how I liked to go out exploring and that Trac came with me often to keep me company. He listened and made various replies when he got

47

chance, but after a while I realised that Trac was perched to my left with eyes drawn like daggers in my direction. Mother must have noticed too, because she quite pleasantly suggested that the three of us might like to go for a little walk outside. The ground was wet but the rain was holding off and Sach quickly agreed. Trac stood up as if under sufferance and led us outside.

Even in the open air, walking beside him, she stayed silent. I walked just ahead of them, chattering on, but Trac made no attempt to join in. I thought how nervous she must be and wondered about a way to get her to talk. Sach had mentioned his young sister, who had a pet monkey.

'I always wanted a pet monkey,' I exclaimed, 'but Trac said I wouldn't look after it properly. You didn't want one, did you, Trac?'

'I wanted one once,' she said, looking away from both of us.

'Trac had a baby doll, didn't you Trac?'

Sach smiled at her from under his long eyelashes as she tried to ignore me.

'Don't you remember? Cypress baby - you gave it to me. I can't think where it is now. Probably in our sleeping place somewhere. We'll have to show it to Sach. It's very pretty.'

'I'd like to see Cypress baby,' Sach whispered to her. 'But I'm sure it's not as pretty as you are.'

Trac looked as if she'd swallowed a pebble and then began to walk faster. I giggled and Sach followed Trac with his head slightly bowed as he overtook me. Her gorgeous green tunic with the opal swans gleamed in the grey, cloud-filtered light. I thought how well matched they were, he in his bright green tunic and she in the dark one, the sunned and shaded sides of a grass blade.

I stayed back a little then, so I don't know what they talked about or whether they talked at all. They walked side by side, not touching in any way and barely turning their heads to each other. Trac was rigid, but Sach walked with a fluid motion, his broad shoulders tilting as though he was very relaxed. I thought perhaps he had met many girls, especially being so good-looking, and I immediately hated them all.

When we returned to the house, Mother had a meal prepared and we sat to eat. Trac played with her food, putting tiny morsels in her mouth though I heard her stomach rumble because I was sat right next to her. Sach hardly looked at her at all and spoke instead to Mother, who asked him all sorts of questions about what work he did and what ideas he studied and what plans he had. I listened avidly to him talk about wanting to take over from his father soon, to give the old man a much-deserved rest. Sach said he would do things differently from his father and wanted to challenge the increase in provincial taxes and negotiate a better trade for our many export goods which were disappearing in volume into the Middle Kingdom. Hoc laughed and said the Han administrators would get a shock, because Sach was very talented in negotiation even though he was still young.

'He's worked with me most of his life,' said Hoc. 'I took him everywhere with me as soon as he could walk and talk.'

'I remember,' nodded Mother, 'how he followed you around.'

'He's a good son. The very best.'

There was a lull, during which I remembered about Cypress Baby. I leapt up from the table and ran into the back room saying I would find it. Mother called me back, shaking her head at Hoc as if I was beyond hope, but I ignored her until I had found the doll, nestled under some old rags in the base of our clothing trunk. I picked Cypress Baby up and brushed off the fluff and dust that had gathered on her. I took her back to the others, waving her at Sach.

'This is Cypress Baby.'

'Nhi, what are you doing? Sach is not interested in your old toys,' said Mother.

Trac snatched Cypress Baby from my hands and pressed her down into her lap, within the folds of her *ao tu than*. Sach, with a mouthful of food, looked from my Mother, to me, to Trac, then swallowed and said,

'Trac, may I have a look?'

She looked up at him and I saw the embarrassment in her face though I could not understand what she had to be embarrassed about. Then she slowly handed the doll over to him. He took hold of it carefully, as if it were a delicate vase, and turned it about, touching the carved features.

'This is lovely. I am sure you treasured it, long ago, when you were a child.' He passed it back to her.

'Thank you, I did,' she whispered and stuffed it back out of sight.

When they left, Sach bowed to Trac and told her he had very much enjoyed meeting her. Trac agreed, stiffly, that it had been a very pleasant day. Mother and Hoc said their goodbyes and I waved madly at Hoc and Sach as they cantered away on their dark horses, towards Me Linh centre where they would stay overnight before returning to Chu Dien.

As soon as we were back inside, Trac rounded on me.

'You mean little fool,' she screamed. 'Why did you do that?'

'Do what?' I asked, tears filling my eyes.

'Go on and on about the baby doll. You made me look like a little girl who still plays with toys. Sach will think I'm a fool.' Her voice rose in pitch and as she spoke she fetched me a slap to the side of the head. Mother was running to us as Trac struck. She grasped my sister's arm and pulled her away from me.

'You must never strike Nhi,' Mother shouted, 'No matter what you think she has done. I will hear an apology for it immediately.'

'Sorry Nhi,' Trac muttered over my howling sobs.

'Nhi, be quiet, it was not so hard,' said Mother, rubbing my head. 'I've given you worse and not heard this amount of noise.'

'But it's so unfair,' I cried. 'I tried my very best to make stupid Trac talk to him. It's not my fault that she's mute.'

'I'm not mute,' raged Trac. 'You embarrassed me. First you jump about all over him, telling him everything about us so I have nothing left to add, then you start telling him stories about me and my doll. How could I have an adult conversation with him after that?'

'Nhi, I think perhaps you should go to bed. I will have a talk with Trac,' said Mother, stroking my hair. Then, bending to my ear, she whispered, 'Don't worry, you did nothing wrong.'

I hugged her and took myself off, as instructed, pleased that I had been proved to be in the right. I thought it would serve miserable Trac right if Sach decided to ignore her and wait for me to be of an age to marry.

The next morning, Trac apologised properly to me, taking me entirely by surprise. She was so humble and kind to me that I regretted my monopolization of her new friend, and apologised for that in return. Trac laughed at me, at both of us, and said that Sach must think we were both mad.

'No,' I said, full of childish love for my remorseful sister, 'He thinks you're pretty. He said so, remember?'

8

I was not pretty. When Sach said it, I thought he was mocking me. The whole of that first day turned into an uncomfortable memory of my own awkwardness. When I watched Nhi talking carelessly to Sach, her bright eyes and full lips telling vivid stories and entrancing him, I felt boring and ugly. Even walking close by him, I felt he only looked at me because he had to, because his father had brought him here to meet me. The only way to impress him was with my intellect, my adult manner, but when Nhi started talking about my doll, I felt such a fool. I was sure Sach was inwardly laughing at us both, two little girls who thought they were all grown-up.

I spoke to my mother about it, after she sent Nhi to bed, and she said I had behaved impeccably well and that a little reserve went a long way towards enticing a man. She said I had done just the right things, even if I felt I had not. And she said that Nhi had acted perfectly as well, because she had shown I had a soft heart, without my having to flaunt it.

'Did you not see the way he held Cypress Baby? Like it was the most precious thing. And his words were very precisely chosen, Trac. Think about what he said, and what he meant. He does not see you as a child.'

But how could he see me as anything else? As soon as I saw him, walking towards our house with his two beautiful swords strapped to his tight, lean body, hair strands flickering past that fine face, with its high cheekbones and strong chin, I felt sick. A handsome man like that, about to take control of all Chu Dien, would not be short of marital offers. He would have the pick of many beautiful women. I felt unreasonably angry at him, even before he entered our home. That spike of resentment needled me the whole day and I could not free myself of it, walking beside him, catching the occasional scent of his sweat, seeing the calluses on his hands from holding reins. The more intimate details I noticed, the more I was taunted with what could never be. Some other woman would claim him. Someone beautiful and sparkling, who could hold his attention like Nhi could.

I nodded at my mother's words of easement, but I did not really believe her. Sach had humoured us, that was all and much as my chest had hurt when I first saw his good looks and confident stride, and much as I had clung to every simple word he spoke in the fleeting time we walked alone together, he was only the first marriageable man I had met and there were bound to be others.

I put that difficult day aside, because I was very busy now, travelling with my mother and helping her with all the business she had to attend to. She was in Lien Lau more often and was more fully engaged in a diplomatic relationship with the local Han administration. Nhi came into Lien Lau with us, but would spend her time at Auntie An's or with another friend or relative. We were not short of associates in the district and Nhi enjoyed spending time with different people and families. Having dropped her off somewhere suitable, my mother and I would ride on to the government building and stable our horses outside. The government building in Lien Lau had been built a few years previously to accommodate the growing needs of the locally based representatives of the Middle Kingdom's distant emperor. There was an older complex of buildings, along with the hall of justice, that housed the majority of tax officials and public servants, but it sat alongside the new three-floor building, which was wide, like a crab, with low, cantilevered roofs at each level. There was a wall all around this new residence, making the lower floor entirely private, even though it sat higher than street level, and a little side gate was permanently guarded. We would go to this gate and rap on it.

'Lady Man Thien,' my mother would announce, as the guard peered out, and then he would step back and let us through the courtyard. Inside, on the ground floor, there were lacquer paintings on the walls, thick, foreign rugs on the floors and all manner of ornamentation. A door at the back led out to a kitchen area, and to the rear wings of the building that stretched out on ground level and housed servants and guards. Up a level was the floor where the Governor conducted his business and he kept the top level private.

Governor Vo Xuan was a wiry man, with springy, nervous limbs and a slim, tall build. He grew a long moustache that ended in two points just below his jawline and his receding hair was scraped back into a bun, leaving his oval face hovering forwards, like an orchid bloom quivering on the stem. He always stood and bowed to my mother and me, and was very courteous, offering us refreshments and bidding us to sit with him, but he rarely smiled. Instead his face would be pressed into concentration, or wrinkled in thought or flat with determination. I found him intimidating but not threatening. He was an intelligent and mostly pleasant man but his appearance was wraith-like and he had an iron will. He was responsible for all of what had once been Nam Viet, so though he was the governor of Giao Chi Commandery, he was also responsible for the Nhat Nam and Cuu Chan Commanderies and the Commanderies in the north, on ancient Trieu Da's soil. In the short time since he had taken over from Governor Tich Quang, he had been successful, maintaining Han control in our regions and increasing the tributes made by our districts to the court of the Han emperor, but Giao Chi was still a frontier place, a danger zone for hostility and rebellion so Vo Xuan was a very careful man.

He was also beginning to consider new arrangements for the Giao Chi people and he began to hint at these on one of our visits to him.

'I would like you,' he addressed my mother, 'to encourage your Me Linh residents to properly register their families with the authorities here in Lien Lau. It is important to value the family and to treat marriage with due reverence, yet in Giao

Chi the rules regarding proper registration are so often flouted. I know that my colleague Nham Dien has experienced the same problems in Cuu Chan.'

'In the countryside, people often do not see a benefit to registering their marriage in the capital,' my mother explained.

'Then you must tell them that the authorities can only take care of their country if they know who is living there. In some cases, whole villages have not been registered and this makes the whole system of trade and taxation extremely unfair.'

My mother gave a little nod.

'And also,' he continued, 'the people should be encouraged to marry and begin families. We are blessed here in Giao Chi with such wonderful conditions for rice-growing and yet only a tiny amount of the land is properly farmed. We need good, strong, healthy families, working the land.'

He looked at me and sighed.

'How old are you?'

'I'm sixteen,' I answered.

'Are you married?'

'We have begun to consider possible matches,' intervened my mother. 'Trac will marry soon, when we have considered her choices.'

'I'm glad to hear it,' said Xuan. 'There are too many who do not marry, or if they do, they part again all too quickly.'

Vo Xuan was mildly disgusted by the relaxed Giao Chi approach to separation. If a man went away, hunting and fishing, for a long period, it was considered quite fair for his wife to declare their marriage over. Since the men in our area often went away like this, marriages and family units were actually very flexible arrangements, with men and women not tied to each other in the same way they were in the Middle Kingdom. For the Han, our family arrangements were morally abhorrent and, most importantly, unworkable for taxation purposes

'We are making plans,' my mother assured him, anxious to

be off the topic.

'There are some young men here in town you may wish to consider. A marriage between your daughter and one of our visiting young Han noblemen might be beneficial. Trac would be well situated if she married into the Liu family clan.'

'I'll consider it,' said my mother looking a little stricken while I sat very still, hardly daring to breathe. Xuan picked up a bamboo scroll from a little table to his left and flicked the document open. The strips of wood gave a clatter as they unravelled and he and my mother went on to the topic of the new canals being dug within our stretch of the Red River. After a while, I dared to look up from the floor, where my eyes had been firmly fixed. Now I understood why I had the new clothes. My mother wanted me married to one of our own before she was pressured into marrying me to the Han.

★★★★★

Nhi disliked the next proposition from the start. She only saw the latest prospect from a distance, as we walked to the little temple where my mother had arranged to meet Trang Hoa and her eldest son, Mai Nhat. I was less nervous than I had been about Sach, but more unsettled. The situation felt more mechanical and arranged than Thi Hoc's gentlemanly approach via Auntie An proposing an unassuming visit. Trang Hoa had approached my mother directly, with a clear suggestion of marrying her son to me and strengthening ties with her district of Khuc Duong. Nhat was from noble family, maybe with even more power than that of Thi Hoc, and my mother gave agreement that Nhat and I should meet. Mrs Hoa said they would be at the water temple mid-morning. Nhi had insisted on coming – at almost twelve years old, she was willowy and charming and rarely suffered refusal. When she caught sight of the young man and his mother, hovering by the shaded pool that sat to the side of the temple, she laughed.

'Oh mother, Trac will not marry him!' she guffawed, pressing her slim hands over her fat lips to stifle her mirth lest they should hear her.

My mother discreetly took Nhi's arm and gave it a nasty pinch.

'You wait here. This is why I wanted you to stay at home,' she frowned, making Nhi sit by the track side. I knew Nhi wouldn't stay there for long. She'd wander off into the trees or perhaps take a long route round to the far side of the pool so she could observe us. I continued on with my mother towards Nhat, who stood with his arms behind his back, surveying the scenery and pretending not to have noticed us. He was very different from Sach, wearing a dark blue tunic, with his hair tied tightly. He should have left his hair down, because it might have camouflaged his rather plump face which sagged at the jawline. With his hands held behind his back, his tubby figure showed and the sheathed blade dangled awkwardly at his side. When he turned, pretending to catch sight of us for the first time, I was embarrassed for him. He smiled broadly and came, with his mother, to greet us.

My mother took charge and introduced us. Hoa smiled at me and admired my outfit. I had not worn the green tunic with the swans that I wore for Sach. Instead I'd picked the silver-grey tunic covered in pink slipper orchids, the second of the more fancy garments Chi had made for me. Nhat nodded in agreement at his mother's compliments but stayed silent. From the front, he was not unattractive, with nice eyes and a rounded face but he spoiled what looks he had with the inane gape still strung across his features.

'Please, let's walk,' I said, desperately, wanting the whole thing over with as soon as possible and Nhat bowed and led the way towards the path that ran between the temple and the pool. My mother and Hoa stayed by the temple, making their own conversation while their eyes followed us.

'You look very beautiful,' Nhat said, immediately that we

57

were out of earshot, spilling the practised compliment before he could misplace it.

'Thank you.' We were both silent then. I waited for him to make some conversation but when he did not, I tried to prompt him.

'Tell me something of yourself, Nhat. I hear your family raises yams as well as rice.'

'Yes, we grow different crops. Then if the rice fails...' He lifted his arms and smiled.

'And what else do you do?' I had studied his face and thought him to be perhaps in his mid-twenties.

'I help my parents. I'll take my father's position when he becomes too old, of course.'

'What is it like, in Khuc Duong? Are there many Han living there? You are much further from Lien Lau than we are.'

'Not nearly so many Han as at Lien Lau, and the few we have are mostly peasants from the Yellow River, brought in to try and increase the crop yields, but they don't know our weather and they don't really understand how we farm the rice. There aren't many soldiers, not like in Lien Lau or even like your garrison here in Me Linh. It's been a long time since we've had trouble. Of course, now there's all this talk about new laws so I don't know what that will mean.' He tailed off, sounding bored.

I nodded sympathetically, and with some compassion. It was becoming clear to me why Mai Nhat was not yet married. His girth spoke of some over-feeding by his doting mother and he appeared to have little interest in politics. When we came across a leaf turtle, crawling slowly by the edge of the waters, Nhat squatted down and laughed at it like a child.

'Hey little man,' he said to it, 'where are you going then?'

The turtle bobbed its pointy brown head, showing yellow stripes down each side and waddled faster while Nhat grinned and tapped its shell.

'They like still waters,' Nhat said. 'Leaf turtles are peaceable

58

creatures. No playing in the rushing river for them.' He stood back up and wiped his hands, dusty from the banking, on the sides of his tunic. We continued walking.

'My mother says you have a sister,' he said.

'Yes, Nhi. She is five years younger than me. Do you have brothers and sisters?'

'A brother, three years younger.' His eyebrows had knitted together and he looked annoyed.

'You don't get on?'

'He doesn't have much respect for his elders,' said Nhat, 'and we disagree much of the time. Still, he is my brother and I love him as I should.'

'Nhi and I are quite close,' I said. 'even though we see the world quite differently.'

'If Thao and I could be close, I would be much happier,' Nhat said, looking at the floor.

'Often the eldest is forced to swallow pride and set the example,' I commented and he nodded, contemplatively.

'You seem much older than sixteen years,' he said. 'Not in looks, I mean you are very beautiful. But also very wise. They say that of you.'

'Do they really? I was not aware I was that well known.'

'My mother's cousin knows your uncle, Mr Hien. Father heard that you studied Confucius and that your mother teaches you the old martial skills.'

'Uncle Hien, I have not seen him for some years but he taught me a lot while he lived with us. Do you study Confucius?'

'Not especially. I know some of the wisdom but I've not the patience for thinking these things through. A Yellow River general stayed at our home once and he talked more of Taoism. I preferred his way of thinking to that of the Confucian intellects I've met.'

We had rounded back to the little temple and my mother and Hoa waited expectantly for us. I turned to Nhat and bowed slightly.

'It has been very pleasant talking with you,' I said and was a little moved to see the gratitude in his face.

'And with you. I very much hope we can talk again soon.'

'Goodbye Mrs Hoa,' I said. 'It was very nice to meet you.'

'Goodbye Trac. Goodbye Lady Prefect.' Hoa bowed to us and then turned away with Nhat, back towards their horses and cart which waited in the shadow of the temple.

I walked with my mother up the track towards where we had left Nhi.

'Do you think we should look for her,' my mother asked.

'No, she will find us,' I said, looking about and seeing no sign of her.

'Perhaps I should have introduced her to Mrs Hoa and Nhat, but you know what Nhi is like. She hasn't learned to conceal her thoughts yet and if she'd laughed at Nhat, I would have been sorely angered. How did you find him?'

'We spoke enough to find some things in common, but he is not a great conversationalist. Neither does he really enjoy politics or philosophy. He seemed a nice man, very kind and eager to please. I would perhaps enjoy seeing him again. As for marriage, I cannot yet say.'

'He hasn't the looks of Sach, or his fire,' observed my mother and I winced at the direct comparison. Of course Sach was more attractive and more keenly political, but how kind a husband would Sach be, forced into a marriage of convenience?

*****

A few weeks later, my mother received a message from Auntie An. Her husband, fishing out on the east coast had become aware of a scandal breaking in the deep water coastal area that we called Hai tan Phong thu, or just Hai Phong for short. He sent their son back to Lien Lau to alert the Lac nobility. Giang had passed on the news to his mother, and Auntie An had immediately set out to the home of Lien Lau's most superior Giao Chi native, a prefect called Ton Vien. From there, the message spread wider, through the ranks of the Giao Chi nobility within Lien Lau and out, to the surrounding districts - to Tay Vu, Chu Dien, Lang Bac, Me Linh and to Lac nobility all along the Red River. The story came through other witnesses besides Giang and over just a few days we heard several versions.

The news was that a Han army Captain had begun trying to confiscate bronze drums in the small fishing ports and river-mouth communities dotted along the Giao Chi coastline. He had taken one from a temple some distance south of Hai Phong, then realising that most of the villages and towns possessed at least one of the large, engraved instruments, he'd decided to go raiding specifically for the drums, continuing north through the unpeopled mangroves and getting lucky in a few isolated townships. By the time he came near to Hai Phong, he had seven drums in his possession and news of his activities had preceded him, such that in the next place he stopped, his men were ambushed by young Giao Chi natives. The incident, resulting in a few deaths on both sides, had drawn in senior Han officials, who had taken custody of both the renegade Captain and the majority of the Giao Chi ambush party, in makeshift premises within Hai Phong. There was outrage from the general populace, bolstered by fishermen and peasants from isolated communities who had trekked to Hai Phong to complain and to recover their stolen property.

My mother said she must go immediately to Lien Lau and speak with Governor Vo Xuan. She was putting on her travelling clothes and I was carefully folding a clean tunic and wrapping it in a large piece of hemp cloth.

'I should go with you,' I said, tying string around the bundle. 'I am old enough now and this is a serious business. It might be dangerous.'

'It might, and that is why you should stay here. Hai Phong is not like Lien Lau.' she replied, but she was looking out of the unshuttered window apprehensively.

'I am old enough,' I repeated. 'I will go and get ready.' I went to my room and packed one of my nice tunics. I was already wearing a rough old outfit that would do fine for the journey to Lien Lau, and perhaps on to Hai Phong. I guessed that Xuan might already have left Lien Lau and we would end up following him downriver. I slipped a hair comb in with the tunic and wrapped them tight, then went to find some food to take with us, along with our seals of status, the imprinted copper discs with their green ribbons that would prove our high-ranking position to all we met. The servant girl gave me some cooked rice wrapped in large leaves and a few pouches of dried meat and fruit.

'Do you want me to stay with little Nhi?' she asked, her long eyes concerned for my sister who was outside practising with her staff. Diep had worked for us for several years and she was our most trusted servant.

'I do not know yet,' I said and went to the doorway that led out onto the front steps. As I walked down them, I watched her twitch the staff, pivoting the carved bamboo forwards and backwards, taking her hands through the sequence of moves that made up the peacock form. Our mother had been instructing us in this subtle defence manoeuvre for several months but was not yet satisfied. Nhi was whipping through the form as fast as lightning, such that she had completed it twice in the time it took me to reach her. Her eyes were closed, lips white with frustration and I called out as I approached, making her open her eyes and blink in the full sunlight.

'I am going with our mother to Lien Lau,' I said. 'This news about the drums is very serious, Nhi.'

'I know,' she replied. 'That's why I'm practising. We should all know how to fight the Han, just like the men on the coast did.'

'Diep has offered to stay and look after you while we are away.'

'I'm coming with you,' Nhi said, flashing an angry look my way as she resumed her moves with the staff.

'We could perhaps leave you with some of our friends in Lien Lau if we have to travel on to Hai Phong,' I thought aloud.

'I'm coming with you, even if you go to Hai Phong.'

'Nhi, you cannot, it might be dangerous,' I tried, wary of her temper.

'Dangerous for you, maybe. I can look after myself,' she shouted and stamped the floor with the staff. She was tall for her age. Her shoulders were very straight, emphasized by her flat chest and muscles that had begun to develop in her arms and legs. All the outdoor play and the more recent serious attention she had given to her training was beginning to show on her young frame.

'I will speak to mother,' I sighed, but she stormed past me.

'I'll speak to Mother myself,' she said, running into the house.

In the end, the three of us set out together. My mother had not yet decided whether she would leave Nhi with friends or take her on with us if it became necessary. We went from Cam Khe on horses, south towards the river jetty in lower Me Linh. I was a reasonable rider but I shared a horse with Nhi and she fidgeted behind me, forever twisting in the saddle or prodding me about something unimportant. It was a relief to board a boat and let it wash us swiftly downstream, though Nhi still sat close next to me. Halfway to Lien Lau, Nhi slumped more heavily against my side, her arms threaded round my waist and I realised she was sleeping – or whatever approximates sleep on a jolting boat ride. She was such a creature of impulse, reacting instinctively to her immediate requirements. My mother sat in front, facing me, her long face stony, hair wrapped up in a blue cloth that swathed her head. She was silent and no doubt thinking about how to approach the situation, or what indeed the truth of the situation might be, so I stayed silent too, thinking about the drums and the Giao Chi men who had died trying to get them back.

The drums were from the time when Giao Chi was Van Lang, those distant centuries when the Red River Delta was governed by Hung kings and the Middle Kingdom was merely a neighbour whose royalty intermarried with our own. In that long dynasty, begun by the hero Lac Long Quan who fathered the first Hung King, our country was famous for its drums, crafted by bronze workers on the east coast in a little place called Dong Son. My mother says the men and women there have been making the drums since seven hundred years ago, though now there are more places in Giao Chi that produce them. The drums are everywhere – in houses, in temples, in official buildings, at track-side shrines, in mountain sanctuaries – and not only in Giao Chi, but throughout all three Commanderies of what was Nam Viet. There are drums in Cuu Chan and Nhat Nam and further still. Merchants, priests and even kings came to Van Lang for the drums, taking them over the mountain borders into the Laos and Khmer tribes. Sailors took them on boats to the southern islands, out in the ocean. No one knows how far the Van Lang drums have travelled. Perhaps to the ends of the earth, rippling outwards to the beat of Quan's heart and Au Co's fairy wings.

There is a secret in the drums, a tidal roar, a monsoon storm. If you beat one, good and hard, then pause, you'll hear another begin to boom. Give it a moment and you will hear a third, a fourth, the rhythm growing like a pulse. The wind will fill with resonance. The trees, in trance, will shake. North, south, east and west, a wave of heartbeats will rise until all the world is in motion. I have heard it twice. Not by then, not as we travelled to Lien Lau, my mother, sister and I. I did not hear it until long after, but I still knew that the drums were important and that it was sacrilege to steal, deface or destroy them.

I was surprised that the Han captain had dared to take the seven drums. They were protected by the spirits of the land, by beast and bird, and everyone held them in reverence. All the detailing, the patterns of birds, boats, warriors and houses standing out in low relief on the bronze, were a message of deterrence and an invocation of the gods. In addition, the drums were large and heavy - great squat, circular objects, with flat tympani at least as wide as an arm is long. The upper sides bulged and the trunk slimmed before broadening out to a splayed foot. They were well over half the height of an adult and at least the weight of one, if not more. To take seven drums and still be prowling for more, was not a simple matter. But then, Han soldiers did not lack for horses and carts. If needs be, they simply took them from the Giao Chi people.

Taking horses and carts was one thing. Taking the drums was another. The Han Captain had directly challenged and offended our most sacred cultural custom and I had a feeling that both sides - the Lac nobility and the Han administration - would be anxious to find a resolution. Nearing Lien Lau, I interrupted my mother's reverie to confirm what I expected.

'Mother,' I said, 'Vo Xuan does not have the resources to fight a war, does he?'

'No, I don't think so,' she said, leaning in closer to me. 'It won't come to that.'

'But will he hand the drums back or will he retain them? Mother, I think he will be anxious to avoid causing a rebellion but he will also want to show that Giao Chi, the drums included, belongs to the Middle Kingdom emperor.'

'Yes Trac, I've been thinking the same thing. Ton Vien will call for the Han thief to be executed, but Xuan will worry that it diminishes the power of the Han army in the eyes of the Giao Chi people.' Ton Vien, the Lac Prefect of Lien Lau, was more openly vocal than many others. In the rural communities where soldiers had settled, people were scared to challenge Han policy, but in the trading capital where the Han administrators were keen to be seen as fair, it was usually easier to speak out and achieve some kind of justice. However, in the current situation,

65

Xuan may not care so much about appeasing troublesome Vien.

'Have you thought of any solutions, mother?'

'It will depend on the specifics of the situation when we arrive, but there are some ways around the problem. The drums could be retained for a while and then quietly returned, or the Han Captain made to accept a lesser charge of failing properly to understand the remit of his orders.'

'Making him incompetent rather than a thief? That may still carry a heavy penalty which he is unwilling to accept,' I said.

'I've got an answer,' said Nhi sleepily. 'Governor Xuan should tell everyone the drums were collected for the addition of a tribute to the Middle Kingdom emperor. He can instruct the bronze workers to make a plaque for each drum, bearing the emperor's name and then send the drums back. Then the drums were never stolen, the Captain is not a thief, the drums are held nominally by the emperor and the locals can rip the plaques off when everyone has forgotten about it.'

I was surprised by her answer. It was not a bad idea.

'Then the detained band of Giao Chi men have assaulted a Han detachment on legitimate business, and they will have to be executed,' said our mother, 'But I can't think of a scenario in which this will not happen.'

'Maybe we should start a war with the Han, then, since we outnumber them and they deserve it,' said Nhi, matter-of-factly.

'All very well for a child of eleven to say, but war means death for many hundreds of grown men and women. If it were that easy, we would have done it before.' My mother stared into middle distance as she spoke, sounding wistful.

'I just wonder,' said Nhi crossly, 'how far the Han must go before the people who truly own this land do something about it.'

I was expecting our mother to make a retort, but she did not. Her eyes were still glazed, but at the corner of her mouth was a tiny smile.

We came to Lien Lau and disembarked at a jetty near the grand administration building. It was quiet in the yard and in the entrance to the building and I knew we had missed them. We found a scribe in the entrance to the older buildings who told my mother that Xuan and his retinue had taken a boat to Hai Phong that morning.

'Is there any further news?' She asked.

'Nothing more from Hai Phong, but we know that four or five other Prefects are making their way there,' the scribe answered, knowing my mother to be the high-ranking Lady Man Thien.

'Ton Vien?' My mother guessed.

'Yes, and Thi Hoc of Chu Dien, along with the Prefects of Tay Vu and of An Dinh. There may be more.'

'I will take a boat to Hai Phong,' my mother told him and he bowed and went to fetch a servant. Another man appeared, this time a Giao Chi man, and he led us back out and onto the footpath from the back of the government buildings which provided a private short-cut back to the jetty we had just left. Here, the boatmen plied a fair trade between Me Linh and Lien Lau and, today especially, between Lien Lau and Hai Phong. Our previous canoe had already gone, but the servant whistled up another from the far bank. Arrangements were made so quickly that neither my mother nor I properly considered leaving Nhi in Lien Lau.

Nhi was a little giddy at the ease with which she had achieved her goal of accompanying us. She sat right at the front, in the tip of the dug-out canoe, while my mother and I sat just behind her. There were two boatmen with us, one stood at the back, with a long oar ready for steering us out of the mooring and down the waterway, and another, older man who sat two-thirds of the way back with another pair of oars mounted on the edges of the boat. It was a small vessel - the larger, more plush transport canoes were already gone - but it was still bigger than the one we had just been in. Some of the boats were huge outriggers, long and fierce with a bank of rowers off each side. Xuan had no doubt taken one of those for himself and his entourage. The smaller boats were sometimes faster because they could traverse the lower waters and rapids where the outriggers preferred deeper, safer water. The rear boatman pushed us away from the jetty and the boat rocked in the water before the older man gave a few quick rows, pushing us into midstream. Then the downward current took us and we sailed swiftly out of Lien Lau.

The Red River twists and turns on its whole course through Giao Chi, catching the light like a sunbeam snake. We were carried along the undulating route both by the current and by the seated oarsman, who faced the rear and took direction from his partner at the back who faced the front. The pair spoke to each other a little, but the breeze carried their words away and all I heard were meaningless clippings. There was the occasional name - Vo Xuan, Ton Vien - which suggested that the drum dispute was the hot topic for everyone that day. I watched the scenery drifting past, the flat little loaches flickering under the surface of the water, the cattle herd on the southern bank gazing mindlessly back at us. The day had turned warm and bright, throwing diamond sparkles over the lush green rice fields. I tried to clear my mind and prepare myself for the arrival at Hai Phong but in truth, I was only dwelling on one question. The scribe said Thi Hoc had travelled to Hai Phong. Would Sach, his eldest son, be with him?

9

I've made it from the battlefield. I turn in my saddle and look back in the direction I've travelled. Still there is no sign of them following but I know they will. Ma Vien will want to capture us. The burden I carried through that heaving mass of warriors shifts and moans in the saddle behind me. We are tied together by a length of tunic, ripped from a body dead on the field. I tied us together to stop her from falling from the horse as we rode and I had to ride a steady course, because I knew that every jolt pained her. My back is still wet with the blood that leaked from her as I carried her out of the ill-fated battle. A hand pats my leg and I look down to see that my friend, General Phung Thi Chinh, has dismounted and is untying the band between myself and Trac. I let her lift my sister down and then I slide from my mount.

'I can carry her alone,' I urge Chinh, who is in no state to care for us and who has experienced far worse horrors than I. Chinh shakes her head. Her ability to talk is gone, it seems, but she hooks one of Trac's arms about her shoulders and I take the other and we heave the Queen of Nam Viet to the bank of the river where we can clean her wounds and slake our raging thirst. We have fought hard for so long and Chinh, especially, is dehydrated. Other women and men are dismounting around us, running forward to help, but they are few in numbers. Everyone has either stayed to fight to the death or has run away.

The grass is soft where we lay Trac down and as Chinh pulls open my sister's tunic, we see the wound across her abdomen where a blade has penetrated deep. Trac's eyelids are fluttering and Chinh leans forward to stroke her head. As she does, her tunic gapes and I see the tiny dead bundle, wrapped and strapped between her breasts. Poor little baby, to come so soon in the midst of all that carnage. Even the Han soldiers backed away when they saw General Chinh fall on her knees mid-fight and clutch her pregnant belly, crying out like a wounded animal.

'Nhi, Chinh,' Trac whispers. 'Where are we?'

'We've come away,' I say. 'The battle is lost.'

'Mother...'

'Mother is... at the front.'

Trac's face creases, her body tensing in grief, and then she gives a shriek as a wave of pain strikes fresh through her wound.

'Try to stay still,' I plead.

Chinh takes the rag that had bound Trac and I together on the horse, and dips it in the flowing, crystal waters of the river. She returns and gently mops Trac's stomach, taking the blood and filth away. Someone removes their tunic and passes it to me to use as a bandage. I take the offered material blindly and it is only after Chinh and I have bound Trac about the middle with it that I see it is Giang, Auntie An's son, beside me. He bows to me, drops his weapons on the grass nearby and kneels by Chinh. Chinh looks faint. She has fought two battles today and lost them both and her face is white as snow. Giang puts his arm about her and holds her, being careful not to disturb the lifeless bundle on her chest. Chinh's own husband is dead, lost at Lang Bac, the first of our battles with Ma Vien.

I stop noticing them after that. I just lay with Trac, my arm under her head, listening to the rush of the river as once I listened to it slapping at the sides of a boat bound for Hai Phong.

★★★★★

I was so excited to have got myself on the river boat. Mother, I know, had intended to leave me in Lien Lau, but I like to think I had proved my worth with my idea about how to deal with the drum problem. I was still worried that they might drop me off in Lien Lau on the way past, so I stayed as calm and quiet as I could until we had sailed by the capital and were safely downriver. Then I perhaps became a bit too exuberant because Mother kept telling me off for trailing my arms in the water and rocking the boat. The weather was so fine for a boat trip - sunny and glorious, lighting up the hills and the fields and dancing on the surface of the water. It was almost impossible not to dunk my hand into that glossy sheen and feel the billowing water buffeting against my palm. I stood up a few times, to better see the passing scenery, but the boatman standing at the back glared at me and Mother fretted and waved at me to sit down, so I tried to contain myself and Mother pacified me with some of the food from the packages Diep had prepared.

When we finally arrived at Hai Phong, my legs felt the wobbly sensation of passing from water to land. The ground seemed to rise up to meet my feet too abruptly, but the feeling subsided within a moment or two and Mother and Trac disembarked impatiently, eager to find Vo Xuan. We were informed by a fish seller that we would find all the action at the people's building in the centre of Hai Phong, where the law was kept and where the local officials and occasional visiting ones were based, so we made in that direction. We had been deposited on the bank of the Cam River and there was a southbound track leading directly into the small town, so we followed this, aiming for the biggest building, the roof of which was already visible. The centre of Hai Phong was a cluster of bamboo and thatch roofs strung along a few streets, with a large marketplace and what was evidently the people's building to one side. Mother stopped and looked about her, then took a short, sharp breath inwards and began a determined stride to the doors of the building. Trac and I followed, aping her confidence.

Inside, a harried-looking young man demanded our names and turned to lead us into a large room where a crowd of people were gathered, listening to some speech being made at the front. We pushed through people and caught sight of the drums, lined up at the back of the room and guarded by a Giao Chi man armed with two swords who was flanked by a younger man and woman. The voice ringing out belonged to a woman older than Mother, who was urging everyone to convene outside rather than in the stifling heat of the people's building.

'The drums will be well guarded,' she insisted. 'They will not be moved until a fair decision has been reached.

The man leading us through the throng went to the right of the room, where Vo Xuan was quietly talking with several other Han officials. He saw Mother approach and greeted her with enough deference to make her status clear to everyone.

'Would you explain to me what is happening?' Mother asked him. 'I have heard mixed accounts.'

'Let us step outside,' said Xuan, his face shiny with sweat. 'Perhaps if we lead, these fools within will follow.'

So back out we went, into the marketplace, whilst curious eyes watched Xuan and Mother. Sure enough, as we left, some people started to wander out, hovering nearby and casting anxious glances back towards where the drums were being guarded.

'You have Giao Chi people guarding the drums,' Mother said.

'Yes. Tran Thi Chau acts as a Prefect of sorts in this whole area now. Her husband is Le Dao. He is the one with the swords.'

'Ah,' said Mother. 'I have heard of Prefect Chau but have not met her in person since she rose to her new rank.'

'This business is most sensitive and I have yet to uncover exactly what has happened. The Captain who has acquired these drums says he did so to give in tribute to the emperor. He says there was no opposition until he was attacked quite unexpectedly just south of here. He gave fight and killed several of his enemy, but two of his own soldiers died. The rest of his Company took the Giao Chi aggressors prisoner and brought them here, the nearest town. We have ended up with a strange situation where our soldiers are guarding the Giao Chi men who attacked them, and Giao Chi people are guarding the drums. The petals fall, caring not where they land.' He smiled.

Mother stared at him for a second then said 'Yes, I see.' She did not like the Han penchant for quoting poetry in the midst of business or politics and for her it was momentarily baffling rather than clarifying. 'Where are the other Prefects? Have you met with Vien yet?'

'He made his views very clear but wished to wait until all the appropriate persons were assembled for further talks. I am pleased with that. I had been waiting on my own colleague, Nham Dien from Cuu Chan, and he has fortunately now arrived.' Vo Xuan was irritated with Ton Vien. I could see that he was angry the Lien Lau Prefect was throwing his weight around, but happy that Vien's actions had turned-tail on him. Now that the Cuu Chan administrators had arrived, they would provide extra support for the Han Captain's argument.

'And how are these talks to be conducted?' Mother looked around the open square, at the groups of locals outside their homes and the angry neighbours from lower down the coastline whose drums were inside the people's building.

'My belief is that we should hold a hearing here, in the square, where all these people can air their grievances, then my administrators and Prefects should retire inside to consider a solution privately.' Xuan was looking about him, at the angry faces and huddled conversations. He had the Company commanded by the Han Captain, and a further several platoons who had escorted the officials from the Cuu Chan Commandery, but though he was well-manned he clearly did not want proceedings to descend into any kind of fighting. Whatever he did had to appear legal and correct. Without such decorum, representatives of the Emperor jeopardised the ruling dynasty's divine right to rule. The Han were our oppressors, but they must be seen to be embracing the Confucian and Legalist principles that the Emperor's court had officially sanctioned.

'I, myself, shall take a neutral role, hearing the complainants. I would like Prefects and administrators to perform the role of asking questions and elucidating truthful answers,' he continued.

Then he looked down at me, all of a sudden, as if he had only just seen me. 'Now then! Trac, I see regularly, but this sweet girl I have never set eyes upon.'

'This is my second daughter, Nhi,' said Mother, putting a hand out as if introducing us, but actually barring his way to me. She gently steered me slightly behind her and Trac moved closer to Mother, blocking me. 'May we begin the process? By the look of this crowd, many will wish to speak and it will take a long time.'

'I suppose we must,' sighed Xuan. 'I'll gather my people. You may gather yours.'

Mother gave a brisk nod and set off towards the people's building. I, too, had seen the Giao Chi Prefects gathered there in the doorway, talking with Tran Thi Chau.

'Nhi, you must try and be inconspicuous,' whispered Trac, as we walked. 'Be wary of letting Xuan talk with you. He would marry us both to Liu men this very day, if he could get away with it.'

I couldn't answer her, for we were already in the company of Thi Hoc, Ton Vien, Tran Thi Chau and several other men and women. Truth be told, I was feeling out of my depth for possibly the first time in my life. I had at last been allowed into the adult circle of politics and I was keenly aware that my strengths and abilities did not lie in tact, diplomacy or dissembling. I dared not say the wrong thing and embarrass Mother, so for once I took Trac's advice to heart. I was happy not to be noticed and to remain quiet, though I felt unnaturally constrained and my hand tap-tapped with a life of its own against my outer thigh.

'Lady Prefect,' said Ton Vien to Mother, with a glancing smile at Trac and myself, 'We saw you arrive but thought it prudent to let the Governor have the first word.'

'What circumstances these are, in which to meet,' exclaimed Mother, who then turned to Tran Thi Chau. 'Lady Prefect, I am from Me Linh. I wish we were meeting in better times.'

'I know of you, of course,' deferred Chau, with a bow to Mother. Chau was taller than Mother, with wider hips and an almost manly jawline. She wore a sword at her side, making me conscious that we were unarmed. Yet it was evident that Mother was the senior person there, weapon or no weapon.

'Vo Xuan has helpfully disclosed his own understanding of events,' said Mother

'I'm sure he did,' grimaced Vien, his fingers rotating a ring of jade and gold that he wore on his middle finger. 'The truth of the matter is that this Han Captain has stolen our sacred property, whether on orders from above or not I do not know. He refused to return it and when challenged, fought honest, local people and killed a number of them. We all accept that the Han govern here in the name of the Emperor and that taxes must be raised, but this is different. This is theft of ancient, spiritual treasure. The temples must be protected. I cannot believe that even the Han Emperor would want them defiled in this way. When Tich Quang took me to the Han court to be rewarded for the loyalty we showed in the Wang Mang time, I knew that the Emperor was a good man, who would protect our Commandery, not do it harm.' Prefect Vien's voice had risen, as if he wished Governor Xuan to catch his words.

I stared past Vien to gauge Thi Hoc's response. I was happy to see a face I recognised, the face of a man I had last observed over our own meal table. He looked worried, the lines on his ageing face multiplied in consternation. Yet when he caught me looking at him, he softened and gave me a comforting smile. He turned to a figure just inside the hall.

'Come, take the Lac sisters inside. I'm sure they need a drink after their journey.' He motioned to me to come forward along with Trac and as I skipped to him, the other man came to join Hoc and I saw that it was his son.

'Sach!' I cried out gladly. 'You're here.'

'Certainly am,' he replied, smiling. Then he turned to Trac

and gave her the most exquisite low bow. She flushed, but managed to return his smile.

'Go on inside,' whispered Mother, to us both, 'Give me chance to speak freely with my friends here and I'll call you back when I need you.' I was already half inside, but Trac had paused, unwilling to leave Mother alone. Mother's eye's brooked no dissension, so Trac, who was thirsty in more ways than one, accepted her dismissal. I stood back to allow Sach to walk closer to my sister, then followed them into the large room where the drums had been stored.

★★★★★

My heart was beating wildly. All down the river I had pictured him, turning his image about in my mind, wondering if my memories had sculptured his features into a false perfection, but here he was in front of me, gloriously smooth-skinned and brown-eyed. He did not have his swords but his manner was still one of absolute, warrior confidence as he showed Nhi and myself back into the hall and snapped at a servant to fetch us a drink. Some low benches lined the room and we settled gratefully upon those. A few persons still hovered nearby, chatting quietly, and the three members of the Le family remained guarding the drums.

'I'm very happy to see you again. I think of you often in your swan-covered silk,' said Sach. It was hard to quell the surge of excitement pressing in the centre of my chest, but I did so. I could not let myself mishandle this meeting, like I had mishandled the previous one. I had practised in my mind how I would behave, if we met again and I was resolved to use the tactic of gentle indifference that my mother had advised. My other aim was to try and uncover his true intention towards me. If his only purpose was to gain Me Linh province through marrying me, then I would rather marry plump, turtle-loving Mai Nhat and keep my political independence.

'I am happy to see you and your father also,' I answered,

sincerely though without passion. Nhi kept blessedly quiet, with her face a little averted. I gave a silent thank-you that she was behaving discreetly. I could not have born another blunt interlude like the cypress baby conversation. Sach gazed at me and now his smile was a little more quizzical. I took advantage of his brief perplexity at my cool response and turned the conversation to business.

'I am concerned about how heated this situation will become. My mother's position puts her in danger from both sides. If she does not fully support Ton Vien, the relations between Lac nobility will fracture. But if she challenges Vo Xuan, I do not know how far he will go to subdue her. Tell me, what does your father think? How will he respond to Xuan?'

'Truthfully, I don't know. My father is old now and not in favour of a fight. He wishes a peaceful resolution but no one, not he nor Vien, will stand by to watch the drums taken from us. There is a line beyond which the Han may not step.'

'We can, then, only hope that Xuan and his officials see for themselves the sense of finding a face-saving way out of this. They cannot wish for war either, surely.'

'They're not in a position to conduct one,' agreed Sach. 'They haven't the reserves, unless Xuan calls on the Emperor for more men, but I don't think he will. He's an intelligent man. I may not agree with his beliefs, nor can I ever be fully satisfied while we are ruled by the Han, but we do have working peace and Xuan will see that it is ridiculous to let the actions of one petty Captain jeopardise that. You shouldn't worry for your mother. I am confident that this will all be settled very soon.'

'Yet Xuan is suggesting an open hearing, where people may say all kinds of things that cannot be taken back. Everyone who speaks puts themselves in danger of future reprisals if they betray clear animosity for the Yellow River Emperor and his clan. I do not think an open hearing is advisable. I think they should seek a resolution privately, without inflaming things further.' This had occurred to me as we were speaking. I was thinking of the way Sach had stated that he would never be happy under the Han, and how if he allowed himself to speak openly like that in future he would endanger himself.

'People want to air their grievances,' shrugged Sach. 'Once the fire has started, it needs to be allowed to burn out a little before cold water is thrown upon it. This is where your mother and my father can make a difference. They must guide our people and protect them from going too far.'

I nodded. There was a kind of sense in that.

'Nhi had a good idea on the way here,' I said, and told him of her diplomatic solution to the crisis. She looked surprised as I spoke and hesitantly moved closer to us.

'That's quite good,' said Sach. 'We are all so immured in the passions of both sides, we have not seen this simple escape. I should mention it to my father.'

'Mother heard my idea,' said Nhi, 'I think maybe she'll suggest it, if it has merit.'

We were all silent for a moment, the whispers of other people's conversations drifting past us. Then Nhi spoke up again.

'Can we see the drums?' She was already on her feet. Poor Nhi, she had been still and well-behaved as long as her energetic body would allow.

'Yes, come over and I'll introduce you to Prefect Chau's family,' said Sach, who had evidently arrived much earlier than us and ingratiated himself with the coastal clan.

We crossed the room to where the three armed people stood. The man in the middle cocked his head at Sach.

'What's going on out there now,' the man demanded.

'Xuan is talking about having some kind of hearing in the square,' I said, moving forwards and looking directly at him. It was perhaps quite rude, but then so was his manner towards us. I was not going to be treated like some passing peasant.

'Le Dao, this is Trac, daughter of Lady Man Thien and General

Lac. And here is her sister, Nhi,' Sach interposed.

Dao nodded abruptly and I responded likewise. He was a gruff man, with a thin tangled beard and thick, muscled shoulders. His hair was loose and his teeth were well-blackened, in the old Nam Viet way.

'These are my children, Le Chan and Le Chien,' he said, gesturing in turn to the girl on his left and the boy on his right. I say girl and boy, but they were young adults, older than myself. Le Chan, I later found out, was about nineteen years old and her brother was seventeen. Le Chan was eyeing me strangely and I wondered if I had offended her by speaking brusquely to her father.

'I've brought Trac and Nhi over to see the drums,' said Sach and Le Dao gave a barely discernible turn of the head to indicate that we could go closer and inspect them. His offhand manner was apparently his natural one. I stepped past his imposing figure to within touching distance of the large bronze instruments, standing squat like giant rice mortars. They were all slightly different, but the patterns and pictures on the surface of the metal were all of a kind – concentric rings of sharp water birds and of warriors in stark feather headdresses, long boats carrying more warriors, and even representations of the drums themselves, carried on long boats across eternal waters. I reached out and traced my finger through a groove, the tiny incised pillar of a stilted house on the shining bronze. Some craftsman had worked this design directly into the wax core onto which the bronze would have been moulded. It was a scene by itself, amidst the repetition of animals and fighters that appeared in low relief above and below the house. I wondered what exactly the pictures meant and who had decided that they should be depicted so. The craftsmen still made these drums but it was to a pattern set many hundreds of years before, and indeed, looking at one or two of the other drums close by, I could see a difference. The warriors and birds that ran around the polished tympani of the newer drums were like stick shapes, compared to the miniature people and animals that encircled the older drum before me. The priests knew the meaning, what few of those spirit walkers were left, but the old ways were dying in Giao Chi, forced out by Confucianism and Daoism. As I touched the bronze, I felt the spark of recognition that came from my Lac blood crying out to its distant forbears. Nhi felt it too, I could see. She stood spell-bound, soaking in all the messages that called to us from the death boats and the temples and the ibises, tigers and elephants and all the many hundred warriors cast in burnished bronze.

Sach cleared his throat and I backed away, aware that we all were being watched. If the full power of these drums was not already evident to the Han, we must not reveal it any further than necessary. Nhi continued to stare, the glow from the drums casting sunset shades in her eyes.

'They are beautiful, aren't they?' said Le Chan, the girl who guarded the drums and I agreed with her that they were. 'Sach was looking at them earlier and he had just the same expression as you. Everyone who sees them is touched by them. Everyone born here, that is.' She looked at Sach and within her defiant, fighter's eyes I saw with sickened heart the gleam of desire. His eyes twinkled as he met her gaze and though he did not speak, I saw how attractive she would be to him, with her long, tanned limbs and her glossy hair and the strong jawline from her mother that, in Le Chan, looked magnificent rather than manly. She already had rounding of her hips and the fullness of breasts ready for babies. I felt punched. I walked a few strides away from them, on the pretext of introducing myself properly to Le Chien, her younger brother.

'Have you had to stand guard long?' I asked him and he said yes, since the previous day, with six hours of sleep during which others took over. While he spoke he looked furtively towards Nhi, whose shining face was still perusing the drums and so I sighed and said I was going outside to find my mother. Le

Chien was nearer my own age and even he preferred another. I obviously had no chance in securing the true affections of Thi Sach. I took Nhi's arm and drew her away. Sach, unexpectedly, came with us.

'You're right. We should find our parents and see what is happening.' said Sach, escorting us both back outside.

We found his father and my mother sitting in the shade, along with several more diplomatic envoys from local provinces. Xuan was organising more seating, since the Han preferred chairs to squatting, and had set some of the soldiers to erecting a canopy that would protect the hastily arranged legal hearing from the strength of the sun. So it was going ahead. I went to my mother and spoke quietly and directly with her. Seat Nhi away from us, she told me, find someone to keep watch over her while you sit with me. I glanced about but could find no one to trust. It was busy in that square piece of land, packed with Han soldiers, officials and diplomats, along with local peasants and all the offended native people from along the coast who had come to demand the return of their drums. There was no one to whom I could entrust Nhi, no one, in fact, who I knew at all. Just when I was about to argue that she should remain with us, Le Chien emerged from the people's building, still armed and wiping a hand over his tired face. I hurried over.

'Chien, are you no longer guarding the drums?' I asked.

'My father says he and Chan will stay inside and that I should keep an eye on things out here and let them know if anything of importance happens.'

'Chien, I have a dilemma. My mother and I must sit in this hearing, but Nhi should not. I have no one I trust to take care of her and-'

'I would be very honoured to look after your sister,' Chien interrupted, desperately eager. 'We will sit over in the shade of the building and I shall take her inside if there is any trouble. You may trust me to protect her.'

81

I pretended to consider. He touched his sword, nervous that he had been too forward.

'I do trust you, Chien. Please keep her safe.'

He beamed at me and we went to fetch Nhi. Once the pair of them were out of the way (but still within my sight – I trusted Chien to protect her from others but his obvious desire was another danger) I sat down with my mother. Eventually, after the usual fussing and faffing that accompanies these kinds of bureaucratic exercises, the hearing got under way. The onlookers moved to the edges of the square and a line of people with grievances stood to be heard. There was no sign as yet of the Han Captain, nor of the Giao Chi men in his custody. One by one, irate villagers described to Xuan the behaviour of the soldiers who had taken their prized drums.

'They came to our temple,' said the first, 'and saw the drum and simply took it. We watched them load it onto the cart and some of us shouted at them to stop, but the soldiers were armed and we were not.'

'Was there any violence?' Ton Vien asked.

'No, but only because we did not dare challenge them.'

The next few men and women said the same – that the Company of soldiers had taken the drums with barely a word to the locals. They had been afraid of the soldiers, and when, in one village, several people tried physically to protect their property, the soldiers had beaten those people senseless. Xuan's scribe made a little notation on his strip of bamboo. I could not have read it even if I had been closer to them. The Han had a written language but we did not and the markings were a mystery to me. Still, I hoped he was recording the unjustified use of violence by the Han against Red River people.

'Did they say why they wanted the drums?' my mother asked.

'No, they said nothing.'

The crowd mumbled and shifted throughout, conscious of the military presence. When all the villagers had been given a chance to speak, the widow of one of the Giao Chi men killed in the final skirmish came forward. She related how the people where she lived, not far from Hai Phong, had heard of the renegade Captain and had ensured that they remained armed in case he descended upon them, for they had a fine collection of drums and some were exceptionally old and beautiful. They had sent a message to Lien Lau trying to alert the governing presence there to the actions of the army, but apparently this message had gone astray because they had not received a reply. Then the Captain had indeed led his men into her town and her husband in response had led an ambush that felled several of the soldiers, taking the Captain entirely by surprise. Even so, there were more Han soldiers than local fighters and some of the local men and women perished on the swords of the Han while the Captain regained control and took the remaining ambush party prisoner. By now, said the widow, who had collected her husband's body from the dirt track where he lay, the Captain could not continue his thievery because he was left with prisoners to control and clear evidence of violence. People from her town had tracked the Company of soldiers as they travelled into Hai Phong where everyone had waited for the Governor to arrive and sort the mess out.

She told her tale as a sequence of facts, her voice steady and even and one would have thought she was unaffected by the events if not for the cascade of tears that slipped silently down her cheeks. I almost felt ashamed of our search for a diplomatic resolution. What this woman wanted was true justice, but there was no such thing in Giao Chi. Vo Xuan bowed his head and waited for her to retire before he called for the Han Captain to present himself.

When he came, he swaggered into the square in full uniform and weaponry with not a trace of humility on his face. Xuan looked at him sternly.

'You may give us all your account,' said the Governor. The

Captain bowed and began to speak. It was, I knew immediately, a prepared response carefully worked out by Xuan to engender an acceptable outcome. It was what I had expected, but having seen the widow speak, my heart ached for an honest result instead.

'My lord governor and all assembled nobles, my love and duty towards the Giao Chi province is outshone only by my love and duty towards the Emperor, in whose name I have assembled these items of such spiritual significance. As part of my post, I am tasked with extracting appropriate tribute from all areas of the province for the benefit of the Emperor. When I became aware of these wonderful objects, I knew that the Emperor would be delighted to see them and assumed that the loyal subjects of Giao Chi would have no objection to providing the Emperor with such pleasure. I intended to gather a selection of the instruments to transport to the mighty Emperor Guangwu, for his perusal. If the inhabitants of the villages I visited had asked my purpose, I would of course have explained it, but none did and most remained mute. Those that spoke were aggressive and hostile to myself and my men. We were surprised and dismayed to be ambushed on our route to Hai Phong, by villagers whose community we had not even intended to visit, and we fought to defend ourselves knowing not what had provoked this violent outburst.'

There were outraged gasps at this. I glanced at my mother and her face was hard as ice as she stared at the Captain. Prefect Vien's cheeks had darkened.

'Why did you not expressly reveal this purpose of yours, when it became clear that local people were hostile to your actions?' Vien shouted at the Captain.

'Forgive me, Prefect Vien, but it is sometimes hard to make oneself understood given the strong dialects that persist on the coast.'

'I think it is more likely that this explanation is a concoction after the fact!'

'How I regret that I did not make my intentions perfectly clear at the time!' answered the Captain, without a trace of regret on his features.

'This is preposterous,' Vien argued to Xuan. 'We can all see that he is lying. The man stole those drums for personal gain and even if he was taking them for the Emperor, it is still a theft.'

'Is it so?' asked Governor Vo Xuan, coldly. 'The Emperor has the right to take what he wants from Giao Chi. Would you argue with that?'

'We owe the Emperor tribute,' said Vien, hotly, 'but we cannot be expected to hand over items essential to our ancient spiritual tradition.'

'It seems we have confusion at the highest levels. It is not surprising this Captain has found himself in difficulty, trying to do the right thing,' answered Xuan.

Thi Hoc, seated just behind me, gave a little pained sigh. He had been silent throughout. Like my mother, he had known how this would proceed and had perhaps been as instrumental in it as my mother. Even so, neither was enjoying the spectacle. Ton Vien stood up and shook his head angrily.

'No, no. I understand what you are trying to do. But you cannot absolve this man of blame. We all know what went on. Why must we pretend otherwise?' He looked to my mother and the other Prefects and received some sympathetic glances, but no one else spoke up.

'It is my job to decide what went on, once I have heard all the evidence,' said Xuan. 'Be seated, Prefect Vien, and let us continue.'

Vien paused seeing that he must either walk away or resume his seat and, no doubt bitterly swallowing his pride, he sat down. The square was silent in those seconds – even the lowest peasants had ceased their scuffling and chatter. The Captain still stood before us, arrogance lighting a smirk across his mouth. Xuan dismissed him and required him to fetch the Giao Chi men, kept prisoner by his company since the ambush. While the Captain strode away, I stood up to look over to where Nhi was waiting with Chien. The pair of them were still there, sat on the outer edge of the crowd, in the shade of the people's building. Conversations in the crowd started to resume and under the low hum of voices, I whispered to my mother.

'Did you plan an outcome with Xuan?'

'More or less,' she whispered back.

'Does Vien not know?'

'Vien won't listen to reason. He does not know how to pick his battles. He's too busy trying to look important.'

At the sound of the prisoners being marched into the square, everyone turned. They came under the guard of the Captain's men, but the Captain himself had hung back. Perhaps, since he had emerged almost unscathed from the hearing, he felt it politic to avoid coming under their gaze once more. The men formed a row before us, facing Xuan resentfully. They were all well-built fighters, confident and undiminished by several nights in captivity.

'We've heard the Captain's account, and the account by the widow of your leader. Do any of you have anything to add?' Xuan asked.

'I'll speak,' said one man, stepping forward. 'I don't know what you've been told already, but the truth is that these Han soldiers have been stealing drums from villages all along the coast. We heard about them, we knew they were coming our way and we decided to protect the drums. We waited on the road that leads into our town, so that if they came without official orders, we would block their way. We were protecting our drums, in the name of our ancestors and on behalf of the Emperor. The Company of soldiers had no official orders so we did not let them pass.'

I glanced sharply at my mother. Had she somehow managed to prime this man with such a clever defence? Her face was impassive. The man spoke some more. A few questions were put to him by the administrator of Cuu Chan, Nham Dien, and so it went on, with the prisoner's friends also giving much the same account. The day was beginning to darken. We had sat in the square for hours and I sensed, from Xuan's increasing abruptness that he wished to draw the proceedings to a close. Indeed, there was no need to prolong it, since the witnesses and evidence had been manipulated to delineate a previously decided result. Finally Xuan called a halt to give a verdict.

'My finding from today's hearing is this: That the Captain and his Company acted in a prudent manner, having become aware of tribute which they believed the Emperor would require and seeking to acquire it; That the men who attacked the Company acted in a prudent manner, being falsely informed that the Captain was not acting in accordance with the Emperor's wishes. Men have already died on both sides, which seems a logical and fair distribution of justice. I order the prisoners to be released and the Captain to continue in his role within the Emperor's army.'

Someone called out, 'What about the drums?' and a few angry voices chimed in, under the falling darkness.

'The matter of the drums themselves will be decided tonight by myself and the assembled prefects of Giao Chi.' Xuan rose and his scribe hurriedly finished off his writing and gathered his strips of bamboo together. That night, the scribe would thread them together, so that the rows of bamboo strips would form a scroll and that scroll would be lodged somewhere within the Giao Chi administration's meticulous records collection. It mattered not to us, who could not, in any case, read it, but to the Han rulers, who set great store by legitimising their actions as conquerors.

★★★★★

Later, when we had all eaten, we came together with Governor Xuan and his fellow Han officials to determine what should be done with the drums. My mother, Nhi and I had all taken refreshment in the Le home, with Tran Thi Chau. Her son and daughter, Le Chien and Le Chan had joined us, leaving their grizzled father in the people's building with a fresh pair of guards. Le Dao was staying put in the hall and some food was sent to him. Conversation over the meal had been muted. Prefect Chau was not a talkative woman in any case, but the day's events had given us all pause for thought and everyone was anxious about what would happen to the drums now. It was unthinkable that they should be sent away, to the court of the Yellow River Emperor, when they belonged here, in what was the Van Lang heartland. Furthermore, allowing these seven drums to be sent away would set a precedent and if it was allowed to happen, soon our entire collection would no doubt be spirited away. Chau commented that Vien was in a sulk over our perceived refusal to support him. He was eating alone, with just his attendants for company, so angry was he with us all.

'It will pass,' said my mother. 'Vien understands what had to happen today and he will forgive our actions.' She exchanged knowing glances with Chau, which suggested to me that the pair had already established a good understanding of one another.

Sach and his father ate with us also and my meal was slightly ruined by having to bear Sach and Chan smiling at one another, her dark eyes flashing. I had sat with Sach just behind me, to my left for the whole afternoon, and I had felt his presence there like a heat against my shoulder for the first hour of the hearing, conscious of whether I was holding my posture sufficiently upright and whether my hair wrap was neat at the back. It had been exhausting and stressful and thankfully I had forgotten about him as we listened to testimony after testimony. But now, here he was again, grasping my unwilling attention. I was almost grateful to escape the Le house and return to Vo Xuan's presence. Xuan had dined in the people's building, with Administrator Nham Dien and officers from the Cuu Chan

Commandery, as well as his own staff. Infuriatingly, when we entered, Sach contrived to be by my side, close enough to brush my arm. My instant reaction was that he was bolstering his own status by affecting to be close to my mother and I.

We had left Nhi in the house, where Chien was overjoyed to entertain her once more. The family's servant was with them and I had in any case relaxed my guard towards the boy as I saw how respectfully he held himself towards Nhi over dinner. Perhaps, I had quietly commented to our mother, it would do Nhi good to have some practice in the company of a boy other than Bao, and she distractedly agreed. My mother was now wholly focussed on what should happen with the drums and how she could manage Xuan, for he was a man who needed very careful management.

He welcomed us back into the hall, as though it were his own, and bade us sit with himself and his group of stern-faced politicians and generals. What one has to realise about an outpost such as the Giao Chi province is that it attracted the fearless among the Han - men who did not baulk at travelling thousands of miles from home, deep into the forests and mountains of a hostile native people. The Han who governed us might be fair and honest, or greedy and callous, but they were, without fail, intellectually sharp and brutally purposeful, even if they adopted perfect manners and acted with diplomacy when conversing with our own nobility. My mother knew what she was dealing with. Ton Vien, who entered immediately after us, either under-estimated them or overestimated his own power. Having a few hours by himself had calmed the Lien Lau Prefect, but he was still fidgety and pursed with annoyance.

'Chau of Hai Phong, my gratitude to you on your hospitality,' said Xuan gesturing about him at the hall and the remnants of the food he and his men had eaten.

'Given with our compliments, Governor,' replied Tran Thi Chau. I have mentioned that she was a tall woman, impressively square-jawed, and this was still evident when seated. Her physicality dominated our gathering, but it was my mother whom Vo Xuan knew he must be wary of. Lady Man Thien sat quietly by Chau, a small smile on her lips.

'Lady Prefect, what do you make of the day's proceedings? All finished in an afternoon. That is Middle Kingdom legality for you!' He smiled at my mother, letting her make what she wanted of his vague statement.

'Highly efficient, Governor, and a satisfactory outcome. Yet we have further matters to settle.' She gazed at a point beyond him, like prey staring past the predators eyes, hoping not to incite the leap, the attack.

'Further matters indeed!' Xuan grinned and his eyes fell upon me, seated a little away from my mother, still with Sach at my side. 'Ah, the lovely daughter Trac visits with us, and with a young man too. Here to help your father, young Sach? I'm glad to see we all know one another and are friends.'

Beside me, on the bench, Sach tensed. I could feel it even though no parts of us were touching, as if the flex of his muscles swept a tiny breeze against my skin. I suppressed my urge to look at him, or to look directly at Xuan and I held my body rigid, my face pleasantly tilted.

'I'm glad to support my father and to work for our province, Governor,' said Sach at last and Thi Hoc murmured to no one in particular that Sach was a good son.

'But where is your other daughter, Lady Prefect? The one I met today?'

'She is sleeping,' stated my mother, 'as she is but a child and very tired from the events of today.'

'Quite, quite,' replied an amused Xuan. 'I too am tired. It has been a long day. I hope no one will prolong it further by complicating the agreement of what will now happen to these items of tribute.' He waved towards the drums. The big, bronze ornaments lined the back wall still but the lithe figure of Le Chan now stood guarding them, her father having come forward to join us.

'That depends,' piped up Prefect Vien 'on what the proposed agreement involves.' He was leaning in his seat, red spots on his cheeks, frustrated but not deflected by all the needling small talk. My mother cast her eyes down, awaiting Xuan's response. It was the question that had to be asked, but better that Vien had asked it. My mother was not a coward. She was marking her time, waiting for the right battle in which to show her true colours. That quiet evening in Hai Phong was neither the time nor the place.

'What else can happen but that these drums go in tribute to the Emperor?' asked Xuan. Vien began to puff, taking in a lungful of air ready to unleash his outrage, but my mother forestalled him.

'Governor Xuan, you ask an excellent question. May I offer a possible answer? One which you might consider or discard as you see fit?'

'Of course, Lady of Me Linh,' said Vo Xuan, with narrowed eyes.

'I must admit, this is not my own idea, but that of my youngest child. An innocent and loving girl who sees harmony everywhere. She said such a beautiful thing, Governor Xuan. She said, let us inscribe tribute plaques which can be attached to the drums which will then return to their homes. In that way, she said, the glory and presence of the Emperor can be further established and proclaimed along this wild coastline. What do you make of that? Isn't there poetry in such a solution? Of course, it is a child's idea, but, sometimes for the better, they see the world in simpler terms than we. I leave it in your hands, Governor, for you see the wider implications of whatever actions you take.'

Throughout her planned and meticulous speech, my mother had let her voice lilt and ride in pretended wonder, but that final sentence was delivered in a tighter tone, carrying the message to Xuan that theft of the drums could not be tolerated and that warfare would surely follow if Xuan persisted. Prefect Vien gripped his hands together so hard that I saw his knuckles turn white. Next to me, Sach moved his arm by a fraction and a loose thread from his tunic touched against me. My mother remained smiling, composed and relaxed. She might have just commented on the weather, so calm was her countenance.

'Poetic indeed, my lady, and intelligent too. Nhi is wasted, sleeping alone in her bed.' He paused, viciously, his double meaning all too apparent. 'She should be here to present her fine conclusion in person, for then she would hear me say that I applaud it. Indeed, transporting them to the Emperor would be, dare I say it, something of a waste of our resources, since the court of the Yellow River prefers ivory and jade to commonplace bronze. So I agree. Let the drums be returned bearing plaques and for a time, the tribute entitlement will be raised, to give due material honour to the Emperor.'

My mother rose suddenly, making me start.

'Governor Xuan, forgive us all, you said how tired you were and we have intruded for far too long, keeping you from sleep. Since we have settled on this most satisfactory answer, may we bid you good night and leave you to your bed?' Still she smiled at him and it must have hurt the tendons of her jaw to do so, because he had given veiled threat to Nhi and also insulted our precious native antiquities.

'Of course, Lady Prefect. Good night to you.' He bowed slightly and my mother turned and swept past me. Chau stood also and followed my mother, her long arms swinging by her sides, and then I followed. Xuan fixed me with a stare as Sach escorted me out and I wondered if the Governor was thinking about his idea of marrying me off to a member of the Liu clan. I shivered and Sach glanced at me. My mother was walking ahead with Chau, conversing quietly and Vien was talking with Sach's father a little way from the people's building. We had found ourselves in the centre of the square and Sach stopped.

'Your mother is very skilled in diplomacy,' he said.

'My mother is very skilled in many things,' I agreed.

'But she doesn't like the Han, that much is clear.'

'None of us likes the Han.' I thought about Xuan's face when he spoke about Nhi and felt revulsion

'I am sorry if I offended you.'

'Offended me?'

'By not being clear with Governor Xuan. When he said you were with me, I did not set him straight. He assumes now that we are intended for each other.'

'The Governor told me I should consider a Liu match. I would rather he thinks that I am matched already,' I said, avoiding Sach's stare. Sach smiled and was about to speak but at that moment his father joined us. As we made our way back to Tran Thi Chau's home, I realised that despite all our polite and cautious conversation, I had still not ascertained Sach's true motives in courting me.

10

From my vantage point in the shade at the edge of the square, I watched the whole hearing. It got very boring after a while, with all the peasant people coming forward and complaining about the Captain's actions and I really only listened when the Captain himself came forward, because I wanted to hear his excuses. He was a nice-looking man. He didn't look like a man who would go round stealing and killing. I thought about how the warty newt, so unremarkable and brown on top, hides the blood-red splashes of tell-tale colour all along its underside.

'Just like a warty newt,' I said to myself and beside me, Le Chien said, 'What's like a newt?'

'That man. Hiding his true colours.'

'Look around, Nhi. Newts everywhere,' he joked, and gestured to the Prefects, his mother and mine included, and all of the Han men, all hiding behind a façade of truth.

'Mother and Trac are excellent diplomats but I lack the skill.'

'More of a Fan Xi Pan yellow bird than a warty newt, then,' he said.

I blushed, not knowing if he was making fun of me or complimenting me. The yellow and pink birds that live on Fan Xi Pan mountain are the most conspicuously beautiful in all of Giao Chi. Since we had spent a long time talking happily together, I guessed it must be a compliment. Words came easily to Le Chien and with my lack of artifice, we covered so many topics that by the evening, I felt we knew each other very well. We didn't talk as much over our meal, instinctively knowing that Chau and my own mother would not necessarily approve of our wholly unguarded conversation, but afterwards, when they all went off yet again and left us alone, we were delighted.

'Nhi, why is your sister so cool with Sach?' he asked me after a while. 'I thought they were intended for each other.'

'Why did you think that?'

'Prefect Hoc and Sach himself led us to believe so.'

'I think Sach is counting chickens before they have hatched,' I laughed. 'Trac hasn't yet agreed, and in fact, has not even been asked.'

'I think Sach will be very disappointed if she turns him down. He seems very taken with her.'

'Do you think so?'

'Oh yes. Before you arrived this morning, he was watching out for her, and when he was introduced to Chan, he made it very clear that he had a woman already. Chan was put out, I think, but then Chan thinks she's entitled to first go at everything. You know what older sisters are like.'

'Oh yes,' I laughed. 'But Trac isn't really so cool as you think. She likes him very much. She just won't say so.'

We were sat in the living area of his parents' home, in the shadows thrown by a small torch braced on the wooden wall. Outside, the sounds of the sea wafted towards us.

'I love the sea,' I said. 'I hardly ever get to visit the shore.'

'We must go tomorrow,' Chien insisted. 'There is a beautiful beach a little to the south. If your mother would stay just one more day, we could spend it there.'

So it was that the next morning, we found ourselves loaded up onto a small cart, with a basket of food and Chien excitedly checking the horse. I was in an especially good mood. Mother had explained to me the agreement with Xuan and I felt very proud that she had used my suggestion, and proud too that all the assembled prefects knew the idea had been mine. Mother was very tired when she returned and told me about the meeting and I almost didn't ask about the beach, but then I couldn't help myself. To my surprise she immediately agreed. 'It would be useful,' she said, 'to avoid the Governor and his men for a while.' If he was travelling back upriver the next day, she didn't want to end up sharing a boat with him. 'We'll go to the beach and with luck, he'll be gone when we return,' she reasoned.

The cart could hold four people, so Hoc drove the horse while Mother, Trac and I were the passengers. Behind us, Chien and Sach followed on foot, chatting amiably together. The track was pitted and thin in parts and we were jolted about, which I didn't mind but it was hard on Hoc who ached after a while holding the reins. We stopped once on route, to give the horse some water because the morning was already sweltering, and then Mother firmly took the driver's seat. I jumped down. I wanted to walk and less weight in the cart would mean less burden on the animal. Trac stayed in the cart, looking up the coast to where Cat Ba island sat in the East Sea, guarding the mouth of the river. She avoided looking at Sach and I knew she was regretting that she had decided to wear her plain travelling clothes from the previous day and not the pretty outfit she had brought. She didn't want sand and sea spray and splinters from the cart to damage the precious silk, but now she thought Sach would be unimpressed by her slightly stained and rough attire. My silly sister had no idea that in her undyed cloth, which had softened through wear, the lines of her body stood out more clearly and she looked more approachable and relaxed than ever she did in her more fancy clothes. Sach's eyes were constantly upon her.

I had none of Trac's modesty. Even though I had yet to turn twelve, I knew Chien was taken with me and I had every expectation that he should be. My face was pretty and I had entertained him well the previous day and on top of that, the status of my family made me a good catch.

When we arrived, I ran through a man-made path between thick shrubbery and out onto the hot white sands. The air was dense and salty and a heat-wave shimmered to the south, blurring the mangrove forest that lined that edge of the beach. The curve of the coast allowed us to look north towards Cat Ba and beyond it, I could just see the faint, turquoise mirage of Ha Long Bay. I cast off my slippers so I could feel the warm grains giving way between my toes and then I ran down to the water's edge to dip my feet in the cool shallows. Behind me, the others were sitting down on the dry sand, Chien bringing the basket of food and Sach carrying a bundle of firewood and kindling. It was nearly midday and Chien was keen to eat, but he ran down to me and splashed in the water.

'What do you think?' he asked.

'It's beautiful,' I said.

'Come and eat, then we'll walk down the shore.'

I followed him back to the others, the sand sticking to my wet legs and feet and Trac shooed at me with her arms.

'Don't get sand in the food,' she complained. She had the basket open and was unwrapping the bundles of meat which Prefect Chau had packed for us before we left. Sach was building a small fire. When he had got it lit we let it burn for a while and then used sharpened, fresh bamboo sticks to hold the turtle meat over the flames. It had been cut into slivers which we toasted and then ate with balls of cooked rice and pickled vegetables. There was a melon for afterwards. Hoc cleft it open with a machete and then sliced it into a dozen pieces. Chien took his and stood up.

'We can walk while we eat these,' he said and I grabbed a slice of the melon and got up, brushing sand from my knees. Sach stood also. He had spotted an opportunity to be alone with Trac.

'Come on,' he said to her, 'Let's leave your Lady Mother and my father to have a rest. My old man tires easily.'

Hoc swatted at him affectionately with the machete and Sach jumped aside laughing. Trac got up and the four of us started to walk down towards the waterline, Chien and I in front with Trac and Sach following. Mother silently watched us leave, eyeing me with that all-knowing face. I could tell what she was thinking and I had to try very hard not to give her my customary tongue-stuck-out face. I'm just having fun Mother, I wanted to say, don't go getting ideas about marrying me off yet. But I knew that we had to think about it and when I did think about Chien in that way, I got a fluttery anticipation in my tummy.

I walked in the edge of the sea, the waves folding over my feet and ankles and Chien left broad footprints to my right, deep depressions that pooled with clear saltwater and blended away behind us. When I finished my piece of melon, I threw the tough outer skin into the sea, watching it sail over little waves before it sank. Sach and Trac kept pace for a while and I could hear the mellow tones of his voice coaxing at her and her polite little replies, vast in their meaninglessness. I thought about what Chien had said the night before, but really it was no proof of Sach's feeling. If he wanted my sister, he would have to fight through her defences. If he truly loved her, he would find a way to reach her and so I resisted my urge to turn round, shake her and tell her to relax. Chien and I were faster, more eager to reach the distant end of the beach where the mangrove forest crowded in, and we left them behind.

'It's a shame your mother, father and sister couldn't come with us,' I said to Chien as we slid through the soft sand and the surf.

'My father is usually too busy for days out like this. When he's not teaching his students, he's brewing up medicines and travelling about to visit ill folk.'

'Le Dao is a medicine man?' I asked. Having seen the intimidating man guarding the drums with his black teeth and wild hair, I would not have guessed.

'Locally he's known for it. People come to him for cures and he takes on several students at a time, teaching them about medicine and other things.' Chien shrugged, unimpressed. 'He tried to teach me but I had no aptitude.'

'Thi Hoc is also knowledgeable about medicine. It is an honourable pursuit.'

Chien laughed at that and dared to give me a little push

that sent me stumbling deeper into the water. It caught at my underskirt, even though I had rolled the waistband over several times. 'Why are you speaking in that serious way?' he teased. I regained my balance and reached to him as if I was slipping. He took my hand to steady me and as he did I threw him over with a simple wrist-lock. He landed with a grand splash. I ran away along the sand, laughing fit to burst at his shocked face as he fell. He caught up with me in seconds, fortunately smiling and holding his hands up to suggest he would not retaliate.

'It's true about you girls then? I heard you were experts in the fighting arts.' He was rubbing at his wrist and arm.

'Mother teaches us,' I said.

'That's more than teaching. You have what I lack at medicine - real aptitude. Teach me that lock. Show me how you did it.'

'It's not hard,' I said, offering him my hand. 'That's right, use your hands to turn it, so my body must follow.'

'Why aren't you falling?' He asked, frustrated, bending my supple wrist.

'It's the height difference. You're taller than me so you have to compensate, you have to feel where my centre is, then take me from that balance. Do you see?' I altered his arms slightly with my free hand and gave a push to his hip to alter his alignment. 'From there it should work.' He twisted again and my arm gave a little. I patted him twice to show he had achieved the lock and could release me.

'You didn't fall,' he accused.

'No, you need to work on it. Throwing someone over with that simple move takes a lot of practice.'

'If only we lived closer to each other, you could teach me,' he said. 'There are people in Hai Phong who can fight, of course, but I have trained with them and still not learned to take someone down with such grace. You have a natural talent for it.'

We had resumed walking, apart from one another again, but the bones on the back of my right hand still held an impression of his thumb. We had touched for such a short time and now, although I wanted very much to touch him again, it was impossible. Instead of chattering away happily, I found myself waiting helplessly for something satisfactory to be said or done. Chien seemed to feel it too, because he went quiet and we just walked briskly, desperate to reach the end of the beach. As we came close to the thick undergrowth, a scent of salt and meat, brackish and inhuman, drifted towards us on a heat haze.

'The mangrove stretches into the sea,' I said, looking at the deep green trees, up to their necks in the tide.

'Or the sea stretches into the mangrove,' observed Chien. 'It carries in the fish and they breed in the swamps. The baby fish swim out when they are ready, or else provide food for the crocodiles.'

The foetid air of dark, wet places washed over me and frightened me and I turned sharply. I saw Trac waving, perhaps twenty cart-lengths from us.

'We're going back,' she called. 'Are you coming?' But she and Sach turned and left without waiting for an answer. Chien stared into the mangrove, biting on his bottom lip and I waited, breathlessly, for him to begin walking back. He grasped me suddenly, with his arms flung around me, pressing his cheek to mine and holding me with such tight passion that I wanted to cry.

'I know you're still a child,' he said, 'but soon you'll be grown. Think of me then, Nhi. We're two of a kind.' He pulled away abruptly and stood staring into my eyes. I swayed in his absence.

'I'm not a child,' I said. 'And I will think of you.'

It was a peculiarly adult bond. The words carried more weight than they should have done. Maybe it was the carnivorous and rotting air of the mangroves that did it, making us feel for a moment that we were somewhere darker and more dangerous than the idyllic golden beach. Instead of feeling elated at this perfect, romantic moment that was occurring, I felt like I was in one of my terrible dreams - the dreams I could never remember. I had a searing need to cling on to Chien and escape, but escape from what, I did not know.

★★★★★

The incident with the bronze drums passed. The plaques were made, the relics redistributed to their rightful owners and attention moved away from Hai Phong and back to the capital. Our journey home was uneventful and the only aspect of note was that Nhi sat quietly for the journey, the spark gone from her usually vibrant face.

'She's smitten,' said my mother, with a nudge, and we smiled at each other. Tran Thi Chau and Le Dao, though not of our status, were respected Giao Chi elite, and their son Chien might be a good prospect for Nhi.

The summer was quiet after that and my mother did not visit Lien Lau for some time, letting the dust settle and ensuring none of it stuck to her tunic. Prefect Vien was more restless and sought out discontent, rallying the traders and the peasants to complain when the Han were seen to take liberties, but Xuan did not respond. The populace might have been ready to quarrel with the Han over the drums, but now that matter was over with, there was no heart for a fight in the hot, drowsy weather. In Me Linh, Nhi and I trained in the early mornings when the heat was not so strong, and we worked for our mother in the long afternoons, since we were of an age now to begin management of our lands and people. The farmers knew us well and so we rode out whenever it was needed, overseeing the crops of rice and millet, yams and sugar-cane. Bao worked the land now and hardly had time to spend with us, but we waved when we saw him and he always shouted a hello through the incessant summer rains, whether he was planting, digging or shovelling old water buffalo excrement into the rice beds.

When finally the hot monsoon downpours receded and the air turned cool, and I was just about seventeen, Governor Xuan invited us to an evening's entertainment in Lien Lau. It was a formal and illustrious summons, read to us by a cheerful little messenger, and required all three of us to attend the administrative complex. I had been there with my mother often now, but never as an official guest at a formal function and I wondered to what purpose the meal had been arranged. Nhi, whose spirits had rekindled within a few days of being back home, was gleeful at the prospect of fine food and dressing up, even if it meant keeping company with Xuan and his colleagues. After all the drama at Hai Phong, life in Me Linh had bordered on dull and even I found myself looking forward to it.

When the day arrived, we packed our nicest clothes into rolls and Bao drove us in a cart to the river, where my mother had arranged for a boat to take us all the way to Lien Lau. The boatman took us downstream, past the great fork and along the lower distributary and finally to the jetty behind the Han complex of buildings. When we alighted we found the path that would take us round the outer wall to the front courtyard and entrance. Xuan had promised accommodation overnight, and though he was not in sight, one of his staff took us down the left wing and out through a garden towards our room, which was part of an old, long, single-storey building bordering the river. In this room, we could rest and then dress, ready for the evening. My mother slept, sensible of the fact that she would have to retain her wits until long into the night, but Nhi and I couldn't sleep, not with the bright, clear day outside and the sweet smell of pollen from the late flowers out in the garden. We sat outside, on a low stone wall that ringed a sunken pool. In the depths, fish flickered their colours and a pale sun hid behind the green lily pads. Nhi gazed at her own face, shimmering on the surface.

'Is the Hai Phong Prefect invited?' She asked me, still staring down into the pool.

'I do not know. I have not heard otherwise,' I answered. She was thinking, of course, about whether Chien would attend with his mother, father and sister. Nhi had turned twelve over the late summer and she was rapidly blossoming into a young woman. If Tran Thi Chau attended, then it was possible both she and our own mother would be seriously considering the merits of a match.

'Sach will be here, of course,' she said, almost bitterly.

'I presume so, but Nhi,' I said, stroking her arm, 'you are the lucky one. Chien loves you and anyone could tell on those few days in Hai Phong. Whereas Sach is still a mystery to me, even though we meet again and again.'

'Do you love him though?' She dragged her eyes away from the water to look at me.

'How can I love a man I do not know?' I answered.

'I think he does really want you, Trac. He was quite possessive about you in Hai Phong. Chien said he practically warned Le Chan that he wasn't available.'

'Ah, well that explains Chan,' I said, thinking of how the older girl had eyed me so strangely when I first met her. 'She did not seem to like me at all.'

'Chan's all right,' said Nhi.

Later we saw Sach arrive with his father and both his sisters. Their maternal aunt had accompanied them also, to guide and care for the girls, who were twelve and fourteen. They had been without their own mother for seven years – Sach had spoken to me briefly about her death on the day we spent at the beach, almost unable to mention her as I was unable to talk about my father. There were introductions all round, before Sach's family disappeared into a room adjoining ours. He went with them and we returned to our own room to begin dressing. I had brought my finest clothes, the ceremonial ones, and my mother was allowing us to wear some of her jewellery. Nhi was anxious to be finished, so she could go and speak some more with Thi Khanh and Thi Kim Cuc. Sach's sisters were pleasant girls, at least on first introduction. They had that air of girls who have been protected by an older brother and had been very quiet when first presented to us, but beneath the polite exterior, I saw that they were fascinated to meet me and I guessed I had been the subject of much conjecture and interest.

Our mother was quite keen that we both looked especially presentable but also that we trod warily through the evening. All the time we were washing and dressing, combing our hair and wrapping it up in silk, she talked about making sure we were never alone with the Han men and she warned us over and over about thinking very carefully before we spoke.

'I wondered before what this evening was for,' she said to us as she fastened jewellery around our necks - blue glass beads for Nhi and a string of polished jade beads for myself - 'and now I think I understand. Xuan is evidently surveying and monitoring the Giao Chi nobility. He will be looking to see what the relationships are between us all and where we are divided. He must be interested in our younger generation, since he has invited them all and he will be seeking to ascertain what marriages and alliances are intended.'

'Really Mother?' asked Nhi. 'Don't you think it's just a ceremonial thing he has to do?'

'Nothing is ever as simple as it seems, Nhi. Just, please, take care tonight and try to stay by me when you can.' She didn't extend the same warning to me and I had no idea if it was because she thought I could handle myself or if she believed I was protected by the outward appearance that Sach and I were intended. Certainly, there was still a risk that Xuan would make good on his idea of arranging marriages between the daughters of the Giao Chi people and the sons of the Liu clan, the family that led the Han.

At last we were ready. I wore the blood-red silk that Tailor Chi had been so convinced of nearly a year ago. Nhi wore the orange, with the tiger-like markings. Our mother blinked at our vivid, womanly appearances, then shook her head and turned to finish her own hair. Poor mother, she had made us glorious but a part of her must have wanted to hide us away for safe-keeping. Nhi skipped out and I heard her banging on a door, calling for the Thi girls. She made friends so easily. I hung behind her, waiting until Kim Cuc and Khanh appeared, and with them came Sach, dressed also in his finest, and handsome enough to make me stare. He stared back and Kim Cuc tittered into cupped hands. Nhi whispered something and all three girls went off into peals of laughter. Their Auntie Nhu came bustling out and waved her hands at them.

'Come along now,' she said. 'None of this silliness!' Then she looked appreciatively at Nhi and I and said how nice we both looked and asked where we had got our outfits. I told her and we had a short conversation about silk trade in Lien Lau while Sach fended off his playful sisters. 'Doesn't she look lovely?' Auntie Nhu said to him, above their bantering.

'She always looks beautiful,' he agreed and his Auntie Nhu gave him a pleased smile.

Hoc had appeared behind Auntie Nhu and shortly after my mother came out too, so that we all converged in the water garden in the growing dusk. A figure hurried across the garden, one of Lien Lau's many Han officials, come to escort us across.

'Just one moment, while I call on the brothers from Khuc Duong,' he said, scurrying off to our left to another low building.

'Mother,' I whispered, 'would they be the Mai brothers, Nhat and Thao?'

'Ah yes. Their mother, Trang Hoa is very ill and her husband, who is still prefect there, has no doubt stayed with her.'

'Will it not be awkward, seeing Nhat?' I fretted.

'No, daughter, don't worry. I sent word to his mother that you had already settled on another. They did not take any offence.'

'You never said!'

'Oh Trac, Nhi was right, you would never have married Nhat.'

I remembered how Nhat had talked to the turtle, bending down like a child, and I gave in with a sharp sigh, but I was angry she had replied to them without speaking to me. Everyone was assuming that Sach and I were a deal already done when we were far from it.

The official returned with two men following. Nhat was just as he had been on our previous and only meeting - rotund and dreaming, gazing about at the garden with a satisfied countenance. He caught sight of me and came happily forward with a jolly bow.

'Trac, how pleased I am to see you again. And this must be Nhi.' He tilted his head to her and she grinned back with a nod. Close up, I could see dark half-moons of sleepless worry under Nhat's eyes and I wondered how his mother was faring.

'I hope your mother is receiving good care,' I said.

'She is, thank you, but she is really very poorly.'

We had all begun walking towards the main building, where a central hall would house the grand reception that the Governor had arranged. Thao was on the far side of Nhat, but slipped round his brother and introduced himself properly to my mother. I turned to say hello, and was startled by the intense young man that looked back at me. I had expected a younger version of Nhat, but Thao was nothing like him. Instead of the plump build, he looked all muscle and his face, though a round shape, was tight-skinned with thickish lips and lean eyes. If I had met this brother, my mind whirred, then Sach may have had some more serious competition. Thao was older than Sach, not by much, but the combined effect of Nhat's obvious acquaintance with me and Thao's confident conversation with my mother had affected Sach. He walked at the rear with his sisters.

Besides my family, the Thi family and the Mai brothers, we found inside the prefects of An Dinh, Cau Lau, Bac Dai and Ke Tu. Ton Vien was there, with his wife and so all the Commandery

Prefects were represented. It would have been a perfect occasion for assassination, in retrospect, but relations between the Han and the Lac were not nearly so bad back then. Vo Xuan needed us, the original Nam Viet noble families, to be on his side, governing the land in the Emperor's name. Xuan himself was energetically working his way around his guests, greeting and studying them in equal measure. The man had a skill for remembering faces and names, as do most people who attain high leadership positions, and when he came to our impromptu little group, he guessed immediately at those whom he had only heard of by name. He spoke to my mother first, of course, and by taking her arm, managed to walk us all to a more central point in the room. Of all the prefects and their families, my mother was the highest, the most honoured. She looked it, too, dressed in a decadent, pearly silk with a shimmering sky-blue wrap around her piled hair. Next to her, Xuan wore a long gown in green silk, which crossed over at the front and fell to his ankles. The points of his sleeves were so long, they almost trailed on the ground by his neat little black shoes with their inlaid pearls.

I looked around as we walked through the groups of people, seeing the various Han generals and politicians and the assembled prefects and sons and daughters, but nowhere could I see Chau, nor any of her family. When small talk reached an appropriate point for me to interject, I asked Xuan if the Hai Phong prefect was attending.

'Not on this occasion, my dear daughter Trac,' he said. 'After all, the defensive coastal region is not really a proper administrative region, and prefect status there is still an informal allocation.'

'I see. Perhaps in the future,' I said, diplomatically and Xuan smiled. Poor Nhi, I felt so sorry for her that she would not see Chien. She pretended to be oblivious to what had just been said and turned to speak to Kim Cuc.

Great benches had been arranged around the sides of the room, with soft mats for sitting or squatting on laid alongside - a friendly gesture by our chair-loving rulers. As the final people arrived, a Han orator banged on a little gong and recited a poem, after which everyone began to take seats and servants appeared, placing covered dishes along the benches and laying out bowls and spoons. My stomach growled. I had not eaten since early that morning and the smell of heavily seasoned culinary treats wafted through the air. When the lids were removed, they revealed partridges and pheasants in rich, fruity sauces, carp soaking in soy sauce and ginger, steaming fresh rice strewn with shredded cabbage, skewered and roasted paa frogs, pickled water chestnuts and all kinds of other creations. The amount of meat on the tables suggested Xuan had spared no expense.

I took my wooden spoon and filled up my bowl with rice, then clumsily used some chopsticks to grasp some pieces of partridge, dunking them in the accompanying plum and berry sauce before heaping them on top of my rice. Chopsticks were the Han way of eating, and we were not as practised as we should have been. Nhi dug in as well and there was a friendly atmosphere as we all enjoyed the food. Sach sat a little way along the table so I could see him but not easily speak to him. To my left were my mother and then Xuan, and opposite sat a few of his men - a corpulent general and several emissaries of the Emperor who had been in Giao Chi for a year or so.

Alongside the meats, rice and vegetable dishes sat plates of fried honey cakes and I devoured several of these, dipping them in the apricot preserve next to the plate.

'Are you enjoying the food, daughter Trac?' Xuan asked, leaning forward to see past my mother.

'Immensely. This is a very fine spread.'

'It's certainly good food,' said one of the emissaries opposite, 'but what a strange way to lay it out. Why have you not used the correct arrangement, Governor?'

'In Giao Chi, the families do not use the method of place-laying which we consider so important,' replied Xuan.

'How would you lay out the food in the Middle Kingdom?' my mother asked.

'We would put meat like this pheasant, on the bone, to the left, along with the millet or rice. On the right, we would put sliced meat, like this pork and also here we would put the soup. The drinks and garnishes would stand beyond these dishes.'

'Isn't that rather awkward in large groups?'

'Not really. These rules are important, Lady Prefect, because they bring order to a gathering.'

'But what about now, when we are facing each other across a table? If we are sharing dishes, whose left and whose right should they go on? I would find it most confusing, most unnecessarily so!' laughed my mother, deliberately.

The emissary smiled, with pointed little teeth, and incredulous snipe's eyes looking down a long nose. 'I am sure you would,' he said with equal spite and resumed eating.

Vo Xuan spooned soup into a clean dish for my mother, who thanked him and began drinking the sour broth.

'I am sorry not to see the Prefect of Khuc Duong here,' commented Xuan, raising his cup towards Thao and Nhat who had caught his eye at the further end of the table. 'His sons say that their mother is most unwell. Have you heard so, Lady Prefect?'

'I have indeed,' my mother answered. 'Poor Hoa is in a sorry state and the medicines don't appear to be helping.'

'Ah, too bad, too bad. Still, at least the boys came. Nice young men, aren't they?'

'Yes, very good sons.'

'You know the family then?'

'Of course,' said my mother. 'The Prefects of Giao Chi are one family. That is why we are so happy and honoured that you have brought us together like this. It's not often possible.'

'But most important. Family is what binds and strengthens us, so it must be encouraged,' said the other emissary who had a more kindly manner, reaching with his chopsticks for the salted pork. 'It is, after all, what our society is built upon. If we forget our places within our family, we cause a break in the chain that holds society together. A father is a father. A son, a son.' He put the piece of pork in his mouth and chewed contentedly.

'What about a daughter?' asked Nhi, speaking diagonally across the table to him and placing her own chopsticks down on the little resting block.

'Ah, a daughter has her place,' he dissembled, and if he could have reached, I am almost sure he would have patted Nhi's head without sparing her a proper glance, but whilst he nodded at her as if to impress his point, he caught sight of her good looks and stared a moment too long.

'You have noticed youngest daughter Nhi, then,' said Xuan.

'How could I have missed her before? Lady Prefect, you have two very lovely daughters,' said the emissary, while the colleague at his side studied us with those black snipes eyeballs. My mother nodded her acceptance of this compliment

Whilst the plates and dishes were being cleared, a musical troupe entered and we listened to a song about the rice harvest sung by a man with a gong zither made of bamboo and dried gourd. The salutary piece was followed by a more haunting melody about two lovers, which a young woman played on her own southern-style zither. With the eating over, we were encouraged to mingle while the music played on and Nhi gratefully sprang up to move closer to the musicians with Kim Cuc. Xuan angled himself around my mother and firmly drew me towards some men, to whom he had promised to introduce me. I felt bloated and sickly from all the food and from the pounding of the drum that had struck up in accordance with the latest tune but I allowed myself to be escorted towards the little clutch of Han who smiled expectantly in my direction.

'Eldest daughter Trac, I would very much like you to meet Captain Gang and General Cai.' Xuan said the names of two other men who were present also, but I didn't take them in. I was looking with some alarm at the anxious and excited grin on Captain Gang's face. He was perhaps in his early twenties, with a small pointed beard and very thin eyes resting in a smooth-skinned, taut face. He put his hands together belatedly and bowed and I returned the greeting silently.

'Captain Gang is new to Giao Chi. He joined his Company on the last new moon.'

'I hope that will prove auspicious for you,' I said, kindly.

'I'm sure it will. I feel that many good things are due to happen to me here. I have been looking forward to coming to Giao Chi and working for the Emperor's great cause.' He spoke quite fast, and with his regional inflections I found him difficult to keep up with. The way the skin moved over his sharp cheekbones as he spoke reminded me of something vaguely reptilian, though not in an unattractive way.

'Captain Gang comes from the Nam Hai Commandery,' explained Xuan.

'Originally my family is from old Ba Shu.' said Captain Gang.

'The good captain here will replace the fellow we had that unfortunate episode with in Hai Phong,' said Xuan, quietly so just Gang and I heard. Then louder he said, 'I hope you two will get on.'

Gang beamed and I returned his smile and agreed that surely we would. I was glad to hear that the other Captain was gone, and in his place this soft-skinned young man did not seem so threatening.

'I am so sorry, but would you excuse me?' I said and the men bowed as I left, moving on as they were anyway, to chat with other guests. I walked with purpose to the main doors, anxious that Gang would see I was going outside for air and offer to accompany me. As I stepped out, I noticed to my relief that he was being introduced to the corpulent General who had sat next to the emissaries through our meal.

111

Out in the garden, the black lacquered evening assailed my eyes and I stepped blindly to the low wall I knew to exist to my left. As I sat down on the cold stone, I was startled by steps behind me. I rose immediately and made to move on but a man's suppressed laugh made me turn.

'Please, sit back down. It is only me.'

He came around me and I made out Sach's profile in the dark. Behind him the branches of the cypress on the riverbank were blooming, plum-coloured against the squid-ink sky. His face came clearer. Now I could see his teeth, grinning at me.

'Why are you out here?'

'For the same reason as you Trac, no doubt.' He sat down on the wall. 'You know, the brighter the lights we surround ourselves with, the blacker it appears when the flames are extinguished. Please sit down.'

I lowered myself back onto the wall. He turned his head to face me and I heard the soft brush of his silk collar against his tied-up hair.

'Have you enjoyed the evening?' I asked.

'Not until now.'

'You are most ungracious.'

'Would it help if I concealed my feelings with some poetry?'

I sniggered, despite myself and he laughed, seeing he had reached me at last.

'But, those Han in there, are they the bright lights or the extinguishers of the flame?'

'Eldest daughter, I was merely talking about the difficulty your eyes were having adjusting to the night, but since you draw further meaning, I'll play along. How about this: their words are the light but their actions snuff the flame?'

'It's not quite right,' I said, folding my hands in my lap. 'Too clumsy.'

His hands were planted squarely on his knees and I watched his fingers flex as he considered a retort. Then, with more gravity than he had thus far displayed, and in a voice heavy with effort, he replied, 'Their words are the sparkle of sun on water that blinds onlookers to the dark depths beneath... When the sun ceases to shine and the words fade to dull reflection, all that remains will be the black void of the undertow, carrying away all those who have waded in.'

'Better,' I breathed, surprised at his eloquence. With my eyesight fully adjusted to the dark, I was gazing into his dilated pupils, almost covering the earnest brown irises.

'Can you see me now?' he asked and I tried to answer but he was already kissing me.

11

Sach's hatred of the Han went deeper than I had realised. He concealed it with etiquette, always measuring his language around Xuan and the petty functionaries that surrounded the Governor, but after those bleak, beautiful words in the water garden I tasted a sarcastic tang in all the polite comments he made, like the lick of a base metal under a gilt coating.

We had agreed to be married, returning into the hall that very night to confirm to both our parents that they could at last be certain of our engagement and celebrating quietly in case Xuan, Captain Gang or anyone else should take offence. Gang had seen me with Sach anyway and I saw him exchange a few words with Xuan, his quizzical eyes casting for a second in my direction as he tried, no doubt, to establish whether I was available or not. Xuan set his sharp eyes upon me and in the tiniest apprehension that tinged my face he read the answer, but I imagine he gave Gang a vague reply. Xuan had not yet given up on capturing me for his Han Captain, but that night at his party he didn't speak to me again. I suppose I had embarrased him.

I didn't care. I was elated. I was the happiest I had been since before my father died. Sach came to visit several times a week after that, despite the long ride in the descending winter, and we spent ages talking together. He watched me train with Nhi and although I felt self-conscious of his gaze at first, over time his earnest appreciation gave me the confidence I had never known was lacking. Within a few months, I no longer felt grateful for his love. I knew I was equal to it. The more I returned his loving smiles and easy laughter, the more he was captivated. I grew into a different person. My mother gave me a compliment one cold winter morning, when the air was touched with ice from the mountains. She said, 'Eldest daughter, you look very beautiful today.' It wasn't the words so much as her tone which struck me.

She sounded enthralled.

I needn't really describe Nhi's reaction to it all. Bounding and giddy perhaps give a sense. Apparently, when I was outside in the water garden with Sach, she had run to our mother whispering, 'Mother, Trac is out there with Sach,' and our mother had told her to hush, she already knew. Past midnight, as I tried in vain to get to sleep, Nhi pestered and whispered relentlessly, asking all about what we had said to each other and whether we had touched. She was so excited for me, and between my good news and her new friendship with Kim Cuc (and, to a lesser extent, with Khanh), she had apparently forgotten all about Chien.

Of course, as I was to realise later, she had not forgotten all about him at all. She was tormented by thoughts of him and by the knowledge that she might not see him for a very long time. Our mother had asked Auntie An to ask her son Giang (who fished some distance south of Hai Phong) to find someone on the coast who might pass messages back and forth, but so far no discreet person had been found and Giang's father was unwilling to let his son perform the task and neglect the fishing work, even infrequently. My mother complained to me about it, saying the man was unhelpful and unpleasant and that Auntie An was better off living so far from where her mean husband worked. I thought it may have been a touch of sourness on my mother's part, but I had never met him and couldn't comment. Nhi knew nothing about these attempts to locate a messenger. My mother did not want to get her hopes up, or even mention Chien, and after some months when Nhi had not mentioned him either, my mother let her efforts rest. 'Perhaps when the weather comes warmer we can visit, or he will come to us,' said my mother to me, privately.

In the cold depths of winter we did not much visit Lien Lau. The temperatures at the very coldest would only just put a shine of frost over the house or maybe ice a puddle, but as a people we made sensible decisions about keeping safe and healthy. Perhaps it came from living in a land roamed freely by tigers, buffalo, crocodiles and snakes or perhaps it was the ever changing weather that flitted from dry cold to hot rain, that wheeled from intense sunshine to harsh winds, swept down from central Asia, but whatever the cause, we adapted cautiously to the circumstances. With the abundant rain we grew rice. When it was cold, we wrapped up warmly and conserved energy. We had such plentiful stores of rice and so many containers of pickled vegetables and sweet preserves made in earlier months that there was no need to do more than strictly necessary. The only exception to this was Sach and his persistent visits, which caused him to ride up through Chu Dien, cross the river and arrive with us, saddle-sore and cold. Eventually my mother invited him to stay over nights with us instead, so that by the moon festival, he was almost living with us. Mrs Chau could barely contain her curiosity, studying the pair of us whenever she was round for her regular gossip and drink with my mother. I am sure much of Me Linh and beyond heard detailed descriptions of our fledgling relationship. If nothing else, at least it allowed the definitive news of our engagement to filter out to the Han and up through their ranks to Xuan. We had the immobilising weather to protect us for a while, but I would have to face him soon and I did not know what his response would be.

Soon after the moon celebrations, Xuan rode out to Me Linh. It was the first time I can remember him coming, so when we received an outrider telling us that Governor Xuan would be there shortly, we were nonplussed. My mother sent Nhi to Mrs Chau's immediately. 'Better that you are out of the way,' she said. 'We will say you are visiting family.' Nhi agreed. She had no desire to be the new focus of Captain Gang's marriage plans.

Sach was not with us that day – whether Xuan knew this or not I cannot say, but spies were working for the Governor even then so it was probable. My mother and I waited alone, while our servant girl, Diep, clattered around nervously, making refreshments for the outrider who sat on the front steps, as well as preparing a meal for Xuan and the three men accompanying him. The outrider had not said exactly who they were. I just hoped Captain Gang himself was not one of them. There was no need for outright unpleasantness. Outside, some of our labourers had sauntered by, ostensibly going to repair Mrs Chau's chicken pen underneath her stilt house, but actually keeping a close eye on our property. In their cart were the wooden-handled tools that would each double as a weapon, and under these, blades, hidden by straw. My mother watched them pass but did not wave. The outrider was watching them too.

'Mother, Xuan must be very determined, to ride out to us like this,' I whispered, anxiously.

'No more so than I had suspected,' she whispered back. 'But it is like the drums - he doesn't have the resources to fight our noble families and he can't stop your marriage to Sach.'

Despite her reassurance, I was terribly nervous - not of any fighting or hostility that may occur, but of the possibility, however slight, that Sach and I could ever be separated. It seemed unimaginable, now that we had become so close. Eventually we heard Xuan's entourage arriving. Diep went out to show the men in and to direct their guards where to rest the horses. My mother and I sat still in the front room of the house, which was filling with the scent of aloes-wood burning in a dish. We rose only when Xuan entered. My mother dazzled him with a smile.

'Governor, please come in,' she bowed. 'Let us serve you some drinks.'

'Lady Prefect,' he greeted her, a touch impatiently I thought, 'You have all met before, I believe?' He gestured behind him to one of the emissaries from the meal, to the general who had been sat with them and to one of Xuan's own staff.

'Yes, we're all acquainted,' said my mother, drawing them in and bidding them to sit down. Diep hurried back in, looking harassed and I guessed Xuan's guards had been teasing her. She went to fetch drinks for us all and Xuan watched her and looked about himself, at the furnishings and personal ornaments of our home.

'Tell me, Governor, what brings you out to Me Linh?'

'I must know my Commandery, Lady Prefect. I have not been here for such a long time and the occurrences here are becoming a mystery to me.'

'I'm so sorry, Governor Xuan. My reports have not been detailed enough. In future I will try and be more comprehensive.' My mother took a sip of her drink.

'It is not so much the crop yields and canal work and so on and so forth that I am interested in,' he said. 'I must know the people too. Who they are and what they are doing.'

'Who had you in mind, Governor? I can easily answer the questions you have.'

'Then tell me, Thien, what is going on with this daughter of yours? I thought you were considering my proposal of a match with the Liu.' Xuan was truly angry. He spoke politely, but I had never heard him use my mother's given name in front of me before and I had rarely heard him speak so directly.

'Governor, I am so sorry you have misunderstood me. I have of course considered many matches and took very seriously your suggestion. The fact is that Trac has become very attached to Thi Sach, who approached us as a suitor before the last rains.'

'You have let her settle for the first young man to come asking,' snorted Xuan. 'Think of the benefits if she would consider Captain Gang. His family are well respected in the Middle Kingdom and he greatly desires your daughter. I know he would care for her.'

'I have no doubt that Captain Gang is a good man and we are so very honoured that he had considered Trac. Equally we are honoured by the attentions of the family Thi. We have known Sach's family for several generations. His father and General Lac were good friends and my late husband would have greatly approved. Yet I waited for Trac to make her choice. If she had chosen another - a man of the Middle Kingdom or one of the other young men of Giao Chi, I would have acceded to her wishes, if he were suitable. Happily, she loves Sach and I will not go against their match.'

'You have decided that most definitely? I wonder if you truly understand the benefits of what I am proposing. The marriage I suggest will bring you many more riches. It will put you higher in the esteem of the Emperor and secure your position within Me Linh and within Giao Chi.'

'I am already secure,' my mother answered, tightly.

'You answer to me, Lady Prefect. I hope you have not forgotten that,' Xuan said.

'No, I have not forgotten. But you cannot order my daughter to marry Gang. You have no authority to do such a thing and the noble families of Nam Viet will not stand for it.'

'Giao Chi!' shouted Xuan, standing up. 'This is *Giao Chi* Commandery and has been for more than a hundred years. When will you people learn to accept that? Have I not been fair? Have you not prospered under me?' He stamped to the doorway, breathing steam through his nose into the cold, draughty air. My mother stayed silent. 'This is the problem with you people. You don't want progress, you don't want morality. You want life to stagnate.'

The General shifted uncomfortably. He did not like the way the conversation had developed and he glanced with some slight sympathy in my direction. The emissary was indifferent. He was the snipe-faced man who had complained about the food settings and he simply stared at us though those round, black eyes. Xuan's colleague was smirking.

'Governor Xuan,' said my mother, after a pause, 'in all other things but this I feel I have tried to respect and serve you.'

'You are not remarried,' said Xuan, facing my mother again, 'and you have not stepped aside either. If you would but understand the role of a man and the role of a woman! Here in Giao Chi, it is all upside down. It cannot go on.' Xuan shook his head. He came back and sat down. 'Lady Prefect, changes will come. I cannot effect them immediately, but one day your people will marry properly. We will record all marriages properly and men will stay in their villages and work the land properly and women will stand behind and below them. High-born girls, and boys for that matter, will accept the matches of the Governor's choosing. All these things will come to pass, even if I cannot make them happen now.'

My mother sat white-faced at his seething declaration of a kind of war on our people. Never before had he spoken to her in this way, making her feel so inferior. Always there had been a deference to her status, an acceptance of her role, but with such open hostility, the landscape had changed. Still, as he had said, he could do nothing to force me to marry Gang, and for that I was extremely relieved. I took heart from it and motioned to Diep, who cowered in the corner.

'Fetch the meal. I expect we're all hungry,' I ordered. 'Governor Xuan, please eat. After all, you've travelled a long way today.' I grinned at him, showing teeth and he twitched, ever so slightly. Then I set too, gnawing eagerly on a roasted leg from one of Mrs Chau's tough old hens and making small talk with the disconcerted General.

★★★★★

'Trac, that was very strange behaviour,' said my mother, when they left soon after. 'What has happened to you? You were behaving like... well, like Nhi when I think of it.' I laughed, which unsettled her even more. She stared at me, her arms helplessly by her sides. 'Have you gone mad?'

'Mother, they have shown us their plans.' I explained. 'Xuan has spoken honestly at last and now we know the Han to be what Sach has always said they are. But they cannot act. They do not have the strength. The Emperor has not sent more armed men, even after the Hai Phong incident. And if they have shown their true colours, then I have shown mine. I am not one of their little puppet daughters. Xuan should know that he cannot rule or control me. Xuan should be scared of me.'

'Quite so, eldest daughter. But really, guzzling the roasted leg? Was *that* necessary?'

My chest gave a hiccup and then we both fell to laughing. When Nhi ran in, worried and frightened, having seen the Han men with their guards galloping away, she stared incredulously at the pair of us.

'What?' she demanded. 'What is it, what has happened?'

Our mother recounted the whole tale, and Nhi's face grew grave and pale as she heard what the Governor had said, but at the part where I ordered the food and ate the hen's leg and asked the General about *wushu* training amongst the Middle Kingdom armies, Nhi giggled.

'Sach will never believe it,' she laughed.

Later, when we were all calmer, we spoke more seriously about Xuan's threats. My mother said she would meet discreetly with the prefects from our surrounding districts and alert them to his foul temper, but she agreed with me that we had only discovered what we already suspected to be true. We knew the Han did not like dealing with women in positions of authority, we knew they wished us to live by their own moral codes and abide by their tax schemes. None of it was a surprise. The only way forward was to maintain peace and politeness so that Xuan would be forced to do the same. His hands were tied by the legalistic notions of the Emperor's court and if Giao Chi remained essentially peaceful, he couldn't attack us, even if we would not marry according to his wishes. In the longer term, I knew, he and his kind would find a way to oppress us, but by then we would be ready for them.

★★★★★

Sach and I married in the middle of the rainy season, when I was seventeen and a half. His father, two sisters and a variety of aunts, uncles and cousins, escorted him from Chu Dien to Me Linh, bringing with them the bride price – jade and jewels, some fine weapons, pottery and silk. In the custom of our people, he would pass this wealth to me and it would remain with me, even if he left. Moreover, once we were married, he would live with my family. It was the way in which things were done. I wore my red silk and he wore green and we spoke an oath that bound us together as a couple. It was a modest affair. I had not wanted to invite other Prefects and nobles because we did not want to bring Xuan's attention down on our heads on the very day of our marriage.

Poor Nhi. She had hoped it would be an opportunity to invite Chien and his family, but our mother thought it best not to do so. Xuan would surely become aware if the Le family passed upriver right under his nose in Lien Lau, and we couldn't invite the Hai Phong prefect without inviting others. Nhi had asked outright for him to attend, speaking his name for the first time in months and, in the way she said it, I finally understood how much she was longing to see him, so I felt bad about disappointing her.

'Once this marriage is completed,' I said, 'then perhaps we could go to Hai Phong. We must just wait for the fuss to die down.' I was caught up in my own happiness. I thought everything would work out just as well for her as it had for me, if only she would be patient.

I could barely drag my eyes from Sach on our wedding day. He was so handsome, with his strong cheekbones and dark eyes and strands of black hair escaping, as usual, from the bun at the back of his head. Despite all the laughter and the food and the conversation with his relatives and my own – for Uncle Hien and Auntie Linh had come with two of their children, and Auntie An had brought Giang and there were others too – we were both just waiting, all day, to be alone together.

122

When the humid night finally drew in, our well-wishers waved us into the room where we were to sleep and Nhi, laughing, put a carved jade rhinoceros to watch over us, while Kim Cuc offered to help me out of my clothes. Sach pushed them out of the room, closing the bamboo door against them and hooking the loop of rope over the bent nail on our side. They fell away chattering, ignoring the scolding from my mother, and at last it was just us two. I fumbled with my outfit and he hesitated then came to help me. I dared not try and take his clothes off. A fear had come over me and I did not know what to expect. People use a great many evasive expressions to refer to what a man and a woman do together but it had never been fully explained to me what would actually happen. Nhi probably knew. She paid a lot more attention to what animals did. I had never asked my mother either. Of course, she had to help me when I bled for the first time and she said it was to do with being a woman and being ready for bearing children. She clarified that I would need to lay down with a man to get a child, but none of that was much help to me either and just as I had once wondered, and still did, how a baby actually came out, I wondered again how the baby got there in the first place. I had a feeling it must involve something sinister, or people wouldn't keep it such a secret. I wondered if it would hurt.

'Don't be frightened,' Sach whispered. He could feel me shaking but he was still eager to take off my clothes and his eyelids looked heavier when he saw my small breasts. He hurried out of his own clothes while I stood there feeling a fool, but as his body was revealed, I stared in fascination. His penis looked so very strange in the moonlight, sticking straight out of his body like that.

'We must lie down,' whispered Sach, and so I did, and he laid with me and that is all I will say about that, except that it was a good end to the day.

12

When Sach moved in, I moved into Mother's *kang*. There was plenty of space and I did not at all resent sharing with her. I was never fussy about where I slept - on the back of a horse, under the stars or next to my sighing mother. The only things that disturbed me sometimes were the faint words she cried out in her dreams - words that sounded like pleading, but barely formed, and the hint of Father's name. I laid awake every time she had one of those dreams. My own dreams were still a mystery to me. Occasionally I would have one of those deep, dark, rushing nightmares and awake on the edge of a scream but Mother would grasp my arm or put a cool hand to my forehead and I would calm immediately. The years of sleeping in with Trac might never have happened. Here I was, a toddler in the arms of Mother once again.

By day, I was anything but, and my adherence to martial arts training had increased. I spent whole mornings practising and in the afternoons, Mother would teach us, with just a break for some soup or a sticky rice ball. I'm not sure how to explain it, but I felt that if I could master each new technique, commit to memory every ancient pattern of movement and find the mystery behind the ritualised steps then I would reach Chien. It makes no sense and I never articulated my confused dedication to Trac or Mother, but I heard Trac say quietly one time, 'She trains so hard because she misses Chien so badly,' and I suppose that is as close as I could have come to explaining myself.

Sach joined us in training too and that was a revelation. I could practice regularly with a strong and able man at last and I found that routines that previously made little sense came alive as I applied them to our fights. I varied the speed and timing of my assaults. I tested the precise footing of my stance. I even fought whilst blindfolded so I could feel the balance and the energy of my throws without being distracted by how I thought the move should look. Trac fought Sach too, but their sparring looked like an excuse for embracing and Mother had to smack her staff on the ground sharply to make them focus. She should have been scandalised, but she was not. Mother's fury at Xuan's contemptuous words had stripped away some of her Confucian veneer and there was a tighter slant to her face these days - a showing of teeth, a baring of her animal spirit.

Speaking of teeth, Sach had begun blackening his. It was the old tradition, and men past a certain age still did it, but the younger generation of the nobility had been abandoning the practice, which was abhorred in the Middle Kingdom. Sach's insistence on blackening his teeth and his encouragement of others to do the same was an outward show of his increasing hatred for the Han and his intolerance for their rule. So, too, was his growing refusal to pin up his hair. He kept it roughly tied back, or even loose on his shoulders. He was becoming a popular figure in Me Linh, since he was a friendly man anyway, and we found that the district's youths who had previously kept a respectful distance from their Lady Prefect's residence now hung around and waited for glimpses of us training or opportunities to talk with Sach. Before long, many of these young men were wearing their hair down. Most had blackened teeth already - it was only amongst the nobility that the tradition had begun to wither.

Sach was also responsible for encouraging Bao to come round and train with us. Mother was not so keen at first. 'He's too familiar with the girls,' she complained. 'He does not know his place.' 'Not so,' argued Sach. 'He's a young man in need of guidance.'

Bao's grandfather had died earlier in that year and their household, like ours was now a heavily female one. His grandmother lived on, restricted by her many ailments to the back room of the house. Mrs Chau was still an active trader between the Lien Lau and Me Linh markets and her two young daughters accompanied her now, being about five and seven. They were old enough to fetch and carry and be of use whilst Bao worked out in the rice fields, labouring just like most of the other local men and women. His father had not been back home for several years. In the early evenings, Bao, who anyone could see was bored with life, eagerly wandered over if he saw Sach on the front steps. He was only fourteen but the heavy agricultural work was already ageing his features and his skin was darkening from constant exposure to the sun. He now looked and acted like a man rather than a child.

I began to sit out there with them too, in the smoky dusk. Sach would take out a small hemp pouch and from it produce an areca nut or two, along with a few peppery betel leaves and some black cloves. Then, with his knife he would remove the green husk and cut a few slices of the nut itself. These slices, he would wrap in a betel leaf with one of the cloves and hand to Bao, who would say a heartfelt thank-you and begin chewing the little package. Then Sach would prepare one for me, if I wished, and one for himself. Trac didn't like the areca nuts. She was wary of anything that altered her senses and even with the rice wine she was always moderate. But I liked the glow they gave me - the pepped up, exhilarated warmth that fired me with optimism and made the colours of life sharpen into clear focus. Father had chewed areca nuts when I was a tiny child and sitting out on the front steps chewing them myself made me feel closer to him. Soon my teeth were dyed quite red from the habit.

Chewing nuts with Bao made me feel comfortable with him again and before long, Sach asked him to train with us. Bao came over in the very early mornings before he had to be in the fields, and Sach sparred with him while I traced my solitary patterns. When Bao had acquired some basic ability, I taught him too, sharing the more superficial movements and obvious locks and throws. He was very respectful, contrary to Mother's initial concerns, and once we got past some of the awkwardness involved in the physical proximity needed for training, it became a pleasant and rewarding start to each of my days. The reward was seeing Bao progress from clumsy, ineffective striving to solid, efficient performance. He would never be an adept, but only a few reached that level. Only a few were worthy of learning the secrets behind all the patterns.

Trac made the most progress in her martial training in those few years after her wedding. I found her new demeanour confusing and unsettling, probably because she had become more like me. I had been the defiant, carefree and spirited one and I had laughed at Trac's over-bearing seriousness, but secretly I had needed it. If I was the untamed horse, then Trac was my trainer. In balance, we made sense. Now, Trac's forthright speech, her occasional guttural laughter and her strident behaviour, both within her training and outside of it, frightened me.

'Why has Trac changed so much?' I complained to Mother. 'She would never have acted like that before she married him.'

'Your sister is happy. Just be happy for her.'

'I *am* happy for her. I just wish she would calm down and be a bit more like herself.'

'Perhaps this is who Trac really is,' said Mother, easily. She was pleased to see Trac so liberated and to have acquired for herself such an able and personable son-in-law.

I bit my lip and knew that I couldn't talk to Mother about the way I felt. She wouldn't understand the dawning sadness that had risen over me. I didn't really understand it either. Why should I miss the days when Trac had been so controlled and muted? Why did her aggressive assaults during our sparring patterns concern me? Everyone else had only compliments for her - how married life must suit her! how much prowess she showed in her martial arts! how she glowed! And indeed, all that was true. So I tried to smile and compliment her too, and I didn't speak to her of how strange she had become in my eyes or how I missed my cautious and careful big sister.

Deep down, I had begun to realise that I was different from others. I thought about the day on the beach with Chien - thought about it all the time - and saw more clearly the meaning of his words. When that dark mood came over me by the mangroves, it had come over him too. He had felt the same darkness snapping at his heels as I had. I hadn't asked him if he had nightmares like mine, but somehow I knew he must. When he said we were two of a kind, that's what he meant. I missed him so much. I knew if there was one person I could talk to about my peculiar feelings towards Trac, it would be Chien. At last, after so much waiting, Mother decided that we could travel to the east coast and that she would speak with Prefect Chau about a match between her son and myself. Trac and Sach stayed behind, authorised to conduct Mother's business in her absence.

It had been over a year since I'd seen him but I wasn't anxious. The journey took forever - the ride over the plain, the careful negotiation of the mud banks which had swelled and spread through the rainy season, the long, churning ride on an outrigger that fought the current at the various junctures to stay on the correct distributaries towards Hai Phong, the wet disembarkation and the walk into a lively town. This time, instead of grim-faced Han and resentful peasants, the track from the river and the open area in front of the people's building were full of busy traders and baskets of fish. A woman crouched by a huge wooden slab, gutting an enormous tuna and slicing parts of it into steaks. I stepped past wooden buckets full of clams in salt-water and past a slab upon which a crocodile had been dismembered. Mother led the way. She glanced at the produce with a sniff and a keen eye.

We went straight to the Prefect's house which, as I remembered from our previous visit, was larger than any of the others that clustered at the centre of Hai Phong, and as we approached, Chien came out.

'Hello!' he said, with a wide smile. 'We got the message that you would be coming, but we didn't know which day to expect you.'

'Hello Chien. I'm sorry it's been so long,' I said, walking forwards to him.

'Where are your parents, Chien?' asked Mother.

'Father is treating a boy who broke his arm yesterday and Mother is down at the river mouth, checking on the catches that are returning today. My sister is with her. But you are very welcome to come inside with me.' He led us into the house which was much like ours - wooden-built and raised up from the ground on stilts. It had a brick day-bed in the centre, near the warm stove and the food preparation area. There was extra space at the back and another sleeping area, but no internal walls. We sat down on the mats that covered the clay bricks of the central *kang*.

'Chien, I want to talk to your parents about a very important matter but perhaps Nhi should mention it to you before we proceed. I'll leave you two for a few moments. How about some of that crocodile meat for later? Will your mother like it?'

'Yes, she likes crocodile,' said Chien, flustered and then Mother was back out of the house as quickly as she had come in.

'I've missed you very much,' I said, as he regained his composure.

'Not as much as I have missed you,' Chien replied. 'This matter that your mother has left us to talk about...'

'She says we can be married. Will your parents agree?'

'Yes, I should think so. And if they didn't, I would do it anyway. But they will agree,' he said quickly, seeing my face, 'because it is an honour, of course, since Lady Prefect of Me Linh is so highly respected.'

I laughed at him, trying to say all the right things.

'You seem older for your years,' he said, staring at me. 'As if more than just a year had passed.'

'I feel different,' I said. 'The visit here changed me.'

129

'It was a strange time.'

'Did you know my sister married Thi Sach?'

'We were very pleased to hear it. We heard afterwards that Governor Xuan had not been happy. Is he frightened of an alliance between Me Linh and Chu Dien?'

'Perhaps, but all the noble families are allies anyway. It's more than that. The Middle Kingdom see marriage and family, and a woman's place within it, differently than we do. I think Xuan had hoped to set an example with Trac – to see her married off to one of the Liu and taken back to the north to live as a Han wife.'

'Oh, I see,' murmured Chien. 'I thought Governor Xuan had more respect for your mother.'

'Only as much as he is forced to show. He would rather be dealing with a man. He was quite rude to Mother when he called on us before the wedding, though I wasn't there. Trac took care of him though.'

'How so?'

I told him about her spirited defiance and he looked incredulous.

'That's something I wanted to talk to you about actually. I've been worried lately–'

The door opened and Mother came back in with a heavy package of crocodile flesh wrapped in leaves, and a basket of clams. Chien opened his mouth in concern at my abrupt silence, but I shook my head. 'Later,' I mouthed and he nodded. I regretted that we had spent precious, private minutes talking when we could have touched hands or even kissed. There might be no chance of either for the rest of the visit.

★★★★★

Mother spoke to Prefect Chau and they agreed together that a match was acceptable. Chau was pleased and even her husband, Dao, managed a smile. Marriage to one of General Lac and Lady Man Thien's daughters was quite an achievement for the son of a minor coastal family. Why had Mother agreed so readily? She was not sentimental and would not have encouraged a match for love alone. I think that she had seen the value of links with Hai Phong, which was starting to grow in reputation as a fishing port and trade estuary. It helped that the family were clearly ambitious, patriotic and competent – worthy people to encourage into Giao Chi politics and potential allies for Mother against the tightening grip of the Han. Of course, Chien was still young – eighteen or thereabouts and untested – but he was as promising as any of the other candidates Mother might have had in mind.

With a match arranged, Mother did not want to stay in Hai Phong for too long. She was wary that Xuan would cause trouble in her absence, perhaps provoking Sach and Trac in some way.

'You are welcome to leave Nhi here with us for a while.' Prefect Chau offered. 'Chien and Chan can escort her back to Me Linh before the winter.'

Mother considered it.

'They are not married yet. I am not sure it is appropriate.'

'But Mother–' She silenced me with a look. Prefect Chau looked down at the dusty wooden floor. Voices rose and ebbed outside. Gulls cried over the East Sea.

'Thank you, Prefect Chau. I will leave Nhi here to become better acquainted with you all. I know you'll take very good care of her,' Mother said at last. She gave a tight-lipped smile from which I realised it was hard for her to leave me there.

She left the following day, after a stay of just two nights, with a promise from Chien's family that I would be returned within two months. I was elated – I hadn't expected to have so much time with Chien, and in my heart over that long year previous, I had nursed a secret dread that I would never see him again. I felt overwhelming gratitude towards Mother as her boat pulled out into the river from the Hai Phong jetty and began its journey upstream. She glanced back once – worry, anxiety and pride holding her face in that same fixed smile - and I waved indecorously. Now I knew how Trac had felt, when she was so happy about being wedded to Sach that she could only believe that everyone else should be happy too.

I had no fears about being landed with a family I knew so little of, in a place I had only visited once before. Quite the opposite, in fact. I couldn't wait to explore the unfamiliar, salty landscape and talk to the fishermen and see all the magnificent creatures, large and minuscule, that they brought in from the open sea. I was looking forward to getting to know Chien's sister, Chan, better too. I had liked her on that first visit, even though she'd been a little huffy towards Trac and I thought maybe she, as well as her brother, would like to train with me. I had no intention of neglecting my martial arts and the open space in front of Chien's family home was perfect.

Each morning, just as at home, I got up early and took my weapons outside - a carved full-size staff that had long before replaced the child-sized training stick and a sword, short and sharp. It was easy to be disciplined because the gulls woke me every morning, taking flight when the earliest fishermen and the fiery strings of the rising sun alighted on the sea. I used my staff to draw a circle in the dusty ground, wide enough for me to practice within, so that anybody passing by would not step within the arc of my blade or staff. Within days, I noticed that people saw the circle on the ground and avoided stepping into it, even when I wasn't practising. I commented to Prefect Chau that I did not intend to prevent people walking across it the rest of the time and I could brush it out, but she said it was just as well to leave it.

'Some of them believe they will offend the Lac warrior-daughter of Me Linh if they tread in it,' she said, 'and others think it is simply sensible to leave the space clean and clear, for your practice. Leave the circle on the ground.'

Lac warrior-daughter? I liked that. I have to admit, I

introduced certain flourishes to my forms that weren't strictly necessary, conscious of the town's eyes upon me. Chien was bursting with pride. He trained with me and although he wasn't as developed in ability as Sach, he learned quickly and intuitively. It was a rare chance to touch. Apart from sitting close and letting our arms brush against each other, most forms of touching were frowned upon in public, and we couldn't often be in private since we were not married. Chien's parents took seriously the promise they had made to Mother and I was under constant, discreet surveillance.

Chan and I got on well - she wasn't fun like Kim Cuc but neither was she self-absorbed like Khanh. Eldest daughter Chan was cunning and calculating, sharply intelligent and without any self-consciousness. Chien called her shameless, but I wouldn't have described her like that. Honest and fearless, yes, and if you act honestly and without fear, why should you bear any shame? She was not married and didn't show any inclination to be so, at least while I was there with them. I had the impression she had not yet found anyone worthy and I guessed from her matter-of-fact congratulations towards Trac and Sach's marriage, that she was not so much heart-broken at missing out on the handsome young man of Chu Dien, as frustrated that a quality prospect had come within reach and been whisked away. Yet Chan was quite a sensual person, with her tall bearing and square shoulders. She walked like her mother, with a wide, arm-swinging gait and her mouth, with its thick lips, was often partly open, showing the black teeth and pink tongue inside. I don't think she was averse to sexual relations. She was just waiting for an equal. Like I said, the family were ambitious.

Le Dao, Chien's father, was the biggest surprise. Under that slightly unnerving appearance of wiry facial hair and glaring eyes, he was a quiet man, almost shy. He spoke quite freely and warmly under his own roof but outside of the home he reverted to the angrily abrupt manner that I know had offended Trac when she first met him. It was as though he compensated for his natural introversion by becoming arrogant and hostile. I wasn't sure whether he liked or approved of me or not, until one day when he asked if I would like to go with him to Cat Ba.

'It means a boat trip on the sea,' he explained, hesitantly. 'But it is a good place to visit.'

'I certainly would like to go, Father Dao, if I would not be in the way.' I was very excited that he had asked, but I had learned better than to alarm him with excessive gaiety, and I had cultivated more serious manners since the locals had started calling me warrior-daughter.

'But you must do as I say and take care. Mother Chao will have my head on the chopping block if any harm comes to you.' He whispered the last bit.

'What was that?' Chien's mother interrupted.

'I'm telling Nhi we must take care on this trip.'

'Be sure you do,' she ordered. 'Better take Chien too.'

'I doubt I could make him stay behind,' answered Dao and I blushed.

Cat Ba is a beautiful and large island which stands in the sea by the mouths of several distributaries of the Red River. I had stared out towards it from the coastline before, watching birds swirling above the shimmering archipelago, descending down behind the pointed, hilly limestone into forests, coves and lagoons that I could only imagine. The people who lived there fished for pearls, shrimp and clams and I had seen their outrigger canoes gliding silently over misty green waters, coming to the mainland to trade their produce. As we took to the waters in a small dugout canoe, the scenery came into a sharper focus and I could pick out, as we came closer, all the tiny islands, the jagged and humped karst up-thrusts and the little bays and coves. Only a dragon crashing down in the sea could have caused this landscape; the legend must be true, I thought. I hadn't yet seen the full magnificence of Ha Long Bay, but the southern tip certainly made an impression.

We skimmed over the rippling salt-water, Dao and Chien having a pair of long oars each, which sliced with swift precision through the shallow liquid jade. A fisherman bowed to Dao as we passed a tethered raft and Dao nodded back without breaking his rhythm. Further out east, I saw a double outrigger gliding fully laden and heading south. I had never seen a vessel of such size – there must have been about fifty rowers, and more people on board, under a canopy of large overlapping leaves resting on bamboo pillars. The rest of the bay was quiet and empty.

The canoe banked on a small beach and Dao and Chien jumped out and dragged it further up so I could alight without getting too wet. Through the trees ahead I could make out a few dwellings and after the men had dragged the canoe well clear of the water, Dao led us towards them, taking a path that had been cut through a stand of cycads, their bladed leaves a dark, glistening emerald. Further up the bodies of these forbidding plants I could see the cones, full of their small, poisonous seeds. I followed Dao into a clearing, where a man sat outside his house, chewing on betel and areca and scraping clean the skin of a small pile of mackerel. Dao greeted him and the pair had a short conversation after which he directed Dao on, through thicker undergrowth towards the people we had come to meet. A climb took us up the northern face of a low hill and here we found another dwelling, but this one smelt very bad and the area around it was ringed with sharpened stakes. Dao emitted a low whistle and the door to the house opened, revealing a thickset woman with coarse, unbound hair and a machete in her grip. She stepped out of the hut and studied us for a brief moment before recognising Dao and hooking the machete back into a strip of leather that tied about her waist.

'He's out,' she said, without any formality. 'Wait out there or in here.' Then she shrugged, turned and went back into the hut.

'We'll stay here,' called Dao and he settled himself down on the rough ground.

'What's that smell?' I asked, sitting down also and glancing around at the stakes.

'Monkey meat,' said Dao.

'What kind of monkey meat smells like that?' I was revolted and could not imagine eating anything that smelt so peculiar.

'Golden-headed monkey meat. It's what we come here for. Well, not the meat, but monkey parts.'

'I've never seen a golden-headed monkey.'

'You wouldn't. They only live here, on this island, but there are huge numbers of them, sleeping in the caves and the high trees. People like her don't notice the smell of the meat any more, although I don't think even she would eat it.'

'What is she doing with it then?' I asked, looking towards the closed door of the dwelling.

'Making monkey medicine. Round the back, where you can't see, there'll be a pile of dead ones waiting for whatever she does with them. They sell the scalps, the golden fur, monkey fingers and they make different types of monkey balm, for which I think she must skin it and cook it, but I've never seen her do it. I don't go in there. I think it must smell even worse than it does out here.'

'And her man, he catches them?' I guessed.

'Yes, he's one of the traders here, but they're all fiercely protective of their monkeys. People who've come here looking to catch a few and sell them on have disappeared and Mother Monkey in there nearly took a slice out of me the first time I came to her door.'

I giggled, although it was not really very funny. The mingled stench of cooked and rotting monkey made the place seem foul, but from our vantage point on the hillside, I could see swathes of Cat Ba that still looked beautiful and entirely untouched.

When the monkey trader arrived, two deep brown langurs with shining golden heads and shoulders lying lifeless across his back, he conducted business swiftly and almost silently with Dao. I understood later from Chien that his father had already delivered several sacks of rice a few weeks before and in return the trader went inside and got the requisite glass bottles of medicine that Monkey Mother, as Dao called her, had prepared. As we turned to leave, the trader hailed Dao as an afterthought.

'You tell Prefect Chau to keep the Han away from here,' he ordered. 'They want the monkey medicine, they can get it at the markets, or send you or one of my other regulars. They come here by themselves, they'll be floating home without heads!' He made a snorting noise for good measure, bowed perfunctorily at Dao and then stalked off behind the hut with the day's catch.

'That's something new,' said Chien, 'the Han coming out here for the monkey medicine.'

'They probably thought they could get a better deal, or like as not, just take it,' said Dao, thoughtfully. 'They will not help themselves by trying to bypass our markets.'

We went back down to the dwellings near the beach and the man chewing the areca nuts was still there, now crisping up several of his mackerel over an open fire. A younger woman, probably his daughter, came out with rice in bowls and some mashed up yam and handed them to us with a brisk nod. Dao thanked her and we went and sat by the ageing fisherman, who broke some cooked fish into each of our bowls. He gave me a fish head, with the briefest of smiles and I sucked out the eyes, which were satiny and delicious before devouring the meat and the crispy skin along with fingers-full of rice and yam. A gang of rowdy children emerged from behind the houses, evidently having been out fishing themselves, for one of the boys was carrying a netted cuttlefish and the others carried clams. They stared at us before going for their own rice and receiving a chunk of mackerel from the areca-chewing cook.

'How many people live here?' I asked.

'In these few houses? Maybe fifteen or so. But there are more houses further along.'

We ate up and I bowed my thanks to the old fisherman and his daughter before we went back through the cycads and onto the beach. The sun was shining weakly through the cloud layer now and it was warmer travelling back. Dao took us straight back to Hai Phong, and though I had hoped he might take us a little further along the coastline of Cat Ba, I contented myself with the fact that he had taken me there at all. I wanted to return and see those islanders again and perhaps dare to speak directly to them about life there but I knew it was unlikely. Dao would not need to return there in the span of time I had left in Hai Phong.

I made the most of my remaining time with them, I can say that much. Chien and I did not kiss; that would have to wait until after marriage, I realised, but he held my hand on more than one occasion and we even managed to embrace when we found ourselves momentarily unguarded. More importantly, I had made firm friends with his family, who would thereafter be my family also. I missed them when I went home. I missed them terribly, but I was very happy to see Trac and Mother again. I had never been away from them for so long before and I had entirely forgotten my misgivings about Trac's recent alteration. Chien had assured me that it took a while to settle down into a marriage and that, no doubt, I would find Trac back to her old self when I returned. He was wrong about that, but he could not have guessed what had happened back home in Cam Khe.

★★★★★

I had worried in Hai Phong about what Governor Xuan was up to back in Lien Lau. True enough, he had left us all alone after Trac married Sach, but that didn't mean he had forgiven our family for the slight of not taking his proposed match. Governor Vo Xuan was an old crocodile, showing just eyes and nose above the water before he made his next move. Yet when we returned – myself, Chan and Chien having made the trip together with an older relation of the Le family - I found that tragedy had already struck from an entirely unexpected source. No one spoke of it during the night that we all stayed, although Chan was clever enough to have worked it out, and it wasn't until we said goodbye to my intended and his family the next day, that Mother fully explained to me what Chan had whispered in my ear.

Chan had said, 'Go steady with your sister, Nhi. I think she and Sach have suffered a loss.' And indeed, Trac did look paler and stranger than usual, though she was still being uncharacteristically gregarious. It should have been obvious to me what had happened, but the vague stirrings of realisation were only confirmed when Mother took me aside and said, 'Trac has lost a baby. She bled five days ago.'

A baby? I stared at Mother.

'She must have got with child before we left for Hai Phong,' Mother went on, 'but it was still very early and she lost it without fuss. There will be another soon enough, though I have advised Sach to wait a while and make sure they are both ready.'

'But why did she lose it? Did something happen? Was she working or training too hard?'

'Not that I noticed,' said Mother, the shadow of a frown creasing her forehead. 'Sometimes it is just not meant to be.'

'They're both physically strong. Is it Sach's fault, has he been wasting his energy?' The men in Giao Chi, as in the Middle Kingdom, practice restraint, holding their seed in to strengthen it, as I had been laughingly informed by Auntie An's servant once.

'Nhi, listen to me. I have spoken to Sach and he has been acting quite correctly.'

'But there must be a reason!' I was getting quite upset. 'Did she eat something bad?'

'Nhi, stop it. This will not help Trac. Babies are lost sometimes - it is the way of things. Be a good girl and comfort Trac. That is all you can do. And please, do not attack her with this kind of question. You will make everything far worse.' Mother glared at me until she was quite sure I was going to remain silent. 'Good. Now go and see your sister.'

Trac was drinking soup inside the house. When I went in to her – which I did not actually want to do, but Mother was watching me – she fixed a bright, unnatural smile on her lips and shooed away Sach, who was trying to wrap a blanket around her.

'Have they gone? Did they get off all right? You will have to tell me all about Hai Phong and what you got up to there.'

I went and sat beside her on the soft mat. Wordlessly, Diep handed me a bowl of soup and went back to the stove and Sach receded into a corner. Trac shrugged the blanket away.

'You should keep that on, The weather's coming cold,' I said.

'Are you an old married woman now?' Trac replied, with a hint of bitterness. We both sipped at our soup. I wished Mother hadn't sent me in. I had no idea what to say. 'It is not like you to be quiet. Are you not going to tell me about your visit?'

'I can tell you, if you really want to hear all about that.' I looked at her, wishing she would mention the baby, because I didn't know how to, but she just stared desperately into her soup, so I told her all about Prefect Chau's bossy command of her family, about the temple I had visited where whales were venerated and about how Chien's mother made offerings to the great whale spirit when the catch was good. I described Dao's unexpectedly kind nature, the fish market that stank to the heavens and the peculiar island of the golden-headed monkeys that sat at the end of Descending Dragon Bay. I talked and talked, and once or twice she smiled or looked up and we could almost have been having a normal conversation.

When I ran out of stories to tell her, I said, 'I am very sorry, you know.'

'I know,' she said. 'Everyone is sorry.'

I sat with her for a while longer and then went out walking.

I passed Bao, out in the fields digging irrigation channels, and he waved at me, as usual. The air was cool and clear, as it should be at that time of year. The world outside was as normal as ever and I hoped that normality would come back to our house, and to Trac, soon. Even my own sadness at parting once more from Chien was of little importance compared with her grief.

★★★★★

Downriver that day, though, nothing was normal. Governor Xuan had been informed that the Le siblings and some unknown family cousin were escorting me back to Me Linh. Ordinarily, I guess he'd have given this nugget of information an indifferent response, but Governor Xuan remembered Le Chan. Her proud figure and good-looking face must have skipped from memory to mind and he saw an opportunity to make good on his promise to Captain Gang's family as well as a chance to consolidate the coastal defensive town of Hai Phong into the auspices of the Giao Chi Commandery divisions. His exact plans and motives, I'll never know, but presumably for the reasons I've guessed at, he intercepted Chien and Chan on their return journey and smooth-talked them into the Lien Lau government building. Once there, he put to Chan the possibility of a marriage to Captain Gang, who was not at that time present, but was with his Company on an expedition south to the borders.

She vacillated diplomatically, explaining that she would have to put the proposal to her parents and eventually, Xuan allowed them to continue on their way. But he wasn't going to let her slip away as Trac had done. Bearing in mind that Hai Phong was technically under his direct control, and that Chan's family had not yet been officially authorised and did not possess the seals of Prefecture, he felt free to act decisively. He ordered the return of Captain Gang, and in the middle of the winter, he promoted Gang to Colonel and sent him to Hai Phong with a full regiment and an open remit to take Le Chan and marry her, at which point her family would pass the status of Prefect to Gang, who would hold that position alongside his army role.

It was a planned military offensive by the Han in all but name. The regiment rode to Hai Phong, whose leading family received advanced warning of the impending assault and, with their backs to the sea, took the last actions remaining to them. Firstly, they sent Chan away into hiding. She took a dugout and sailed up into Ha Long Bay to hide amongst the thousands of tiny islands and caves that even the Han could not hope to penetrate. Then Prefect Chau and her medicine-man husband waited for the assault and Chien waited with them.

Why he didn't go with Chan, I cannot understand. Why didn't he get in the canoe with her? Why didn't he think of me? I think I'm over it, but poking at the wound, I find that it does still hurt, even nine years later with so much water under the bridge; even while I lay here holding poor wounded Trac by the riverside.

13

My sister is crying. She thinks I do not know, that I am insensible with pain and drifting already into the starry heavens, but a drop landed on my own cheek a moment ago and her soft breath as she holds me chills the damp spot on my skin. I do not know what she is thinking about. Her son, perhaps? So far away from her now, and probably never to be held by her again. I hope it is not me and my sorry state that have reduced her to tears.

I hate this sticky, itching feeling of blood drying on my sides. The bandage they have wrapped round me has slowed the flow, I can feel that much, but still it pulses slowly and if I were to shift position, I know I would feel that knifing agony though my middle. If I stay very still, just like this, I can bear the tender ache and the pin-pricks of mortality. Was it only last night that I spoke with my Generals? Chinh looks so horribly changed. She is on the periphery of my vision, white and skeletal. I cannot see who else is with us - I dare not move to look around - but I know our mother is not here. Nhi says she is still at the front, though I doubt the front exists any longer. Soon Ma Vien will pursue us all the way to this riverside, hacking through everything in his way. I should hate him - he has killed so many of my army and no doubt he is coming here to kill us - but I do not. I feel connected to him. I feel we are in balance, General Vien and I. He came here, to my Nam Viet, to remove me and I stood against him, to turn him away. We are each performing a clear role and being what we must be and I cannot hate a man for that. Ma Vien has slaughtered many thousands, but he has done so honestly and cleanly, without lies or prevarication. I would rather meet Ma Vien on the battlefield any day that go back to those terrible days of Vo Xuan and To Dinh - men who came here to profit and exploit. What Xuan allowed to happen at Hai Phong - that was terrible and, immortal creatures protect me, what To Dinh did- No. Later. I just cannot.

In Hai Phong, Le Dao, Tran Thi Chau and Le Chien were murdered. The boy who was Nhi's first love, along with his two serious and hard-working parents staged a resistance when Colonel Gang brought his regiment to the coastal town, and Gang, in fury at realising Chan had eluded him, cut them down. That is to say, he cut down Chien, who ran to protect his parents and then he forced Chau and Dao to take their own lives. It is something they had anticipated, I am sure. That is why they sent Chan, the flower of their future, to hide in the caves. I know, from Chan's few messages to us back then, that they tried to send Chien away also - that they did, in fact, believe him to be gone, but that he returned. He knew Chan would be safe; he believed in her strength and that she would bring a terrible revenge down on the Han one day, but he felt that he had never proved himself and that his time had come. He saw that this was his fate - to be a good son and sacrifice himself for his parents, so they would see how he honoured them and how he distinguished himself at last. Nhi lashed out when she heard this - at Chan who had not held him back and at his dead parents who had allowed him to act so recklessly. Perhaps her grief was easier in the early days, when she could simply believe that Colonel Gang had caught and murdered Chien. To know that Chien had chosen his parents, above the future he could have had with Nhi, burned her.

Chien's death dragged me past my own misery and into caring for Nhi, and so I began to live again, while my young sister grieved and suffered. I still cried sometimes, strictly when no one was looking, for that little life that could have been, but I had lost it so soon - before it had quickened - and these things happened to nearly every woman, my mother said. I saw all adult women differently after the miscarriage - no longer were they chatty or shy, traders or weavers, pretty or ugly, Prefects or peasants; they were all one long procession of women mourning for some little bundle of bloodied rags. There was a kinship in the loss – I had joined the ranks of married, child-bearing women who suffered silently. At least my baby had been unformed. My mother told me the tale of how gossipy Mrs Chau next door had lost a baby, not ten days after she birthed him. Mrs Chau – who could have known? Beneath her vocal and trivial exterior must lay an ocean of pain at which I had never guessed. No one talks of these things and so we never know.

Nhi did not speak much either. If I tried to describe her attitude, I would say that she acted as though somehow, she had been proved right. It was as if she had already known everything that would happen there in Hai Phong and that her grief was not so much sadness at the loss of Chien as fury that it could not have been altered. It was a perception I formed over months, from the little, embittered things she let pass between her lips and the way she attacked air and ground with her staff, smashing wildly through her daily training. Then, inside a year, she was recovered. It was as simple and as complicated as that. She emerged one day, with a smile on her face and life began again for her also. I asked, once, how she had got over it and she said she had seen a peacock in her dreams, opening its glorious tail feathers. Nothing ends, she explained, life is always beautiful.

And life was beautiful, then. I was into my nineteenth year and Sach and I were inseparable. On a night, we practised the usual art of control, so that Sach was always very focussed on my pleasure and restrained himself from completing the act, to improve his own vitality. Always we were silent. He never spoke when he kissed or held me and I made myself feel faint from inadvertently holding my breath, not wanting to break the spell of what he was doing with any sound. In the daytime, like all couples, we didn't kiss or touch and his presence, a finger-span from me, set the same thrill though me as it had before our marriage. Even more important to me than all the intimacy we shared, was the bond he was forming with Nhi. She reminded him a little of Kim Cuc, his youngest sister, and he treated her in much the same way. When I saw her smiling and talking eagerly with him, I was filled not only with warmth, but also with relief. He eased the burden of care I had always felt towards her. He was an asset to my mother also, availing himself of any opportunity to assist her. In those respects, I could not believe my good luck.

With the cloud lifted from Nhi, she regained the inner balance required to progress with her martial training. Was I jealous when I watched her move with such controlled animal force? I suppose I must have been or I would not have thought to ask myself the question. I knew I would never be quite as good as her, though I was a close second, but the envy that may have nestled within me was easily surpassed by the pride I felt towards her. Mrs Chau beamed when she saw Nhi putting Bao through the fundamental routines, and I saw that Nhi's skill was not just in her practice of the arts, but in their dissemination. Her openness to people meant that she could bring out of them what they did not know they possessed, and although she had to be selective about who she taught, soon there was an array of men and women approaching her during her daily sessions. She turned away those who were arrogant and simply wanted to fight her to prove something and took on instead the people who she warmed to, even if my mother and I were dubious about their ability. She inspired her students and she was much-loved by the people of Me Linh.

One day, a woman from Tay Vu arrived at our home. She was erect and proud on horseback, but swung herself down with such an approachable smile that Nhi greeted her almost as a friend.

'I am Chinh,' she said. 'Phung Thi Chinh, from Tay Vu. I've heard about the training you do and I wish for you to teach me.'

'You've come from Tay Vu?' asked my mother, coming forward in disbelief and Chinh smiled and bowed. Sach stood by also and he nudged me. 'You and your sister are becoming quite famous,' he said.

146

'I am Trac,' I said to the woman and she gazed at me through fathomless eyes.

'Ah, I know, of course. It is an honour to meet you all.'

She was so deferential that one had to like her. In the course of that first day, we discovered that she was quite skilled herself, possessing the forms and movements of her own familial branch of martial arts. She was as cautious as we were about sharing such privileged secrets too soon but we trained very effectively together and she stayed with us in our home for a time. She was, of course, from a noble family, and when my mother inquired further she discovered that Chinh's particular branch of the head Tay Vu family did indeed have connections with our own, distant but discernible. My father had been born in Tay Vu, the large district watched over by Mount Tam Dao. It was a well-settled place of plains and hills, nestling within rivers and lakes, where the thousands of inhabitants raised huge rice crops on the saturated land. It was exciting and comforting to think that people downriver in Tay Vu had begun to talk about us and that we were so highly respected.

Yet, equally, this was dangerous.

'Mother, if we have such a growing reputation, do you think Governor Xuan will become angry again?' I asked.

'Quite possibly,' she replied.

'Should we be careful in how we proceed?'

'One should always take care,' my mother advised. 'There is a time for stillness, a time for preparation and a time for movement. Think on that, eldest daughter.'

Preparation, then. That is what we were engaged in, though I did not know what the preparation was for, and some instinct prevented me from enquiring. I have stood on the plains, in the hot, dark night time, and felt the swell of humidity that rolls in before the storm begins. First comes the wind, cloying and heavy, then comes the growl of the immortal lion in the heavens, then comes the lightning crash from the hand of the star god, before the rain assaults the ground, battering the houses and engorging angry rivers. My mother's words made me think of that swell, that first wave of heat, portending the storm to come, and once my mind had attached to that idea, I could not shake it off. Every conversation, every piece of news from Lien Lau, sensitized me further to this feeling that we were preparing for something big.

Sach had none of my foreboding, but all of the anticipation. He had moved from the stillness of childhood, into the preparation of early adulthood and was more than ready for some kind of action. Always, he had chafed at the Han imposition on our lives, even before he had fully understood it, but etiquette and filial obedience had prevented his overt demonstration of restlessness. In my mother's company, he found himself freer to speak of what angered him. At home, his ageing father had been focussed on reinforcement of their position and bringing up his two motherless daughters, but in my home, Sach discovered a different set of priorities. My mother was trained in the martial ways – one could say they had been her first love and they certainly were her great skill – and she had a born resoluteness of spirit that prevented her from contemplating defeat. She was not concerned with bolstering her position in the Giao Chi Commandery – for my arrogant mother, that position was a given – and neither was she overly protective of myself and Nhi. She had trained my thoughts and actions from babyhood and she had loosed Nhi to wander the wilds, knowing that was the right path for her youngest daughter. My mother was not the same as Thi Hoc, who had a man's concern for worldly achievement and protection of the home. My mother's heart was set upon the Way. She had a vision of our destiny, but even she could not have said how it should unfold. She followed the Way as one follows a star in the night – blindly and with faith.

I do not think she spurred Sach on purposefully. In fact, I do not think my mother particularly calculated more than a few moves ahead, because she was so open to the Way. It was more that she found a kindred spirit in Sach. When he began speaking his mind on subjects such as the increasing taxations, exploitation of agricultural land for Middle Kingdom consumption, enforced trade cooperation, and most controversially of all, new marital policies, she encouraged him. She sympathised with his righteous indignation and she validated his anger. She began, I do not doubt, to be confirmed in her opinion that we were the generation to throw the Han from Giao Chi – to make it Nam Viet once more – but she did not force it. She let us grow into it. I am not angry at her for that. How can I be, I, that have profited more than any from her good guidance? If I have suffered, it is because that suffering was part of the Way. It was not my mother's doing.

Even so, the suffering was some years away yet. The heartlands of Giao Chi stayed for a time under the rule of Governor Vo Xuan and slowly the animosity faded. I think Xuan had realised the danger of forcing change too swiftly – he had tried to force me into marriage and failed, then he had tried to force Chan into marriage and failed. His only success, if you could call it that, had been to exterminate the head family of Hai Phong and bring the coastal town under a form of direct rule, but even this achievement was proving to be a double-edged sword as hostilities crackled under the surface. There had been rumours that Le Chan was gathering an army of warriors and although Governor Xuan snorted derision upon this drifting story, he had pulled back his military imposition from Hai Phong to calm the waters.

The first time Sach and I were summoned together into Xuan's presence must have been two years after our marriage. We were quite the adult couple now – myself at eighteen and him at twenty-two. Xuan received us courteously but his eyes were as cunningly appraising as ever. At first, we danced around the necessary small talk, until Xuan raised the reason for our meeting.

'In my discussions with your father, Sach, he has intimated that the time may have come for you to succeed to his Prefect status.'

'I do not presume myself worthy to assume his duties,' answered Sach, with the required filial politesse.

'Naturally,' said Xuan, an ambiguous smile curving his lips, 'but nevertheless, he assures me you are more than qualified and that you will relieve him of the tiresome journeying that he finds difficult now.'

'I see it is necessary. It would please me greatly to give my father some rest.'

'He also assures me that now you are older, you understand something of the subtle balance which we in Giao Chi strive to achieve. You are lucky, in this province, you know, that the old systems have been retained and that the Lac Lords are still respected. No one wants war here in Giao Chi, do they? Yet, every so often I hear on the breeze that this person or that person is dissatisfied or offended and that they seek to cast off the rule of the divinely inspired Emperor. I have to be certain, when I accept any new Prefect, that they are not one of those people who are going to cause such problems.'

'I have no plans to start a war,' said Sach, 'and I am not dissatisfied. Yet I must be honest and say that some of the reforms that have been talked about cause me concern.'

'Reforms?'

'I've heard it said that marriages must be registered here in Lien Lau. Also that the peasants and labourers will be versed in Confucianism. Some say the taxes are to be raised higher, and new rules introduced to increase the rice crops.'

I shifted on my knees. We were knelt at a low table, taking warm drinks as we, or rather they, spoke. I was uncomfortable with the direction of the conversation. The room seemed to draw closer about me, like a web.

'This is just talk. Nothing has been changed yet and neither will it be without the consent of the Prefects. But let me tell you this - those who are older and wiser understand the need for some changes, as will you, dear son, as you learn more about the duties you have inherited from your father.'

Sach bowed his head. I glanced at his face. He was very slightly flushed but content with himself. I could see he had been pleased to speak his mind. I was less pleased about that. I did not trust that Xuan could be negotiated or reasoned with so openly and as he turned to speak directly to me, I was more than ready to dissemble if I must.

'Your Lady mother has, as you will know, no such plans to step aside. I hope this does not frustrate you.'

'Not at all,' I said, remaining calm but furious that he had dared to suggest I was so rudely eager for power. 'My happiness comes from serving my mother in all things.'

'And from serving your husband,' he corrected.

'Naturally,' I echoed. Now it was Sach's turn to shift in discomfort. Notions of servility by women to men were not the Nam Viet way.

'And how is sister Nhi? Is she well? Not yet married, I understand.' And there it was - the sharpened stick I had been expecting, right into the well-spring of grief for my sister's loss of Chien. He had asked on purpose, even though it undermined his own agenda of re-establishing good relations with his Prefecture.

'No, not yet married. But very well.' I pictured a blade behind him, about to pierce him. I imagined his scream as it struck.

'I've heard you and she run an excellent *wushu* school.'

'Have you?'

Xuan smiled. I smiled. I showed teeth. Their blackness repelled him.

'And so! I must let you continue on with your day,' he said, rising. 'Sach, my clerk here will prepare for you the new seals of Prefect status. We will meet regularly, especially in these early days while you find your feet.'

On the surface, we had concluded a civil, productive meeting. Sach was even pleased with the outcome. He had feared that Xuan might somehow prevent the inheritance of the Prefect status and, now that he was to be honoured with the copper, green-ribboned seals, he felt he had his foot wedged inside the door. Once in, he believed he could right so many wrongs and set the future of Giao Chi back on a more acceptable course. On the way home, he insisted to me that the administration would be forced to give in to the demands of the Prefects, if only they could organise themselves better.

'What conceit is this?' I asked in astonishment. 'Do you really believe that your father, and my mother and Vien and all the others, have failed us by some lack of organisation?'

'No, you are twisting my words,' he argued. 'I am saying that they have not always presented a united front. I plan to return to Lien Lau and talk with Ton Vien very soon. I think we'll find we have much in common and I already feel that your mother and I agree on many points.'

'Perhaps, but I do not believe she will agree with you about the way forward. If it was so easy to negotiate with the Han, my mother would have done it herself.'

'But your mother has so often put herself opposite Ton Vien and others,' he said. 'Times have changed. Now she can be more open about her true feelings. Xuan has been forced to concede on more than one occasion. He has realised the limit of his power and knows he must step more carefully with the Lac.'

'I doubt Le Chan would agree with you,' I said, kicking my horse into a gallop and pulling away from him. I felt like crying, but I was not sure why. After all, my husband's analysis was well-reasoned. Governor Xuan had agreed to a diplomatic backing-down over the stolen drums. He had shied away from forcing me into marriage with Gang. He had also pulled troops

152

away from Hai Phong. He was a cautious man and not an overtly violent one. Why, then, did I feel this tearful frustration? On the jolting ride home, I wondered if I was pregnant again and experiencing the altered perceptions that accompany the condition. It was easier to believe that, than to listen to my gut telling me that the Lien Lau administration could not be trusted - that they had murdered Chau, Dao and Chien and that they looked upon the Lac lords with the same patronising amusement as they would look upon dancing water puppets.

Sach sensed something of my mood, because he left the topic alone, and presumably recounted to my mother the content of the meeting whilst I was out of the way. The next day, we trained together and then walked to the market in the sheen of golden sunlight, and I felt better. In Me Linh, we were the honoured couple and not a single person passed us without a bow or a word of greeting or a small gift, pressed into our hands like an offering. It was enough to make anyone feel better and I reminded myself that this was my daily life, here in my beautiful town, far away from the cesspit of the Han government in Lien Lau.

It was on one such precious day as that, when the sun shone hard and broke through the morning mists and made steam rise from the ornamental lakes near the temple, that Mai Thao came visiting Me Linh. Thao was the younger brother of Nhat, my one-time suitor. I had not seen either brother since the feast in Lien Lau, where Sach had formally proposed. We had heard, however, that their mother, Hoa, had died following her long illness, though her husband continued as Prefect of Khuc Duong. Thao - the younger and more aggressively ambitious brother - was acting as his father's second, relieving his father of the more arduous work in much the same way as Sach had relieved his own father. When he arrived in Me Linh, he let his presence be known and we immediately invited him to stay with us.

Thao did not have the angular grace of my husband, but had instead a fighter's unlovely attractiveness, with his bullish lips and drawn eyes. His shoulders were very wide and he had a small, muscular waist. His hands were squarish and perfectly still and he held conversation with ease, charming my mother as he had at the feast and quickly finding common ground with Sach. It was upon Nhi's arrival, though, that he was wrong-footed.

She had been out most of the day – I do not know where, as she was still prone to wander – and she had not heard that we were receiving company, so she strode into the house in a wanton manner and handed me an uprooted slipper orchid with a flourish, chattering about how she had scraped her shin reaching it high in a tree, but didn't it look unusual and wasn't the colouring beautiful? It was sometimes hard to reconcile the meditative martial artist of the early mornings with the excitable young woman who returned from her afternoon strolls, but after seeing her black state following Chien's death, I always took pleasure from her giddiness, where before I had experienced impatience. Now, with Thao standing open-jawed behind her, she prattled on oblivious to my amusement, until our mother helpfully intervened and suggested to Nhi that she meet our guest. She turned to face Thao, who of the two looked the most unsettled, and his eyes widened. To his credit, he closed his open mouth.

'Second brother, I remember you,' she remarked.

'And I you, second sister,' he replied, although his confused countenance was telling a different story. How could I have missed this one? his eyes said. His intense stare softened. 'Have you been out walking?'

'I go most days,' she said, 'after I have trained.'

'Perhaps, Lady Prefect, I could walk with Nhi tomorrow,' he said, to our mother.

'Oh, are you staying? Very well then! And do you train? You look as though you must,' said Nhi, with her usual directness.

Thao, bemused, nodded, then seemed to recapture his wits and gave some kind of answer about the martial traditions he had studied. I smiled behind the grotesque bloom my sister had handed me and slipped outside to see if I could find somewhere to wedge the thing. She had prised the roots carefully from whatever nook she had found it in, and I expected it would take if I found it a sheltered spot. She brought these flowers home almost as an offering to me, not noticing that I cared little for them. I took the orchid round the back of the house where a tangle of dried old roots from a long-dead tree had broken the surface soil. There were a few flowers here already and I heaped up some dirt and scraps of rubbish and balanced the sorry-looking specimen within, wrapping some of the green, tubular roots around the older, decaying tree roots. When I stood, wiping my dusty hands down my sides, Bao was behind me.

'Hello Bao,' I said. 'Have you finished early today?'

'I had a visit,' he answered, looking at the orchid. 'Not enough sun here. It will die.'

'Who visited you, Bao?'

'He was Han. From the Governor's office.'

'One of Governor Xuan's men visited you? What did he want?'

'He wanted me to spy on you, eldest daughter Trac. On you and Sach and also on Nhi and your mother.'

'And what did you say to him, eldest son Bao?'

'I was not sure what to say. So I stayed silent and he asked if I was a mute. The other workers said nothing and he took me to be simple, but he said he would return and that if I gave him information, he would give me a reward.'

'Then what happened?' I asked, with a chill running down my shoulder blades like the tingling caress of a finger.

'He left.'

'And that is all?'

155

'Yes.'

'He did not hurt you? Threaten you?'

'No. But I thought if I refused his request, he might have done so. It seemed sensible to stay silent.'

'Very good, Bao. Very good indeed. Now here is what you must do. When the man returns, you must play simple again, but give him some information. Governor Xuan is just keeping an eye on things but we do not wish him to know everything, do we?'

Bao shook his head. I noticed that instead of his usual weather-worn complexion, his skin looked paler.

'Bao,' I said, making him look directly at me, 'Everything will be all right but you must do as I say. I will tell you the things to say to the man and he will be satisfied. He will be relieved he has something to report to the Governor. Now tell me, does your mother know of this?'

'I came straight to you,' Bao said.

'I will talk with your mother. She may herself have been approached. Now when this man returns, tell him that Lady Man Thien's family are hosting a visitor – a man you do not know. That will do for the first occasion.'

'Are you hosting a visitor?'

'Yes, we are. If pushed, tell him you think the man may be a suitor for Nhi but that you are unsure.'

'Is he a suitor for Nhi?' Bao asked, with rounded eyes.

'I am unsure,' I laughed.

'You seem very relaxed about all this,' Bao accused.

'Why should I be otherwise? Governor Xuan wants to know what his Prefects are up to, that is all. All the noble families experience such intrusion.'

Bao nodded, but looked uncertain. After all, my father, General Lac, had been Prefect for many years and never before had Bao's family been asked to spy. In truth I was unsettled and, once again, I felt the storm surge in the air.

On the second day of Thao's visit, he walked out with Nhi. Sach and I followed, as escorts, at a respectable distance, whispering occasionally about Bao's news. During the previous evening I had told Sach of the latest imposition by Governor Xuan and he had accompanied me to speak with Mrs Chau, whose absolute amazement and disgust at such tactics had belied entirely to me the fact that she had been approached and had most likely agreed to part with information for reward. I had never entirely trusted Mrs Chau although I did not blame her. She could hardly pretend to be mute, like Bao, and an outright refusal would have brought awful pressure upon her, yet I was wary that, unlike Bao, she had not come straight to us. I forgave her that. I had lost a second barely-there baby not long before and I was thinking of our mutual sorrow, rather than her suspected perfidy.

You would think, wouldn't you, that if I cannot speak long about my father, then I should not be able to speak long about these part-formed babies. It was different. The four babies were never really there. They hadn't limbs or voices. They hadn't movement or sight. I mourned so terribly at the time for the loss of the child I had imagined, but now they are to me the delicate sparks of hope, delivered to the immortal beings before worldly suffering could extinguish their beauty. It did not feel that way at the time, when I cried in the night, letting tears flow down my cheeks and over my earlobes where they wetted the hair at the back of my neck as I stared into the wooden roof and wondered what I had done to deserve such loss. I can still almost feel it - the desperate, gnawing hunger for a soft, breathing baby in my arms; the agony of that horrendous lack. If I seek out the pain, it sears through me, just as this real wound to my stomach burns me each time I move. It's still there, wrapped carefully, like bitter slices of areca nut inside a betel leaf.

Walking behind Nhi and Thao, Sach and I debated whether

Mrs Chau would betray more than she should to the intermediaries sent by Governor Xuan. My unease had grown overnight, but Sach was quick to reassure me.

'What can he learn? By what method do we offend him? Let his men spy on us. They will learn nothing,' he whispered to me.

'But we do not follow the Han ways. We do not lay our tables in the way they have shown us. We do not perform the ancestor rites they have tried to teach us. And what about Confucius? There are a thousand ways in every day that we offend the Middle Kingdom philosophies,' I said, in a hushed voice.

'None of those things really matter,' Sach assured me. 'Xuan is worried about discontent simmering into violence. That is the kind of thing he's looking for - plans and alliances that directly threaten him. Not how we choose to live.'

'I am not so sure. What about the clerks and their money? He must care about our lack of adherence to Han custom, if he's willing to do that.'

An edict had spread throughout Giao Chi, stating that for families who married and lived in accordance with prescribed Han customs, a reward would be issued. This reward was to be drawn directly from the money, minted in the Middle Kingdom, that the clerks and officials in Giao Chi received as pay. Though it looked like a gesture of goodwill, most of the officials were natives of Giao Chi, so it amounted to us paying for our own kind to marry - a redistribution of wealth within our own ranks.

'It shows he is dividing to conquer. Don't you see? Of course, ideally, he wants them to change their ways, and some will, drawn by the lure of the coins, but many will retain their own customs and there is nothing Xuan can do about that.' Sach's voice had risen slightly and on the path ahead, Thao threw a curious glance back towards us. I smiled and lowered my eyes.

'Quieter,' I murmured. 'We do not know Thao's sympathies yet.'

'Oh? I thought you knew the family quite well.'

'I met his brother once, that is all,' I said. Sach was silent. The air of his unspoken jealousy hung around us and I sought to mollify him. 'You may be right. I will not worry about Xuan's spies. But please, we must be careful how we speak and to whom we speak in future.'

'I am always careful,' he answered. We picked up our pace to keep Nhi and Thao in sight. My sister was walking gaily, ignoring the calmer pace which Thao was attempting to set. I watched him watching her, trying to engage her. For a single heartbeat, the hairs on the back of my neck rose in the chill belief that it should have been Chien walking with her and that the ground underfoot should be sand, not soil. Then the rain clouds began to roll shadows across the hillsides and the four of us turned for home.

★★★★★

I mourned for a long time. At least, it felt a long time. I mourned until the ten thousand things said enough is enough and I started to see beauty in everything again. Yet the darkness of Chien's death was inside me now and part of my spirit was his. I liked Thao but I couldn't smile coyly at him or allow my arm to remain where he might brush against it. Thao understood. He asked Mother to consider him if one day I should be ready to marry and then he left us in peace, after his short stay in our home. Perverse as I am, I missed him when he'd gone, but it was just as well. I didn't want to torture him with my ambivalence.

At fifteen, I was now fully matured. Trac and I stood at equal height and we were reasonably evenly matched in our training. Her skill was her power – she swung her *kiem* hard and she could throw me with ease. My skill was my speed. I was agile and prescient. I smelled the blow before my opponent could shape it. Of course, there were others in Giao Chi who were formidably equipped to challenge and teach us. When Phung Thi Chinh came visiting, I learned new moves, new patterns of footwork and new ways to turn an opponent's joints and render them immobile. We went north a few times, following rivers quilted with water hyacinths, upstream, to the mountain forests of the hill people, searching out the skilled masters of the ancient Au Viet line. We took rice with us to pay for our training. In the hills, they produced rice, but not in great quantities like we did, low down on the delta, so they welcomed such trade. I made friends with a good number of families and Trac and I earned their respect. Mother came with us those times - her name was known in the hills and it was she who gained us entry into the lofty, cloud-shrouded villages where little lines of houses backed neatly into the sloping landscape. She was ever worried, though, that we were leaving Me Linh unprotected and so Sach remained behind while we went on those trips. Secretly, I was glad. I liked having Trac back to myself again and I always thought she fought better when he was not distracting her. That seems awful to say now, but I can't tell untruths; there wouldn't be much point in my story if I did.

I hadn't had much cause to hate in my young life and I'd always been of cheerful disposition but I found that there was a hard stone in my heart after Chien was killed. It bit into the tender centre of me, like a pebble underfoot in the rice threshing pit. When I trained, I imagined that the stone was sharpening into a weapon to be inflicted on those I blamed for his murder - Governor Xuan and Captain Gang. Xuan had allowed it, Gang had committed it. Trac had murmured some half-hearted excuse for the young Captain (now, in fact, a Corporal) but I had silenced her. He was responsible - he killed Chien and one day, he would pay, as would Xuan. She let it go, backing away from that conversation like a ibis skips from the crocodile at the water's edge. She knew I could never let it go and she was aware, therefore, of how consumed with frustration I was when I learned that Governor Xuan was leaving Giao Chi to return to his native Middle Kingdom.

What was an impedance for me was a relief for everyone else

and as the news quickly spread, I had to hear what good fortune it was, and how perhaps fairer taxes and regulations would now be considered. Xuan, it was assumed, must have offended someone or else been judged to have been doing a bad job and surely that meant that whoever came next would have to do things differently. I was angry. In my anger at missing the opportunity to avenge Chien, I stubbornly refused to be optimistic. Xuan was just old, I said, and had been recalled so that a younger, stronger man could take his place. Things could just as easily get worse as get better. Xuan had a leaving ceremony and incense burned on his procession route out of Lien Lau, but I was not there. Mother went, with Trac and Sach and I stayed behind. After my terrible mood, they would have been frightened that I was going to try something stupid – a sword in his side as he passed us, perhaps – and they would not have let me attend anyway.

The clear intention to kill Xuan had actually come upon me as a tangible desire only when I learned of his leaving. Before that, I had nursed an incoherent hope, but I had never quite said to myself, I will kill those men. Only when he was leaving did I realise that was what had been crystallising inside me. Then, with Xuan's departure, the sharp stone had to be more finely shaved, pointed solely as it now was in the direction of Corporal Gang. I wouldn't let him escape as Xuan had.

I had learned that Corporal Gang had moved further inland with his men. He was in charge of a vast swathe of newly cultivated rice-growing land – wide fields to the east of Lien Lau. His men, like many of the Middle Kingdom army, worked the land to produce grain in tribute for the Emperor, and there were generations now of settled Han – soldiers who had arrived, worked, carved out their own home and family and who would never return north. It had been over one hundred years since they first threw over the Trieu Dynasty and whole Han family lines were lacing their blood into the land that was ours. If only

Xuan had peacefully resigned his commission and settled into an old age in Lien Lau! Then I should have had him. I think I would have sliced his stomach apart and watched him die slowly. But he had gone, and in his place came To Dinh. Fat, hairy To Dinh, with his ingratiating smile and furry tufts above his ears that would not be tamed into the bun at the back of his head. His eyebrows nearly met in the centre and beneath them he had black eyes, shiny and plump like the dark diamonds on a pit-viper's back. Where Tich Quang had been a respected diplomat, and Vo Xuan had been a greedy administrator, To Dinh was a crafty zealot. He had Quang's cunning and Xuan's acquisitiveness but behind all that, he possessed an almost fanatical desire for reform.

Governor Dinh settled in and met with all his staff – those within Lien Lau and those further afield. He made a trip to the Commanderies south of us – Cuu Chan and Nhat Nam – the southern limits of Middle Kingdom influence. Below these Commanderies, the lowlands thinned to a strip passing between mountain and sea until they reached the Pass of The Mountain Clouds, and beyond this was virtually unknown territory. In the very far south lived the people of the Phu Nam, whose port on the tip of the land serviced the trading ships, but we knew little of them other than the gossip the traders bandied about. We knew they grew rice, like us, and that a grand river flowed through their territory, just as the Red River flowed through ours. Their river was called Me Kong and their port was Oc Eo. But none of this was To Dinh's concern. He went as far as Nhat Nam and that was all. I doubt he even saw the Pass.

Two crops of rice were planted and harvested before I first met Dinh. I went with Mother and Trac, though Sach had an audience separately, to represent Chu Dien. We were there as the Prefect family of Me Linh and a joint audience would have complicated matters for our new Governor (or so he said).

I didn't like him from the start. I usually have a feel for a person as soon as I meet them and I don't often change my mind. Dinh was charming and over-bearing and bowed excessively low to Mother when he received her. He bade us sit with him, while a servant poured drinks for us and brought little fried treats. In his seated position, he struggled to conceal his rotund belly with his martial uniform. After the introductions and the niceties and the basic report of agricultural progress and productions that Mother was expected to make, Dinh lost little time in launching into what was to become his most passionate subject.

'Is it not shameful,' he said 'that the men of Giao Chi are so uncaring about their families? That they swan off whenever it suits them, to wherever the hunting and fishing is good? Would it not be better for families to stay together, as they do in the Middle Kingdom? And do you not consider it a travesty that Giao Chi women can so easily dismiss one husband and take another? They would not have to do this if only their original husbands would stay close and take what should be a natural role of providing for and protecting the family.'

'The men of Giao Chi must hunt. They must fish. It is the way they live,' my mother answered, without tone. She had a lot of experience in meeting and managing new Han officials and was almost immune to this kind of talk.

'It is an old way, but not the best way. Hunting and fishing is so unreliable and it leaves women and children unprotected and alone. If men would but tend to their own land and grow more rice, then it would be better. The province would grow stronger.' His unpleasant glare was fixed upon my mother.

I think he expected a response, but my mother stayed silent. He sighed and flexed his chubby fingers.

'Lady Thien, I would like you to do me the service in Me Linh of encouraging the locals to tend larger tracts of land. We need more canals, more dykes, more paddies. Tell the people, more rice! The Emperor decrees that Giao Chi must produce more rice and I am determined to satisfy him. Tell the men to stay at home and work your fields. Tell the women to remain true to their men. If they wish, they may now come to Lien Lau and properly register their marriages. It will give them more protection, so their family is respected and lawfully approved. Will you share this message?'

'I will tell the people all you have told me,' she replied and bowed her head. To Dinh continued glaring. It was his natural expression, the black, piggy eyes straining from his face.

'And the young must marry. A strong country needs strong families bearing strong children. Sons and daughters must be married, when they come of age.' He looked directly at me and I looked back. He was grinning, though his stretched lips attempted to hide it.

'Our children do marry,' my mother said, attempting to draw his eyes back on herself. 'Often they marry quite young - Trac has been married for a long time now and we are beginning to consider matches for Nhi.'

'Excellent. I can see that you and I think alike, Lady Thien. You wish, as I do, for Giao Chi to grow strong and proud, yes? For it to be a jewel of the Middle Kingdom, loved by the emperor. The way to this is through strong families, bearing strong children and growing more rice, always more rice.'

My mother stayed silent. She could not entirely agree that amassing grain for the Emperor was a progressive step for the Lac, but it would have been foolish to speak out at that early time. The time for action hadn't yet come, but one thing we had learned was that our troubles were far from over. Xuan, as I had stubbornly anticipated, had left the way clear for one even worse than himself.

14

At the start of the new year, To Dinh had arrived and we duly began our regular meetings with him. Xuan had left his network of spies relatively intact, but the one and only delightful thing about To Dinh was that he all but gave up using them. He did not trust that these agents would give him accurate information and, like any fanatic, he didn't think he needed them. He wanted to control everything himself, directly, and he used our regular visits to Lien Lau to re-emphasize the familiar, tedious points about taxation and about marriage. I found him quite repulsive but was glad to be rid of Xuan, whose sly references to Chien's death angered me. I also could never forget the way Xuan had barged into our house and threatened us before my marriage to Sach. With To Dinh, it was a new start, even if he presented the same old challenges. I saw him usually with my mother and only occasionally did Sach and I report to him jointly. He found it confusing to speak with me in the presence of my husband on issues that he considered were the preserve of men. It was just easier to represent our two provinces separately.

This, though, raised the same troubling point for To Dinh as it had for Vo Xuan. I could see that he did not approve of the intermarriage between the ruling Lac nobles. Though it was an inevitable fact of life that we would, as a race and a class, find mates amongst one another, he foresaw the danger of us banding together – the strengthening of the Lac Lords, whose hold on the Prefecture of Giao Chi was an obstacle to the progress of Han rule. It was in his every smile and bow, the disdain he truly felt for us and the desire he had to repress us all and allow Han nobles to take our places. The more he could break us apart, piece by piece, the closer he would come to overturning the Lac Prefects. When he met Sach and I together, I am sure he saw the very picture of what he wished to destroy. He remained subtle, though, and he rarely talked about his ideas of social reformation to us when we met him together. He reserved those conversations for myself and my mother, perhaps thinking that as two dimwitted females we would not be able to resist the compelling truth of his arguments.

His primary enterprise was to create a more comprehensively taxable social system. We had known something of the Han desire for this from years before, when Mrs Chau had spoken of widespread dislike of Xuan's proposals. This distaste had not stopped Xuan from gradually forcing through new rules about who should be taxed and when. Now, To Dinh's biggest problem was finding all taxable people and bringing them to account if they did not pay up. Giao Chi is a complicated province, with huge tracts of forest, varying from inaccessible swampland to high mountain ranges and in between there are tropical forests, great stone outcrops, limestone ridges and fast-flowing rivers. The coast is a mystery of caves, mangrove forests and more limestone outcropping. All in all, a good place to hide, especially for a native population who know how to traverse the wild countryside and are not averse to an unsettled existence. To Dinh, however, had spent long years previous to his appointment formulating the simple but revolutionary solution that he expressed to my mother and I.

The answer, he believed, was to insist upon everyone becoming married and to make registration of marriage a legal requirement, and non-marriage between certain ages a criminal offence. Of course, he was doing his best to keep the idea of marriage and taxes separate in the mind of the populace, since tax was such a hated concept. Instead of saying outright that he wished to create registered, taxable family units, he talked about the importance of family, of fealty and propriety, of protection for women and their children.

The truth was that To Dinh was grossly offended at the sexual proclivities of the native women who would have children with one man and then so easily discard him if he offended her. That was not correct, he asserted. Women should remain with the father of their children. Women should remain *in the care of* the father of their children. He couched it all rather more subtly but the gist was apparent. To Dinh, along with the hordes of men from the Middle Kingdom who had settled to work and rule in Giao Chi, could not at all understand or accept the way our lives and families worked and he thought their own way was superior.

For To Dinh, as for the rest of them, it was unusual to be conversing and dealing with women at all. His regular meetings with my mother, and with other important ladies of the Giao Chi nobility were of a kind he had never had back in the Middle Kingdom. He had a conception of social relations with women, but before coming to Giao Chi, would have laughed at the idea of having business or political relations with one. Now, after a short period of acclimatising, he had effected an approach that served him in these dealings, but he still did not accept the central and previously unquestioned role of women in Giao Chi.

His distaste for women in business, his revulsion at their marital independence, his desperate need for more grain taxes to please the emperor, all had coalesced into a clear plan – make everyone marry, make them register the marriage, make breaking up a marriage (or refusing to enter one) unlawful and use the registered information of family units to keep track of all the taxable people, who would now have to grow more and more rice to fulfil the requirement. It made me angry and it made me scared. There was something in To Dinh's tone with my mother that suggested iron resolve behind his silken speech.

'The day is coming when To Dinh will use real force,' she said to me. 'Have you noticed how Lien Lau gets busier and busier with soldiers from the north? When To Dinh becomes exasperated that Giao Chi is not bending to his will, then he will employ those soldiers to force his will through. He has no love for Giao Chi. You can see in his eyes, when he talks of the Middle Kingdom, that he misses his homeland. He only wishes to strip Giao Chi of what it can provide and rebuild our country as a monument to the Emperor.'

'How will he force people to marry? It is not possible,' I said.

'Anything is possible. Trac, we must be cautious. To Dinh is a greedy and a cunning man who already resents the Lac nobility he is forced to work with. We must be seen to be in agreement but we must slow his hand.'

So it was that during To Dinh's first summer as Governor, we were already quietly undermining the new rules he was attempting to set in place. The Lac nobility was stirring from slumber, and none was happier about this than Ton Vien, the Prefect of Lien Lau who had been such a thorn in the heel of Vo Xuan. Vien came to visit us, sensing the new mood and having received an invite from my Mother.

'Better here than at my home,' he exclaimed, barely inside the house. 'Dinh watches everything I do.'

'I thought the spying had stopped,' I said, looking over at my Mother in concern.

'Ah, well he's not as bad as Xuan in that respect, but you know, one Governor is much the same as another. They all want the same things. They all do the same things.' Vien appraised me with heavy lidded eyes that sat high in his thin face.

'Come and sit,' I said, offering him the low bamboo bench, but he bypassed that piece of furniture and squatted on the rattan rug, feet flat to the floor as he folded his chest against the fronts of his thighs. Nhi did likewise and my mother took the bench, her knee joints not being as supple as they once were. I sat alongside her. Sach was by the cooking surface, dishing out some food which Diep had prepared and left for us earlier.

'The spies Xuan had reporting on us are no longer very active,' my mother explained to Vien. 'I wonder why that should be, if he continues to spy on you?'

Vien smiled. It was a smile to cover his embarrassment, quite different from the one he had worn when he greeted us.

'Ah,' said my mother with understanding, and she glanced at me. 'Dinh does not perceive us as a threat. He is not very interested in what we do.'

'I think so,' said Vien. 'But more than that-' he paused and we waited. My mother smiled and bowed her head, forgiving him for what he had to say. 'The truth is, he finds you distasteful. He takes genuine exception to dealing with a Lady Prefect. He is the same with all the women he encounters.'

I wondered for just a moment if Vien's apparent embarrassment was part pretence - if he was actually enjoying seeing Lady Man Thien insulted. She had, after all, failed to openly share his outrage during the Hai Phong drum dispute. He had resented then her lack of support and her clearly superior standing to his own. Gratification in her discomfort would not be surprising, but I believed then that Ton Vien was at heart a good man - that was why he had been so passionately offended by the Han Captain's theft, and why now he displayed such awkwardness.

'The more fool him,' Nhi commented. 'If he wants rid of us, he should watch us all the more closely.'

'I consider it fortunate that he underestimates us,' said my Mother. 'And besides, an insult from the Han should surely be considered a compliment.'

Vien laughed and recovered his earlier ease. We ate some of the cold cooked rice from the little bowls Sach had passed around, and took shreds of beef from a shallow bowl in the centre.

'In seriousness, however, we are facing real problems with Dinh. He is much more determined than Xuan ever was to push these new laws into action.' Vien put his bowl down. 'I think he is more dangerous.'

'I agree,' said Nhi. 'Xuan was a logical man. He didn't push at the closed door, but simply attempted to lever it. Dinh will push.

169

He will break it, if he has to.' She moved her hands as she spoke, miming the actions she described.

'I have not found him so intransigent,' said Sach. 'He has a vision for Giao Chi and perhaps it does not accord entirely with our own, but I have found him willing to debate and discuss the issues.'

We all stared. Sach had been so outspoken against Xuan that we naturally expected him to have formed a similar opinion of Dinh. He looked at our incredulous faces.

'Does he not discuss openly these issues with you?' he asked, looking around.

'As you have heard,' answered Vien, 'he hates to discuss anything with women, and he is quite conscious of my fixed views. We have meetings that are perfunctory at best.'

'Sach, my son,' said my mother, 'I think perhaps To Dinh sees the opportunity to win young minds round to his way of thinking.'

'You mean he thinks I can be swayed?'

'He is ingratiating himself with you,' I said, impatiently. I wished I had not allowed Sach to have his private audiences with Dinh. He was a clever young man and very brave, but Dinh was an extremely intelligent adversary, with years of tactical diplomacy to draw upon. I am not saying that I myself was any better prepared to deal with a man like To Dinh than Sach was, but my natural reserve and suspicion made for a stronger defence than Sach's energetic eagerness. 'Oh Sach, you must be careful. You think he is debating issues with you when in fact he is testing you, hoping to mould you to his cause. When he sees that he cannot, you will become his enemy.'

'I think you are exaggerating the dangers, wife,' said Sach, his skin turning pale with anger as he looked at the concerned faces gazing back at him. 'I am quite aware of the diplomatic complexity of philosophical discussion and I can assure you all that my conversations with To Dinh have been appropriately conducted.'

"I do not doubt it. It is To Dinh's conduct that I fear.' With this quiet comment, I sat back. It would not do for me to offend my own husband in the presence of others. I loved him. I did not want to belittle him.

'The truth is that I find him easier to talk with than Xuan ever was,' Sach explained. 'Yes, Dinh has his strange ideas, about which he is quite passionate, but he is an educated and articulate man. He cannot fail to appreciate the veracity of my counter-arguments. I have an opportunity to sway *his* way of thinking. Do you not see that? He is new to this role and of course he will be excited to make changes at first, but he will calm down and then he will find that he has become reliant upon certain of his Prefects to assist him in governing this complicated Commandery. I hope to be one of those Prefects. If we are not to fight - to throw them out completely - then I must shape my destiny in their shadow. Vien, you of all people should understand. It's all or nothing. Either we fight them and rid the country of them completely or we work with them, because we have to. What other choice is there?'

Vien looked sharply at Sach. He did not appreciate the reference to his abortive attempt to challenge Xuan at Hai Phong, and the political isolation that followed. My mother simply sat with a small, curving smile on her lips. I looked at Nhi and she looked back at me. The door clattered suddenly against the bamboo frame. Out on the plains, the warm winds had picked up.

★★★★★

It was not all about To Dinh, in those days. I have made it sound as if politics and diplomacy were all that occupied us, but of course, they were only a small part of our daily life. The martial training continued - our house in Cam Khe, or rather the scratched circle in front of it, was becoming regarded as a school for such training and Nhi ran what I suppose could be

171

termed classes. They ran each morning when we had finished our own private training (which was not all that private, because everyone came early to sit and watch). In the mid-morning and early afternoon, we would each conduct whatever business we had to attend to. For Sach and I, this meant liaising with the labourers and the farmers, dealing with whatever disputes and difficulties arose. We were most often called upon to settle arguments over payments.

In Giao Chi, the people did not use money. The Han had their coins - round, bronze pieces with a hole in the centre for stringing them together, or sometimes the coins would be in the shape of tools like spades and forks, or even knives, but these tool coins were much older. Funny little things. We used trade instead. Most commonly, payment for work was in rice, though sometimes it was supplemented with produce from other crops - yam, sugar-cane and the like. If workers wanted other goods, they would use part of the produce to buy them - a quantity of rice for a piece of silk, for example. It was a system that worked because it was well managed by the female traders. Women like Mrs Chau knew, day to day, how a measure of any goods should be balanced against another. She, like all her kind, knew all the gossip from Me Linh to Lien Lau and beyond. She could tell you when and why a crop in Khuc Duong had failed or what the markets in Hop Pho Commandery were paying for glass jewellery or how many bandits had recently been apprehended on the silk route through the north-west mountains. The information she picked up coalesced in her mind, like tattered hemp stitched together by a measured thread of reason. Here, in this patchy pattern, lay the value of every trade commodity. Of course, Mrs Chau's ideas did not always correspond evenly to those of her counterparts and there was much haggling and bartering to secure deals that felt fair to everyone, but it still felt a lot easier than coins.

I liked our afternoons of travelling out into the countryside and meeting the overseers. They were all very deferential and I surprised myself by learning and remembering the names of hundreds of people across Me Linh – the overseers themselves, but also their families and many of the workers. I copied the example that Nhi had so often set, feigning an interest in the lives and experiences of these men and women, until I found that my interest became genuine. I still did not have the great love of nature that Nhi possessed, but I could appreciate the beauty of a ripe, green paddy field, calculating the crops therein. I could examine a newly dug canal and understand the engineering decisions that had been made with regard to depth and direction. When I became knowledgeable on the waterways and the hard work that went into diverting and managing them, I found the kind of purposeful desire for progress that my father must have felt, all those years ago when he was out commanding the construction of some of the earliest run-offs and flood banks.

Sach was also equal to the task and the Me Linh people liked him. They responded to his warmth and to my intellect and between us we made a good pair. I wanted to see Nhi happy, like we were happy. I saw no reason why she should go on wasting her young life mourning Chien. Also, more importantly, To Dinh was sounding just like Vo Xuan whenever we met – pushing for Nhi to be married just as Xuan had once pushed for me to marry. I wondered why my mother had rushed me into arrangements with Sach when she did not appear to be pushing Nhi at all. Was she not in just as much danger of being married off to one of the Han? There was a whispered rumour that a girl from the south had been kidnapped and boated up the East Sea to the island Commandery of Chau Nhai, just off the coast of the Middle Kingdom, in order to secure a marriage.

'We should invite Mai Thao again,' I said to my mother while we prepared partridges for roasting one late afternoon. 'It has been long enough.'

'Nhi was quite clear. She is not ready yet.'

173

'That was long ago – we have passed through two rainy seasons since. Why do you not want her to marry? She must, or she will be in danger.'

'She must come to it by herself, just as you did.'

I laughed at that.

'It was hardly by myself, Mother. I seem to remember you had a lot to do with it.'

'I merely put opportunity in your way,' she answered.

'Well then, let us put opportunity in Nhi's way. Mai Thao will visit again, on the slightest pretext, I am sure of it. Perhaps now she will find herself ready.'

My mother nodded.

'You are right, of course. I have let her tread her own way, but she has hate in her heart and it must be tempered. If anyone can do it, it will be that sturdy little rhinoceros.'

'Mother!' It was true, he did have the muscular bearing of a charging, horned rhino, but the carnal associations in her analogy were quite rude.

'What?' She asked, innocently, and I shook my head, laughing again.

★★★★★

He did come to visit – my mother acted soon after our conversation and sent a message to Khuc Duong with the silk wagon that passed through Me Linh. It was just a verbal message, as they all were, since we did not write, and the silk seller promised us that she would deliver it to the home of the Prefect as soon as she arrived there. She was on an almost direct route to Khuc Duong. Even so, the speed with which Thao accepted our vague enticement was almost indecent. He had been waiting, we knew, for just such a message to arrive, and waiting for two years at that. He was a man of serious intent. I liked him for it.

Nhi had been told in advance, out of necessity. We did not want her to become distressed at his sudden appearance, but she surprised us with her nonchalance.

'If he must come, he must come,' she sighed, when our mother explained that she had asked Thao to represent his father in discussions about the latest dictates from Lien Lau.

I tried very hard not to mention his impending visit, nor even cast an unwary smile in her direction and she said never a word about it. When Thao arrived, he greeted her with all the gentle reverence that one would offer to a priceless artefact and they did not speak further for two days. Certainly, there was no suggestion that they should go walking together. There was more distance between them than there had been on his first visit, and after three days I began to despair. When we sat together for a meal late that afternoon, I decided we had all been patient enough.

'Do you know,' I said to Thao who sat at my mother's side, 'that when Sach first came to visit me, I was so nervous that Nhi took over and told him all the things she thought he should know.'

'Is that right?' said Thao, looking more than a little nervous himself. Nhi flashed angry eyes at me, but I continued.

'When we were out walking, she talked on and on about us wanting a monkey pet, and then about a doll we had when we were little.'

'Cypress Baby,' Sach said, smiling at me with a touch of sadness.

'I was so embarrassed. I thought she was making me look ridiculous. We fought afterwards, didn't we Nhi? But I realised later how much easier she had made things. If she had not been there, I think I would have been so cold as to scare Sach away, when in fact we were perfectly suited.'

'More rice?' Nhi asked me.

'Just a little,' I said.

'Maybe if you talk less, you will be able to eat it,' she said, smashing the spoon of white grains into my wooden bowl, her cheeks flaming.

'Some for you, Thao?' She asked, in a quieter tone.

'Yes, please,' he said, watching her tap the mound of rice into the bowl in front of him. He looked directly at her. We pretended not to see and my mother began a new conversation, but I saw the look, and it said that he had understood my message and that he would not give up on her. More importantly, the answer her eyes gave back was one of equal promise.

★★★★★

Thao stayed for eight nights. He slept on the *kang* in the unused room next to Trac's, at the back of the house. When I fell asleep each night, I was uncomfortably aware of his solid, masculine presence just beyond the door of the main living area that I shared with Mother. He was silent – not a snore or a cough – but the lightest sound of the mats creaking as he turned would wake me. Fortunately, Thao was quiet by day too. He didn't pester me with needless chatter, but he trained with me each morning and our practice became conversation of a kind.

His physicality bothered me. I thought about this when I evaded him in the afternoons. Chien had been a beautiful young man, but he was a dreamer and in my memories, his slim body moved with an ephemeral elegance. It was as if he was never really of the world; as if he had been dying even when I met him, though the thought made no sense. Thao, with all his muscular prowess, was as present and immovable as the mountains. The more I looked at Thao, the more Chien receded. It hurt me, even though the worst sting of grief had passed. Thao understood, just as before. He tried very hard to be still and quiet, to blend softly into my environment without offending me, but that was as possible as a buffalo wading through a stream without splashing.

'I have had a thought,' he said, on the seventh day of his visit. 'It concerns myself and you and the memory of Le Chien.'

I closed my eyes and nodded. He had lost patience. It was time for him to propose and I must decide once and for all what

I would do. I waited for him to continue.

'Chien was your first husband. I wish to honour him so that you will take me as your second husband. I have heard that Corporal Gang, who murdered Chien and his family, is stationed east of Lien Lau.'

I opened my eyes and stared hard at him.

'I know this,' I said. 'What of it?'

'I will kill Gang. That is my gift to you. Then you and I will marry.' Thao stood with his legs wide and his hands on his hips, above his sword belt.

'Thao... that is my task. I will kill Gang. I have sworn to do it.'

'Then let me help you,' he said. 'Together we will avenge Chien and he will give his blessing on our marriage.'

'You talk as if you knew him,' I accused, but it was good to hear Chien's name on Thao's lips. I no longer felt so traitorous.

'I know that he made you happy. I know that he was a good young man. All of Giao Chi knows this. That is why some young people have run off to join his sister. Everyone was horrified by what happened at Hai Phong.'

'People are joining Le Chan?'

'Yes – not many so far, and the Governor does not take it too seriously, Chan being a woman – but Chan's army is slowly growing.'

'I had heard something of it, but I thought the numbers were very small.'

'No one wants you to rush off to Ha Long. That is most probably why few have spoken to you about it. You do more good by keeping yourself safe here.'

'I will do good by killing Gang,' I said, 'and then perhaps I will join Chan.'

'No, Nhi. Chan's army is of outlaws and angry youths. It is not the place for you. With your skills, you would be wasted. Don't you know you and your sister are two of the greatest martial artists in the country? If war breaks out, you will be leaders, not followers, and an army will come to you.'

'You really believe that?' I asked, and I saw to my astonishment that his eyes became glassy with tears. It was because, for the first time since he had known me, I had allowed myself to speak as an unsure sixteen-year-old. He put out his hand and took hold of mine.

'I do believe that,' he said. 'Will you let me help you? I will get you to Gang. You kill him and I will get you away again without being caught.'

'When?' I whispered.

'At new year,' he said, 'when everyone is celebrating. It isn't long to wait.'

'New year,' I agreed. 'Then we will marry.'

Thao smiled and squeezed my hand before letting it drop. He left the next day. We were careful to show that our courtship was proceeding, but we did not tell Mother anything about our agreement. Nothing was going to stand between Gang and I.

★★★★★

Thao asked Mother's permission to take me to the celebrations in Lien Lau. He had friends there with whom we could stay and he offered for Trac and Sach to come also. Mother agreed readily, so pleased was she that I was beginning to respond to Thao's overtures. We boated down in a cool, twinkling afternoon and disembarked in the market town. Thao's friends were friends also of Ton Vien and his family and thus we found ourselves happily received. We had a room to stay in, the four of us, so Trac and I had a raised bed on one side of a curtain, and Thao and Sach made up a place to sleep on the other. Thao led us out into the town to look at the shop fronts, all decorated with jade and ribbons. Vendors were selling rice alcohol and skewered frog legs. Thao gave Trac and Sach each a cup of the strong drink. We walked about in the cold, building an appetite before returning for the grand meal that Thao's friends had prepared. I sat between him and Trac, and I barely spoke. I am sure Trac put it down to my mixed feelings about Thao, which was convenient. Thao made sure Trac and Sach drank more rice wine and as they became more giddy, I became impatient.

Finally, it was time to retire, and we went to our makeshift room, settling down in our appointed areas. Trac lay on her back with her head still, trying not to mess her hair and before long, her sighs of discomfort turned into faint snores of inebriated exhaustion. I slipped from under the coarse jute and around the curtain. Sach was alone on their pallet, snoring like his wife. I found Thao just beyond the door, strapping his sword belt on and he handed me my own weapons without a word. The house had two exits and we were able to sneak out of the right-hand door and down the little steps at the front without passing the people who were still up, eating and drinking.

Outside, along the thin street, two horses had been tethered. Thao had arranged it. I wondered if any of his friends knew what we were plotting. We mounted up and cantered through the moonlit streets, taking care to avoid any of the revellers wandering back to their homes. Once outside the town limits, we galloped at speed. We knew roughly where we were going, but there was still every chance that we could become lost and waste precious time. My sword pressed along my thigh and my heart pounded.

We were looking for new fields - empty and surrounded by raised borders to hold the coming floods. We knew Gang had his home near these. We knew also that we should pass a smaller selection of roughly-erected houses where the men of his regiment slept and ate. Eventually we found the right place. The moon was still high in the sky, plenty of night remaining. We rode as close to the houses as possible, then dismounted and left the horses. Lights shone from between ill-fitting wood planks and the occasional guffaw echoed out through the milky darkness. The grandest house was one of those with firelight still seeping through cracks and I altered course, to approach the house from behind. Thao followed. As we came near, I could pick out individual voices, yapping away in their Han language. Would I remember Gang's or recognise his face? I worried not, since I had barely met him before – it was years ago at Xuan's feast that I watched him talking with Trac. Kim Cuc and I giggled about it, like we giggled about everything that night. As I remembered her high-pitched laugh and the touch of her fingers upon my arm, I had another flash of memory, piercing and bright. 'I feel that many good things are due to happen to me here,' I had heard him say in the lull of the music before the conversation was again drowned out, his blurred face half obscured from me by Trac and one of the Generals. Even at the time I had thought it an odd thing to say – a desperate statement rather than a true belief. I had pitied him then, but I did not pity him now.

Time slowed. We waited while the moon passed overhead. I listened to their drunken voices. Thao nudged me, a question in his eyes and I shook my head. Wait, I mouthed to him. We were in the shadow of the house, moonlight filtering past us onto the rice fields. No one would see us, even if they left the house and walked across the land at the front. I should have been terrified of discovery but I felt no fear at all. I felt no joy either, and even my impatience from earlier had evaporated. I felt nothing, but I knew everything. I knew that the men inside would drift off to sleep. I knew that Gang would leave himself open and vulnerable. I knew that I would move silently inside and pick him out at once.

The wavering reeds of conversation had thinned, and there amongst the stand of voices I heard him, unsteady but nasally imperious.

'He's here,' I breathed to Thao. Yet still we waited, while our bones grew cold and the moon travelled on across the sky.

When finally the voices inside had quietened, we came out of the shadows and climbed the few steps to the door. I opened it and went inside. The room was dark. A handful of figures lay draped about - on the floor, on the low brick day-bed. Others crowded a wide *kang* at the back. I walked amongst these men, glancing at faces and dismissing them, until I came to the one I wanted. He lay with his arms curled around his chest, the stench of alcohol on his sleeping breath. He was fast asleep. I turned to Thao, who was edging towards me, and made a motion with my arms. He understood and came to my side. Thao was strong; Gang was relatively slight. Even so, Thao grimaced as he bent down and lifted the sleeping man like an infant. Gang wriggled in his dreams and gave an inebriated snort but then settled like a child into Thao's arms. Thao breathed heavily as he trod though the dark house, back to the door and the steps. I followed, checking behind us, but all the men were still asleep. Down the steps and out onto the delta, I made Thao keep walking with Gang in his arms until he could go no further, the sweat running down his cheeks. He dropped Gang to the ground in the middle of a rice field, half-way back to our horses.

Gang shrieked as he hit the floor, waking from one nightmare into another, and he rolled instantly to his front and tried to stand. I kicked one of his arms away from under him and he fell back onto his face.

'Who are you, what do you want?' he gasped, rolling to his side. I levelled my sword at his face. He had spoken in his native tongue, which I understood but never spoke. He swallowed and tried to study my face. 'Who are you?' he repeated, this time in our language.

'I am Nhi,' I said. By my side, Thao stretched his aching arms, which shook uncontrollably from the strain of Gang's sleeping weight.

'I don't know you, Nhi,' said Corporal Gang. 'Why are you doing this?'

'I know you, *Captain*.'

'Is this about the girls? Because I can pay you. I have money at the house.' He gestured back, hopefully, looking from me to Thao and back again.

'Where are the girls?' I said, understanding at once what the revolting man must be talking about.

'They're, uh, gone now. Sold to a different regiment. But I have the money, I have the money and you can have it. It's in the house.'

'I don't want your money, Captain Gang, and this is not about girls you have stolen. I'm here about Hai Phong.'

Gang's face froze, his mouth partly open in some aborted attempt to plead further.

'You're Le Chan.' he said, when his words finally came. 'Or from her army?'

'No, I am Nhi,' I repeated. 'I am Le Chien's wife. Chien, who you murdered.'

'No! No, I was just doing my job. Governor Xuan sent me there with orders. The Le family resisted. I had no choice.' Gang scrabbled in the dirt, trying to back away from the point of my sword which had come to rest in the soft hollow at the right-hand base of his neck. If he had any sense, he would grasp the blade and roll, fetching a sweeping kick to my legs with his right one and felling me whilst taking my weapon. It was what I would have done, though it might mean losing fingers. But Gang had no sense - or if he did, his fear had pushed it from him.

'You wanted Le Chan so you murdered her family. Say it, Gang. I know it is true.' I stared down at him impassively.

'It was a mistake, I am sorry,' he wailed. 'The Governor said to use force!'

'And what about the girls? Did the administration tell you to steal them too?' I pressed with my sword and the blood came, making him squeal. He was a coward. 'The mistake you made was in coming here to our land. Good things will not happen to you here, only bad things. Very bad things indeed.'

I drew back my sword and the instant I did, he made the

move which I expected. He leapt to his feet in a clumsy attempt to run. I thrust my sword through air, then skin and flesh and guts. The moon slid sadly across the sky and a bird lifted suddenly from a distant tree. I pulled the sword out and Gang gurgled, still standing. I swung the blade in a wide arc and sent it cleanly through Gang's throat and out through the back of his neck. For a moment, he hovered there staring at us, then his body fell away, the head rolling sideways and coming to land apart.

'Clean,' said Thao.

'I was going to gut him. It seemed... unnecessary.'

We stood looking down on him. Blood was pooling in the dry, empty rice field, seeping into the soil.

'There is a difference between revenge and torture,' said Thao. 'I am glad you didn't prolong it.'

'We must leave now,' I said, wiping my sword clean on the dead man's clothing and re-sheathing it. 'The night is almost over.'

When we returned to Lien Lau, we found Trac and Sach awake in the room we were sharing. The moon had dipped and dawn was about to break. My sister and her husband squatted on the floor silently, waiting and as we entered, my heart jumped.

'Where have you been?' Trac whispered, angrily. 'I woke and you were gone.'

Sach stared hard at Thao, who returned the look.

'I went to kill Gang,' I whispered back, mindful of other ears in the house, beyond the flimsy wood and bamboo. Trac's eyes widened. She and Sach shared a shocked glance.

'And did you do it?'

'Yes, I did.'

'And Thao here helped you?' she asked and I nodded. 'Well then. Good. I thought the pair of you were... and I did not want to wake all the... well, anyway. Clean yourselves up. You are dusty from riding. You can be the one to tell our mother. She will have to know.'

Trac was good about it. After all, I had gone behind her back and put myself in danger while she was supposed to be looking out for me. I had expected, when I saw her sitting there waiting, that she would be furious, so the calm way in which she let it go was a surprise. She was clearly relieved that I hadn't been out copulating covertly with Thao. Perhaps that's why I escaped without lengthy chastisement.

Mother was not so calm. She received us home two days later with a stony face and clenched hands. She met my eyes and immediately I knew that she knew.

'It was you,' she said.

'How can you know of it?' I evaded.

'News travels, Nhi. Especially news about a beheaded Han Corporal in the centre of the Commandery. And I suppose you all were involved?' She looked around at Sach, Trac and at Thao who had accompanied us home.

'Just Thao,' I said. 'What are people saying? Do they know it was me?'

'If they knew it was you, do you think you would still be standing here?' Mother hissed. She couldn't shout. She didn't want Bao or his mother or any other passing pair of ears to overhear. 'Everyone thinks this was Le Chan's revenge. They believe she or someone from her army did it. There is speculation that Dinh will try to hunt down the offender, but he hasn't the same family links to Gang as his predecessor and trying to track Le Chan down would take more effort than he can spare. With any luck, nothing will happen.'

'If he blames Chan, I will have to take responsibility,' I said.

'No! You certainly will not.'

'But I must.'

'Chan is hidden away, biding her time and training her army. It's no harm to her if Dinh thinks she killed Gang. If anything, it enhances her reputation. Makes her more feared by them. She's safe from them for now, but you are not.'

'This is the first time you've admitted she's got a proper army,' I said. 'Why did you never talk about them before? Why must you hide things from me? I'm not a child.'

'I've never hidden anything from you. You are the one hiding things, like this stupid attack on Gang.'

'It wasn't stupid,' I seethed. 'It was for Chien. It was the only way I could feel free to marry, which is what you're all forcing me to do!'

I stormed away from them, down the steps and out onto the plain, even though I was weary from our journey back from Lien Lau. I regretted my words as soon as I had said them – not for Mother's sake, but for Thao, who had made a fair deal with me and who would never force me into anything. He stayed behind with the others – none of them followed me – and when I returned hours later, he had gone. Trac was settled inside, repairing a tunic. Sach sat out on the steps, chewing betel and areca and watching the sunset. I sat down beside him and he wrapped up a leaf and nut for me. Wordless, I chewed.

'Since you are not going to ask,' he sighed, 'Thao has returned home and will call on us soon. He took no offence. Lady Mother is sleeping. She had no rest last night, after she heard the news late yesterday afternoon. She was very worried about you.'

'You're not my father,' I said, with sharp pleasantness, 'so stop talking in that way.'

'You realise what could have happened? If they'd seen you or worse still, caught you, Dinh would have executed you. He still could, if he gets wind that it was you.'

'I'm not afraid of Dinh. And there was never any chance that they would catch me. I would have killed them all.'

'I don't doubt it, but still, we worry. You're young, Nhi. A better fighter than any of us, but so young. I almost cannot believe that you did what you did.' He gave a single, incredulous laugh. 'I bet Gang could not believe it either.'

'I think he knew it was coming. He had that hunted look in

his eyes, as if he'd done many bad things and was expecting some kind of revenge. He'd stolen girls. I don't know where from, but I can guess what he did to them before he sold them on.'

Sach whistled through his black teeth.

'He told you this?'

'He thought I was looking for them.'

'Good, then there are other suspects to confuse Governor Dinh - the families of those girls, whoever they are. I'll make sure a rumour is spread about his camp activities. It will make it harder for Dinh to pursue justice for Gang's murder if what you say about him is true.'

It was all very sensible, but I was feeling peeved. Gang was the first life I had taken and yet I could not claim him. I had the heart of a killer, but the ego of a sixteen-year-old girl.

★★★★★

Later that same year, Thao and I married quietly. Governor Dinh had let Gang's murder pass unavenged, for all the reasons we had expected, but also because he was concentrating so hard on all his reforms. Things were being set into motion that we had long dreaded, and among these was the law which stated that all marriages in the Giao Chi Commandery must be reported to Lien Lau's administrative officials. There were also new laws about the way in which hair must be dressed, laws against teeth-blackening and laws about repossession of Lac land by incoming Han nobles. The taxes were being raised again and more soldiers were appearing on the streets.

It had got so bad that Mother called meetings with the Lac Lords. They gathered in secret, or under careful pretexts, never quite sure whether there were spies amongst them, but taking the risk anyway. Sach attended as Prefect of Chu Dien. Thao's father came from Khuc Duong, Ton Vien from Lien Lau and even the lady we had trained with, Phung Thi Chinh, came from Tay Vu with several others.

I found it frustrating - all this underground talk of how best to undermine Dinh's advances and how to rebel without being seen to rebel. Everyone was looking for the political way out when they all knew it was impossible. I felt we were wasting time. I wanted war, but even Thao did not entirely agree with me. He was worried we weren't organised enough.

'All this secret discussion,' he said, 'is necessary in order to develop an alliance. We have to know each other and to share information first.'

I didn't agree. Obviously we needed a strong leader to follow and I was dismayed to see that in all of these meetings and half-hearted sabotage plans, no one was coming forward to lead. Sach, maybe a little, but not enough. Even he could not quite bring himself to openly declare hostility to the Han. He still went along to his meetings with the Governor in hopes that Dinh's fanaticism could be tempered and that laws could be repealed.

It was a troubled start to my marriage – not least because Thao was uneasy about leaving Khuc Duong to live with me. According to our customs, the husband joined the wife's family, and I was not about to leave my family and move to him, but in those difficult times, we decided to compromise. We consummated our marriage and he came to visit when he could. Occasionally I went to him, but weeks passed without us seeing each other. This situation had one huge benefit. Thao and I had not reported our marriage to the supposedly correct authorities. Neither had we, as prescribed by the new rules, sought approval for our union. Yet, because we were still living apart, few people beyond our trusted circle knew that we had actually married. For the time being, we weren't under scrutiny. No one ever seemed to question what would happen when our marriage came to light. I'm sure Sach thought he could explain it to Governor Dinh, if it became necessary. After all, he and Trac had defied Governor Xuan by their marriage and got away with it. It was, as I said, a troubled time – not just for me but for everyone. No one knew by which rules we were supposed to be playing any more.

15

Nhi said I was different when I was married. She said Sach brought something out in me that no one else ever did. I smiled more, apparently, and I was more inclined to be forthright than diplomatic. Perhaps I became more like him in thought and manner. I imbibed some of his optimism and self-belief.

In the cold of winter, Sach received word from his father. Armed soldiers had been to the house in Chu Dien to inform Hoc that his two daughters, Kim Cuc and Khanh, must marry and the ceremony be conducted in Lien Lau, according to the new Commandery laws. In addition, further taxes were payable. It was not a shock to us, although Sach's hand curled around the sword-hilt at his hip while the messenger spoke. We had recently received a similar command ourselves. Ours insisted that Nhi was of age to marry and also reminded us of unpaid taxes – both personal and provincial.

'Governor Dinh is pushing us too far,' said Sach. 'These taxes cannot be raised, they are unjust.'

'And I can't be married off, since I have a husband already,' put in Nhi, humourlessly. 'This shows the Governor is cracking his whip across the whole Commandery. What happens now?'

'I'm going to speak with him. He might yet listen to reason and if he does not, he must hear the objections of the people. No Governor before has acted so aggressively. To Dinh must be reminded of the example set by his predecessors. Tich Quang would never have behaved this way.'

'Tich Quang was before your time,' my mother said. 'You do not know what he would have done. Each Governor has moved us further under the control of the Middle Kingdom. It is easier for Dinh to enact these reforms than it would have been for Quang.'

'Even so, Dinh must be reminded of his responsibilities.' Sach swept a hand over his hair. It was tied back, thick and glossy. 'It is criminal now to cut one's hair. Criminal! Why must Dinh make it so? Hardly anyone cuts their hair short. He is set on making trouble where there is none. Well I will make trouble for him. He cannot ignore the children of Lac Long Quan!'

I looked from my mother to Sach in alarm, blind-sided by his sudden discharge of anger but empty of any response. He strode out to our sleeping room at the back of the house and jammed the door closed behind him. We stood mutely, the three of us, watching that door. From within came his frustrated sighs and the scrunching sound of his blade against hair.

'Spirits protect us,' whispered Nhi and she, consciously or otherwise, fingered the edge of blue fabric that covered the hair piled on her head.

'I must go with him to see the Governor,' I said. 'I will represent Me Linh, Sach will represent Chu Dien. The Governor surely cannot ignore us both. Can others be persuaded to join us?'

'I do not know,' admitted my mother. 'They are in favour of waiting.'

'Waiting for what? Until there is no country left to call our own? Sach is right that something must be done, but talking to Dinh isn't the way. We must gather our strength now, before it's too late,' said Nhi. She had ceased gazing at the door and I saw the fire creeping into her eyes.

'They are not ready,' insisted our mother. 'I wish that they were, but they are still afraid of the Han. They do not believe that anyone can truly stand against them.'

'Ton Vien believed once,' I said. 'But he has lost some of his passion for the fight.'

'And Thao would fight, but his father holds him back,' complained Nhi.

'They need an example to follow,' I said. 'Which is why Sach and I must face Dinh. Then others will see that he can be challenged and that his word is not law in Giao Chi.'

'It is a dangerous course of action, eldest daughter.'

'But necessary,' I said.

The shearing sounds had stopped and beyond the door all was silent. Then his footsteps came and the door opened. Sach came out to face us, loose hairs falling from his shoulders and a ribbon of blood on his cheek from a small cut on his ear. Behind him, in our sleeping area, black tresses lay scattered on the floor. He had taken his hair as short as the dagger would allow, so that it fell in a ragged fringe across his forehead and stuck out at odd angles around his head, the length ending abruptly at the nape of his neck. It needed some tidying up, but the initial effect was not unappealing. This was what the men of the Au Viet must have looked like, when they came down from the hills with the warlord Thuc Pan nearly three hundred years before - bold, conquering faces framed in short, vicious black. I felt a shiver across my spine and crossed the floor to Sach. I smoothed down his hair and brushed away the strands that were tickling his neck. Then I helped myself to his dagger and set about trimming off some of the more obvious clumps. He stood still, but I noticed his hands were shaking. It could not have been easy to cut off a lifetime's growth of hair and I sensed that he was on the cusp of regret for what he had done.

'There, husband, you are a true Au Lac now,' I said, and, ignoring the presence of others for the one and only time in my life, I kissed him on the lips.

★★★★★

We left the following day, just Sach and I. Nhi and our mother had agreed to spread the word that Sach and I were presenting a formal challenge to the Governor's reforms. They would travel to Me Linh's borders and speak with all the nobility they could. Nhi would send word to Thao to return to Me Linh, and messages would be sent further afield. We had not yet even spoken with Dinh but already it felt like the storm's heavy raindrops had begun to fall.

On route, Sach's appearance earned him many blatant stares. We passed Han soldiers, who could have taken him into custody, except for the fact that he carried his copper seals, proving his Prefect status. We passed labourers and traders, children and craftspeople who all eyed his short hair and black teeth with a kind of awe bordering on fear. Few short-haired men were seen. They were a relic of a bygone age. I do not know how Lac Long Quan and his Hung descendants wore their hair – long and loose or plaited or pinned, or short and ravaged – but the Au Viet who came after had worn theirs short. Everyone knew it. They had blackened their teeth and cut their hair and decorated their terrifying bodies with intricate tattoos. Then came Trieu Da, that man of the Middle Kingdom who became more Viet than Qin, and gradually the Lac Viet in his servitude grew their hair long but they wore it differently than the northmen. They made a distinction with their hair – they were different than the Emperor's true people. Then came the Han, and they said hair was sacred. It must be grown long to honour the ancestors. 'None shall defile their bodies with ink or dye or take a knife to their hair,' said the Han philosophers. 'Our body, our hair and teeth and skin and bones are a gift from our parents – a living legacy of the blood of our elders – and we must preserve them as wholly as we can. That,' said the great thinkers of the Middle Kingdom, 'shows our filial obedience.'

But who were they to say so? They had followed a path of logic, but their logic was flawed with the morality of their culture, and morality is the death of the Way. They said we must preserve the body. Our ancestors said we must *decorate* the body. Why should the former be correct and the latter be a sin? Both are ways of honouring the gift of flesh and bones that we have been given. I was never one to dismiss Confucius out of hand – I wanted to understand the ideas this ancient man had sown amongst the great tribes of the Middle Kingdom – but now that I did understand the wisdom he had left behind, I saw that it was lacking in some vital ingredient, and besides that, the application of his ideals was no longer pure. Confucius said the governing man should be like a wind to the swaying grass of the peasants. His own adherence to virtue and piety should press the lesser men into correct behaviour. But the Han were like a scythe, slicing through our people and cutting down the ones who would not bend. The Han were wrong to do this and Confucius was wrong on one fundamental point - the common people of Nam Viet are not grass to be walked upon. Perhaps they are so in the Middle Kingdom - I cannot say for I have never been there - but it seems to me that Confucius enormously underestimated the ordinary men and women. I agree that some are mandated to rule - that the immortal creatures imbue only very few noble people with the aptitude and wisdom to become great leaders - but we ignore the masses at our peril. That much I had learned since the naive days of childhood when I talked with Uncle Hien.

When I took sideways glances at Sach on our way to see Governor Dinh, I thought about all the people who were being forced to adhere to the Confucian way - all the men with their hair aping the Han top knots, all the couples marrying in the new fashion, all the families building ancestral shrines where before we had sacred places for honouring the animal spirits. None of it was overtly terrible - who does not like to remember with reverence their long dead grandparents? - but the gradual erosion of our identity was terribly sad, and all the more so given that under the silken sheen of change lay the hidden blade of force. In Sach I could see a new path forwards, where men and women could be encouraged to remember the ways of their own ancestors, not those of the ancestors of the Han. I could almost imagine the Han administration being forced to accept that they could share in the plentiful trade exports from Giao Chi but they could no longer subjugate the Lac to the will of the Emperor. Beyond a shimmering layer of doubt lay the

Nam Viet of my dreams. For much of our journey to Lien Lau, the emerald-green mountains and the cool, alluvial plains shone supernaturally under my determinedly ambitious gaze.

It was only when we entered the imposing and undeniably grand complex that housed the Giao Chi administrators that my earlier euphoria began to wear off and the reality of what we were about to do stole into my chest again. Of course Governor Dinh would see us, the excited clerk insisted, as he scurried away, whispering to others along the corridor and drawing out more scribes and servants to witness the aberration that had dared to present its sheared head for audience with the highest authority in the land. I glared at these feeble men and they flinched under our combined attitude - myself with my hands on my hips and my legs apart as if ready for a fight and Sach with his nonchalant stance that suggested he might just as easily use those black teeth to rip out a person's throat as to chew on a rice-ball. I thought, this is who we are. There is no going back now. We are the ruling Lac Lords and we can no longer, in good conscience, hide it from anyone.

After leaving our weapons outside, we were shown into Dinh's usual reception room where he already waited, standing between two personal guards. We walked forward and greeted him. His upper lip snarled as he eyed Sach.

'Have you been the victim of an assault, Prefect Sach? For only a criminal act could explain what I see before me.'

'Governor Dinh, we are here to challenge the new laws, including those regarding personal appearance. More importantly, we've come to make clear that the noble families of Giao Chi cannot and will not pay such unjust levels of taxation.'

'Tribute, Prefect. What you are required to pay is *tribute* to the Emperor.'

'Tax, tribute, it's all the same.'

'And you claim to speak for all the noble families? If so, why are the other Prefects not here with you?' Dinh waved a dismissive hand through empty air. 'You are a lone voice, young Sach, and always have been. I had hoped you would learn more appropriate thought and behaviour, but you have shown yourself unwilling and egregious.'

'Sach is not alone,' I said. 'I am here for Me Linh. You cannot ignore two provinces as powerful as ours. The others will follow when they see that we have spoken out.'

'I doubt that,' Dinh sniggered. 'This Commandery is full of weak-minded fools. There is no organisation here except what we have given. You would be running around the hills chanting to animals and rolling in half-planted rice paddies if not for the good governance we have given to you.'

'How dare you?' I spluttered, almost lost for words. 'Giao Chi has an ancient and revered history. We were raising an abundance of rice before the Yellow River people had even learned how to grow it. You came here for the riches of our land. Do not pretend that we are the lesser people for we are richer and stronger than the Han.'

Dinh shuddered, as if he'd had to repress deep laughter in his fat belly. On his face was a wide smile that he was struggling to suppress. Behind us, the door had opened quietly and a number of guards filed in, lining the wall. Obviously the clerk had been sent for reinforcements as soon as we'd been shown in.

'Has it truly come to this?' asked Sach, glancing round at the armed guards. 'Must you force the Commandery into war because you do not like the way we marry and the way we wear our hair?'

'Dear son, it is about so much more than that,' said Dinh, earnestly, his amusement now subsiding. 'Have you not listened on all those occasions when we have talked? Have you not explained to your errant wife how heaven's mandate decrees that the Middle Kingdom must rule Giao Chi, and must rule it according to the proven ways? I have done as Confucius once taught – that is to treat you with kindness and attempt to give you clear instruction, since you are backward in thought, but now I see that I cannot help you any longer. I will not have you calling into question my correctness in ruling this Commandery. I have observed every principle of good management and I have been kind to the people, punishing only when every attempt to reform has been rebuffed.'

'How can you say such a thing?' I interrupted. 'Yes, you have directed the building of waterways and the enlargement of rice fields, but you have also taken land from the people and given it to your soldiers. You have brought trade to our towns, but you have insisted on preferential rates that cripple the sellers. Worst of all, you have ignored all the abuse – the women and girls that are stolen, the men summarily executed. And you have set terrible sentences against people who are just following their own traditions.'

'We are speaking at crossed purposes, like two swords striking pointlessly,' he said. 'I will not continue this discussion. The guards will remove you to the prison, where you will remain until trial. Happily this will take place very soon and we can bring this unfortunate unpleasantness to a clear end.'

'I welcome it,' said Sach. 'You do not know what you have brought upon yourself.'

The guards took hold of us. They shoved us disrespectfully out of the room and directly out into a courtyard. From there we were marched the short distance to the cells. They pushed us inside together and I fell slightly against Sach as one of the guards gave an additional thump to my ribs.

'One day I will rip that man's arms from his body,' I swore.

'I don't doubt it,' said Sach, looking into my eyes. 'You could have turned on him then. Even unarmed you would have won.'

'So could you,' I said, 'so why have we walked into a prison?' I glanced around the foetid little room. Three others squatted on the dirt floor, observing our arrival.

'Because we are making a point to the people of Giao Chi.

They will never rise up unless the injustice is made plain and they can no longer ignore it.'

I studied my husband's face, fixed in resilient defiance. I had never grown tired of his looks, though it had been six years since we had married. The sheer edge of his cheekbones, the angle of his jaw and the high forehead still invited the touch of my fingers as they had at the very start. The skin across his chest and stomach was as soft as the seed heads on a summer grass, as smooth as a willow bud, even though the muscles beneath were hard as bamboo. His words made me shiver. I knew exactly what he meant. In order for the noble families of Giao Chi to be provoked into war, something terrible must happen to some of their own. The injustices against peasants may rankle, but a direct attack on the Prefects could not be ignored. It was a fitful night's sleep in the miserable cell, pressed against Sach's warm body, dreaming of going to my death with him in order to breathe new life into our people.

★★★★★

I strode along the thoroughfare, swinging my arms and pretending a vague interest in the market stalls and shop fronts along the way. Ordinarily, Lien Lau was a friendly place, but on that day, tension hung like a dark cloud. Shopkeepers loitered by their doorways with sombre expressions and people hurried by with downcast expressions. Pairs of Han soldiers patrolled through the streets, hands on the hilts of their swords and as we crossed a street to take the turning towards the large government buildings, a gong sounded several times, resonating through the chilly air and making me jump.

'Excuse me,' I said, to a woman carving bowls outside her shop, 'What does the gong sound for?'

'There's a trial today,' she said. 'It sounds more days than not. Today is a big one, though - lots of prisoners. Haven't you heard?' She stared at us curiously and I smiled and walked on. Inside, my stomach was heaving.

'If it's a public trial, we can blend in,' said Thao. 'They won't notice us, Nhi.'

'But how will we get them out?'

'Let's find them first,' he said.

We rounded a corner and immediately I saw the silk banners and huge, bamboo scrolls, with Han words painted all across them. They hung either side of a grand doorway where a crowd of people spilled out into the courtyard. The people all faced into the tiered building and from inside, the monotonous tones of a court official drifted out. We hurried over, joining the press of bodies. I stood on the tips of my toes, straining to see into the hall. I could make out a line of seating at the back, where the unmistakeably overweight outline of To Dinh sat in the centre, other members of his staff to his right and left. An official in the sidelines was speaking and seemed to be calling out the charges against one unfortunate woman. I tapped the man in front of me. He looked round excitedly.

'Who's being tried today?' I asked.

'This woman's the second. There are a few more to come, and they say a Lac Lord is being tried. It's not normally as busy as this, but a Lac Lord being tried... that's something new.'

I stumbled back, as horrified by his happy indifference as by the confirmation that Sach was indeed in such a dire predicament. There had been no mention of Trac and the man had turned away again, so I had no idea whether she was with Sach or even in Lien Lau still.

'We need to get closer,' I said, grasping my husband's arm. 'We can't see them from here.'

We pulled back from the crowd and assessed the building. There were a few high windows but people were already standing on boxes looking through them.

'I can throw them off,' said Thao.

'It would draw attention. We mustn't end up in a fight.' I looked up. There were two cantilevered roofs, slightly upturned, like a pair of tiled smiles, one each on top of the first and second stories. The building was wide and all the people were at the front and sides. The soldiers were patrolling out on the road. The back of the building appeared to be quiet. I led Thao around the side and along past the people on boxes to the back. Once we were out of sight, I felt the walls. They were a mixture of wood and brick, and rough enough to gain a handhold. I scaled the wall and then threw my arms out to grasp the overhanging cantilever. It took some effort and I dangled precariously for a moment before swinging myself to gain momentum and then throwing my legs up and over. Thao was already scrambling the wall and he was up and beside me within a few seconds. We had made a clatter and we flattened ourselves as still as toads, low against the shallow slope of the roof, hoping no one inside had heard us. From below we could hear the scraping, coughing, shifting sounds of the public gathering, providing the backdrop to a raised voice that rang out above the other mumblings and occasional cries.

Thao shook his head at me. No one had heard us. There was too much noise inside. The second storey was windowless on the rear side so we did not have to worry about anyone looking out and there were few vantage points that would allow passers-by and guards to notice us without deliberate effort. The problem now was to find a way to see in. The roof was well-constructed and sturdy, but it was also shallow and the roof tiles were small. We felt along for any that were loose and when I found some that shifted in my grip, I began to work them out. I nearly lost my footing once or twice, but eventually I was able to move several and give myself a direct view down through into the hall.

'Can you see them?' Thao asked. 'What's happening?'

I shushed him and pressed my face hard up against the hole. Directly below was the line of officials. To Dinh was to our right. I could have thrown a dagger into his neck with ease. In front of them stood a short, elderly man, bound at the wrists with his head dropped low. Someone came to lead him away and another bound detainee was brought from my left.

'The prisoners are on the left,' I said to Thao, 'But I can't see them from here.'

I wanted to scream with frustration, so desperate was I to catch a glimpse of Trac. In the justice hall below, someone was reading out a name and charges. The most senior administrator, who answered only to the Governor himself, issued the sentence, committing the prisoner to hard labour for a period of ten years and the prisoner shuffled away. I saw blood on his legs.

'The woman said there are trials most days,' I said, my voice rising. 'At this rate they will force hard labour on half the population of Giao Chi. The charges are not even clear and that man had been tortured.'

'Keep it down,' warned Thao. 'Can you see Sach or Trac yet?'

I strained my neck and there, on the left and finally moving into my line of vision, was my sister. I could see the side of her - down her left arm and leg - though her head was still out of my sight. I gasped and then I turned aside from the hole in the roof and vomited that morning's noodles down the clean, grey roof of the law hall. Thao fastened a bone-hard grip about my upper arm, holding me as if he expected me to faint away to the ground. I spat and wiped my mouth against my sleeve.

'I'm all right,' I said and he loosed his grip. 'It looks as though they will be next.'

'Let me see,' he said, forcing me to move sideways. He twisted his face against the hole. I looked towards the river. In the distance, the cajeput trees stood motionless and exposed amongst the winter-faded grasses of the savannah. I hoped my mother was getting word to all our people - Khanh and Kim Cuc, Chinh, Vien and all the other Lac nobility who would surely descend on Lien Lau and prevent whatever travesty of justice was being played out. And yet, I worried, it is all happening too fast. How can my sister and her husband be free one day and detained the next? How can it have come to this? My stomach churned again but there was nothing left to throw up. I experienced a sharp and violent anger towards all those who had sat in the subversive meetings and talked about resistance without actually providing any.

'Cowards,' I hissed. 'They did this.'

'What?' Thao looked up, disoriented.

'Why couldn't Prefect Vien have done what Sach did? Why couldn't *he* be the one to challenge Dinh's reforms? He has longed for the chance and yet he has let Sach and Trac be the ones to face the Governor's wrath.'

'There isn't a leader among them,' said Thao, quietly. 'But all is not lost. There is time to get them out of this mess. Dinh might request payment of a tribute, or give a labour sentence from which we can help him escape. We don't even know the charges yet.'

He surrendered the spyhole to me and I looked through again. This time I could see both of them, in full. They were calling Sach's name - 'Prefect Sach of Chu Dien Province,' the voice said, 'Thi Sach, son of Thi Hoc, charged with insubordinance towards the laws of Giao Chi. And also Trung Trac, his wife, daughter of Lady Man Thien who is Prefect of Me Linh.' They both moved forward.

'They've used our family name,' I said to Thao. 'They haven't used the name of Lac that Father went by.'

'Probably on purpose. They will not want people to remember that Trac is the daughter of General Lac so they have used his other name.'

'I cannot remember the last time I heard it,' I murmured. 'We were always just Trac and Nhi and Father was always General Lac.'

The clerks below were calling for silence so the senior administrator could speak.

'This is an unusual case,' the disconcerted official began, but

To Dinh cut him off.

'As the primary witness to this man's treachery and disrespect, and indeed that of his wife, I will now give a full account.'

The administrator, of whom I had only a top-view of shiny black hair in a top knot and shoulders clothed in padded brown silk, shuffled in his seat but stayed silent. Sach glared at the ineffectual law lord and then turned a contemptuous gaze on the Governor. He stood very proudly, even though they had bound his hands and he was weapon-less. There was no blood or bruising that I could see, unless it was hidden by his tunic and trousers. I studied Trac and found to my relief that she, also, looked unharmed. Her eyes were heavy-lidded and her mouth down-turned, as if she had taken a sip of the sourest soup. She didn't look pretty, but she did look formidable.

'I have long suspected that this young man harbours ill-intent towards our great Emperor and the benevolent rule which the Middle Kingdom bestows upon this young Commandery of Giao Chi, but I had thought that by coaxing Thi Sach into a fuller understanding of the complexities of...' To Dinh droned on and on. I listened to the words but they danced like blossom in a wind. I lifted my face to Thao, who was watching in case anyone saw us there on the roof.

'Governor Dinh is making the case. The senior administrator is silent.'

'Is there a charge?'

'Insubordinance to the law. They will convict him without any doubt.'

'But it isn't a crime to disagree with the law, only to act against it,' said Thao.

'I'm not sure that's true any more. And besides, if the hair is not enough, to prove their point they need only make him smile,' I said.

'Would they really impose a harsh sentence upon a Prefect just for black teeth and cut hair?' Thao asked.

'Perhaps, perhaps not. But it will prove Dinh's point – that Sach is inherently dangerous, especially as a Prefect.'

I looked back into the hall. Dinh was still speaking. He was recounting the things that Sach and Trac had apparently said when they confronted him – how Sach had challenged the many new legal reforms and Trac had insulted the Emperor and all the people of the Middle Kingdom. None of it interested me now. I just wanted to know how they would be sentenced. They looked very fine, standing in front of the ugly Governor and I hoped all the people watching would see that this is what Giao Chi men and women should be, and could be, if only they would stand up for themselves. The Governor's voice swam back into my consciousness and I realised he was reaching a conclusion.

'...and so it is clear that Thi Sach has shown open disregard for the laws of this Commandery and has no intention of rectifying his attitude. He has violated Imperial law. There can be only one sentence and that is death!'

There was a gasp and shuffling. It was what I had expected. I had prepared myself for this. I knew To Dinh would seek to make a firm example of Sach, and that he would use the distinction of Imperial law, rather than the usual statutes, in order to gain the death penalty, but I had been clinging to more hope than I realised and now a deep desolation filled me. The senior administrator coughed awkwardly.

'May the prisoner speak, given that he is a Prefect and that the charges are, well, somewhat... shall we say, ideological?' he asked.

'By all means,' said To Dinh, smiling.

'All that the Governor has said is true,' said Sach loudly, his voice ringing through the hall so that even Thao, leaning close beside me, managed to hear him. 'The reforms which this Governor has introduced are suffocating our country. We must not allow our ancient culture to be destroyed. We are the children of Lac Long Quan and the Han have no right to take away what is ours. I have tried to make progress by peaceful means with the Governor but to no avail. Now he sees he can silence me only by executing me. His actions contravene the principles of legality which the Middle Kingdom claims to uphold. If the Governor executes me, he gives a lie to the Emperor's mandate to rule. So you see, Dinh,' he spoke directly to the Governor at this point, 'if you kill me, you will bring down the force of our people upon your illegal rule. If you let me live, I will continue to speak out against you. It is your choice.'

Silently, I applauded him. Silently too, the assembled public watched To Dinh and waited. In their faces I could see confusion, shame, distress. These people had come for entertainment. They had not expected to hear a call to arms. Neither did they want to see this handsome, eloquent epitome of Giao Chi manhood publicly executed.

'Death,' said To Dinh. 'And for your wife, imprisonment with my permission to take her own life, if she can find the honour to do so. That is the sentence. As for your people, here they are. Do you expect them to fight for you? Their lives are good. They have rice, they have families, their duty is to the Emperor and they know it. Giao Chi has no *force* that can stand against the Emperor. His reign is mandated by heaven and by your opposition to his progress, you are the one acting illegally.'

He looked sideways at the senior administrator who hesitated then nodded. A scribe was hurriedly scribbling down the sentence, but he had made, in so far as I could tell from the inactivity of his brush against the strips of bamboo, no recording of Sach's words, nor indeed of the Governor's. A guard came forward to escort Sach and Trac from the hall and I caught one last sight of their impassive faces before they were hustled out of view.

★★★★★

If the rules by which we played were changing in the year

leading up to Sach's arrest, at the point of his death sentence, they were thrown away completely. I was stunned by how quickly we had descended to that terrible point. I hadn't wanted it to be my sister and her husband who went to the Governor, but I knew why they had to do it. Someone needed to start the cart rolling by standing up in public and saying that the Han oppression must stop. They were so very brave and Sach spoke so well and so clearly that all the people listening would understand and pass on his words.

We scrambled down from the roof and came round the side of the building. One of the officials who had been inside was just coming out and Thao dragged me back against the wall. When the crowd started to push out into the courtyard, we joined their throng. The few prisoners bound for hard labour were already in a cart on the road but there was no sign of Sach or Trac.

'What now?' Thao asked me.

'I don't know,' I said. I turned to face my husband. 'We can't try to free him. We would destroy what he has just created – the legend of his sacrifice.' Bitter tears were threatening to drop from my eyes, but I blinked them back. 'See the soldiers?'

I pointed to where the official from the hall had gone. He was speaking up to a mounted Captain whose horse was impatiently striking at the dirt with a hoof. Behind, several more soldiers on horseback were appearing.

'They're going to look for me,' I said. 'I saw To Dinh speak to the official just as Sach was taken away.'

'They will be hunting for your mother too. They'll want to remove anyone who might try to avenge this. We have to warn her.'

'We can try,' I said, 'but I doubt that we can get there faster than that Captain.' The soldiers were already cantering away down the street. 'Besides, our mother is travelling herself. They will struggle to find her. The one person we can help is Trac.'

The crowd had spilled out and away from us and the

courtyard in front of the justice hall was empty. I walked back towards it, round to the far side.

'There must be another door.' I stopped and pointed at a gateway through the high wall surrounding the building. 'That gate leads to the one-storey building over there. I think that must be where they keep the prisoners before trial.'

'Then they'll be leading them out this way any moment,' Thao said. 'If we can intercept them and overpower the guards, we may be able to get Trac away. But will she thank you for it? Maybe she intends to make the same sacrifice as Sach.'

'I don't care. One dead Prefect will start the beat of the drums. A second dead leader is just a waste.' I wiped the back of my hand over eyes that had already begun to dry and walked across to the gateway. It was unsecured and we let ourselves through into the scrub land at the other side. Something had taken over inside me. My will was directed by that shiny, sharp stone that Chien had left in my heart. I knew, before it happened, that the guards would certainly walk this way - that they would be chatting and full of easy arrogance. When finally they pulled the gate open and stepped through, Thao and I were on either side, flattened against the wall. I let the first guard get just ahead of us, followed by Sach and Trac walking side by side, and then I sliced the throat of one of the guards who walked behind. He fell, staggering and sloshing blood onto the flattened yellow grass and the first guard turned. I drew my long sword and gutted him before he could even draw his own weapon. Thao had taken a third guard, but two more were pushing past their fallen comrades with fury in their eyes, and they were shouting loudly.

Trac held her hands up wordlessly and I used the dagger in my left hand to cut the rope that bound her wrists. I was momentarily grateful to her guards for not using chains. As her arms fell free, she reached towards me and drew my second sword, a shorter one that was still tied into my belt. Then, hardly breaking her gaze from my own, she decapitated the next guard to reach us. I smiled happily amid the rising sea of scarlet but another guard had reached Sach and was dragging him backwards and we could hear the clattering of footsteps in the yard beyond. Thao, bloodied from several kills, tried to pull the gate shut, but the headless guard's body lay in the way.

'Go now,' yelled Sach, his hands still bound and, as I now saw, his ankles bound too. 'Go now, Trac.'

She froze for a heart-rending second and I saw the look that passed between them. It seared me down to the bone. Then she broke away, in a sudden, violent pelt towards the river. Thao and I followed without a glance behind. It haunts me still, that I didn't look back. I wonder how Sach felt as he watched us running away. Was he filled with deep desolation and horror or did he rejoice in Trac's escape, believing his own sacrifice to be so necessary? I do believe it was the latter, and not just because it is the happier alternative. After all, I've sent others away to safety, whilst I have remained in serious danger, and always my own fear has been out-weighed by relief that those I love are far from harm. Indeed, the worst pain is that which comes from the harm done to loved ones, not the harm one endures personally. Trac suffered more than Sach ever did, although she cannot accept it.

The three of us ran like civets to the river, following the stretch of scrub-land, scaling a wall, crossing a decorative courtyard and another wall before we reached the bank. The guards were pursuing and we could hear the shouted commands as they tried to organise themselves against our unexpected attack. They didn't know how many we were and perhaps they wasted time securing Sach, because we reached the water unimpeded and they were only just coming over the courtyard wall onto the banking as we dived into the Red River and swam hard downstream, the current speeding us on to the main jetty. The shout went up along the river front, but not in time to prevent Thao from reaching a docked canoe, throwing the unfortunate owner into the water and dragging us aboard. We struggled up, clothes having become a dead weight and muscles clenched in agony against the cold. Thao gave the angry boatman a crack with the oar to keep him from clinging on to his vessel while I grasped at a second oar and then we slipped away with the current, paddling as hard as we could. A few boatmen watched in astonishment, but they were Lac people, not Han, and they were not inclined to stop three fierce, home-grown warriors.

'I am Trung Trac,' my sister shouted at them as we sailed away, 'Tell the Governor his days here are numbered.' She held up my sword, which somehow she had kept hold of while swimming. It was clean of blood now, rinsed in the river. My dagger, held between my teeth while I swam, and remaining there now as I paddled, tasted warm and bitter from the man whose throat it had cut. My long sword was lost in the depths. By the time the guards reached the jetty, we were being carried out of sight and I would guess the boatmen, entertained despite the theft, played stupid and did not allow them to board easily, gaining us precious time.

'They'll follow on horseback,' shouted Thao, pounding the black ribbon of water with his oar. 'We must take to land before the next curve or they will gain on us.'

'You make your way north and find our mother,' Trac answered. 'We will go south. They will not expect that.'

Thao didn't answer. I could tell he did not like receiving her orders and perhaps was wary of parting from me, but he deferred and after a little longer, we pulled the boat into the southern bank. Trac jumped out.

'Take care, Nhi,' Thao said, as I followed her.

'You also,' I replied. 'Find Mother. We must raise an army. She'll know what to do.'

'We will go to Nhat Nam Commandery, right to the mountain cloud pass if we have to, and return with a force that Governor Dinh cannot ignore,' said Trac.

Thao nodded and then angled the canoe across the river,

being drawn along for a short distance until he banked clumsily at the other side. I didn't wait to see him disembark, but set off after Trac, the two of us running at the same frantic pace that we had set in Lien Lau. It was essential that we cut south before the troops from the town intercepted us. If we could make it, we would be fairly sure of our safety as the guards would likely only look for us along the river and north into the provinces neighbouring Me Linh. I was a healthy young woman, fighting fit and energetic, but nothing had prepared me for the breathless, muscle-tearing pain of that run, soaked to the skin, first with river water and when that had burned away, with my own sweat. How much harder must it have been for Trac? We were running towards our liberation and our future, but every step took us further from the love of Trac's life, who would now die at the hands of To Dinh.

★★★★★

Night time found us under cover of thick forest. We had evaded the Han troops and taken a south western route, crossing the lower branch of the Red River to head slightly further inland. We were still on foot, so the distance we could cover was limited, but now that we had reached the sprawl of dense woodland beyond the delta, we felt safer. As darkness drew on, we found a place within a stand of beech trees to rest. There was a small stream, at which we drank, and then I left Trac alone while I went in search of something to eat. It was dismal beneath the tree cover, with a dank mist settling. Out on the plains, it would be a persistent drizzle but we were protected by the thick levels of branching above us. A mouse-eared bat swooped in panic a finger's width from my cheek but I didn't startle. I was only angry that I hadn't caught it. Somewhere in the blackness a dhole howled and I heard the shift of air, terminated by a soft thump, that signalled a colugo gliding through the canopy and coming to rest on one of the tall conifers.

The dense foliage was a challenge, and twisting tree roots,

along with low, winding branches, conspired against a body that was already taxed beyond ordinary endurance, but I persisted upstream and eventually I came upon what I had been looking for - a paa frog as large as my hand, sitting on a rock and camouflaged by its warty, grey exterior. I could barely see in the darkness. There was the faintest moonlight filtering into the under-storey but I moved on instinct rather than sight. I unwound my hair wrap and held the fabric in my hands, moving closer to the flat-headed creature. As soon as I came within touching distance, I threw the fabric over him and grasped him tight, bundling him into the thick, jute cloth while I took out my dagger. Then I exposed his body and dispensed with his little life in haste and let the blood drain down into spongy undergrowth. The fat, spine-covered limbs ceased twitching and I wrapped him back up and made my way back downstream towards Trac.

She had gathered some old, rotting wood and like me, her hair fell down in loose, damp coils over her shoulder. Her dark silhouette gestured sideways and I could just make out her soggy hair wrap, wrinkled over flattened shrubs. Nestled on top were two tiny loaches.

'I used Bao's old technique,' she whispered, 'but I wish I'd had a proper net.'

'Mountain chicken,' I responded, swinging the dead frog down beside the little fish. I helped her to get the fire going with the little flint set I always kept secured to my body in a pouch. It took a while because we didn't have enough dry moss and fibre, but eventually we raised a flame, and then the old branches and pieces of bark started to take. The weariness was overwhelming, but I knew we must eat before we slept. I dismembered the frog, taking out the inedible innards as best I could. The loaches we left whole, sticking them on the end of the short sword and roasting them in the flame until they crisped up a little. We had one each, the little bones cracking in our teeth and then I roasted the parts of the frog - legs, arms, head, carcass. There was a surprising amount of meat for such a small animal, and the muscle tension in our bodies meant we did not need very much to fill our stomachs. After drinking some stream water from cupped hands, Trac rinsed our hair wraps and hung them over a branch to dry in the fire's heat. I climbed several trees until I found sturdy branches for sleeping on.

'Can we not sleep down here, by the fire?' asked Trac.

'You can if you like,' I said, keeping my voice down, 'but I prefer to be higher up. If a bear or a leopard blunders this way, I would rather they missed me.'

'I think they will smell us up there anyway,' sniffed Trac.

'Maybe. But there are snakes and spiders and shrews and all kinds of other things creeping through that undergrowth. Any one of them could give you a nasty bite.'

'They all climb trees too,' said Trac, but she seemed persuaded and I directed her to a neighbouring tree which she climbed easily until she found the branch I recommended. We were about the height of two people from the ground, but reaching out, we could have touched fingertips. Below, the fire continued to crackle and smoke drifted by us into the damp night.

'Nhi,' she whispered.

'Yes?'

'They'll kill Sach. I won't ever see him again.'

'Yes Trac, I know. I am sorry.' There was a long lull. The night sounds of the forest encroached on us and reached a feverish volume in my head. Then she spoke again, and with her words, the crescendo of the beasts receded.

'When it happened to you, with Chien, how did you get over it?' Her voice was full of desperation and longing. I knew it well, that terrible feeling, and I knew it was surmountable.

'I had a dream one night, eldest sister. I saw a beautiful peacock in my dream and as it opened it's bright blue tail feathers, I felt a swell inside my heart as if my breath was connected to its very movement. I knew then that all of life is beautiful and that nothing is lost because nothing ever ends. When I awoke, the world seemed glorious again and I was part of it. I was the delta and the river and the mountains and the sea. I was the island in the gulf and the swamp on the shore and the tiger in the forest.'

She didn't answer that. I didn't mind. It would take time for her to understand, but when she did, she would be as free as I was. The pain would reside in a sharp, shiny heart-stone and, together, we would be unstoppable.

16

The route south was hard and fraught with dangers, but for the first few days, I was barely conscious of my own fatigue or of the fierce, prowling eyes that marked our progress through the deep forests. All I saw was Sach, standing before me with his wrists and ankles bound. Nhi guided us through the wild land and I followed her lead, drinking when she said we should drink, sleeping when she said we should sleep. Our movements were so constant that in my warped mind, it felt that the world was turning through us - that we were in fact standing still, an arm's length apart, and that the forest was rushing towards and past us. We were ceaseless and silent and nothing existed beyond the narrow horizon of tangled trees.

We were making for the Truong Son mountain range, but we stood barely a chance of getting there without assistance. Looking back now, I am incredulous that we survived those first days at all - we were chilled and half-starved and at the mercy of bears, tigers, leopards, snakes and all the other insidious, lethal killers that lurk in the Nam Viet wilderness. The nights were painfully cold, the temperatures dipping beyond the daytime chill as the winter monsoon winds swept down from the north. We followed trails through the undergrowth when we could, but much of our energy was expended on fighting through the thick, uneven and twisted terrain. For five days, we saw no other people. Then, on the sixth day in the mid-morning, we were startled by a raucous barking and slapping sound directly ahead of us.

'What is it?' I cried to Nhi.

'Doucs,' she answered. 'Something's frightened them.'

We climbed up a twisted rhododendron and swung over to the lower branch of a great conifer, fearful that a large predator might be about to pass our way. Within a few seconds, a tribe of monkeys swung through the canopy overhead, their organised silence now in stark contrast to their initial agitation as their red legs streaked through the foliage. We waited but nothing else appeared. After a few moments, Nhi shinned back down and I followed. She set off in the direction the doucs had come from.

'People' she said, to my unasked question. 'I think there are people this way.'

I caught up to her and we stumbled on, tramping over ground that had become more sparse over the last day. It was still dismal under the thick cover of the evergreens, but we were no longer clambering over a gnarled under-storey in near darkness. Orchids decked the trunks and branches of conifers, and ferns hung in the canopy. Ahead, we could see light filtering into the forest floor and the ground had become hard and rocky in places. We had come to the southern tip of the Hoang Lien Son range. I should have been glad to see the weak rays of late winter light. I should have welcomed the proximity of other human beings who could help us, but my first reaction was aversion. If the world out there did indeed still exist then Sach was dead. My husband and I had both left the world for a time, but now I was coming back into it and he was not. I stopped.

Nhi stopped also and turned, but did not look directly at me. She looked into the rich, heavy upper storey where a whole world of creatures lived, never bothering to trouble themselves with the ground, far below their alien feet.

'Are you about to tell me that life goes on? Or that it is beautiful?' I asked, with a hint of bitterness.

She smiled patiently but still did not meet my eyes.

'I thought you'd stopped to look at the leaf-birds,' she said. 'There is a pair just above us.' She pointed up but I refused to look. She knew full well I had not stopped to look at the scenery.

'From now on,' I said, 'I am in command. I am the eldest sister.'

'Of course.'

'We are Trung Trac and Trung Nhi. The sisters Trung.'

'If you wish.'

'I mean what I have said - we will raise an army and return to Lien Lau.'

'I know.'

'Good.' I set off walking again. She waited until I had passed her and then she followed in my wake. I thought I might have upset her, but as I overtook her, I was sure I saw her smile again.

★★★★★

Our encounter with the villagers was most successful. We sheltered there for two nights, rebuilding our strength as we accepted bowl after bowl of fresh, steaming rice. They fed us on pheasant and frog meat also, and one of the old ladies brewed up a soup with some special bark and herbs that tasted incredibly bitter but was apparently sure to replenish us. While we were there, we told them about what was happening in the capital and they listened in rising anger. Of course, we embroidered the facts just a little. People needed to sense an immediate and dangerous threat to their own livelihoods before they would take up arms, so Nhi and I told them To Dinh was planning a campaign to the western fringes of Giao Chi and that very soon he would come, demanding higher taxes and forcing them into Confucian ways and Han rituals. It was not far from the truth. I told them that my mother, the famous Lady Man Thien, was in the north raising an army and that war was coming. They cast anxious glances between themselves and some of the younger people gave swift and excitable promises to fight.

My mother was indeed in the north, though I did not know at the time what was happening to her. Thao had caught up with her near the northern borders of his own province, Khuc Duong, where she had already assembled a number of significant warriors. From there, they headed north, to the Zhuang tribe. The Zhuang had been assimilated into the Middle Kingdom, just as we Lac had been, but like us, they kept to their own ways. They, too, were feeling the pressure from their Commandery administration and would be our natural allies, especially as the Zhuang and the Au Lac were closely related. Yet at that time, for all we knew, our mother could have been captured or even killed.

The village supplied us with sturdy pack horses to take us south, for which we promised to make recompense, and one of the young women offered to guide us, at least to where we could pick up a lesser-used trade route on the Truong Son. Cong was a lithe girl, slim-built but with a wide face and sun-squinted eyes. She helped us pack some basic supplies onto the horses - a blanket each, cooked rice and pickled vegetables wrapped into tight leaf packages, a machete for use in foraging and a staff each, since we were short on weaponry. I believe they would have equipped us with long swords if they could, but they had no such fine equipment. What cherished items they did have resided in their small temple, which we visited before we left. It was a darker, somehow more serious place of communion that the one in Me Linh, with paintings of wild animal spirits on large stones and numerous effigies of the immortal creatures carved from animal horn. In the centre stood a bronze drum, ancient and hallowed, a great beating stick laid by its side. I contemplated it as I made my pleas to the heavens and as I honoured the great animal spirits. By the time we rode out from the village, one of the small boys was beating out a slow and persistent rhythm on the old metallic beast and its low, ringing heartbeat followed us through the sparse forest, carried on the cool wind to all the surrounding communities.

We had taken three horses and though they were strong animals, they tired quickly with the increasingly mountainous terrain and we had to stop frequently to rest and water them. Each time we came across a running supply of water, we paused, knowing that we would make more progress that way in the long run. Cong was friendly but she was not a great talker, which suited me and Nhi just fine. The only conversations we did have were about martial artistry, and given a willing student, Nhi could not help but examine and correct the girl's fighting techniques. There was plenty of opportunity, in the days it took to reach the Truong Son. Cong, true to her word, had delivered us into the foothills, but she showed no signs of wanting to turn back. We never actually spoke about it - she just carried on riding with us and we didn't turn her away. She was a good hunter and she did have an aptitude for fighting, which Nhi was nurturing.

It was when Cong brought down a saola that I began to believe she had the makings of something more special than simply a hired warrior. We had rounded a stand of trees and come upon three of the magnificent, sleek, brown beasts, kicking their heels in a glade. They were still some distance from us, and due to the wind direction, had not picked up our scent. Cong immediately slid from her horse and drew out the bow she kept fastened across her back. She slipped an arrow into place and released it before I had even brought my horse to a full stop. The lethal shaft whistled through the woodland breeze and implanted its sharp head deep into the neck of one of the saola. It reared and bleated hoarsely. The other two mammals tucked their horned heads low and broke away, their large hooves beating a track out of the glade and up the escarpment, following the line of a tumbling mountain stream that fell through the evergreen hillside. As they raced to safety, Cong aimed another arrow at the wounded saola. It caught in the ribs and the animal staggered, losing its back legs for a moment, but as it struggled to rise, Cong stowed her bow and set off towards it at a sprint. That was no mean feat considering the uneven forest floor, but she sprang across as if a series of stepping stones had been placed neatly in her way. Reaching the saola, she threw herself against its heavy side and grasped hold of one of the long, backward sweeping horns. The beast fought, trying to throw her off and even breaking into the semblance of a canter, but she wrestled it down to the ground,

217

pulled out her nicked and battered machete and pressed it hard into the saola's throat. As the blood was spilling we brought the horses nearer.

'That was excellently done,' I congratulated her.

'It'll make a change from green chicken,' she answered breathlessly, meaning the fat frogs that had formed most of our diet for days. She stroked the wide, white spots that coloured the saola's cheek, one arm still wrapped around the beast as if in an embrace. Nhi and I dismounted and in honour of the slain beast, we each took a fingertip of his blood to our foreheads and thanked the great spirit of all the saola for its sacrifice. It was the way of the ancients, the way that existed before the Han came. Later, Nhi and Cong hacked off the horns, each about three hand-lengths, and then skinned the dead saola before dismembering the body. I cleaned and prepared the hide and hung it from a branch. The work took most of the afternoon so we stayed in the glade that night and ate meat, roasted on the fire. The metallic odour of blood lingered in the air, but I did not mind it.

★★★★★

At the Ca River, we faced a large community, filled with languorous individuals. Their tepid welcome was warmed by our travelling stories and, with the exception of some of the drunken husbands too sodden with rice wine, their tempers were inflamed by our retelling of the injustice at Lien Lau. There was a Han camp within half a day's ride to the east and the villagers were no strangers to the ambivalent demands that Middle Kingdom soldiers were wont to impose.

Of course, it was not easy. I had to tell the tale of Sach's death as if I already knew exactly what had happened to him - as if I had been there and seen it done, when in fact his sentence could have been commuted or he could have escaped. But if you are waiting for my return to Lien Lau in anticipation that my story has a happy ending in the arms of my husband, then I must be clear now – Sach died, and in much the same way as I told it, over and over again, in all the towns and villages we passed through. Deep down inside my soul, I knew it was true and so the words were not a lie. They were just very hard to say. It helped to have Nhi there with me, stiffening as I spoke, and even Cong, standing guard-like just behind, had become a source of strength. In the Ca River town, I honed my performance because I knew that everything hinged on inciting the rage of the Lac people.

'My husband, Prefect Sach of Chu Dien province, has been murdered by Governor Dinh,' I told them. 'The Governor will murder all the Lac Lords until there are none left. It is false to say the Prefects are safe. We are in as much danger as you all are. Every day, the courts at Lien Lau convict ordinary people of acts that are not criminal – acts such as blackening our own teeth, tattooing our skin or cutting our hair – but these rituals are what the Lac have always done. We are not Han and we do not worship Confucius. Yet soon there will be no Au Lac people left – our bones will be ashes and Lac Long Quan will weep in the heavens and our souls shall never join him unless we fight these invaders. Join me and we will avenge what these monsters from the Middle Kingdom,' and here I spat on the floor, 'have done to our country. With my blood, I will restore the Hung lineage and I will see that my husband's honour lives on while those who murdered him are slaughtered. I vow that I will do this.'

People cried, so I knew I had made an impression. I demanded, at Ca River, that those who were serious about fighting join us immediately. Previously, it had been important to put some distance between ourselves and the vicious intent of Dinh's mercenaries, but we were well away now and, like as not, Dinh had no idea where we had gone. It no longer mattered if our pace was hampered by extra followers; we were building an army now, not running away. We picked up men and women from that town, and we acquired better weapons, including new long swords each. I put Cong in charge of keeping order amongst the rabble and so she became my first General. She smiled her usual wide, silent grin when I titled her thus, so I did not know if she was embarrassed, happy or proud. It was probably all three and more besides. She had been a simple mountain girl raising crops and obeying her family, and now she had found herself at the forefront of a new, national army. I wondered what her family back north made of her continuing absence.

Our journey south carried on, but we varied our route according to where known settlements existed. My plan was to gain reinforcements along the Truong Son and then turn east, towards the Hai Van Pass on the coast, from where we could begin a northern expedition up the coastline. Beyond the Hai Van Pass, the people were different – we knew that some foreigners with darker skin had begun to settle there, and that the Han had not tried to colonise that far south. It was, to all intents and purposes, a different country, and one we had no intention of entering. There was no reason to suppose that the Cham settlers would assist us, nor that the Tai tribes across the Truong Son Mountains would help – many of them had migrated from the north in recent generations under pressure from the Han expansion and would not be eager to provoke Middle Kingdom wrath. In the far south, beyond the Chams and the Tais and the Khmers, were the people of the Nine Dragon River – the Me Kong. They were too far away, too free of the Han threat, to care at all. Turning back at the pass of the mountain clouds was the only course of action.

We came at last to that furthest point of our progress without encountering the Han at all. Our numbers had swelled, but insufficiently and I had begun to fear that I could not draw enough warriors to my side. At the pit of my belly, a snake of doubt coiled, hissing in To Dinh's voice that Nam Viet could offer no force to threaten him. I looked at our encampment with pride, but also a terrible sense of responsibility. Unless we could attract more followers, we had no chance of taking Lien Lau. Nhi, who was planning our course, had led us directly to the Hai Van Pass, believing the sacred boundary would inspire us all, and we had camped just north-west of the patrol, looking out towards the green peninsula that stretched into the smooth blue waters of the gulf. It was a fine day and the clouds that gave the pass its name had lifted. The warm weather was breaking through- a reminder of how long we had travelled. I guessed it had been a little under two moons. The high limestone hills gave us plenty of cover and protection and we rested for several days, breathing in the thin, salty air. On the third day, the mists and cloud descended and the bay below was swathed in swirls and wisps, the jagged lines of the surrounding hillsides a forbidding and murky green against a grey, opalescent sky. As our line of sight shrank, danger increased, and we moved out, riding north along the high paths and tracks.

I was, by now, well-armed and attired. I had a new wrap for my hair in a bright green cloth and I carried two swords and a carved, sharpened horn from the saola. Nhi carried the other horn, and both were long, black and deadly, with strips of leathery hide wrapped around the base for a hand grip. The rest of the hide was Cong's, and after it had dried as best it could in the dank forest air, she treated it with the brains from the animal, stamping and rubbing it in along with a liberal amount of her own piss, and then washing it well in one of the many streams. It was not a perfect job, but the pelt was soft and warm, and the dark, glimmering brown sat well around her shoulders and made her authority as General quite clear to those who might have looked on the slim, young woman with disbelief. It lent her an unusual, barbaric look that was not without its advantages and I wondered whether I should have taken it for myself.

We came, by and by, to the next series of villages on our route. Our scout had gone ahead, to check for soldiers and to announce our arrival and so when we cantered in to the main settlement of houses, the people were already gathered. There was, as usual, excitement and interest mixed with some caution and a hint of fear and I gave my usual, rousing speech and call to arms to the half-naked and cautious men and women. They whispered and debated, and I became aware that some of them were discussing a kind of trade.

'Will you make deals even while the future of your children is at risk?' I asked, impatiently. One of the loin-clothed men smiled awkwardly and came forwards.

'If you're as invincible as you say, you will accept our challenge before you take our best fighters.'

'That depends on what your challenge is,' I said. 'I do not have time to waste.'

'It won't be wasted,' he assured me. 'If you can do this favour we ask, many will follow you from here, and from the places further along the track.'

'What is the favour?' I repeated.

'Many times, a tiger has come. It takes children and even grown men and women. See here.' He pulled a woman close to him and lifted her withered arm, gathering her ragged tunic to one side at her waist to reveal a gouge in her side that had healed in thick, ruddy welts. Just above the scar, the underside of her unharmed breast showed, the soft colour of ginger root peel. 'The tiger tried to take her and it bit into her arm and body. She dragged herself free as people ran to help her with spears, and the tiger gave up, but it was seen by four others. Tell him, Tuyen.'

The woman pulled her tunic back around herself with her good arm. The other hung limp now the man had released it, the fingers completely still by her side. She didn't speak, just nodded her concordance.

'Why don't you hunt this creature down yourselves? There are many of you, and only one tiger.'

'Some tried, but they could not bring it down and one was killed,' he replied. 'Since then, we've all lived in fear. It's got a

222

real taste for human blood now and we daren't travel through the old paths to the fishing places in case it comes.'

'So, you are saying if I kill the tiger, you will all agree to fight with me?'

'Everyone who's fit enough,' he shrugged, giving a toothless smile.

'Then I will do it. The sisters Trung will kill your man-eating tiger.'

'*Hai Ba Trung!*' shouted Cong, suddenly, '*Hai Ba Trung!*'

'*Hai Ba Trung!*' our small army instinctively repeated. The villagers, half-naked, uneducated people, gaped, over-awed.

'Feed and shelter my warriors. My sister and I will return when the deed is done. General Cong, you're in charge here.'

We dismounted and walked into the palm forest. The shorter trees and undergrowth had been cleared so at the outset we walked easily and were quickly out of sight of the village, but we soon came to denser thickets, where the terrain was lumpy and bladed palms stood squat and at odd angles beneath their towering cousins. When I went to grasp a branch for assistance, Nhi smacked my hand away and pointed to the creamy eyes lurking in the moss. I had nearly put my hand down right on a horned pit-viper.

'I thought you were invincible,' she snorted, pushing past me and taking the lead. 'But no, still as dumb as always. Couldn't spot a turtle in a temple.'

'It was an oversight,' I said, indignantly. 'I have a lot on my mind.'

'Then stop thinking,' she said, 'or you'll get us killed. 'Do it like I do it - feel the forest. Breathe it, smell it, hear it. And, for the sake of the immortal creatures, look at it!'

I pressed my lips together. She was not entirely teasing, and she did have a point.

'You made me think about Nhat just then,' I said, as we clambered through rhododendrons and past climbing lianas.

'Why's that?'

'Just the turtle thing. He was so fascinated by one at the temple, that first time we met. Do you think Nhat has joined his brother?'

'What? No. I hope not. Thao gets very frustrated by Nhat and they don't agree on many things. Besides, Nhat is probably settling into the mountain village with his new wife's family.'

'I am glad he finally found a woman,' I said. 'Are you missing Thao very much?'

'No, not really,' she answered, without even a pause to consider. 'I know he'll take care of himself, and I'll see him again.'

I marvelled at her stoicism, then thought it might mean that she did not love him as she had loved Chien. Perhaps real love was only supposed to happen once. Poor Thao.

The shrubbery was giving way to spongy, swampy patches of land and we had to be more careful of our footing. We were moving into the mangrove, where the land and sea mingled in a brackish melting pot of plants and creatures. The buzzing of insects was louder and there were more noises from the undergrowth, along with the occasional splash of things moving in nearby water. Filtered, green light coloured the humid jungle, rendering life in shades of emerald and jade. Further in, the black, tangled roots of the mangrove trees looped and twisted above ground and we were clambering, leaping, contorting in order to keep moving. The thick mud sucked at our feet and the cloying, decayed air filled our noses. Sweat slicked my temples and upper lip and under my tunic I was damp, but my heart beat steadily and my breathing was not laboured. We had travelled a very long way, had run the greatest race of our lives, and our bodies were stronger for it.

'This way,' Nhi beckoned, and we ducked under a fallen and rotting trunk and through high, thick ferns to the very edge of a pool of water. The tidal swamp was wide and shallow, the surface pocked by mosquitoes and flies, and broken by rounded mangrove roots, curling through the salt-water like solid nets. We squatted on the muddy banking.

'I can hear him,' I whispered to Nhi.

She nodded, and began scooping up mud and wiping it onto her face and arms. I copied her. We wiped the foul-smelling brown paste onto our skin, our clothes and our hair, having discarded our head-wraps. The mud slicked our dark hair back from our faces. My chest thudded faster. I could hear padding, out there in the monstrous stands of myrtle and palm.

'Sit very still,' breathed Nhi, through her slimy, brown mask.

Like unfinished clay figurines, we watched the other bank, hearing the padding stop, then start, then stop. At times we thought he had gone, but then the gentle padding would again commence, and once we heard a whoosh and a growl and the startled flutter of birds. We had squatted for a long time, before a black-faced spoonbill emerged on the far bank. He came close to the water, splatting splayed feet into the wet mud, child-like and child-height. Then, carefully, he waded into the water and lowered his black bill into the shallows, sweeping it back and forth in a hunt for food. He closed on a tiny fish, the water cascading from his bill as he jerked it back to swallow the unfortunate meal. Then in he went with the paddle-shaped black probe again, stroking through the water for more. Behind the gentle swish of the water, came the soft, soft padding and I tensed. Two shining eyes, large and inhuman, loomed in the green. I wondered why the bird had not heard the pad, pad, pad of the pink-nosed predator. I could hear it, clear as day, thumping through my skull to the beat of my heart. We watched him come through the leaves behind the spoonbill until the whole of his orange and white body framed the snow-white bird. A step, another step, gently lifting and replacing each paw with exquisite delicacy while the spoonbill went on wading and swishing.

His mouth opened and he sprang, all long teeth and claws

225

flying, an unearthly growl vibrating from his chest, but in mid-flight upon the bird, the waters themselves seemed to launch up at him, green-ridged and equally toothed. Caught in the middle, the spoonbill flung itself aside then rose up and ran away, like Au Co, in a flash of white feathers. The tiger's killing jaws caught upon the scaly head and front legs of a crocodile. The tiger roared and instinctively pulled back, towards the mud, dragging the crocodile with him. I had stopped breathing. The tiger twisted over backwards onto the bank, with the writhing crocodile on top. They were out onto the land, but the crocodile was attempting to pull the tiger back into the water, into the murky pool where he could pin and drown the tiger. The tiger kept a desperate hold on the crocodile, tensing the whole of his magnificently striped body around the reptile and biting hard into the leathery neck. Searching and biting and tearing; I watched his jaws, working swiftly but mechanically upon his opponent. This crocodile was not prey, it was an accident. The pair were evenly matched – two top predators coming upon the same, hapless young bird and finding that their mealtime had just escalated into a fight to the death. The bright stripes of sun-coloured fur were blackening as the tiger wrestled in the mud, but the crocodile was beginning to capitulate. The tiger had bitten through something important. Bloody gashes, like ripped red silk, were opening up on the crocodile's neck and his swiping tail had slowed. Finally, the tiger threw the quivering body off, pinning it and biting a hefty piece from the throat, which he ate with an impassive determination. His top coat was dark and filthy, but his underbelly was starkly white- and black-striped, the fur matted with wet from the crocodile. He chewed, mauled the head again to be certain and then sat down heavily in the mud, ears flicked back showing soft pink insides, dirty shoulders shaking with exertion. We did not move a muscle.

He pushed himself up to standing after a while and tore himself huge pieces of meat from the carcass, ploughing through them with the sturdy gusto of one who has earned a good meal. It took a long time. Then he walked, defiantly, into the salt-water and rinsed his beautiful coat. He gave a great shake and the spray flew so far that flecks reached our muddied faces. Then he played in the pool for a while, splashing at darting fish and grooming his fur, before finally exiting and strolling past the dead body on the bank with barely a second glance.

As his newly-washed rump and curled tail swaggered into the trees, we got up and waded into the pool, making straight across to follow the sated tiger. In the deepest point, the water came to our waists and I felt the flick of tiny creatures and the hard tangle of roots. We moved slowly and quietly – not for fear of other predators in the tidal swamp, who would surely have fled at the recent commotion, but for fear that the tiger would hear us and turn around. On the far bank, we re-coated our lower bodies and our clothing with the stifling, rotten-egg-scented mud. The crocodile's mutilated face stared blankly past us. We slicked the foul dirt on and then continued on through the myrtle and the stunted palms, tracking the sunset-orange killer whose meaty breath clung to the air. We knew he would sleep soon, after such a big meal, and then we would strike. I was not surprised the last gang to hunt him down had failed. This tiger was pure predator, entirely honed into a murderous excellence. He had given us a lesson in his strength and ability. If a crocodile could not bring him down, then nothing else in the world could match him. Nothing but us, and then only if he were tired and sleeping and we were very fast and efficient.

We came close to him, stretched out on drier land, under a shaft of sunlight stabbing through the trees. The warm rays turned his fur to fire and made his teeth sparkle. He was fidgeting and preening, making himself comfortable, turning his great head one way then the other as if working his aching neck muscles. His fat, pink tongue lapped once or twice at his long-whiskered muzzle, satisfied and proud. Eventually he laid himself out, with a growl that could have been a yawn. We stood still and waited. Babblers and laughing thrushes twittered above us and the heat of the day intensified under the canopy. His chest rose and fell unevenly. Flies descended and his hard tail flicked, still conscious. A tree-shrew scampered past, pausing to sniff at our legs before suddenly racing away, little eyes wide. Butterflies came and went, bright colours catching the ethereal forest light. I saw a barbet, high up through layers of branches, livid green against muted leaves with a head like a target for crossbow practice, feathered in yellow, black, blue and red. The shadows moved slowly. Our tiger stilled, in his spot of golden sunshine. I counted the risings of his ribcage, one, two, over the distant, shrill call of macaques. Eight, nine, the slow, lifting chest rippling soft, lustrous fur, twenty, twenty-one, under the cacophony of leaf-birds, horn-bills, woodpeckers and magpies, all warbling and echoing in the humid edge of the mangrove. When I had reached one hundred, I said 'Now,' and Nhi nodded.

We walked into the tiger's space, carefully but without hesitation, and drew our short swords for the close-in kill. We were within striking distance, about to aim the first blows, when a languid eye opened, the black markings above it painted into a permanent, menacing frown. A large, black pupil swam in an ocean of liquid green beneath his furred lid, and on the surface of this verdant mirror we saw ourselves with swords raised, as if we had been painted there on his eyeball for all time.

'The Jade Tiger,' I whispered, caught in his unending gaze. Nhi gasped, then the tiger's white muzzle peeled back and his mouth opened into a furious chasm of killing teeth. I pierced his heart with my sword and Nhi thrust in her own blade. The tiger roared and howled and we pulled back our swords and leapt clear as he sprang up on his feet, the blood spilling onto the ground beneath him. He pounced at us and I aimed a slashing blow to his throat, slicing as his heavy paws felled me. Claws closed in on my upper arm, punching holes into the flesh and making me scream as I fought to get out from under the suffocation of his body. Nhi stuck him again and as he flinched, I squirmed free, the gnash of his teeth skimming my ear and the side of my head and leaving a raw wound. As I rolled away, he launched himself at Nhi, grazing her side and sinking teeth into her shoulder, but she kept on with her sword, stabbing him and darting from him. He roared again, but no longer as loud. The life was draining from him into the forest floor and his pain must have overtaken his fury. He slumped, back end first, then front legs buckling and sat there in his spot of sunshine, licking weakly at his muzzle and looking past us as if we were incidental to his suffering.

Nhi raised her sword again, but I waved it down.

'Just let him die now,' I said. 'He will not let you end it quickly, so we must wait.' She nodded. The forest, though stuffed with the shrieks and calls of the ten thousand things, sounded eerily muted now the roaring had stopped.

'I'd forgotten about him,' said Nhi.

'Mother only said it once, and you were very small,' I replied.

We stood and waited for him to die and he punished us by taking a long time to do it. The light was fading and our bodies were exhausted from the long day of stillness and the sudden burst of fighting. I was not sure which was the most tiring and I thought of our mother's oft-repeated insistence that the great leader practices stillness before movement, though I was not sure whether she had ever meant it quite so literally. Perhaps she had - she knew about the Jade Tiger, after all. Where was she now? Was she with the Zhuang or had she returned to Me Linh? Was she already besieging Lien Lau with her own forces? Or was she captured? Executed? I looked at the dying tiger and thought, I have to be faster and stronger. I have to get to Lien Lau with my army. They said I must kill the tiger first and then I would gain support - well I have done it and now I will make sure everyone knows it.

When he had laid down and stopped breathing, we went

to him and made sure he was really dead. Then we worked very hard to skin the animal neatly, keeping the face as intact as possible. Nhi was better at the kill and the butchery, but I was better at skinning, and it had never been more important than now. I cleaned it up, scraping off strands of sinew and levelling my blade so it would not tear through. Nhi hacked a good, straight branch from a tree and gathered lengths of vine to tie the tiger's legs together. We passed the branch between the legs and tested the weight, hoisting the skinned body up. The branch would hold, and we could just about take the weight. I draped the skin over the long branch and we lifted our kill up, tented in a shroud of his own skin, myself at the front and Nhi at the back, with the branch ends balanced on our shoulders. Nhi carried it on her unharmed shoulder, the other bandaged over with moss and leaves and bound with vines because the blood would not stop coming. I had soaked up the blood from my head wound with handfuls of moss, and it stung like fire but I left it open to the air. It was not so deep, and the punctures on my upper arms ached more, though they had clotted.

If it was hard making our way through the mangrove the first time, it was near impossible whilst hefting the weight of a dead, man-eating tiger. We had to walk towards the west, into easier terrain, then head south to the village, and it was full dark when we returned. We paused as we came in sight of the houses and regained our breath and composure. We were blood-covered and filthy, stinking of bad eggs and sweat and we were pained, aching and breathless too, barely capable of putting one foot in front of the other any longer. We rested until we could at least breathe easily, then I put the tiger skin on, the head hooked over my own and the hide cloaking my back and shoulders. We hoisted the tiger again and walked into the village.

'*Hai Ba Trung,*' gasped Cong, who was sitting in the open tending a fire with several others. She had probably not expected to see us for several more days. '*Hai Ba Trung, Hai Ba Trung!*'

There was a corresponding rattle and stamp of people in their houses, opening rickety doors and coming down front steps with lit torches. Our followers streamed from a rough camp in the trees and stared at me and Nhi, standing with the tiger on the branch between us. The people of the village gazed in slack fear at our muscle-bunched, blood-slathered bodies and at the striped tiger skin over my shoulders. Cong's eyes gleamed with satisfaction and pride. '*Hai Ba Trung*' she kept barking, in her toneless salute. Two Sisters Trung. And all the village joined her.

17

Riding north, they came to us in their hundreds. Phung Thi Chinh joined us near the Cuu Chan Commandery's base with a force of her own and she became one of Trac's senior Generals. We had more women than men, and the sight of that alone must have bewildered the fleeing Han. When we ousted their Cuu Chan division, the Han Colonels staggered at the sight of Trac, swathed in her tiger cloak, the long teeth still attached and framing her high forehead.

One of them wailed, 'Xi Wang Mu!' and the cry went up among their lines, 'Xi Wang Mu!' Queen Mother of the West. The heart went out of any pathetic resistance they might have attempted and they scattered. Half of them were probably devoted to the Kunlun Mountain goddess whose animal spirit was the tiger and some even fell to their knees in front of our horses, making it a lot easier to kill them. The Han soldiers who escaped north carried the terrifying tale – Xi Wang Mu has arisen here in the country of Giao Chi and she is angry with us! We laughed about it, round the fires in the night. Through the Lac people, stories spread just as quickly, but their tales were of the Two Sisters Trung and the Jade Tiger.

Our numbers swelled daily and when we crossed into the Commandery of Giao Chi, we heard the drums that were beating day and night. Chinh had told us, when she had met us in Cuu Chan, that the drum wave had carried right across the Commandery to the East Sea, and up into the mountains too, but hearing it was different than being told of it. From all directions, the rhythm pulsed and, depending on the wind strength and direction, sometimes we could hear one, sometimes several and occasionally a whole percussive union. I didn't know the language of the beat, but there were still just enough people who did and the code was deciphered and passed on. We made our way up the coast with our army under Trac's relentless direction. We were still quite far south of Hai Phong when Le Chan's unit joined us.

I say her unit but, of course, it wasn't that at first. Le Chan had raised and trained her own army, in the water caves of Ha Long Bay, and she had her own hierarchy of Generals and Captains. In the years since I'd seen her last, she'd broadened to become even more like her late mother. Her face had taken on the worn, leathery appearance of one who has had to live roughly and on her wits. She looked me up and down appraisingly before she submitted herself in a bow. I reined in a sentimental reaction to the vestiges of Chien that shone through her features but I still greeted her warmly enough. She was my sister, of a kind.

'You've been very successful in Cuu Chan,' she acknowledged. 'I have told Trac that my army will join you for the assault on Lien Lau.'

'I'm very pleased to hear it,' I said.

'I hear you are now married into the Khuc Duong family. Thao, isn't it?'

'Yes, though I haven't seen him since we left Lien Lau. I think he's with my mother, but I can't be sure.'

'We've heard that your Lady Mother is moving south. I've told Trac I can send messengers from my own ranks - they know how to travel without being seen.'

'I'll discuss it with my sister. Thank you.'

'Sometimes I cannot believe this war is finally happening,' she said. 'I have waited so long for it. How have you done this, Nhi? How have you raised so many to your call, when they would not come for all that happened at Hai Phong?' Her tone was hurt, softly accusing.

'It is heaven's choice. Trac and I followed the Way and it led us here.' I looked at her, helplessly, and she nodded.

'That is one way to put it. We all saw, at Hai Phong, that you were special.'

I couldn't find words to answer that. It was a kindly

233

compliment and one which I could not dispute – Trac and I were leading an army and it was useful if people thought we were, in some way, special or different. Yet, as far as I could see, I was no different than Chan or Chinh or any of the other strong women leading our divisions. Trac, yes, was a force to be reckoned with. Since she had put on the tiger skin, she had become hard and abrasive. Her natural intellect cowed everyone under her command and General Cong had unwittingly set a highly deferential tone. They all called her 'Trung Nu Vuong,' – Queen Trung – and they used the same title on me sometimes, but I brushed it aside. I did not want to be Trung Nu Vuong. I was not a queen – how could I be when I was second daughter? I didn't have any need of a title, but Trac had said that I should be her second-in-command of the army, so the Generals had started calling me Commander.

Le Chan settled in with us, and we got on, but we were not as comfortable with each other as I was with Phung Thi Chinh. Chinh was lively and eager, not embittered like Chan, and we trained together without the awkwardness of uncertain etiquette. Chinh wasn't afraid to sweep my feet from under me if I made a stupid error and I didn't have to concern myself with whether she felt condescended to as I taught her some technique or other. We both shared the same desire to perfect our martial skills and she, I'm sure, didn't care that I was younger. Both of us took an interest in teaching General Cong, whose confidence had grown considerably throughout our long journey. She needed more intense instruction if she was to hold her own against the formidable Generals and factions now being created within our army. Chinh and Chan were just the beginning; soon Mother would join us, and with her, Zhuang rebel leaders from the north. Prefect Vien would presumably come to us, along with Thao's father and we already had Prefects from both Nhat Nam and Cuu Chan, tussling to establish their place in our army. I didn't want Cong pushed to one side. Her loyalty and fervour were invaluable and, more importantly, entirely genuine. The army was growing very quickly, and women like Cong provided our eyes and ears. Trac and I both knew that the key to our assault on the Han was discipline. Without it, the Middle Kingdom administration would slice through our revolt like a knife.

However, the closer we came to Lien Lau, the easier the challenge appeared. We had fought at several towns, unseating detachments of Han sent to forestall our progress, but we outnumbered them easily. Governor Dinh had underestimated us - either that, or he just did not have the necessary resources to rebuff us. Trac believed he would assemble in greater numbers at Lien Lau, and that we would have the true fight there. I agreed. It was imperative that we establish Mother's location and situation before we came closer to the capital city.

As we moved our army north-west into the interior, south of the Red River, Le Chan's trusted messengers returned. They had found Mother's faction north-west of Me Linh, where it was circling round, trying to group with us. Mother had previously sent horsemen to get word to us, but these people must have been intercepted. The routes around the Red River Delta were in chaos - crammed with assembling Han units and with Lac men and women trying to get to our army. The soldiers were detaining as many Lac as their prisons would hold, but summary executions were now occurring in response to the overcrowded jails. As riots broke out on the streets, Governor Dinh was panicking, and cracking down hard. Mother sent a message with Chan's men once she had learned of our numbers and position. She asked us to close on Lien Lau in three days and she would do the same. We would join in a crescent around the south west of the capital and push Governor Dinh's resistance against the river.

'Will he cross the river into Tay Vu before we get there?' Trac asked. 'It will ruin our offensive, and he still has plenty of time to decamp to the north. What do you think, Nhi?'

'I don't believe he'll move his defences,' I said. 'He won't want to lose Lien Lau. His pride and arrogance will keep him there. Mother is right. We should put all our force to the south-west of Lien Lau, rather than wasting her division on the north banks of the river.'

'Can we keep ourselves hidden on the approach?'

'I don't see why not – we have three days, so we can take the lesser routes. Harder to travel, but more inconspicuous.'

'Good, we will do that. The less that To Dinh knows of our size and strength, the better.'

I agreed, and so did our Generals. Governor Dinh was notoriously supercilious and we imagined he would underestimate our threat. There were regiments and even whole divisions under his administrative office that he could call forth, yet he had not done so. Besides the three Commanderies we had already swept through, he governed a further six, to the north and over on the island in the East Sea. Granted, some of these Commanderies were already defending themselves against the uprisings led by Mother and the Zhuang – perhaps Governor Dinh did not want to leave them unprotected. It made me smile, to think that we had effected such a coup. I peered into the grand, unfolding dream and saw the myriad, graceful forms of our warriors, each swinging blade, each twisting fighter, each thrown and bloodied enemy, layering together to build our victory. My humility grew. Trac's did not. I cannot afford to be humble, her black eyes said, for I am Trung Nu Vuong. Only in the dark spaces and unseen places did I glimpse my sister, hiding wide-eyed behind the Queen, clutching a wooden doll.

We closed on Lien Lau, after the agreed three days. Our army left a wake of flattened vegetation and excited children and grumbling old people coerced into handing over food for our troops. We were Queen and Commander, riding at the front, Cong, Chinh, Chan and twenty further Generals following with their vast divisions. On the plains over which Trac and I had sprinted, not three moons before, we joined with our northern ranks. There, under the yellow sun by the Red River, we met with Mother. Our horses drew up to one another and Mother bowed her head. 'Trung Nu Vuong,' she said. Trac and I dismounted and bowed. 'Lady Mother,' we replied. She took us each by the shoulders, grasping hard and feeling down our arms, as if she could detect the fractures to our souls by this rough interrogation.

'How well you have done!' she whispered. 'They are telling the stories of *Hai Ba Trung* as far away as Thuong Ngo. You have made my job easy. And is this him?' She went to Trac's horse and ran a hand over the fiery pelt draped across its rear. Her eyes half closed as she stroked the fur of the Jade Tiger, then she opened them as if brought up by sudden thoughts, and strode back to us. 'Come, you must meet your newest Generals, and Nhi, your husband waits for you.'

I looked beyond her, through blurred eyes, to where Thao straddled his mount. He threw himself down, permitted by Mother's words to approach. She moved past me and I longed for one homesick moment to feel her loving hands on me again, then Thao was before me. I refocused on his rounded face, his eyes drawn tight and anxious into dark lines against the sun. He opened his lips to speak then withdrew the words that hovered in his throat, swallowing them back in a short cough. His tunic had loosened and a bead of sweat ran over his pronounced collarbone and down towards the hidden ridges of his muscled stomach.

'I have thought of you every day,' I said. The slits of his eyes burned into me and I saw the itch of his arms, wanting to hold me. We bowed to each other.

'I've missed you,' he grunted. 'It was unbearable.'

'I'm here now,' I comforted, amused by the depth of his relief. Perhaps if I did not have flashes of foresight, I would have felt the same desperate tension at his absence. But three moons is not a long time to wait, especially when accompanied by a sister who has no such joy to look forward to.

We walked behind Mother and Trac, as Mother made the necessary introductions. The Zhuang wore their hair short and their skin tattooed. Some of our own people looked the same, aping the style Sach had set before his death, but most still wore their hair in buns. It was easy enough to distinguish the separate groupings but I had to concentrate on remembering names and numbers. I had no doubt that Trac would forget half of them within minutes. I was always better with people. Out of the haze of new faces, finally we came to some we knew well.

'*Hai Ba Trung!*' a pair of voices exclaimed, and exposing their blackened teeth in sharp, strained grins, Khanh and Kim Cuc stood before us.

'My sisters,' Trac acknowledged, her guard lowering, permitting a genuine smile to reach her lips. 'I am very glad you are here.'

'Of course we would be here. He was our brother,' said Khanh. 'We were very sorry for you.'

'Yes, of course,' Trac recoiled. I remembered that Khanh had always been abrasive. Whether she intended it or not, I wasn't sure, but my body tightened instinctively. She had reminded my sister of her grief and wrong-footed her greeting in one ill-considered stroke. Trac's eyelids lowered and her long face became serpentine. Trung Nu Vuong. She moved on. I ignored Khanh and spoke to Kim Cuc.

'We've heard such stories, it's been a medicine to us all,' she confided. 'When we heard your army was growing, we were so proud and we did the best we could to bring people to your cause. To our cause.'

'And we're very grateful,' I said, reflecting her warmth. 'Sach is terribly missed, but his sacrifice will rebuild our country. I'm happy to see you, Kim Cuc, I truly am.'

'Khanh and I are leading a division together,' she explained. 'We have about a thousand people, from Chu Dien province.'

'Then we'll see each other when the Generals convene.' I left her and caught up with the others. I thought, if only Kim Cuc was the elder sister and I didn't have to deal with Khanh! The woman troubled me, and though my evidence was scant, I trusted my gut. I would set Chinh and Cong to keep an eye on her.

★★★★★

In the afternoon, three Han officials cantered across the broad plain, through the whispering savannah grasses that separated our army from the boundary of Lien Lau. Their faces were sternly set, but the high-pitched voice that spoke for them all betrayed their nerves.

'Governor Dinh demands that you surrender yourselves to the mercy of the Emperor,' he squeaked, looking up at Trac. He had not only our entire army to fear, a short distance away, but the disturbing vision of my sister on an elephant. One of the Nhat Nam prefects had gone to some lengths to acquire the beasts, thinking to strike yet more terror into the hearts of the Middle Kingdom men, who were not so familiar with the large mammals as we were. General Chinh had fallen about laughing earlier, when Trac hoisted herself up, waving away the rebuke of General Cong's disapproving glare. Mother, standing some way off, had spared an amused smile, before returning to the work of assembling our front line. We had just spoken with the Generals and agreed to attack immediately the army was arranged and ready. The sensible people were resting, gathering strength for the short, fast march on Lien Lau and the heavy fighting that would surely follow. Trac was teetering in her padded silk seat, high in the air.

'Careful you don't fall off,' I called, making Chinh howl. Trac had glowered down at us both while loyal Cong stood by, tightening the seat straps.

Now she glowered at the Han men who had come to us, not with pleas or apologies but with a message of defiance.

'Stop now, disband and the Governor may be light-handed with your punishment,' the shaking man was saying. He glanced uncertainly at his two companions, who remained pale and silent on their horses. I studied the one furthest left from me. He was familiar... then I had it - he was the Senior Administrator. The man who had allowed To Dinh to make a travesty of the trial. Had Trac recognised him too? She must have done - she knew him better than I did, having met with him on several diplomatic occasions. My stomach twisted a little. This man must have been present when Sach was killed. He was responsible for it, almost as much as Dinh himself.

'My punishment?' She laughed. 'That, you have already... *administered*. Was it quick, or slow, when my husband's head was hacked off?'

At last, the man on the left looked directly up at her, knowing himself addressed, but he didn't speak and his eyes were full of sad resignation. His down-turned mouth and his defeated hands, slack on the reins, spoke a hundred words.

'Trac,' I broke in, understanding, 'this is a stall for time. Dinh is escaping.'

'Then let us send our friends swiftly on their way, with a message Dinh will understand.' She stared down at me and I responded immediately. I spurred my horse to the administrator's side and whistled my sword through his throat as the other two men twisted hard on their reins and jerked their horses away. Blood gushed from the rent and his twitching face fell backwards in the parody of a guffaw. I sliced a second time and removed his head clean off. It fell, bouncing, into the spiky grasses where it rolled to an ignominious stop. I caught the body before it fell sideways and threw the reins over it, securing it as best I could. Then I dragged the silk sash from my own waist and tied the ankle tightly to the stirrup. The horse, strutting and anxious from the deathly odour, took just a light tap to goad him into a gallop towards his departing friends.

Behind us, the army was on its feet. Mother was in the saddle and from this perspective, I could discern the three vast sections of our attacking force. Four people were leading the second elephant towards us and I groaned. Had I not shown that I was better off closer to the ground? I looked up at Trac.

'Well done,' she said, tonelessly. 'Now get on that elephant.'

'You owe me a new sash,' I answered, retying the flaps of my long tunic, but I obeyed. When we were in the throng, then I would dismount and she would not stop me. I had a river of blood to let in her name.

★★★★★

We rode over the plain on our lumbering elephants and I swallowed my slight concern that I might indeed fall off, as Nhi had so wittily cautioned. Ahead, in Lien Lau, the remaining populace panicked. They hid in houses - or, if they were Han, or related to Han, they tried to flee across the river. Drowning swimmers dragged already full boats to the riverbed, trying to cram themselves in. Those who had shed clothes, weapons and possessions managed to fight the current and some of them reached the far bank, but many were pulled under by clutching hands of other drowning folk. The Han army issued forth from the main entrance to the town and met us in a defensive line. We outnumbered them, but they were still a formidable opposition. Or they would have been, with some inspired leadership. They seemed to be having difficulty coordinating their activities and as we clashed into their ranks, I saw some of the Han Generals looking bemused, as if impossible events were unfolding and they could not be expected to respond. Others fought desperately and with skill but their army had no heart. Their Governor had been on the first boat over the river, fleeing to safety and leaving his deputy to face our wrath. I hoped he had seen the headless body returning, dragged raw and bloody across hard dirt by its

241

silk-strapped ankle, leaving it's sorry head to be trampled by Lac warriors.

My elephant crashed through mounted cavalry and I swung my long sword at the lower heads of the Han. This, I thought, is how it should be: them lower than I. But I did not feel anything. As I trampled screaming foot soldiers and slashed at the spinal cords of men on horseback, I was a void. Logic and reason assaulted me. You have fought all this way back to Lien Lau, but you are chasing a ghost. The country will mend, but you will not. My brain tried to solve this intellectual puzzle while my body went about the business of killing.

Nhi was to my right. She was screaming and grunting with the effort of the fight and men fell away in torn heaps from her charge. She had abandoned the elephant, and the beast had been commandeered by one of Cong's Captains, who was using it to good effect, stemming the number of Han soldiers that could reach Nhi so that they came as a steady stream and not a torrent. The Han were attacking our mid-section most vigorously, presumably because they believed that the loss of *Hai Ba Trung* would be a killing blow to our army. The fight was now predominantly on foot, with most of the Han cavalry unseated. On the flanks, Le Chan and my mother were driving deep into the Han weak points, so that although we were being pressed hard, our army was, in fact, taking the advantage. We were encircling them, and driving them to the death points of our finest fighters. From the elephant, I could see it all, and the Han could see me. They looked at me with dismay and revulsion and I gazed at them with no emotion at all - just the pure and unequivocal knowledge that they all would die.

We pushed against them, their numbers depleting, and I watched all my foot soldiers slashing and stabbing, throwing and snapping. Necks broke and arms wrenched. Blood pooled on the dry ground. The throng looked chaotic, but there was a kind of order, as warriors sought each other out, Middle Kingdom honour pitting itself against Lac Viet fury. The clangour rose to deafening levels, but still I could hear the battle cries that Nhi made, as if she were the thread that tied me to the fight. I saw her move through the patterns of our youth – the leg placed here, the arm following though, the shoulder dropping, the slight twist that brings the opponent flying off balance and onto his back with a thud. Her repertoire was extensive and she went seamlessly from forms I knew into forms I did not, wreaking havoc upon men's bodies with the subtlest invasions, locking joints and breaking bones and finishing them with the short sword, dripping scarlet, that she passed effortlessly from hand to hand. Her tied tunic had fallen open and the long pieces of silk shimmered with wet blood, and obscured her lithe body from the thrusting points of Han blades.

So it went on. I pushed the elephant forwards every so often and our net drew tighter around the Han, until isolated Companies were surrounded by mocking Lac warriors. From within Lien Lau, a drum boomed to a rhythm that I recognised as a victory salute. Parts of our army were already in the town, securing our success. The living Han cowered and some begged for mercy, which they did not receive. Others fell on their swords, grimly determined to retrieve some dignity from the calamitous situation. Nhi bent double with her hands on her knees and breathed deeply. Cong started her *Hai Ba Trung* chant. Thao ran towards us from his own Division to find Nhi. I remember it like that – a series of isolated mental pictures, all frozen into stillness, lacquered onto my memory, as if my own life were more fable than reality.

I find it hard to recall the sequence of events after the battle. The army entered Lien Lau. I think there were some attempts at outrages – Lac wives of Han soldiers threatened with death and worse; that kind of thing – but I ordered all such summary trials to be stopped and widows and their children to be set free. Such actions would have been unnecessary and without honour. I was in the Justice Hall, where last I had stood with Sach, hearing reports on losses and casualties from my Generals. There was a flicker of burning relief in the centre of my chest that the important people, the ones I cared for, were still alive, and that my best Generals and fighters had scraped through also. My mother came to me as soon as she could and stood close, advising and organising and occasionally whispering prompts to me. I was twenty two years in the world – I needed her guidance, even if I had become Trung Nu Vuong. Nhi stayed close also and although I could not tell them so, I was glad that they did.

It comes to me now that Nhi had survived her grief over Chien by burying it deep within, where it somehow became a source of strength to her. Perhaps I was weaker or maybe my afflictions were too many – my father, all the babies and then Sach. I could not encompass the scale of the pain within myself. It ripped me in two, and so I was one person standing behind another. I was a façade, an edifice. I was the tiger and I was the reflection in its eye. Only Nhi and my mother could have told you which was real. I no longer knew.

18

We took Lien Lau. Then we crossed the river and drove the Han further north. There was no catching up with Governor Dinh. That self-righteous coward had cut his hair short and run away. Some said he'd cut away his top knot to show to the Emperor that he accepted blame for the loss of Giao Chi. Only criminals and barbarians had their hair shorn in the Middle Kingdom. Others said he did it to look like a Zhuang man, so he could pass unmolested through their territory. We didn't care. As I had learned to live with Vo Xuan's escape from my revenge, so Trac would learn to live with the escape of To Dinh. He'd been disgraced and in some ways, that was better than killing him. His people were an intolerant brood. The Middle Kingdom would never forgive or forget his incompetence. The important thing was that we had retaken almost all the old Nam Viet territory.

There was only one place we wanted to be when all the fighting died down, and that was back home, in Me Linh. The Kings of Van Lang had always ruled from Me Linh. It was sacred ground. We came home in the middle of the rains, marching south after forcing the Han back as far as we dared. I ordered Le Chan to take her Division to Hai Phong. They would watch the coast from there to Ha Long Bay and mobilise if the Han showed signs of a coastal attack. The Zhuang wing had stayed in the north, to defend their new borders. I sent the southern Generals back to the old Nhat Nam and Cuu Chan regions and they resumed the duties they had carried out as Prefects, the only difference being that they were answerable now to Trung Nu Vuong, instead of to a Han Governor. The men and women in their ranks returned to their villages and towns. In our delta, Chinh and Cong settled their Divisions in and near Me Linh, along with Mother's own Division. Khanh and Kim Cuc released most of their ranks back to the rice paddies of Chu Dien, but they themselves stayed in Me Linh with a small force of guards. Me Linh had a new royal family and a moderate sized army. The latter was soon put to work building the necessary housing along with a new home for myself, Trac and our extended family. The town was bustling and happy, and war had ended in time to reap the first bountiful crop of rice. A golden sun lit the rain that cleansed our bloodied land and the nights were deep and peaceful.

'How does it feel, to finally live together properly?' Thao asked me. He had settled the Prefecture of Khuc Duong on a cousin, now that both his parents were dead – his father had passed on during the time I was away.

I kissed him on the lips and he wound his fingers through my hair, long and loose in the darkness. His breath tasted of cinnamon and his hard torso beneath mine was warm, damp with sweat. I laid my face back down on the smooth swell of his chest. Thao wrapped his tree-trunk arms around me.

'When we're alone, I can be happy,' I said.

'She should find another man. Until she does, you will feel this burden.'

'Then I'll always feel it. But I don't mind.'

'What if I mind?'

'Trac is removing all the taxes,' I said, changing the subject. 'Tomorrow we have to decide on the wording of the declaration.'

'They must understand that tribute is still expected.' He meant the Lac Lords – the noble families, the Prefects and leaders. The abolition of taxes was crucial. Where the Han had said, you must pay for the privilege of lordly status, we would say, you are Lac Lords by birthright and cannot be taxed upon it. But we must also ensure that they remembered who was responsible for restoring their honour. The Lac Lords had once supported the Hung Kings, long before the Han, before Trieu Da and Thuc Pan. Now they must support Trung Nu Vuong.

'Trac will make her meaning clear.'

'What if that is not enough? The people of Nam Viet have

short memories. Half the army has returned to the fields. We have no real control over Cuu Chan and Nhat Nam. They may not send anything. Even here, the Red River families are already looking to their own interests.'

'Then we have to remind them that without *Hai Ba Trung*, they would have no interests independently held from the Han. How can they be so ungrateful? We have just fought a war for them!' I shifted, angrily.

'Ouch, be careful,' Thao gasped, lifting my hips and repositioning the delicate part of himself that I had just accidentally squashed.

'Now, see what you have done. I was happy and then you brought all these worries to mind.' I kissed him again, hard this time, and with clear intention.

'There is no satisfying you,' he laughed. 'Warfare has made you a demanding woman.'

'I don't know what you mean.' Although I did know. Our love-making had never been as feral as it was the night following Lien Lau, but it was now always uncompromising, committed with a sense of endurance and passion that bordered on violence. I had almost forgotten what it was like before, when first we were married and all his advances were tentative, as if he was scared he would hurt me. Now we engulfed and devoured each other, falling asleep afterwards in a suffocation of limbs that was unbearable in the monsoon humidity but from which neither one of us ever removed ourselves.

In the morning, I went to Trac. She barely slept any more – only four, maybe five of the blackest hours. She'd lost weight and it showed on her face, hollow cheeks disturbing the oval. She wrapped herself in the best silks and hung jade from her ears and glass beads at her throat and disguised herself as Queen.

'This is what we should say,' she began, without preamble, as if we were continuing yesterday's conversation, '"We, Trung Nu Vuong, end all tribute to the court of the imposter Emperor. He carries not the mandate of heaven and we do not recognise his authority. Trung Nu Vuong rule with the guidance of the spirits of our land and with the love and support of the people. The Middle Kingdom see this ancient bond of the Lac to their Hung sovereigns and run with fear."'

I told her, I'm not a Queen, you alone are the Queen. She pretended not to hear. I sighed. 'The rest of it is good, it should make our position clear.'

'You think so? Not too vague? Some of our Lords are touched by stupidity.'

'They'll all understand that you expect tribute to be paid. Whether they do it or not is another matter, but you can't make it any clearer. They must show their support or face consequences.'

'And you, as my second, what consequences do you propose?'

'That depends on what kind of Queen you want to be.'

'The kind that holds on to her land.'

'In that case, tread with care. Show your strength through benevolent behaviour and then, if they still hold back what should be yours, banish them. Send them north.'

'To add bodies to the northern armies?'

'Men and women like that will never fight for us anyway, and they will be an impedance to the Middle Kingdom, these fools who are inconstant and disloyal by nature.'

'I'm not changing the wording,' she said, snapping back to my earlier discomfort. 'It is safer if you are regarded as requiring tribute also.'

'You mean, if you die, I take your place.'

'Something like that.' She turned her attention to people approaching us. Her hair was wrapped in silk, the deep green of the Ha Long waters under mist. At the back, a tendril of black kinked loose against her neck, a thin, drowning wave of youth and freedom.

She gave the orders for the abolition message to be spread

wide, around the old Commanderies of Giao Chi, Cuu Chan and Nhat Nam. It would go by mouth. The Han had taken with them their inks and their strips of bamboo, and what supplies and archives remained would sit untouched or be destroyed. At Lien Lau, there was a room full of missives that would never be sent. Han families, waiting for news; unless their sons and husbands had escaped the battlefields, they would never hear it. At Me Linh, all official communication with the Middle Kingdom was over. The five mountain passes that led north were closed and Le Chan watched the sea. The seed of our independence needed protection if it was to grow. Khanh disagreed. Khanh, as always, with something unhelpful to say. After the adjustment of taxes, which she had murmured and concerned herself about, still she went on, with the little pokes and digs that unsettled our governance. I'd had her watched, but nothing had come to light. She was diligent, dutiful and composed, even in her private hours. There were no secret alliances, no empire-building behaviours - certainly no hint of malicious intent towards Trac, but in our meetings and in our courts I felt her presence burn the back of my neck. Before she even spoke, I was ready to catch her words and probe their rainbow patterns in my net. There was always *something*. She scattered grains of doubt on the floor and let them adhere to the soles of the unwary, where they would be picked off and examined later, their origin forgotten.

'Trung Nu Vuong is correct, of course,' Khanh said, later in that first year of Trac's reign, 'the mountain passes should stay closed, even if the traders complain and struggle. If we have to do without the exchange of goods, the passage of silks and all those things, then we must accept it, because it is the only way to keep our country safe. Isn't it?'

Isn't it. Just two words and Ton Vien, who I had not trusted since his uncanny ability to remain alive and far from danger during the war, was looking sideways at nothing, with a question in his eyebrows. Isn't it, and Kim Cuc was nodding at the surface meaning, but with a frown, as if someone else was rocking her head and she didn't know quite why. Chinh, alert to the double-meaning in all Khanh's interjections, stared directly at her and I replied that yes, it was the only way to keep us all safe. Some people will have to go without the latest designs and ornaments for a while, I said, but in exchange, their lives will be their own and their children will grow up free.

'Now I understand you,' whispered Thao afterwards, as Khanh filed demurely past us with a vacant countenance. 'I thought before that you were being too sensitive, too protective of Trac.'

'And now?'

'She has an agenda, doesn't she?'

'Yes, but what is it?' I hissed, careful not to let Kim Cuc overhear us. 'Cong reports that she is entirely well-behaved, except for this constant, quiet undermining.'

'She is waiting for your sister to fail. She is taking the ground from under her, one small stone at a time.'

'But why?'

'Because she wants it for herself.'

'No, not quiet Khanh. She's a follower, not a leader.'

'Are you sure? I think she is just waiting, and you have misread her patience for contentment.'

We both looked, my husband and I, at the receding figure of Trac's own sister by marriage. She held herself very upright and her arms swung by her swaying hips. I watched the placement of her feet and the set of her shoulders. She had nowhere to go that day, but there was a purpose in her stride and a peculiar urgency of physical attitude. That was what gave her away. I grazed my fingertips against the back of Thao's scarred hand, secretly, in thanks. I had chosen well, when I married him.

★★★★★

What can you do though, about a foe who sits quietly, making comments that others believe are completely innocent?

250

I tried to talk to Trac, but she flinched from discussion of Khanh, as if questioning her loyalty was some kind of slight on Sach.

'She is like him, you know. She asks the questions he would have asked.'

'That's not it,' I said, shaking my head. 'She puts ideas into people's minds. She's subversive. Thao sees it, and Chinh. They both agree.'

'I know she is not easy to like, but she tries hard. If she offends me, I will remove her from our court, but I cannot punish her just for speaking her mind.'

'Just, be wary of her. That's all I'm saying. Don't let her needle you.'

What Thao had suddenly seen so easily in that moment of clarity, Trac could not, and it was hard, then, to put into words exactly what Khanh had done wrong. When forced to explain it, I became confounded. Mother said, what difference does it make anyway? She can't unseat either of you. You're too powerful now.

Mother ran Me Linh with an iron grip. There was not a lord in the locality who had not given tribute to Trung Nu Vuong and she set the etiquette and disciplined those who did not bend to it. Even Chinh was once turned away from a gathering when her approach to Trac was what Mother considered 'ungracious.' From Mother's perspective, we were untouchable. There was not a lord in the land to rival our claim to power. We even held the sacred seat, the old land of the Hung Kings. Me Linh, once the power base of the ancient Lac, was now the modern heartland of the new country and if some of the families downriver in Lien Lau and across the rest of the Tay Vu region had not yet been forthcoming with tribute, then neither were they prepared to force the issue into a challenge. None of them wanted to lead, none of them particularly objected to Trac's governance. What they did object to was the closing of our northern borders.

In Nam Viet, we had forests, full of wildlife and vegetation. We had grassy plains on which the water buffalo and the elephants roamed. We had the mangroves, all down the east coast, trapping and growing our fish. We had ivory, rhinoceros horn, south sea pearls and fire-lit amber, fragrant wood, perfumes, coral and shell, exotic feathers and more bamboo and rattan than we could ever use. More than that, we had rice. Rice in the hills, rice on the flats. Rice where the terraces had been built, rice in the paddies that Han legions had dug. Rice, growing in two crops every year, more rice than we could eat. We shouldn't have had to go to the Han for anything. What more could the Middle Kingdom give us? On the contrary, we had been giving them the goods they desired for generations - our people died on horseback, for heaven's sake, trying to get fresh oranges all the way to the far distant Han court before they rotted, so demanding was the Emperor of our bounty! But people are never satisfied with what they have. They want more, they want different. More and different, they think, is better. Greed opens doorways that were better left closed.

…Open the northern borders! Why doesn't she open the northern borders? Is she afraid? She thinks the Han will come again and defeat her. Maybe they will. Maybe that is better? The Han traded with us, after all. My shop has not been restocked with silks since before they left… My Han husband ran away to the north and I want him to return… Are we really better without them? They weren't monsters, were they? Tich Quang, now he knew how to rule. If only To Dinh had never come. But the others weren't so bad … Opening schools, teaching philosophy, we didn't really mind that, did we? And what if they come back, really angry, and take their revenge? Will she stop them again? She's a woman after all. I know, our women have always been stronger than Han women, but even so… Isn't a woman's place under her husband? Didn't Confucius say…?

Whispers in the wind, malevolent seeds in the dark earth. The legacy of Lords looking to their own, selfish interests. The legacy of cowards. Those seeds have grown, they have blossomed and their fruit is here on the riverbank. Trac's blood in the grass.

Chinh's baby dead at the breast. Me, youngest daughter Nhi, forever parted from my son and husband.

19

Late, always late! Clean up, child, your sister is waiting

★

Yes, Mother. Here's a fish for tea, Diep. It's gutted and cleaned

★

Never mind the fish, did you not you hear our mother?

★

Girls! Into position - no, legs too wide, more like this. And into the peacock form. Remember balance, poise, and circling, circling, good. Continue through your forms

★

Little sister, you leave yourself wide. Please focus

★

Wide? There, ha! You didn't see that coming, did you?

★

Enough. You are enacting the noble forms of the grand animal spirits, not sparring. And you were open. Not much, but your attack was a compensation. Sometimes great strength comes from opening at the right time, but mostly, our spirit must be preciously guarded. Close yourself, permit no entry. It is a time-honoured tactic

★

Like Trieu Da

★

Just like Trieu Da, eldest daughter. You remember he closed all the mountain passes? He seized his moment and took all the south under his mighty wing. Even the northern Empress of the Han could not outwit him. Her armies fell to a foul disease and she died herself, the war unwon. Trieu Da. on the other hand, lived for an age, until his hair had whitened and his son's son was an old man. And this grandson, Trieu Van, ruled when Trieu Da died, but not for long because he was so old himself, so that when he died, his own son, Trieu Anh, ruled

★

And then Trieu Anh died and his son was a useless child whose mother mated with a Han ambassador. We know

★

You have a talent for reducing the bloodshed and misery of your forebears to inconsequence, youngest daughter. Please leave, if I am insulting your superior knowledge

★

Sorry

★

Evidently, you do not need me to remind you of Lu Chia, the leader of our armies?

★

Please, Mother. I'm sorry. I haven't heard the whole story.

★

Lu Chia stopped the Han Queen Ku, Anh's widow, and he fought the Han soldiers, whom she treacherously drew from the north. Lu Chia killed young Trieu Hung, who would have been a puppet for the Han. He killed all the Middle Kingdom people he could, but he did not close the passes

★

Why not?

★

Yes, why not, Mother? Surely he tried?

★

He tried, but he forgot something. He forgot that the most dangerous passes - the slippery slopes lined with deep fissures - are the pathways that cross the human soul. Lu Chia tried to close the mountain passes, but fear and foreboding had leaked through and weakened the resolve. Here comes Lu Po-te, cried the Lac Lords, he is the Wave-Calming General. He has five armies and we are outnumbered. So battle commenced but Lu Chia fell and his bones were crushed into the dust, and behind him, the remaining Lac Lords bowed and gave gifts to the Tamer of the Waves

★

They gave gifts?

★

They submitted to the Han, yes

★

Did no one fight back?

★

One man did, yes. Would you like to hear about him?

★

Yes, tell us Mother. Was he a Lac Lord?

★

Of a kind. He was descended from the Hung, a more sacred line that that of Trieu Da or even Thuc Pan. He lived through the battle and retreated to Tay Vu, where he held out with his warriors for a year, trying to build an army and entreating the Lac Lords to support him. But they wouldn't. They all called him the King of Tay Vu, some unkindly and with a snigger for who, they thought, would want to be king of that swampy place when they could be Lords of the Han empire with all the treasures in the world at their feet? The King of Tay Vu was brought low by the crossbow of one of these upstart lords, a pitiful creature who used his kill to gain favours and titles from the Han. The resistance was obliterated

★

I know that was all long ago, but... father was a Lac Lord. Would he have given in like those ancestors did?

★

Your father would have given in to no one, but our past is not as simple as dividing the people into good and bad, honourable and weak. It is about the constant push and pull of the tides, it's about the struggles within ourselves as well as the struggles between ideas. None of it is ever resolved, and our stories circle through time, reflecting only what has gone before. Thuc Pan, Trieu Da, Lu Po-Te - there's nothing much to choose between them, and the only defining characteristic that enabled them to achieve what a thousand other ambitious men could not, was their focus upon an idea, a belief. Do you see how the lords fell back because the Emperor called his General a Tamer of the Waves, and because rumours were spread of the five armies? Sometimes, ideas are far more powerful than human might. This is the lesson to learn

★

Forgive me, but if history always repeats itself, then why does it matter anyway? No battle is ever truly won or lost

★

But, eldest sister, no form is complete unless it meets its opposition Precisely correct, both of you. I am glad to hear that my teachings are not in vain

20

'Ride now,' she says, 'Or you will never outrun them.'

'I cannot leave...' Giang looks down at Chinh, huddled next to me.

'She's with us. She'll go with us,' murmurs Nhi, and poor Giang, he looks as if he will cry then but he nods and turns and takes the horse that has just been brought.

'Goodbye cousin,' I whisper and he turns, aghast and bows very deeply, horrified into silence that a voice still comes from the limp body of his rent and bloodied queen.

'Cross the river past the bend. You'll make it over easily enough.' Nhi has cast a glance at me, but this is her last chance to get a message through, to say something important to Thao and little Hung and she is not distracted. 'Tell Thao that he will always be my true husband. Tell Hung that I am his mother for as long as the stars shine upon him. Tell them I made a good end. They must keep themselves safe. The time for fighting is over, for a while. Tell them how we died. You understand? The Han will give out different accounts but you must tell this truth. It matters, for Hung and for the future.'

Giang listens and repeats it all back, six times over, until she is satisfied he has remembered her exact words and until he describes our deaths properly, in the way she wants. When he rides away, Nhi stands with her back to me until he is out of sight. Beyond her, a clutch of figures are frantically assembling branches and cloth.

'Is that for me?' I rasp, tasting blood at the back of my throat. She drops down beside me, with a little laugh.

'Yes,' she says, 'Do you want to take a ride on it?'

'Tell them to stop it. They should just go, the fools. I would not last a horse's length.'

I twist my head back, staring at the blank, distant sky. The sun has hidden his face. There is no chance of me leaving here on that crude stretcher, but I understand that it helps those people feel better to make it. Maybe they will start to run when they hear the pounding of hooves.

'What are we waiting for?' I ask her.

'For him, of course. I want him to see that we're beyond his reach.'

'He will want heads for his Emperor.'

'But he won't have ours.'

'I might die before he arrives.' The blood is in the corner of my mouth. Soon, it will spill out in a thin crimson distributary, mapping the valley of my cheek.

'I can carry you. I've done it before,' she says. 'And anyway, it's not far, is it?'

*****

I am thinking of distance, of how long it takes to get from one place to another and of all the landmarks one looks out for, to measure the passage and secure the course. A life can be remembered in these signs – the same twisted tree in fourteen different seasons, the rut in the path that never was filled in, the leaning stilt house that was there in the year Nhi was born, but which collapsed into the river before our father died. Then there are the landmarks you see only once – for me, the pass of the mountain clouds, the Ca River, the glade where we killed the tiger. Added together they all tell a story, but I am confused abut the order now. I see the streets of Lien Lau bathed in sunshine, but it is winter I am thinking of. I am in the old village, Cam Khe, but wearing the dress of a queen, which cannot be, for I never went back. Then the scene changes again and someone hands me a baby. I expect it to cry and be angry, to be Nhi, but it is a different baby, hairless and silent, with a thumb already in the mouth. It is not my baby, I never had a living one.

'He looks healthy, doesn't he?' asked Nhi. She had laboured over more than a day, bringing forth this surprisingly reticent child, who had clung on inside, like my babies had not. The woman who had helped with the birth was gone and the placenta had been cleared away, along with all the bloodied rags. In my arms, the baby was warm and fat, face creased into a map of Nhi's womb.

'You made your mother work too hard,' I admonished him. He stared at me and then abruptly turned his head into me, snuffling like a small animal. 'Here.' I placed him back on Nhi and when, after some struggling, she had him affixed, I passed her some water.

'Thanks. I have this raging thirst,' she said between great gulps.

'I know. Our mother was the same.'

'And it hurts again. Should it hurt this much?' Her face was pinched up, mouth as puckered as the baby's. Diep thrust a finger in the corner of his mouth and broke the seal, grasping Nhi's breast and re-inserting the nipple with the same nonchalance as one would shove a foot in a slipper. My sister grimaced, then sighed, 'Better.' Diep nodded and sat back down.

Our mother came back into the room. She had the old cloths for baby's bottom, collected over moons past and she deposited them in the corner.

'Feeding well? Good sign. Where is Thao?'

'Gone to tell all his friends,' I said. 'He was here until just a short time ago.'

'Your father made me soup,' she grumbled at Nhi.

'Thao makes horrible soup,' Nhi answered. 'I would rather he went and enjoyed himself for a while.'

'I'll fetch something to eat,' said Diep, leaving the room.

'I can bring him back,' our mother offered.

'No, truthfully, let him be. I think he's a bit shaken,' Nhi insisted.

'That buffalo of a man? Still, they're the worst. Think they've seen it all, then a baby's head pops out and they faint. Chinh and the Thi sisters want to see you, and Cong is stood outside like a statue. Uncle Hien is waiting for news also, but it won't do to have them all in here.'

'Let Chinh and Cong in. Tell the others they must wait.'

'Khanh won't be happy,' I warned.

'I don't care what Khanh thinks. Send her away. And Kim Cuc with her. She'll understand.'

I let our mother deal with all that and when the two Generals came in, I left them with Nhi and went out to take some air. The birthing room was hot and oppressive from the loaded fire in the little stove, but outside, the mid-winter evening was cold. Uncle Hien was chewing areca and betel with a placid smile.

'You look happy, Uncle,' I said, approaching him in the quiet dusk.

'It's a new start, all this.' He gestured back towards the house where Nhi and her baby lay, and out towards the other new buildings, elevated and leggy on the river plain. We had selected this site, near the main Me Linh town, within the rounded curve of the river, where Da and Hong joined. It gave excellent access to the waterways and was within the most developed part of Me Linh. Above us, in the lee of the Hung Mountain, Cam Khe slumbered. Was Bao still up there, and Mrs Chau? I had not seen them since my arrest. Perhaps they fought for us. Perhaps they died. I would have to check.

'Be careful not to throw away what is still useful,' my uncle said.

'What do you mean? The Han have given us nothing of use.'

'Now, Trung Nu Vuong, is that really true? What about the schools, the courts? What about the army bases they have built, which your own forces now use? Giao Chi produces more rice than it used to - look around, our paddies have multiplied at least five-fold in just a few generations.'

'We no longer say Giao Chi,' I said, stonily.

'My apologies. Old habits take a while to die out.' He smiled. 'I am just saying, it wasn't all bad.'

261

'Uncle, I respect your wisdom and your many years of experience, but on this, I cannot agree. You nullify my victory with this subservient talk.'

'Not at all. You have given us the freedom to follow our own path. There is no disputing that the heart of this country is behind you.' He twisted his fingers through his small beard. 'Do you remember how we used to discuss philosophy? You understood Confucius well.'

'Confucius was a Middle Kingdom man. His ideas make sense only in the Middle Kingdom. Here they are unnecessary. Here, he is already a relic. The schools will no longer teach his ideas.'

'Then what will they teach? What learning do we have to offer instead?' My uncle was aghast. He stared at me as if I had broken some precious belonging of his.

'We will build our own knowledge. We have wise people, who never forgot the old ways. We have skilled craftspeople who construct our canals and drainage. We have many excellent warriors who practice martial arts equal to anything the Han can display. We have our own systems of trade which have worked for many hundreds of years and which the Han have never fully understood. If there are to be schools, which in themselves are a Han invention and not of my liking, let them be places to share our own knowledge, rather than dens of debate whose final conclusion must always centre on the ascendancy of the Emperor and the subjugation of the Lac!' Breathless, I grimaced at him.

'Trac, you were once such a good student,' he said, sadly.

'I was confined by the restrictions of Middle Kingdom thinking. Now I think for myself. I hope that you can too.' Uncle Hien looked straight back at me as I spoke. His eyes were black like the night, dark pools over which his beetle eyebrows lowered like thunderclouds, but he was lost, not angry. I was the angry one. He cowered under my scrutiny and I felt the rush

262

of what it was to be Trung Nu Vuong, superior to everyone in the land. They feared me, more, perhaps, than if I had been a man. They feared me because I had overturned the rules they had become used to under the Han. Secretly, inside every man uncertain of my rule, lurked a hidden belief that women could not rule. Confucius had said it was so, and they had listened to the words of Confucius for too long.

'It will take time to get used to the changes,' I said, taking pity on him, 'but we will never bow our heads to the Han again.'

'*Hai Ba Trung,*' he whispered. 'How is your sister?'

'Very well. The baby is greedy and fat. Nhi needs sleep.'

'As do I. I feel the years now, in my chest. I'll come back tomorrow, see her then.'

I had not thought of Uncle Hien as an old man. He looked little different than back when he had stayed in our home; serious, pensive, eyebrows a little more unruly and a few lines around his thin lips, but nothing more. I had a thought, fleeting and sly as an eel in the stream, that the older generation needed to die out for us to be free of Han influence. How else was I to fight this notion that the Han were somehow naturally superior to the Lac? That they possessed some esoteric understanding beyond our own? That women could not rule and should be, as Confucius said, obedient to their husbands? You can fight an idea, a thought, but believe me, it is harder than engaging in armed combat. The more you try to root out the errant notion, to slice it from the uncertain mind which bears it, the more it seeds and spreads. Ideas and beliefs survive best in opposition. If there is no opposition, they slumber unquestioned, barely making their presence felt, but when someone takes the sharp stick and seeks to dislodge them, they unfold exploratory tentacles and expand in ways you hadn't expected. The Trung victory should have told the masses that the Lac were strong, equal to the Han. It should have inspired them and encouraged them, yet what did people do? Fret and worry because it beggared belief, because somewhere down the track, the wheels would surely come off the cart. Oh yes, I understood what Nhi had tried to tell me about Khanh, but if I poked Sach's sister, she would not recoil. She would turn sharp fangs against me. She would speak to every insecurity that her fellow nobility privately held. She would opt for a policy of appeasement, of negotiation with the Han, and all the men and women who were scared would leap from me to her, like tics on a cornered beast.

A tear bordered on the lower lid of my left eye. I felt it tremble then reabsorb, to join the thousand other unshed drops.

★★★★★

Nhi was a natural mother, more so than I think I would have been. She lifted Hung and cuddled him, brushed her plump lips on his bald scalp and put him to the breast as if she were replacing a necessary part of her anatomy. I was simultaneously admiring and repulsed. She named him many days after the birth, when we were certain he would live, and when the bad spirits had hopefully lost interest. Every time I said what a fat, ugly boy he was, she scowled.

'You were ugly too, but you turned out well enough,' I softened. Would she rather I drew those bad spirits back with ill-conceived compliments? At least I was not as harsh as our mother, who threw out these insults, designed to protect him, ten times a day and in a tone of voice that distressed him into a wail.

When Nhi had fully recovered from the birth and Hung was named, content and safe from supernatural predation, she returned to my inner circle. Hung came too, at first, but when his increasing inquisitiveness made concentration impossible, Nhi allowed his care to transfer to Diep. Diep, knowledgeable about all things child-related, confidently cleaned, entertained and fed him, cooking and mashing rice and sliding gooey blobs into the corners of his mouth on her long fingertip to satisfy him for the periods when his mother's breasts were absent. I could have coped without Nhi for longer, but not well. Khanh was no easier to manage and Ton Vien, that ageing peer of my mother, was a thorn between my toes.

Vien still had responsibility for Lien Lau, and Lien Lau remained our biggest market town, but power had slid north-west, to Me Linh. The seat of the Trung Queen was growing and people, resources and trade were sliding in our direction. Vien had once been the most vocal of the Lac Lords, renowned for his mettle and his righteousness in challenging the Han, but his enthusiasm had sapped long before the war. Why his courage and clear-sightedness drained away is anyone's guess, but my unkind assessment is that Vien was essentially a vain and arrogant man. He liked to challenge the old Governors because it made him feel important, and they tolerated it because it made them appear fair and benevolent, but he never actually wanted to risk his power and position to gain real freedom for Nam Viet. A crooked official, would you say? Maybe not so bad. Maybe he just yearned for the old days, when Tich Quang had governed us and when the Han Emperor had received Ton Vien, with many other Prefects, to give his divine thanks for their loyalty in the Wang Mang time. But I am biased and to me he is a self-serving coward. I have never forgiven him for letting Sach do what he would not.

In his daily work within Lien Lau, he did me good service, but in the regular meetings at Me Linh, he chafed at the bit. He thought we should open the way for trade. I knew who whispered in his ear. He questioned the order of precedence in our new hierarchy, though ever so tentatively, suggesting that I consider remarriage and that I would benefit from the guidance of a husband. Which man did he have in mind? Oh, he'd not given it much thought, but perhaps someone older, someone with experience? The bile rose in my throat and my nerves tingled as my muscles imagined loosing my sword and taking off his impudent head. Surely he could not think that I would join with him, an ageing widower packed with scheming intentions? I reminded him that his whole idea of marriage was a Han imposition, that we no longer required such official, ritualistic ceremonies and that women in Nam Viet accepted only as much guidance from their men as their men received from them. Unlike my uncle, who spoke from the heart when he questioned the loss of Middle Kingdom teachings, Vien was a man with an eye to a more worldly game. He had no especial care for Confucius, beyond what personal benefits could be reaped by following such edicts. My uncle believed that Confucius was wise and that his format for living made a kind of divine, inarguable sense. Vien just liked the promise of power and status that lurked behind the guidance. Both were wrong, both were dangerous, but only one was morally reprehensible.

Nhi came back to full strength just in time, as it happened. Having wondered whether there was any slight chance that the Yellow River Emperor might disregard his losses in our tiny, inconsequential sliver of land, we discovered that his intentions were quite opposite. The Zhuang warned us that preparations for a major assault were under way in the Middle Kingdom and that a grand appointment had been made.

'Who will come against us?' I demanded to know.

'He is titled The Wave Calming General. His name is Ma Vien,' explained Chinh. She visited the borders regularly to receive news from the Zhuang. 'He's a Zhao man, very loyal to the emperor. Used to be Grand Administrator of the Longxi Commandery.'

'A career General, one of their finest?'

'Very much so. He's been appointed with great ceremony and honour and the emperor thinks highly of him. He has a reputation for toughness, fairness and discipline.' She touched her fingers, passing off each of the attributes exactly as she had been told by the Zhuang.

'Which way will he come? North-east?'

'He's built an army from three Commanderies so far. The Zhuang think he'll add a fourth. That gives him many thousands of soldiers. Twenty thousand, say our informants.' Chinh shuffled uncomfortably. 'They're saying he'll come by boat, not land. There is a fleet harboured up the eastern coast of the Middle Kingdom.'

'Then an attack is imminent?' cried Khanh, standing up from the relaxed squat she had adopted. 'There is no time to negotiate?'

'We will never negotiate with the Han,' I said, as sweetly as I could. 'You should know that by now. Perhaps if you are so keen to converse with the men who murdered your brother, you should leave now, before battle breaks out once more.'

Khanh glowered, but stayed silent. Kim Cuc, eyes slitted at her troublesome sister, said 'What are our orders, Trung Nu Vuong?'

I nodded for Nhi to take over and she bowed back.

'Chinh, you leave for Hai Phong tomorrow,' Nhi said. 'Brief your Captains tonight. Kim Cuc, take your division to Chu Dien and wait for instruction. Mother, you'll hold Me Linh with our reserve forces while Cong and I go to Tay Vu. Thao, we need orders sent out for our Cuu Chan and Nhat Nham lords to bring together their fighting forces once more. They should meet us at Tay Vu.'

'Can we expect help from the Zhuang?' I asked.

'I don't know,' Chinh admitted. 'Perhaps, but not in the numbers we saw before.'

'Le Chan has grown her defences along the coastline,' Nhi said. 'They'll gain us time, until the old Nhat Nam and Cuu Chan divisions get here.'

They dispersed, each about the business Nhi had delegated, none of them voicing the biggest concern – that the southern parts of the new Nam Viet might not respond at all.

It was hard enough drawing together our local armed force.

Over a year of peace had seen people go back to field and family, and though Cong's permanently assembled division was more than ready to repair to Tay Vu, Chinh had more trouble gathering the extent of her companies in such a short time. It was three days before she could set off for the coast, and with reduced numbers at that, but all the while, Nhi reassured me that Chan would have the situation, if situation there was, well in hand. Don't forget, she said, Ma Vien has not reached his fleet yet. Chan will let us know if he is sighted. Probably, we'll see four new moons before he even boards ship, she said. But any news was old news. Agitation twisted in my belly, not from fear of fighting, but from anxiety that my planning and execution of the defence of Nam Viet would fall short of the mark. I barely slept, running scenarios through my mind, pushing divisions around the imagined contours of Nam Viet, the way a child pushes stones in the dust. Move our mother to Tay Vu? Spread the army along the coast? Pull back all the army to Lang Bac and wait there? I am not an indecisive person, but I am a tactician, and tacticians must forever reconsider and reassess.

We went to Tay Vu, Nhi and I, leaving Hung behind in the care of Diep. Thao stayed in Me Linh also, much to his frustration. I will not hear it, Nhi said, when he tried to insist on coming; Trung Nu Vuong must go into battle and you must keep her son safe. It was the first time I'd heard her pull rank on Thao, but even then, she could only call herself a queen in the third person.

So, in the wintertime, we camped at Co Loa with about a quarter of our army. Co Loa, that ancient citadel of Thuc Pan, was in the region we called Tay Vu, where diverging branches of river had rejoined to annex a huge plain of lakes, hills, marsh and paddies. Patches near our encampment were boggy but the land had begun to recover from the summer rains, and the site we chose was more than bearable, situated as we were within the old ramparts. Not far away, just across the river, south of our position, Lien Lau was preparing its own defences. Ton Vien was taking care of that, supposedly leaving me one less thing to worry about, but not only did I doubt his conviction and faith in our cause, I knew that if the Han even made it past us to Lien Lau, nothing mattered anyway. The main reason I did not order him, and the families who fought for him, to join us was because I preferred him to stay away from me. Similarly, Khanh was down in Chu Dien, where her insidious manipulation could not wind its malodorous way through the bulk of our army. They were my reserves. I would call them later, once I had word that Ma Vien had landed.

This time round, preparing for war felt harder. The zeal was faded, the people restless. We were pushing through a cold winter, where the temperature dipped lower than I remembered for many years. Nhi had originally recommended installing our army on the heights of Lang Bac, but I overruled her. Co Loa was more protected from the elements and we could always take to the higher ground when the Wave-Calming General came close. Wave-Calming General, indeed! It took me straight back to my mother's lessons of long ago and I wondered if she too had permitted herself a small smile when Chinh revealed the title. The Emperor was playing a clear game of intimidation - we have cracked you before, his appointment said, and we will do exactly the same again. It might work on people of Ton Vien and Thi Khanh's cowardly persuasions, but not on me. I had no personal fear of this venerated Ma Vien, who was, apparently, older in years than my father would have been, if he had lived. I worried, on the surface, about the trivial details inherent in running a country and ruling an army, but these were cerebral concerns; tortures of the intellect, rather than the heart. When I laid awake at night, cogitating and ruminating, the agonies were never in my chest. They never made me want to rush, heaving, to the door to spill my last meal. They never made the tight ball of pressure settle against my rib cage, the way it had when

I looked into Sach's eyes and knew I had to sever myself from the gaze if I wanted to live. I only ever have to take myself back to that moment, standing by the hall of justice, for the sweat to bead sickeningly at my temples, for the ache of a long distance run that was yet to come, and has long since finished, to creep agonisingly up my legs.

Sach; so recently lost to me and yet as far removed as the heavens are from earth. I had lived almost two years without him and if I had learned anything from that hideously long race to safety, it was that the first sprint is the most intensely painful, but that the muscle-burn and fatigue of the mid-section is the most lethal – that part when it is as far to return as it is to go on, and the mischievous spirits whisper to you that it would not be so bad just to rest a while. That is where I was now and that is why I had no fear of Ma Vien. If he had stolen into my camp one night and put a sword to my neck, I might have thanked him for saving me the trouble. Or perhaps I'd have still fought. The evidence suggests so, for haven't I done just that? Fought on and on, to the very end?

I have to face it. I am not a martyr, not a willing one, at least, and not even to my own grief. I had heard, after we returned to drive Governor To Dinh away from our Nam Viet, exactly how Sach had died. I was lucky that I'd had three or four moons to imagine the very worst and to travel some way along the path of bereavement. They executed him the day after Nhi and I ran, which meant he'd had a night to ponder my escape, to know that I had got far, far away. I hope that cheered him. In the morning, they brought him out to face quite a crowd – his notoriety now increased hugely by his wife's dramatic escape. He looked well, so the account went – no signs of torture, just the dishevelment of captivity. He was impassive when the charges and sentence were spoken, keeping his eyes closed and his mouth in what had appeared to be a smile. Then, when told to kneel, he produced another short, inflammatory

270

speech before his executioner drove a foot in behind his knee and forced him down. On his knees, he closed his eyes once more, and the stolid Han swordsman whirled his blade through Sach's neck, severing the artery at the back and slicing through his throat and out into open air. No spluttering, no suffering. I had seen beheading performed clumsily during battle - the wedged sword, the hacked juncture between shoulder and head, the sticky grooves chopped inaccurately across the back of a head - and had harboured secret terrors that Sach might have died screaming, gurgling up blood past a badly lodged blade, but his death had been fast and clean, over in an instant.

People seemed to forget that we had once been a normal couple, happy and intimate. Sach belonged, no longer to me, but to everyone who bowed their heads at his memory. Their pride in his sacrifice transmuted into a feverish zeal, mimicking happiness. The memory of his death enriched them and they were surprised when, at mention of him, I could not match their teary-eyed smiles or upbeat praise. Instead I detested their words as one might detest a theft of precious belongings. With each retelling of his death, or invocation of his courage, they carried him further from me.

★★★★★

Winter, long and indifferent, passed us by and still Ma Vien had not been sighted. I travelled around the Red River delta, checking on our divisions in Chu Dien and Lien Lau, and spending some time on the coast, at Hai Phong and further north into Ha Long Bay. The fishermen bobbed patiently in their small canoes, oblivious to the threat beyond the islands of the dragon, that littered the calm waters of the bay. Nhi came with me, and apart from a brief period when she returned to Me Linh because little Hung was sick, we stayed together, as much for outward show as for mutual support.

When the cold weather lifted and the warm drizzling rain began, I had the dawning premonition that Ma Vien was not coming. Whether it was true foresight or simply the optimism of entering a new season, I cannot say, but I was looking for a final sign – some breathless information arriving on horseback from the Middle Kingdom, perhaps – that would confirm in me that it would be correct to release my army back to their crop production, an endeavour just as crucial as preparing for a Han onslaught. It came in a form I had not expected, but the sign did indeed come.

'What is happening to the sun?' Cong cried out, amongst general consternation in camp. We were back in Tay Vu, our disgruntled army working unenthusiastically at some waterway repairs and developments. Men and women stood around, staring at the sky and rubbing strained eyes. I joined my sister and Cong, who were gazing heavenwards with the rest of them, rubbing and shading their eyes.

'It's disappearing. It's turning black,' Nhi said, and so it was. A spreading darkness, like a slow, inky tide, was moving across the sun's golden circle and though it hurt our eyes to watch, we all stood transfixed as the day darkened and the source of our warmth succumbed. A tenebrous light settled – a soft, dusty yellow glow that was not day time or night time, but which might have been the end, or the beginning of something. Just as cries were ringing out and panic began, a splinter of bright white broke out from behind the black, lifting the gloom. It grew to a curved blade of brilliance and refilled the world with light.

'What was that?' asked Cong, little expecting an answer.

'Ma Vien is not coming,' I said, sure now as I could be. 'The Han have threatened us, but they will not attack yet. The danger has passed for now.'

'Are you sure?' asked Nhi. She still gazed up at the emerging sun. A short distance away, in the grassy marshes, a group of people consoled a man. He was wailing that he could not see anything and he rubbed at his eyes frantically.

'Disband the army, Commander Nhi. We are wasting our time and energy here.'

Nhi turned to Cong. They were silent for a moment, looking at each other, up at the sky, back to me, then Nhi said, 'General Cong, make preparations for our move back to Me Linh and inform Lien Lau and Chu Dien of our plans.'

Cong bowed and backed away, moderately dazed. She already revered both of us, and now she must have believed even the heavens moved at my will. Solid, young Cong. I miss her very much. Such untainted devotion is hard to find.

'Shall I recall General Chinh?'

'Yes, do so.'

'Trac, are you certain of this? We've waited the whole winter and now suddenly he's not coming? Maybe... maybe that wasn't a sign for you. Maybe it was a sign for him.'

'Trust me, little sister, as I have trusted you. I do not fool myself that the sun darkens its face for the fate of a single queen, but I know that something has stopped Ma Vien from coming. It has been too long, Nhi. If he could have sailed, he would have done so. We have other work to get on with rather than simply waiting for him.'

Yes, that was it. Not foresight nor magic at all. Pure logic. Even so, that blackened sun; I did not like it, even if it did portend a reprieve. I did not like it at all.

21

When I was apart from Thao, I didn't think about him much. It sounds callous, but it's not that I didn't have strong feelings for him. I did - I loved his muscled, broad body and the tangible boundary it created between each day and the next. I loved the territorial angst that tortured him as he tried not to impose himself upon my day, only occasionally veering near to me on some pretext, just to remind everyone that we were a couple. And there was Hung, of course, with his father's tough little shoulders and my pointed chin, a perfect, almost-walking and talking monument to our marriage. I loved Thao for making me a mother.

But then we were apart, and Thao could no longer wander past to catch sight of me in the day. Every night that passed without his being able to lay urgent fingers against my skin, was a night in which he doubted me. The stoicism he forced upon himself when I ran from Lien Lau was only possible because he saw there was no choice. My leaving for Tay Vu was different. It *was* a choice; my sister, above himself and Hung; Our new nation above our marriage. The precedence was simple, as far as I was concerned but I hadn't duly considered Thao's feelings. At the time, I honestly did not realise how severely he missed me and how, while I was comfortably preoccupied in one thousand tasks and duties, he was dwelling on my absence. I wasn't dwelling on thoughts of him, so I never understood that he could not stop thinking about me. His inability to bear distance between us was a product of our intensely physical relationship. If he couldn't reach out and touch me, he was dissatisfied. The opposite was true of me. His anchored, solid presence in the world, that beautiful, animalistic bulk of muscles, gave me a centre from which to venture out, always knowing he would be there for me to return to. I soared and he sank.

I returned home to Me Linh when Trac ordered it, to find

Thao no longer there. Diep told me he had taken a trip back to Khuc Duong, his home province.

'What about Hung?' I demanded. 'I told him to stay here with our child.'

'Hung has been fine,' she said. 'There is no need to worry about his care.'

'War looms on the border, and you think there is no need to worry? He should have been here, with our son.'

'He felt he had to leave,' she said, helplessly, glancing around as if planning her escape. Hung played on the floor between us and she made to pick him up, but I pushed her back.

'Why?' I said, holding the front of her tunic in my fist. I had known Diep since my childhood, but such a cold anger welled inside of me that I could have knocked her to the floor.

'Please, go to your mother. I am too afraid to tell you,' she whimpered. 'Go to your mother.'

I released my grip and stepped away from her, a dread settling in my stomach. Hung watched us curiously and, beyond the dread, I felt a tinge of pride that his eyes were like Trac's – sharp and constant. Yet, on the heels of that pride came the fury that Thao had left this precious child here in Me Linh when I was relying on him to be Hung's protector. What use was the man, if I couldn't trust him with our own son?

Diep went shakily to Hung, joining him in his play and keeping her head down. I gave Hung a rough cuddle and left them to find Mother. I stormed back to the area by the temple where I'd last seen her. It was deserted, apart from a few people working on the structure. The temple was half-finished and thick lengths of bamboo and rattan were piled about on the ground. With every step, my anger flared. Where was she? And if there was important news about my husband, why hadn't she told me when I arrived? There was noise coming from nearer the river where the horses were being unharnessed, and I followed the sound of voices, eventually hearing Cong, shouting commands above the racket.

'Where is Lady Mother?' I shouted at her, and she pointed up towards one of the new houses by the river. I nodded a thank-you and stalked up to the house she had indicated. Mother was just coming down the steps, Trac in tow, and the pair of them came immediately towards me.

'Mother, I need to speak to you,' I said, as she kept on walking, pulling me away with her, back towards our own, grander home where I had left Diep and Hung. Trac and her entourage disappeared into the tumult surrounding Cong, and finally Mother and I were walking alone, away from the little house by the river.

'Thao has gone to Khuc Duong. Is that true?'

'Yes, Nhi, he is visiting his home there.'

'Why, Mother? I told him to stay here with Hung. How could he leave him at a time like this? What is so important in Khuc Duong?'

Mother sighed. She stopped walking and turned to face me. We were on the track, midway between the new temple and our home.

'Diep didn't tell you?'

'Diep sent me to you.'

'Just as well, by the look of you,' Mother observed. 'Now I want you to control yourself. Thao has gone to Khuc Duong at my suggestion. He was pursuing a course of action most unwise and I intervened.'

'What do you mean?'

'Thao was lonely, or so he said when I spoke with him, and he began a relationship with the daughter of one of the traders, newly moved here from downriver.'

I gasped. My stomach revolted with the empty, flipping sensation of panic and fear.

'A relationship?'

'The term is too polite, in all honesty. He went with her

276

in the night. Copulation is all it really was. They were never together in the daytime and few people know anything about it.'

That didn't make me feel much better. It was too close a comparison to my own relationship with Thao and in any case, the thought of other breasts in his hands, other flesh wrapped around his own, another supple, naked woman pressed into his rippled torso, was horrible to contemplate.

'Where is this woman?' I asked.

Mother cast a guilty look towards the river. I caught on.

'In that house!' I shouted. 'Where you and Trac were?'

'Not any more,' she answered. 'Trac has sent the whole family back downriver.'

'By the Jade Tiger, I would have ripped her apart. You should have left her here for me to finish.'

'I did,' Mother huffed. 'It was your sister who decided that was unnecessary.'

'My sister did not have the right. Unnecessary? What does she know of it.' I exhaled, storing my anger with Trac in reserve. 'So you banished Thao to Khuc Duong?'

'Not exactly. I saved him from himself, Nhi. I was very angry with him, but I know that he loves you.'

'Loves me? Was he thinking of me when he was rutting with that low-born scum?'

'Nhi, calm down. You know Thao. He'd do anything for you, I do believe that. But he's a man. Weak, useless on his own. You shouldn't leave him alone for so long.'

'Chien would never have done this to me,' I scorned, 'and we were so very far apart. There was a man who truly loved me. Thao just wants a warm hole to stick it in!'

Mother's mouth opened up in wordless disgust. I had thought of her as unshockable, but even she didn't want to hear words like that from her daughter's lips. When she gathered herself, she said, 'Chien was just a boy, what you had was not a true marriage,' but I didn't want to hear it and I left her standing in the track, while I went to take over the care of my son.

★★★★★

It turns out that Trac was right to release the army back to the Lac fields. I'd had my doubts, though I would never have displayed them. She was vindicated even before Chinh was halfway back across the delta with her division. Ma Vien had suffered a calamitous setback in port. Having been assured that everything was in order – the ships ready for departure and the Han army ready to board – his fleet commander died. Now this, alone, wouldn't have ruined Ma Vien's plans; there are plenty of eager, ambitious and competent men in the Middle Kingdom, waiting to take over such a role. But when the fleet commander died, people began taking inventories and checking his records. Questions were asked of his subordinates, because a suspicion had been dawning for a while that something did not add up. Now, the truth was emerging and when we heard it, we laughed fit to startle the spirits. Ma Vien did not have enough ships. There was no possible way under the stars to squeeze his gargantuan army into the waiting boats, and the recently deceased fleet commander had, whether by intention or not, grossly misled the Wave Tamer. We pictured them, massed on the shores, spilling from the decks and wondering why they could not all fit. There was much hilarity in Me Linh about the misfortunes of this tired, old, Middle Kingdom General. It was an error of enormous proportions and would delay Ma Vien for a long time – at least as long as it took to build more boats.

I expected Trac to be happy. The news not only justified her actions in disbanding the army, it also gave us more time to prepare, but within half a day, she was indifferent again – long-faced and blank. I wanted to punch her. How many years, I thought, is she going to mourn in this self-absorbed manner? We all have our miseries to contend with, I snapped to Mother, but she has to pull herself free. Hush, Mother said to me, you're just

278

angry about the girl. And so I was. I wanted to chase the dirty little creature down to Lien Lau or wherever she was hiding, and let her taste the edge of my sword. I had nearly floored Diep, I had spoken rudely to Mother and I was no longer speaking to Trac unless I had to.

Trac had said to me, and I struggle to remember accurately because I was so angry, 'The girl is very sorry. You must leave her alone and go to see Thao.'

'I'll go after her,' I threatened. 'You can't hide her from me.'

'You will not,' Trac had replied, without even raising her voice.

'How can you let her go, after the disrespect she has shown me?'

'Go and see Thao.'

'If I see him, I'll kill him too.'

But I didn't go downriver. Neither did I travel to Khuc Duong. I immersed myself in the little boy, whose clinging hands and innocent smile alleviated some of the hurt and fury that burned in my chest. I had a job to do, in the aftermath of our recent preparations for war and many matters kept me busy. I tried not to think about Thao, or what he was doing in Khuc Duong.

I turned my attentions forcibly to the politics of Nam Viet and the planning that was still necessary for whenever Ma Vien managed to invade. Trac's subdued reaction to his delay had set me thinking. She was, despite the attendant depression that cloaked her like a rain cloud, highly intelligent and perceptive, and I could not dismiss her restraint as pure melancholy. I considered our position. The army was relieved, barring Mother and Cong's divisions, which stayed more or less assembled in the Me Linh vicinity, but they did not number more than several thousand. Khanh and Kim Cuc were in Chu Dien, and their fighters were all back at work in the fields. Ton Vien had relaxed military conditions and training in Lien Lau. Chinh had left a detachment on the coast, where Le Chan was fiercely patrolling the bay, but the rest of her division had been released. Nothing had been heard from any of the Nhat Nam prefects since the Zhuang warned us of the Wave Tamer, and Cuu Chan had provided, and then eagerly withdrawn, only half the numbers we had hoped for. I knew all the details – it was my role as Commander, after all, and I had given the orders both to assemble and later to disband. It had been, as far as the practicalities went, a reasonably successful endeavour, with no major incidents, internal squabbles or outbreaks of disease. We could have hoped for more support from the south, but since Ma Vien had never actually landed, their loyalty hadn't truly been tested.

Yet I felt uneasy as I reviewed all this. What speed they had all shown, hurrying home to the crops! Where was the heart for the fight? Why was Nhat Nam silent? Khanh and Kim Cuc had not yet returned to Me Linh. Were they planning to remain in Chu Dien? Khanh was closer to Ton Vien, if she stayed there. Was she spreading rumours, stirring up discontent in Lien Lau and Chu Dien, just as she had tried to in Me Linh? But aside from Khanh and her petty games, why were we not overrun with support? Over the mountains to the west were displaced tribes from the Middle Kingdom, as well as indigenous peoples who hated the Han and were constantly under threat from the expansion of the empire. I understood why they had not risked their lives to support us in the beginning, but none of them had shown willing to join us in repelling the Emperor's new army, even though we had proved our worth in battle. The Zhuang were cagey, still talking with us, but conducting who knew what kind of negotiations with the Han.

It might have been my current marital woes that made me draw the conclusion, but I began to see that rather than being victorious and strong, Me Linh and her queens were alone and vulnerable – a little cluster of honour and integrity surrounded by potential disloyalty, deceit and indifference.

'I'm recalling Khanh,' I said to Trac, at one of our frosty work discussions.

'What have you heard?' Trac looked up sharply.

'Nothing - yet.'

'I see. She will not come. She will make the excuse that her husband needs her in Chu Dien. Then you may send a detachment to bring her here.'

I nodded, surprised. Trac had always defended Khanh in the past and I had despaired of ever getting her to see the danger the woman presented.

'Kim Cuc can stay in Chu Dien, if you agree,' I added. 'I've no worries about her.'

'Send Chinh to spend some time there, just to be sure. And you should be contemplating a trip, also.'

'I will not go to Khuc Duong,' I said, standing to leave, as I now did when our discussions became personal.

'I have heard that he is very unhappy,' she said, getting up and barring my way.

'Maybe he should go to Lien Lau and find the girl to cheer him up.'

'He does not want her,' said Trac.

'How would you know? How would you understand anything about this, after perfect Sach who never put a foot wrong? To you it's all so simple and easy. Just because you lost your man, I should forgive any bad behaviour in mine.'

She flinched and stepped aside. I stamped away, not for the first time, but on this occasion I was assailed by guilt. I went down to the river and squatted on the bank. Hung Mountain was a silken blur through the heavy rain and my clothing was soaked in moments, but I watched the silted waters surging by and wondered what messages Trac might have received. I had ordered everyone not to give me news of Thao and consequently no one but Trac dared to mention him to me. I hated him for what he had done. I hated him for making me so angry. I hated him for what he had just made me say to Trac.

'That was cruel.' Mother's voice behind me made me jump.

'I know,' I said, standing up and feeling the water run down my arms. 'But she doesn't understand.'

'Are you so sure?' She edged closer, standing almost at my side. In her hand was a very large banana leaf which she held over her head, letting the rain cascade over the sides. 'She was very angry with that girl. She only let her go so you would not cause offence to her clan by killing her, and so that Thao would not feel responsible for her death.'

I sniffed, unimpressed.

'I thought for a moment she might have done it herself, though.'

'Oh?'

'She hit the girl, quite hard. I think she broke her cheekbone.' Mother shrugged, turning to leave.

'You never said.' I was quite astonished.

'Do you need proof of the way your sister feels about you? For that matter,' she added, over her shoulder, 'if you would listen to any news, you would know how Thao feels about you too. If you are going to change your mind about seeing him, I would do it soon.'

'Why? Is he going to end our marriage?' I snorted with derision.

'Thao would never do that. He can't live without you.'

I sniffed in contempt as Mother walked away, and I wiped the rainwater from my forehead and eyebrows. The deluge was easing and the landscape across the river was sharpening into clearer focus. A small herd of water buffalo were grazing out on a low stretch of the plain, tiny black beasts in the green. Words floated back to me, unbidden.

He's very unhappy... he can't live without you... change your mind... do it soon

A piercing pain gripped at the centre of my chest as I

understood what Mother and Trac were trying to tell me. Stupid Thao! What was he thinking? I turned in horror towards home, breaking into a run as I realised what my fool of a husband was considering.

★★★★★

In riding towards Khuc Duong, I came closer to understanding Trac's agony when she ran away from Lien Lau. For the whole of the ride, my entire being centred on the single desperate need to arrive in time, while Thao was still alive. The more I pleaded silently with the Jade Tiger not to take him, the more I became convinced that I would be too late. Can you imagine feeling that desperate pull and yet dragging yourself in the opposite direction as my sister had done? My skin was chaffing under the *ao tu than*, which I had pulled loose. Halfway on my journey, I dragged the damp robe completely off, and rode in just my *ao yem*, the little square of cloth which covered my chest and was tied with thin string around my back. I didn't care. Down in Nhat Nam, half the people still walked around naked - even on the outskirts of my home village of Cam Khe, some of them couldn't be bothered with clothes. No one was going to be overly concerned with the sight of me in my underwear, although it gave my hastily assembled entourage a wide-eyed moment.

The real surprise was Thao's. I found him at his old family home, gawking from the front steps as twelve of Me Linh's finest fighters galloped after me into his village. A couple of geriatric chickens skittered aside and some of the local children came running out as we pulled to a standstill. I vaulted off my horse and ran to him and in that moment, all things were forgotten. I was just so relieved to find him alive and well. I grasped at his thick arms to check he was real and then pulled him to me. I think the rain and the ride might have affected my wits. He broke out of his stupor and hugged me back, hard, crushing me against his chest. Against my legs, I felt the bulge of his hard penis and, even though it stirred a longing, I wrenched myself free from his grasp and fetched him a hard blow to the side of his head. He reeled sideways, caught off-guard, then regained himself.

'I deserved that. But...' he gestured feebly at my attire and I glanced down at my rain-slicked body, vest water-tight against my breasts.

'Is this what she looked like, too?' I asked, and pushed past him up the rickety steps into the big stilt house. One of the servants - or she may have been a cousin - stared and then turned to get me a drink. I squatted on the *kang* in the living area that, in the night time, was where Thao's parents used to sleep. Thao followed me in and sat beside me. In a corner, sandalwood burned and filled the air with peaceful scent.

'She looked nothing like you. She was a mistake.'

'So I have heard.'

'You were gone a long time. Even when you were in Me Linh, it wasn't like I hoped it would be. You're always with your sister.'

'I'm Commander of Nam Viet. What did you expect?'

'Nhi, I don't want to fight. I'm sorry for what I did.'

'So sorry that you would die for it?'

Thao looked away. His normally erect shoulders were slumped and he poked at the floor with a stray twig.

'Don't ever consider it,' I said. 'If you'd done it, I would have been very angry.'

'Angry?' He managed a small, sad smile.

'Broken. I would have been broken,' I said, looking at the wall, away from him. Peculiar, how neither of us could look at each other though we had been married for several years and had a child together. He sneaked a hand into mine and gripped it tightly. I looked at the veins, standing out on his thick wrists and said, 'I cannot promise to always be with you and Hung, especially while the Han threaten war, but I'll try not to leave you for so long in future.'

'Whether you are with us or away, this won't happen again,' he promised. 'I'll remember you riding here to save me, in your vest, for all my life.'

I blushed. It was the kind of thing Chien might have said, but coming from Thao it made me shy. I had known him longer and in a thousand more ways than I'd known Chien, but in some ways, we were strangers.

★★★★★

The relief when Nhi and Thao returned home was huge. Was it selfish of me to want to see them together again? If Thao had been a licentious sort of man, then certainly I would not have pushed her, but Thao was nothing like that. My mother's description of his sordid liaison with the trader's daughter sounded more like a man in misery than a man giving in to temptation. As for the slut he had fallen in with, she was older than Nhi, and nowhere near as pretty and by her own foolish account, she had simply walked up to him with her tunic open and her bare breasts displayed, after he'd had too much rice wine one late night. Of course, there were other times when he had not been drunk, but I hit her almost as much for being ugly and stupid as I did for mating with Thao. How could she presume to think that he could love her over my sister? Her father had been heard in public to say that his daughter was going to be marrying into nobility, so the whole family had clearly been colluding to push the pair together. I had no qualms about banishing them from Me Linh, and given the threats I had made, I expected they would keep their heads down from now on.

I needed Nhi to be happy, so I did not have to worry for her, but I also needed her focused and by my side. I needed Thao too. There were too many serious issues to deal with to be troubled by strife within our family. Khanh had done just as I believed she would, apologising for her inability to come to Me Linh, and saying she was in Lien Lau enjoying some rest with relatives as she was pregnant.

'Pregnant? That's a good try. What does Kim Cuc say?'

Chinh had visited both Chu Dien and Lien Lau, returning home for further instruction. She smiled in that wide pretty manner she used to have.

'Kim Cuc says it is news to her, also.'

'I see. Who is she staying with?'

'Cousins of her husband. The husband's aunt is a good friend of Prefect Vien. They live close by.'

So Khanh was in Lien Lau, cosying up to Vien just as I had anticipated. I felt an unexpected wave of boredom at her predictability.

'Bring her back,' I ordered. 'Choose some people you can trust - discreet, intelligent people - and have them stay on in Lien Lau. I want to know what they are saying in the markets and on the streets. See if you can find a woman called Chau, from Cam Khe. She spends half her time in the Lien Lau markets and will know better than anyone what the mood in the town is.'

'Your old neighbour?' Chinh ventured. 'I could go to Cam Khe first, rather than searching her out in Lien Lau.'

'If you wish,' I said, impatiently. 'She has a son, Bao, and daughters. They might be useful.'

★★★★★

Chinh found Bao. It was not hard - the boy had risen to something of a leader among the labourers of Cam Khe. He was muscled and darkly tanned and the churlish attitude that distorted his features in his younger years had relaxed into a more adult expression of confidence. It had been only a few years since I had last seen him, but he had matured into, if not a good-looking young man, then certainly a hard-working one.

'Bao,' said Nhi, 'You haven't changed a bit!' She crossed the floor of our house, under the heavy drumming of rain upon the roof, and drew him to the back of the living area where Hung sat with my mother, rolling glass beads along the flat wooden boards. 'This is my son. Do you think he looks like me?'

'Very much so,' Bao said, nodding and smiling awkwardly at her and politely addressing my mother. He had no idea how to respond to this warrior queen whose five-year-old self he had once chased across plains and played with in the river. He gazed at her as if she were some foreign creature, speaking a different language. With me, he was easier. We had never been close and he had always deferred to my authority. There was no change of circumstance except that for once I was genuinely pleased to see him.

'Bao, come and eat,' I ordered, rescuing him from his confusion. 'I want to hear what news you have.'

'Of course,' he said, hurrying to squat down by me. Nhi joined us and at the other end of the room, Hung babbled restless words and struggled down from his grandmother to toddle over to us.

Though it was the first time Bao had visited, we had been receiving information from him and his family ever since Chinh found him, about three moons before. Bao's sisters brought the messages, meeting with Cong on the waterside after they had conducted whatever business they had in Me Linh's market. Gossip, rumour, scraps of nothing and then, hidden amongst and patterned within, the mood and undercurrent of Lien Lau. Thanks to them, we discovered that Ton Vien was trying to persuade some traders to break the line in the north east to import silks he had been promised were just beyond the boundary. We heard from them also the drunken things his servant had overheard him say to a guest about the false rule of the Trung Sisters. Mrs Chau reported that Kim Cuc had been into the town several times, though whether or not she had visited Ton Vien, she could not say. In the markets, according to Bao's sisters, people discussed whether Trung Nu Vuong would remarry but there was no appetite for a new overlord - one sister married is enough, people said.

Hung clutched to his mother and eyed Bao warily.

'How is our friend, Vien?' I asked.

'Busy,' answered Bao, without hesitation. 'He's riling up the traders, getting them worried about the loss of exports, and it's starting to work. Some people are struggling – there's not enough demand here for the pearls, the feathers and other luxuries. They're trading in the bay now, rowing out to the Island Commanderies with goods, but you'll know all this from the Hai Phong Generals?'

I nodded. Le Chan had kept me updated about the shipments, going both ways across the gulf. I knew that trade was going to be the biggest problem, but I thought the markets would have recovered now. We had all we needed – if only people would reorganise and redistribute sensibly instead of trying to exchange piles of rice for unnecessary silks and glass from the north. There was a taste, in our land, for Middle Kingdom living, but it had to be stamped out while the embers were low. And here was Vien, stoking them up.

'They've had meetings,' Bao continued. 'Vien has arranged them, but he's made it seem like the traders have done it themselves. There have been two or three small gatherings so far. My mother was invited to the last one, which is how we know. She's already given the names of everyone there to Chinh.'

'Good. And what are they saying, at these meetings?'

'The traders are just worrying, you know how it is. Complaining that they can't make a living and that we can't ignore our Han neighbours. They're saying a route should be opened just for trade, and that the Han would probably want that as much as they do.'

'And what does Vien say?'

'Mother says he is very careful not to say much at all, but that he asks questions to which people give the answers he wants. Do you understand? I was not sure what she meant.'

'I understand,' I said. 'Auntie Chau describes Vien very

accurately. Now, has Kim Cuc been back to Lien Lau lately?'

'Yes, she has,' said Bao, pushing a clump of sticky rice between his lips. He chewed and swallowed. 'And this time she did go to see Vien, but no one is quite sure how close they are. It was only four or five days ago.'

Just after Nhi refused Kim Cuc's request for her pregnant sister to be returned home, then. Was Kim Cuc looking for support from Vien? Would she ally herself with him if we refused to let Khanh go? It was not as if we had imprisoned Khanh in dreadful circumstances. She was living in a house a little inland from the river, could have visitors if she chose, but was simply not free to travel. Curiously, her stomach had grown no bigger and I was interested to see at what point she would fake a miscarriage. My orders to detain her specified the need to keep my sister-by-marriage safe during her expectant period – a reason Khanh did not believe for a moment, but which was hard for her to argue with. I must have looked concerned, for Bao was quick to reassure me.

'We'll have news soon. Vien's servants trade information willingly. My mother will find out what Kim Cuc is up to.'

I nodded, to show that was an end to *that* conversation. Bao was a spy and an old neighbour, but I required only his information, not his opinion or implication. He moved on, indifferently fluid, poking at Hung and making faces which forced a smile from my little nephew. Nhi was quiet and I knew that she was pondering Kim Cuc's loyalty. We shared a look and I knew that we were both thinking we would not wait for Mrs Chau to send a message. This mess with the Thi sisters was getting out of hand and it was time we went to see Kim Cuc ourselves.

★★★★★

We went together. Thao came with us, and Cong with a handful of her best-trained men and women. Chinh was already stationed near Chu Dien with a reserve force. My mother stayed

289

in Me Linh and Hung, despite a few tears and protestations, eventually waved goodbye from Diep's arms. I felt bad, taking both his parents, but I wanted Nhi with me, and Thao was unwilling to be apart from his wife so soon after their reunion. There was not a question of Hung accompanying us. Me Linh was safe, but the mood in Lien Lau might be volatile, and even in Chu Dien, there might be plotting against us. We had majority support, we thought, but could Vien or Kim Cuc be capable of a sneaky assassination? I could not ignore the possibility. Khanh had not realised until the last moment where we were going, and she hurried to us, asking for us to take her home.

'Not in your advancing condition,' I said, shaking my head. 'I have lost too many babies myself to allow that,' and she had the grace at least to lower her head and hide her burning cheeks.

Chinh was not forewarned of our approach so she met us with some surprise on the road, after our journey south-west from Me Linh, and escorted us towards the Thi homestead. She knew that Kim Cuc had seen Ton Vien, she said, but not what they had spoken about. In her estimation, Kim Cuc was no more friendly with Vien than political diplomacy demanded. Yes, Chinh had passed on our refusal to allow Khanh to come home, but she believed Kim Cuc had been unsurprised at the answer to her request.

We tethered our horses by the water trough and Cong surrounded the house with her guards. Kim Cuc waited, dark-eyed and unsmiling by the house steps. A breeze agitated her loose dress and the long ends of her sash swayed against her legs. Her normally pretty and rounded face was more gaunt. Had that happened during the war and I just had not noticed? She bowed to us and led us inside, very properly. Cong followed to the bottom of the steps and waited there with Chinh. The guards stood unmoving in the light wind, a frozen ripple around Kim Cuc's home.

'You do not seem surprised to see us,' I observed, following her into the darkened living space.

'It was only a matter of time,' Kim Cuc replied, with the shadow of a smile.

Nhi glanced at me as I inhaled sharply.

'What will you do with her now? Though it's not a crime, is it?' Kim Cuc squatted down as she spoke, though we remained standing.

'What do you mean?' I asked.

'Pretending to be with child. You can't punish her for that,' Kim Cuc said.

'So it is a pretence?'

'Isn't that why you're here?' she faltered. 'I assumed she must have been found out.'

'We are here to talk to you,' I said, 'about why you visited Vien after we refused to allow your sister home, but it is helpful to know that you and your sister have indeed been faking her pregnancy.'

'No, no! That's not it at all,' Kim Cuc said, clasping her shaking hands in front of her. 'Please let me explain. I didn't-don't know if she's faking or not. I think so but I can't be sure. I do know that she's been having conversations with Vien that are... inappropriate. Her husband, too. When you recalled her to Me Linh, I was *glad*. I didn't like what she was thinking, what she was saying. But she is my sister. I had to call for her release and I have to try to protect her. When you refused to let her go, I was just so angry. Not at you, but at Vien, for encouraging her and getting her into this mess. I went to beg him to see reason and show proper loyalty and respect to Trung Nu Vuong. I asked him to intervene on Khanh's behalf - to promise his own good behaviour in exchange for her release - but he laughed and would not. That, he said, would suggest he had behaved improperly. I left in disgust.'

I squatted down opposite her.

'Your sister does not like me, does she?'

'No.' Kim Cuc looked directly into my eyes.

'She is jealous of me.'

'She's jealous of the power you hold.'

'But you feel differently?'

'Yes, of course.'

'Then why did you not come to us when Khanh began plotting against us?'

'Because she is my sister. My older sister. How could I go against her?'

I sighed. How could I argue with that? But Kim Cuc misinterpreted the sigh as disappointment with her answer.

'You should understand how I feel,' she accused, big dark eyes flashing with a wet sheen. 'I lost Sach, like you did. I lost my father. I fought at Lien Lau, in all that horror. I only have Khanh and now she's gone there's just me, in charge of all this.' She gestured out to the plain of Chu Dien, the rice fields, the little markets, the swamps, the waterways, the garrisons of soldiers left over from the Thi division, all of it now controlled and managed by her slim and shaking hands. She gulped down a sob and righted her face again.

'Not *just* you, Kim Cuc,' I said. 'You've forgotten that you have more than one sister.' I reached out and smoothed her cheek with my fingertips. Kim Cuc was small and frightened. She was what a different Nhi might have been like – a Nhi who had not wandered the plains as a child, a Nhi whose father had comforted and protected her. The pair were almost equal in age, but it was funny now, to think that Nhi might ever have turned out fragile.

'I can't send Khanh home to you, little sister, but I can send assistance. Chinh will stay on to help you and I will have my own mother come and visit for a while. There is nothing my mother does not know about territory management, and though she can be harsh, I think you'll find her comforting. Now, what of Khanh's husband?'

'In Lien Lau,' Kim Cuc answered. 'He's afraid you'll imprison him, so he dare not stay in Chu Dien.'

'Does he think my rule does not extend into that town,' I laughed. 'Well, I am glad that he is not here bothering you. I expect we will find him with Ton Vien, cooking up some trouble for me.'

Kim Cuc relaxed a little at my tone. I think she was regretting her emotional outburst and she tried hard now to cover her previous distress. Nhi had not spoken in the very short time it had taken for me to establish that Kim Cuc was not conniving with Vien against us. Now she strode to the square gap in the wooden wall that looked out upon our horses and soldiers, and she called a command to Cong about changing the horses for fresh ones.

'We should go to Lien Lau. We're in the wrong place here. I hope to see you soon, sister,' she said to Kim Cuc and embraced her with a hard pat on the back. They broke apart and Kim Cuc bowed to me, long and low and then I was out the doorway with Nhi, going down the steps to where Cong was fetching new horses and others were scurrying to swap saddles. Our whole conversation in the Thi house had taken only moments.

'What are you thinking, Nhi?' I asked very quietly as we walked together.

'We go to Lien Lau for the night. Let Vien stew knowing we're there. In the morning, he'll come to us, as he should, and we'll see what he has to say for himself.'

'It could be dangerous,' I mused, looking at our small guard. 'We have not got the numbers.'

'Since when has Lien Lau been out of bounds to us?' Nhi asked, exasperated. 'Remember, Trac, there are far more people with us than against us, even in Vien's town. Otherwise, he wouldn't confine himself to treacherous late-night conversations and incitement of the traders.'

'That is a fair reflection of the situation,' I agreed. 'But are we needlessly stirring the pot? We may be creating a fight when we do not need to. There is no grand conspiracy.'

'I think the time has come to stop all this nonsense. How long can we let Vien get away with this behaviour? The more the people see him acting so disrespectfully, the more they will come to believe that you are the weak, illegitimate ruler he says you are.'

I nodded, anger outweighing caution. Nhi was right, something had to be done. But how would people feel if I imprisoned, banished or, worse still, executed an old and respected Prefect?

★★★★★

Overnight, Cong sent two of the guards to track down Khanh's husband. Mrs Chau was not in town, or it might have been easier, but even so, we had other informants who were able to tell us the district in which he was staying and the exact home was quickly identified. By the time Vien dragged his bitter old self into our presence, Khanh's husband had already been quietly imprisoned.

I was tired – we had not got to Lien Lau until late and when dismal sunlight filtered in through an early morning cloud bank, I was not sure I had actually been asleep at all – whether the ruminations I had been subject to all night were conscious thoughts or dreams. Nhi was sprightly, though. She was always excited about defending my honour.

'You should have let me know you were coming. I could have arranged a better reception for you,' Vien said, after greeting all of us – myself, Nhi, Thao and Cong. He had so much experience of diplomacy with the Han that he seemed entirely unabashed in our presence.

'The beauty of ruling all of Nam Viet is that I can go where I want, when I want, Lord Vien,' I quipped and he smiled, readying a similarly light-hearted response. Vien was used to conversational games. He boated across the surface of words, finding the current that would take him through tricky waters. I did not let him reply. 'Do you know another good thing about ruling the whole land? I hear everything that happens. I know every word spoken and I know the words you have spoken, *Lord* Vien.' I spoke his title as if I could remove it at will, which, of course, I could.

'But words without context are-' he began, still trying to smile. I cut him off.

'Which noble would you replace me with?'

'What?'

'I said, which noble person would you replace me with? Would you prefer Khanh as your queen?'

'No, Trung Nu Vuong, I-'

'Would you prefer to be king?'

'No, you are queen, Trung Nu-'

'Perhaps you would like the Han to return, so you can bow down to their emissaries once more?'

Vien stayed quiet now, realising this was not a battle he could win. My directness had taken him off balance. The outspoken indignation at Hai Phong almost ten years earlier might have come from a different man.

'The passes will remain closed and Thi Khanh will remain in my custody. Nam Viet is ruled by Trung Nu Vuong and if there is any further dissent from you on that point, I will have you driven in chains to the northern borders and cast over to into the Middle Kingdom as a plaything. There are some angry Han ex-prefects up there, you know, men who would like to take their retribution on a real *Viet* Lord.'

Vien nodded. Then he bowed. He paused for just a moment, wondering if he was expected to speak, but I looked away and he backed from my presence. Nhi and Thao looked thunderously towards him and he fled, probably all too aware that he had narrowly escaped some serious kind of punishment.

'I am not executing nobility,' I said to them, before they

could argue. 'Thao, go and frighten the young man in our jail. Find out what you can, but do not kill him, then offer him a relaxed period of detention with Khanh, if he agrees to soften her for us.'

'Is that wise?' asked Nhi.

'How else do we turn Khanh? And if she will not be turned, what will I do with her?'

'It would be easy for her to pretend loyalty while planning revolt.'

'I know, which is why I need Thao to render her husband so terror-stricken that he will answer to us before he conceals his wife's deceit.'

'Torturing the man might just inflame him,' said Nhi.

'Doubt it,' Cong butted in cheerfully as Thao strode away with a grimace. 'The man's a coward. He'll be pleading for his life before his blood is even spilt.'

Cong was correct about that, though it did not prevent some blood being spilt, but it would take time to see if the husband could bring Khanh into line.

While we were there in Lien Lau, news came at last of Ma Vien - another Vien to cause me trouble and worry. Delayed by his errors in fleet organisation, Ma Vien had set upon another course of action. We thought he would build more boats, but Ma Vien could not wait and he had an eager army, whose enthusiasm he could not allow to evaporate. Instead of sticking to the plan to invade by sea, Ma Vien was coming by land. How would he do this? He was at Hop Pho Commandery with twenty thousand men, no direct route to us by land and all his provisions loaded uselessly onto ships. Only Ma Vien could envision it, could cause it to happen. This man was a plague to me. The grand Wave-Taming General was *making* a road. His army were digging and building as they travelled along the coast and, more horrifying still, the fleet we had thought was dead in the water, sailed alongside, provisions readily available for Ma

Vien's advancing troops.

Sometimes the flash floods pour through villages, water rising swiftly when the rain causes the rivers to rise or the water-logged land can take no more. It happens suddenly, with barely time for panic, and everyone leaps into action, moving the children, kicking the livestock and pets to higher ground. The sudden, sharp attack spurs everyone into a flurry. But silently and slowly, the constant river erodes the banks, taking whole generations to shift ten paces to the left, or to carve a new stream where before there was a field, a pen, a house. The flash floods recede eventually, but the force of erosion is almost unstoppable, constant as an army with pick axes and shovels.

22

I wish I could say that Thao and I were perfectly happy after I had forgiven his lapse, but it wasn't so simple. There was just so much to do. I had Generals and divisions scattered across Nam Viet, all of whom were supposed to report to me, but many of whom scarcely bothered. Within Me Linh, I was ultimately responsible for the security of our family and however much I delegated to Cong, I still liked to know exactly what was happening. Mother went away to Kim Cuc's for a while and that increased the burden of work. I was still at Trac's side, as much as I had ever been. Slowly, the arguments restarted – Thao wanting to know why I was so late to bed, Hung stirring beside us, his sleep disturbed by voices filled with mutual irritation. We went round the same old circles, me citing Trac's need for my support, him insisting that I had deeper responsibilities to him and to Hung. Then I would be stung, at his implied criticism of my mothering and we would both fall asleep angry and unsatisfied. Trac was much the same as she had been for these past few years. Though she was capable and efficient, a good queen, her eyes were clouded as if a grey veil had been laid over her. She became more like herself in moments of urgency, such as when she confronted Ton Vien, but even then, it was the feral Trac, the toothed, tiger-hearted warrior that emerged. Not the big sister of old – not the gregarious, laughing, married creature that had so disconcerted me, nor the sharp, logical, protective girl who had to be dragged out into the fields to play. There was a secret at the heart of why I spent so much time with Trung Nu Vuong, and it had little to do with the demands of our work. I was watching all the time for the real Trac to make an appearance, for her mantle of grief to finally be cast off. I missed her terribly, and the feeling only grew over time. I had no words with which to explain this to Thao. He wouldn't have understood even if I had tried.

At the end of the rains, Mother came back from Chu Dien, leaving Kim Cuc in a much more settled state. Chinh stayed on there, ostensibly to support Kim Cuc, but according to Mother because she was infatuated with some distant cousin of the Thi sisters. Mother wasn't particularly impressed with or interested in this romantic development so her answers to my impatient questions were brief and dismissive and I had to wait for Chinh to visit before I could pry properly into my friend's new relationship. Chinh was a lively, intelligent woman and I'd never seen her captivated by a man before, though I think there was someone, long ago, before she first came to our home in Cam Khe to train with us. Aside from my personal interest, I had an interest as Commander of our army. Chinh was the General I trusted the most, not counting Mother of course. Chinh had more experience and skill than Cong and she was far closer and more devoted to us than Le Chan or any of the one-time Prefects who now answered to Trung instead of Han. She was more necessary to Trac and I than she was to some man from Chu Dien. Yet, I knew I wouldn't stop her marrying if that was what she wanted to do.

In the wintertime she came to Me Linh to ask permission. She didn't have to - we weren't enforcing any of the old laws to do with getting married - but she wanted us to know and to approve. She brought the man in question, who was older than I'd expected and wore a confident and mature expression. He was vaguely familiar. A Captain, maybe, from Kim Cuc's division? He was tall but stringy, with a squarish jaw, wide nose and quite dark skin. He spoke softly, but in a low, resonant voice so that his words hummed together.

'By trade, he's a craftsman,' Chinh explained to us, as Nghiem Dat folded betel leaf with Thao, 'but since the war, he's maintained a garrison in Chu Dien.'

'What sort of craft?' Trac asked, watching Dat with Thao. The pair were getting on well, to my delight.

'Carpentry, lacquer-work, horn-carving,' Chinh shrugged as if she could go on, but didn't want to boast. She was proud of him. It shone in her face.

'But now he's a soldier?'

'For now,' Chinh nodded. 'After all, Nam Viet has more need of warriors at present than it has of artists.'

'I wish more men of our country realised that,' said Trac. She looked approvingly towards Thao and Dat, and then to my surprise, Thao scowled at her and turned quickly away. It was so fast that I nearly missed it. I looked at Trac but she was as impassive as ever and I assumed she mustn't have noticed. Later, after Chinh had taken Dat out for a walk down to the river and Thao had gone outside to spit the remnants of his betel and areca away, Trac caught me by the arm.

'What is wrong with Thao?' she demanded. I should have known his glare would not have escaped her.

'Why don't you ask me?' said Thao, who had heard her clearly through the wooden wall that separated us.

She went to face him as he returned to the living area. 'So?' she said. I stood still where I was, afraid of what he would say. Thao could be so unpredictable, and, when he was angry, he didn't care about hierarchy or manners.

'You make a slave of my wife, then ask me what's wrong? When will you let Nhi spend some time with her family? She's with you all day, every day and it's draining the life out of her. *You're* draining the life out of her.' He jabbed with a finger as he spoke and I winced at the offence his words and attitude must be causing to Trac. 'Do you know what Hung asked me the other day? "Why does Auntie make Mother so sad?" How long, Trung Nu Vuong, before you stop ruining the lives of those around you?'

I hurried between them then, stepping in front of Thao like a shield against the wrath I was sure must be about to flow from Trac's permanently attached short sword. Thao was biting at his bottom lip, not exactly remorseful for what he'd said, but realising from my quick flight across the room just how far he had stretched familial etiquette. I could get away with ranting at Trac occasionally, but no one else could. I looked at him with horror, then swung my head to face Trac, lifting my arms instinctively.

'He's sorry, sister. He shouldn't have said any of that. Please forgive...' But I tailed off because Thao was silent behind me and I knew my apologies were meaningless if he wouldn't give his own. Plus, Trac was staring at me curiously. I coloured under her gaze, feeling exposed and embarrassed. I wanted to drag Thao from the room, but her black eyes pinned me there.

'Are you sad, little sister?' she asked. 'Sad because of me?'

I couldn't answer. I would never have said I was sad because of her, but sad for her? Yes, I was that. Sometimes, over these difficult years, I had been angry at her, but mostly it was sadness. I hadn't realised it showed and now I had no answer. She gave me a tight smile, then a blank stare at Thao, before turning abruptly and striding into her private room at the back of the house. We stood like carved fools for a moment, then I launched myself, fists swinging, at Thao.

'How could you?' I hissed, as he caught at my wrists and held me away from him, his face open-mouthed but dumb. I ran out, down the steps and away from the house out towards where the new temple stood. I would have run to the river to stare into the flowing waters, but it was crowded near the banks these days and I couldn't allow the people to see my tears.

★★★★★

It was a horrible night. Thao tried to hold me and I pushed him away. I put Hung between us and turned my back on both of them. Trac had stayed hidden away for the rest of the day and Mother, who had been apprised of events by our long-suffering servant, Diep, advised me not to disturb her. In the morning, when I woke up, I felt the flare of joy in a new day discoloured almost immediately by recollection of the previous day's events. I slipped from under our winter blankets and pulled my *ao tu than* tight around me, careful not to wake Hung or Thao, who were wrapped against each other on the heated brick bed. Outside, fastening my sash, only the barest light rose from the horizon and no voices yet broke the dawn. I swung my long sword in a high circle, flexing my arms and dropped into an attacking pose, left leg well forward, body lunging, sword forward. From there, I spun myself upwards and to the right, using my left leg as leverage, turning in the air to land facing the opposite direction at an imagined second foe. My sword cut through the dust-coloured morning in near silence, just the whispered slice of blade through air and the soft pressure of my feet, twisting and landing on the winter-hardened earth. I hardly felt the cold - the soles of my feet were stronger and thicker than the soles of any Han shoes. My hair fell from its wrap as I worked through my forms and I pricked the falling length of material with the point of my sword and flung it to one side, where it crumpled to the ground, a small hole now evident in the weave. My hair, thick and black, coiled on my shoulders and down my back. A weak sun lifted in the distance, but the heat came from my own body - tiny rivulets of sweat beginning to work their way beneath my vest and dress. I felt a muscle twinge in my arm, from the tiger bite, and old strain from the fighting at Lien Lau where I had wielded my sword so tirelessly, and rather than resent the pain, I welcomed the reminder. My eyes were closed. I saw them falling in front of me again, those vicious Han fighters. I killed them over and over. The first I realised that Trac was watching was when she spoke, so I've no idea how long she was there.

'You used to draw a circle on the ground.'

I stopped, opened my eyes. She stood too close, grin on her face.

'You used to make more noise,' I replied

'I'm a tiger queen now, have you not heard? No one hears me coming.' She laughed and raised her sword. The metal glinted silver and I put my own one to it, clashing metal. Then we went through the sequence again, one of many that we knew by heart. She stopped my blade and I stopped hers and neither of us had any fear that the bright, sparkling edges would find flesh. Thao and Hung came out onto the steps and over at the main house, Mother watched from the doorway. Cong came by, fear in her eyes that we were training with sharpened swords, but she knew better than to interrupt. I heard Chinh shouting to Dat, 'Come on, this isn't something you see every day,' but, save for registering their presence, I ignored them all. The sweat was a slick under my breasts and across my shoulder blades. How long did we fight? Through so many forms that were as natural to us as breathing, until our pace ebbed and the sun was so fully up that it had disappeared behind the clouds, until finally we had to stop because we were hungry and the crowd had grown embarrassingly large.

'Very good, Commander Nhi,' Trac bowed to me.

'Likewise, Trung Nu Vuong,' I said, bowing back.

'Good morning,' she called to Thao and then walked towards them, ruffled Hung's hair and gave him a great big smile which he returned with something like awe in his eyes.

'That was magnificent,' said Thao, with his head bowed.

'Yes, I know. She *is* good, isn't she?' I heard Trac say deliberately, still smiling, before she went to chat to some of the people still hovering around.

I went and joined Thao. Hung attached himself to my legs.

'What was that?' Thao asked. He looked as though someone had hit his head with a block.

'That was Trac,' I said and the beam of my smile was enough to knock him out all over again.

★★★★★

What was it she had said? She saw that peacock and came

303

back to life? That was how I felt, except it was not a dream of blue-green feathers, it was the vision of Nhi before me, unable to deny what her husband had said – that *I* made everyone unhappy. It shocked me out of the remnants of foul depression and into the brightness of a new day, where life did not have to hinge on painful memories. It was about the timing too. I was ready to hear it. A year earlier and I might have struck Thao before Nhi got in the way. As it was, I reeled away from them both and went to consider the fact that a little boy knew me only as a miserable, oppressive aunt – that all I had been, before, meant nothing, if he could not share in it. From there, I understood that the past is truly ephemeral and that we have to tie it to our present. My memories of happiness with Sach, of growing up with Nhi, of sitting in my father's arms, meant nothing to this little boy if they were hidden from him by my grief. The happy times may as well have never happened, if I let them be clouded out by misery. I had to protect the right memories. If I went on the way I was going, Hung and everyone else who came after would only remember the deaths, the losses. That was not what I wanted at all. I thought I was honouring Sach by clinging to the pain of his loss, when in fact I was losing him entirely.

It was like looking down and realising I had fastened chains around my body, then immediately stepping free. I looked back at the pile of discarded links and wondered that I had ever been able to function with all that draped around me. My splintered self had begun to heal.

Chinh and Dat married not long afterwards, making their home in Chu Dien, near to Kim Cuc. We missed Chinh's cheerful presence in Me Linh, but she was more useful to us downriver, in the busy delta region, and of course, she was a Tay Vu woman at heart anyway. Secretly, Cong was pleased, though she would never have admitted it. Much as she liked Chinh, there was always a tension between the pair, each believing that she was the most senior and respected of the Trung Generals. Oddly the one thing Cong was not so enamoured with was my change in mood. Sometimes she looked almost disappointed with me and I understood that, just like Hung, she had known me only as the avenging widow. Whilst Hung was delighted with the new side to his aunt, perhaps Cong felt that I had lost something - that I had in some way betrayed the mask of *Hai Ba Trung*, which she had helped fashion. Her favourite topic of conversation was the advance by Ma Vien. Without a war on the horizon, Cong would not have known what to do with herself. It was our fault - we took a young girl who was eager and without direction, and moulded her into a child of the battlefield - so we could not complain if she insisted on militaristic training for everyone of age in Me Linh, nor if she expanded the Me Linh guard force to larger proportions than anyone anticipated. She had a gift for warfare. Whilst Chinh was the more accomplished martial artist, Cong was now the more brilliant General.

It was because of Cong's burgeoning competence that I felt fully able to order Nhi to spend some time with Thao and Hung. Thao's hard-flung words had pierced me and although I smarted from his insolence, I gave him what he wanted - time with Nhi before Ma Vien came. I watched them often, without them realising. Thao, walking with Hung on his shoulders; Nhi leaning into Thao just enough to lightly brush their outer arms. They took Hung out walking or on the horses, for rides over the hills and plains and I watched them blurring into nothing in the distance; watched again when they returned. Sometimes, when my heart was strong, I wished they would keep going, over the far western hills and into the hidden valleys, and never come back.

23

The second phase of our war started like this: The news spread down the coast that Ma Vien was through to the existing tracks. His progress would be much faster now. His army was too large to blockade in the north. He would trample his twenty thousand men all the way into the Red River delta and wait for us to attack. Le Chan drew in her forces to the east and held them ready. The Chu Dien and Lien Lau regions prepared in earnest. Me Linh quivered with angry anticipation.

I toured the delta as much as possible over the time we had, inspecting the assembling divisions and armouries, and talking with the Generals. Nhi and Cong came with me: my mother and Thao held Me Linh: Chinh assumed overall command of Chu Dien and Lien Lau, with Kim Cuc and Ton Vien reporting to her. Every day dragged on, far into the star time and every morning began before light. There were hundreds of people who wanted to speak with me, thousands who needed to see me and I could not neglect a single one. The fear and the fury fought for supremacy – would these masses surrender to save their own lives or would they summon their courage and battle the Han again for the future of our country? Everywhere I went, I whipped up passion for the cause, and occasionally I horse-whipped lazy Captains or run-away soldiers or dissenters who shouted obscenities. Dotted amongst the majority who hated the Han were a few who doubted me. I saw the eyes of powerful men who resented my leadership because I was a woman and because they had been raised on Confucian ethics that disparaged the very notion of a female leader. But they were few, and the voices calling for surrender to the emperor were usually taken care of by the rest of the crowd, if not by my own guards. I welcomed some hostility – it gave me a fine prompt to raise my speech to a strident, fiery crescendo. I didn't take them seriously, these fools who wanted to lay down their bodies as a stamping ground for Yellow River feet. What kind of people were they, anyway? Not mine. Confucius said, I would not take in my army anyone who would try to fight a tiger with his bare hands or walk across the River and die in the process without regrets. All well and good, you pompous old shit. Your emperor can keep those cowardly bureaucrats and the Tiger Queen will take all the fine warriors who fear nothing.

That is, in fact, the kind of thing I said. Nhi and Cong approved. They flanked me whenever I spoke and when I'd finished, Cong riled the people, whether they were conscripted village folk or organised companies, into chants of '*Hai Ba Trung*' and 'Trung Nu Vuong' as Nhi and I rode regally away. We never, ever called Ma Vien the 'Wave Tamer,' when we made our speeches. I would close the pass that our ancestor, Lu Chia, had forgotten about – the pass of Middle Kingdom words and ideas that led direct to the human heart. I spat my enemy's given name on the floor. Ma Vien, pah! Just a man. We have vanquished the dirty, thieving Han before and we will do it again. Easy as that.

Our private conversations and orders were necessarily very different, more realistic. Le Chan sent terrifying updates on the scale and preparedness of Ma Vien's marching columns. Reports came to us of whole villages crushed by the onslaught, their stores raided and inhabitants sent fleeing across the countryside. Stand aside, we urged the outlying regions. Let the Han army through to where we can fight them. Ma Vien's fleet, which once we had laughed at, sailed up the river with all his army's provisions, making for the wide lake at Lang Bac.

'How far will you let them come?' fretted Ton Vien in Lien Lau. Chinh ordered him to hold firm; the garrison at Co Loa would slow them down. Ma Vien would most likely come to a halt there, near to where his fleet would surely dock. All of the Red River delta teetered on a knife edge. The garrisons in Lien Lau and in northern Chu Dien were braced. The Me Linh division began its march to join them. Companies and Divisions of the Trung army snaked their way through the limestone hills and sediment-covered valleys, across tidal flats and tropical forests to converge on the Lac heartland. The men and women of the temples pounded the great, bronze drums. Le Chan drove her forces inland, from the east.

Then, the drums stopped. Four moons after Chinh's wedding, we stared across a major artery of the Red River and witnessed the hazy, distant aura of twenty thousand Middle Kingdom soldiers settling into the eastern end of the marshy plain of Tay Vu. They were on our ancient battleground and they were waiting for us to fight.

★★★★★

When the glorious rains fell by the bucket-load, Ma Vien was swamped, even up on the high ground of Lang Bac which he had taken over. Getting close enough to really see his troops was difficult - mostly they were just a minuscule, blurry outline in the wet, opal shimmer - but occasionally, when the sun burnt through the teeming clouds, we could make out the tiny figures of men struggling to assemble materials and build shelters, their mallets and hammers thudding through the thick humidity. We had Lien Lau, and the various garrisons of Chu Dien, so our army were cramped but comfortable enough. Out there in Tay Vu, the Han were sodden, pelted continually by the thunderous monsoon assault. Their tenacity was impressive - unimaginable lengths of road built behind them and still they worked on, out in the weather under the eyes of their enemy. They were career soldiers, single-minded and fully trained. They were more dangerous than the cowards we had ousted from Giao Chi, Cuu Chan and Nhat Nam, not three years before.

'I might have a problem holding Le Chan back,' Trac confided to me, many days into the stand-off. Spies edging close to the Han encampment were bringing back reports of green-faced men, vomiting and shitting in the long grasses away from their camp. They said the air around Lang Bac was starting to smell.

It was the best news we could have hoped for. If we were on the brink of watching the Han army die from some pestilence, we should surely sit back and enjoy the view, not charge in and waste our efforts where nature was likely to carry out a more thorough job.

'She's impatient, but she'll see sense. I know Le Chan. She's not a fool.'

'You do not know her really, though. It has been many years, little sister, since your visit to Hai Phong.'

'You think she'd disobey your orders?'

'Probably. Le Chan began forging her army long before we made ours. She has never felt the same loyalty to us as the other generals do. But she has not the numbers to win. She will only do it if she can persuade more people to her way of thinking.'

'They're dying of disease. Everyone should be made to understand that our chances are improved by letting illness reduce their numbers.'

'The way some of our generals see it, we should rush in now and defeat them while they are unprepared and weakened, not wait for them to recover.'

'That doesn't make any sense. Have you seen them out there? One or two might have caught a river fever, but the rest are hardly unprepared. Trac, these soldiers are not like anything we've faced before. We all laughed at the idiots who ran from Cuu Chan, but they were the weaklings of the empire. They were the cheats and liars and greedy scum that tried to make a fortune out of our country. All the good men went back, after Wang Mang. All the shitty men stayed here. That was what we fought before, the shit that was left. But these are men of honour and bravery – men in the mould of Tich Quang, not To Dinh. Our army outnumbers them, but our army's skill is not equal to theirs.'

'I know, I know.' Trac sighed. 'But it does no good to know these things. How can I explain our tactics to my disaffected

Generals, if by doing so my logic makes clear that they are out-skilled?'

Le Chan must realise, I thought. Surely she could see how dangerous twenty thousand Han soldiers were, even against three times that amount of our own warriors. Or, maybe, she couldn't. After all, she was an uneducated woman – just a girl from the coast who got caught up in the lecherous scheming of a licentious governor. Equally, many of the people outside of our very close circle were schooled only in the ancient ways of our land, with a confused smattering of Confucius on top. Even within our circle, there was Cong from her remote village, who had never interested herself in learning the history of our former oppressors and who would burn any strips of ink-marked bamboo that she happened to find. Trac had been the one to say, most forcefully, that we did not need educating in the ways of the Middle Kingdom – that Confucian ideology must be obliterated – but without truly knowing our enemy, we were blind to the dangers.

Trac and I were educated. We had taken for granted that other people knew the things we knew, but in truth, few had mothers and fathers that had passed on the history of the Middle Kingdom or that talked about politics while they ate. How many knew that thirty years ago, the Middle Kingdom had been torn apart by its own rebellion? That Wang Mang had tried to establish a Qin dynasty and that many good, strong Han had fled south, looking for a place to flourish? I hadn't thought about it much either, as a child, when Mother talked in snippets about these events that seemed so archaic to me – taking place, as they did, before I was born – but it made a perfect sense now, looking back on all that had passed in our lifetimes. Father never had serious problems with the Han, did he? Not the way Trac or Mother remember it. Not the kind of trouble we've had since. When anyone talks of Governor Tich Quang, they can't help the note of respect that enters their voice. Get them to speak the name of To Dinh and they crease their face in disgust. You see, when Wang Mang, of the Qin tribe fell, and the Han took over the Middle Kingdom once more, men that had escaped down here to Nam Viet went back. The honourable men, the ambitious men, the men who wanted close service with their emperor so their talents and achievements would be recognised: they slowly left, over the years, and the ones who stayed were the ones for whom distance from the emperor equalled freedom for personal tyranny and gain. The crooked men, the men in whom ambition was not tempered with humanity, stayed and took advantage of our country until we could stand it no more - until *Hai Ba Trung*.

The men in Tay Vu now were of the first kind. They were the upstanding men of the Middle Kingdom - Generals who waged war according to clear rules and custom, Captains who trained their soldiers in line with principle, and soldiers whose hearts and minds were bound by discipline. Like I said before, they were dangerous. To me, there was no question about it. We should sit tight and wait. I gave the orders daily to that effect.

In all that time before battle, I rode back to Me Linh only once. It was, of course, to see Hung, who was there in the care of Uncle Hien and Auntie Linh. Their three children, all older than Trac and I, were leaders in our division, answering to Cong, though I didn't know them very well. They'd always lived in the north, staying there even when Uncle and Auntie started to spend more time in Me Linh. With the arrival of Ma Vien, our cousins had rejoined the army, and Uncle and Auntie took charge of Hung. In actuality, it was Diep who still cared for my son and I knew, despite the motherly attentions of both Diep and Auntie Linh, that he missed his father and me very much. He hid it well, under that sombre countenance that had somehow skipped sideways from Trac and down my line, but underneath his composure, he was at heart just a two-year-old boy.

'Where's Father?' he asked as I clutched him into my arms.

'He's in Lien Lau, Hung, serving Auntie Trac.'

'Oh.' His shoulders slumped

'But you'll see him soon. I'll send him back to visit.'

'Did you fight Han?'

'No, Hung, not yet. But the Han are getting sick with river fever, so that's good news. It will make it easier for us to win.'

'Will you win, Mother?'

'I'll try my best,' I said. Having run out of questions for the time being, he led me towards a corner of the room where two groups of pebbles and stones faced each other menacingly across a shred of old blue silk. Two of Mother's old bowls, chipped but cherished, that normally languished in her lacquered cabinet, were upturned. I guessed they were supposed to be Chau mountain and the Lang Bac heights. I raised an eyebrow at Auntie Linh.

'She'll never know,' mouthed my aunt, squatting down behind Hung while he explained to me who each of the stones were. Once I knew who was who, I helped him rearrange everyone into a more accurate formation. Hung was thrilled and he ran outside to collect twigs and sticks, so we could represent the Lien Lau and Chu Dien garrisons, and yet more stones for all our soldiers. The room was very silent after his feet clattered down the front steps.

'Will you win?' Auntie Linh asked me, echoing Hung and staring down at his little armies.

'If enough of them die from the fever, yes. Otherwise, it will be hard.'

'Your Uncle, he sometimes says,' she swallowed and picked up a stone General, rolling him between her fingers, 'he says that it would not be so bad for the Han to win. He says that we've made our point and that if we surrendered now, life could go back to the way it was long ago, when he was a child, when the Han respected the Lac.'

'And what do you say, Auntie?'

'That he is a dreamer and a philosopher, Nhi. I don't agree with him.'

'Then why tell me his thoughts? Do you want me to order his silence on the matter?'

'No, no. He wouldn't speak openly anyway. Just to me. The thing is, I wonder what will happen if you... lose.'

'Win or lose, Auntie, there will be a sacrifice. It's just a matter of how many.'

'I fear the revenge,' shuddered my aunt, 'I know I shouldn't and I feel a coward for even thinking about it, but the Han can be very cruel. Your Uncle fears it too - not for himself, but for the people, for everyone.'

'If it goes badly at Tay Vu, Thao will come for Hung. I've given him orders to follow the Red River far up into the mountains. You should go too, but don't encourage others. Hung will have a better chance if the group is small and inconspicuous.'

He burst in then, arms spilling over with debris for our miniature battlefield and Auntie Linh was prevented from further discussion. I welcomed the restriction. Auntie Linh's voice was tinged with the faint note of panic and I knew that conjecture and speculation would increase her anxiety, not lessen it. As for myself, I couldn't contemplate failure for more than a moment. Like a muscle trained a thousand times to wield a sword correctly, my mind should only travel the path of victory. If it practised defeat, I was doomed.

★★★★★

This time, I could not pin the discontent entirely on Khanh or Ton Vien. In fact, Khanh was on my side and believed we should wait for the vomiting and diarrhoea to do its worst to the Han army. Her husband had encouraged her into a measure of obedience and respectfulness, but her better behaviour had more to do with her intelligent analysis of the situation. The woman was a troublesome pain, but she was cautious and calculating and, for her brains, I had allowed her to join us near Lien Lau.

Still, she was partly responsible, along with Vien. She had sown the seeds that got certain people thinking that a woman could not be fully trusted to lead, unwittingly ruining any imagined chance she had of taking my power for herself. She had allowed Ton Vien to raise, in private, the Confucian concerns that females were inferior and now, Generals who chafed at my refusal to attack, began to wonder if there was a truth to this undercurrent of subversion. The unquestioned allegiance to *Hai Ba Trung* was fracturing as Generals met with each other and discussed the position, and as messengers ran between the grand Divisions, carrying official orders and replies, but also passing along gossip and chatter. It was no less than I had expected. What was essential was to keep control of the army and hold them back until they could no longer be restrained. I was disappointed and worried to find that I was already at that point. Ma Vien's men were still dying, their morale was suffering, but the gift of time that this gave us had been thrown aside by my own, impatient people.

I could hold them no longer. I ordered Nhi to round up our divisions and she obeyed without argument, scenting which way the wind was blowing, just as I did.

They had been back to see little Hung, separately, but I did not ask her or Thao about him. I had no living children, but those little bundles I had burned to ash had given me some small sense of the tearing pain that accompanies parenthood and I knew better than to mention him. Besides, our garrisons and camps were full of children and all I thought whenever I saw them was that Hung was, at least, far better off away from there, safe in Me Linh. I am sure Nhi told herself the same thing.

As preparations got under way to move our troops to the north-west, where we could cross the river undetected, shielded by the Co Loa garrison, I sent Nhi to discharge Chinh and redistribute her duties among Kim Cuc, Khanh, and Chinh's husband, Nghiem Dat. It did not go according to plan. Chinh rode to see me, swollen tummy most obvious by now.

'Trung Nu Vuong, please don't remove me,' she pleaded. 'If you do, I will fight anyway, but you won't have the benefit of my command.'

'The baby,' I said, in answer. I glanced pointedly at the modest bulge in her dress. We had learned that Chinh was pregnant during our encampment and I had planned for some while to relieve her of duty before battle commenced. It was frustrating to lose a key General, but that was just the way it must be.

'I can fight better than most, even with the baby. Besides, I'm safer, mounted and at the rear, than fighting on foot, which is where I'll be if you remove my command.' Phung Thi Chinh's eyes were slitted, but not in anger - more in anxious desperation.

'Is this about proving yourself to us? Because I do not expect-'

'No, Trac. Listen, everyone must do their part here, or the Han will overrun us and what chance will the baby or I have then? They'll know me as General Chinh. They won't care whether or not I'm pregnant if they get behind the lines. I'll be just another head on the list, to be parcelled off to the Emperor. Let me be. I have plenty of time before the baby comes.'

I looked her up and down dubiously, but it was true that she remained agile enough to ride a horse and wield her sword. She carried well - the bump was low on her frame and her skin, hair and teeth all shone with health.

'This is your last chance to go,' I said. 'Run to Me Linh. Go to the mountains if we fail.'

'No,' she answered, shaking her head. 'I will not.'

'Then stay. Stay and see it through,' I said.

She smiled and bowed and ran back to her horse as if I had given her a great gift, rather than a sentence of horror. I wondered what Dat made of her desire to fight. Maybe he would be glad to have her by his side as war raged around them. Did he prefer her to die with him, if it came to that? Sach's face as he looked at me for the final time loomed clear in my memory, but now I felt I knew his answer. I had been right to go, right to run from a battle I could not win. Now, the situation was different - the battle could be won, and in any case, it was the very last chance. I could not blame Chinh for refusing to leave.

★★★★★

'Did I get it wrong at Tay Vu?' I ask, spitting blood as I try to push the words past my cracked lips.

Nhi looks round, startled. She has been watching the horizon, the darkening path between the hills where a sorry glint of fading sun has escaped the cloud cover to rest on golden cypress high on the ridges and paddy grass in the valley.

'I've never known you to be wrong about anything,' she replies and there is a muffled sound, half laugh, half sob from the pale, shaking figure of Chinh, just beyond my clever-mouthed sister.

'Should have... waited,' I said, fighting for air.

'It wasn't possible. The army would have broken apart. The slaughter would have been worse.'

'Worse? How?'

'Nhi's right,' says Chinh, and her voices floats, high and thin in the calm air. 'Half the army had lost confidence, without the southerners. And the rest were so arrogant they believed that waiting was cowardice. It had to happen when it did, or half the army would have fled and half would have fought and died.'

'Died anyway,' I manage to breathe.

'But they died gloriously,' said Chinh, 'and made a legend of you.'

It is hard to feel like a legend, when my vision is full of pinpricks of light and holes of pulsing grey, and when my hands and feet feel so cold I am not sure they exist any more, whether in fact those parts of myself have already died. But I accept Chinh's compliment silently. I am not sure it matters though. The war is lost, legend or not. Nhi must see my dejection because she answers my thoughts.

'The idea is what's important, Trac. Don't you remember? An

idea can crumble a mountain. It can hold back the flood or raze the trees. What we've given to the Lac is an idea of what they can be. It's up to them what they do now.' She shrugs her sharp, dirt-smeared shoulders. 'We're just two people. We've done all we can.'

'They'll fight again,' says Chinh, the barest hint of a smile on her bloodless lips. 'This country will be ours one day.'

The pair of them make me feel a bit better, but I am a realist at heart, not a dreamer like Nhi. All our generals are gone. Our army is obliterated. Who will fight? There is no one left.

When we entered the eastern Tay Vu plains, our army was less than that with which we routed the Han not three years earlier. We outnumbered Ma Vien's forces but of Cuu Chan's seven districts, only four had responded to our call, and the refusal of all five districts in the old Nhat Nam Commandery to join us was dispiriting. We made it over the river without Ma Vien realising, and there was some advantage in the timing of our attack, because his forces were surprised when they understood that battle would happen imminently. We set up camp opposite that of the Middle Kingdom men, far enough back to discourage skirmishing, close enough to spy. In the darkness that night, when our camp fires drove away the flies and Nhi talked with Cong, Chinh, Kim Cuc, Khanh and all the other Generals who came to be briefed, I could see the camp fires of Ma Vien's men and their indistinct shadows, as if a dark river reflected us.

The morning dawned, grey and damp and I armed myself over the clothing I had slept in. Riders came in through our rear guard with a message from Le Chan. She was circling Mount Chau and would attack on the eastern flank. Behind those riders were the elephant handlers. They walked the great creatures into camp fully ornamented and stood them out front, for Ma Vien's appreciation. They were different animals from before - one of the elephants from three years ago had died soon after from an infected wound and the other was in Me Linh, living out a tethered existence as a kind of ceremonial pet.

My mother stayed close by me, giving orders and relaying information back to me. Nhi and Thao were walking the line, checking in with the Generals. I had nearly forty of them, and most of them women. I was sure Ma Vien had never faced an army like mine before. Over the flat, silted old flood plain, I saw only men, armoured and indistinguishable from one another. They were stamping out morning fires, forming themselves into groups. There would be no meeting in the middle to discuss terms of surrender. No doubt Ma Vien had heard what had happened the last time the Han sent me an envoy.

Of necessity, I was distanced from my Generals, who each commanded large segments of the army. Down the line, I saw the unmistakeable profile of Chinh and beyond her I could make out Kim Cuc. Closer by, Cong lashed the Me Linh division into order with her growling tongue. The army massed into organic form around me, taking on a life of its own. My pride overtook my gnawing sense that this attack was an error of good judgement, and instead I allowed myself to revel in the beast I had created. Nhi returned and confirmed that all was in order.

We were ready before midday. I had been scanning the troops opposite and measuring our progress by theirs so we would not suffer a premature offensive, though I did not think that was Ma Vien's style. When we formed ourselves and moved forward from the camp debris of fires, carts and shelters, Ma Vien's army moved forward too and there he was, at the head of it, dead-centre. He rode a huge black horse and the small, overlapping plates of his armour moved with his torso like the scaly skin of a snake. His sword was unsheathed, but he slowed his horse on approach and let his troops pass around him, like waters parting for a rock and then rejoining. We marched and rode to the centre ground, but the Han stopped before we did and the front ranks raised metal-embossed shields. As we braced, a wave of arrows soared into the air, like a flock of birds released, then spliced down towards our front line. Me, my mother, Nhi and Thao were deep in the ranks and high on the elephants, easily out of range of the volley of death that rained down. We continued our progress over the fallen, wailing bodies and our own crossbow-carriers were returning the assault, but I saw that the well-equipped Han bowmen were preparing another release.

'Charge,' I shouted. On my right and left, Chinh and Cong echoed my command, and the Lac army moved out in haste, running through the arrows that came for a second time. We were slightly too far away to be running already, but better that than to suffer a third hit. The trained crossbowmen had taken perhaps a thousand Lac men and women down before a single Han had died. Our mounted fighters broke against the Han front line first, and the steaming clash of metal and horse flesh filled the horizon. Breathless warriors followed in on foot, swords swinging and though the Han front line sheared through a good proportion of our front-runners, their line was in fact broken, and our people were making it through into their tightly packed ranks, dragging them out of formation. To my right, I saw the approaching haze of Le Chan's division. Not yet, I willed, not yet. I wanted the Han fully focused on us so they would leave their flank open. It was too late, though. They had seen the new threat and were scrambling to brace themselves on a second front. Ma Vien had turned his horse abruptly and was directing units towards the east. Le Chan drove forward, and a second impact shuddered through the ranks on both sides. Behind me, my mother, who shared my elephant, let out a loud cry of triumph at the sight of Ma Vien's army being squeezed. Nhi and Thao, on the second elephant looked frustrated. I knew, as I had known last time, that Nhi would be down from that beast and fighting as soon as she could. I imagined Thao was holding her back, reminding her of their son back home in Me Linh, waiting for their return.

The fighting was in close now, and we were far behind it.

Chinh stayed back, as she had promised, but Dat and Kim Cuc pushed forward, along with Cong on my other side. It was getting difficult to see them, now that tactics had done their part and blood-lust had taken over. The shearing of limbs and the deep thrusts into flesh happened at such speed that the ground ahead was matted with blood and bodies. Our elephants had come to a standstill - Ma Vien's army was holding its ground.

The battle remained evenly balanced for a time, the line between our two armies not moving in either direction, even though Le Chan's enormous division was pushing from the flank with all the fury she could muster. Then, in the space between us and the front line, a rent opened up and Han soldiers poured in. Dat had gone down. His company were flailing against the better equipped Han soldiers, with their iron plating and protective helmets. One of Dat's men tried to pull him up, but as Dat struggled onto all fours, a finishing strike came from a Han soldier, who drove his sword deep into Dat's side, then dragged the reddened blade out to continue fighting. Nhi and Thao rode their elephant forward, crushing a few of the advancing Han and reaching down to hack at the enemy with their long blades and sharpened staffs. My mother and I were taking the same action, and there was no shortage of Han to take care of - they aimed for the elephants and tried to climb up to reach us. We choked off their assaults until they directed their energies instead into slicing at the elephants tough legs. Han cavalry were perilously close to us, and when they got their horses near enough, we had to fight hard to defend ourselves. Cong turned her unit and reassembled a larger part of the Me Linh division around us. We lost some ground, but we repaired the line.

A few arrows whistled through the air. The Han crossbow experts were trying to panic Cong's formation into breaking apart again. Despite the heavy offensive from Le Chan on the flank, somehow Ma Vien's army was pushing back hard, and if anyone's line was beginning to crack now, it was ours. I ordered

Nhi down from her elephant to assume command within Chinh's division.

'Where is she?' yelled Nhi, sliding down the ropes and mounting a horse that one of the foot soldiers had commandeered.

I scanned the fighting and located Kim Cuc and Khanh. They were too far forward, having some success at cutting through the enemy, but in danger of being encircled. As I ran my eyes over the carnage behind them, I found Chinh, on foot and fighting alongside a Company of about fifty.

'There,' I shouted back to Nhi, pointing. 'Go and get her back on a horse so she can get her captains into line.'

Nhi spurred her mount and Cong's guards parted to let her through.

'You should ride up the line,' said my mother, behind me on the elephant. 'There are whole regiments being wasted.'

I turned in the wide, perching seat and looked west. It was true. Two of the Generals from Cuu Chan were hanging back, and the Lien Lau division was badly placed.

'Cong, follow Lady Mother's orders,' I shouted, to my faithful General, who was still fending off a determined attack. She shouted back an assent, and I slid down to the floor and mounted the waiting horse that had been reserved for me. I knew when I began to ride about that I would draw the offensive – it was my head the Emperor wanted most of all – but behind the line I was still reasonably safe, especially as I galloped towards the Lien Lau division. I made it to the General, a man appointed by Ton Vien since the Lien Lau Lord claimed to be too old to fight, and he received me with wide, unblinking eyes, like a startled stripe rabbit.

'Half the division must fall back,' I told him, as my horse reared and twisted beneath me. 'March them in behind General Kim Cuc.'

'That leaves us exposed here,' he answered.

'Exposed to what? The fight is there.' I pointed to where Ma

Vien's troops were aiming their most fierce attack, and where I could now see, to my relief, that Chinh appeared to be mounted and in full command again. She was riding behind her troops now, forcing them forwards and directing some of the Chu Dien units towards my own Me Linh division for support. 'Take half the division, now!'

He nodded, still unblinking and shouted some commands at his various captains while I rode on to the Cuu Chan Generals and repeated my message. I succeeded in repositioning several of the divisions, so that our attack regained its focus, but I could see, when I got my horse through to Cong, that Ma Vien had done great damage to our army already. On the far edge of the battle ground, I could see Lac being tied up and dragged away alive. Why were they taking prisoners? Then I saw some of our soldiers in the distance drop their swords, and I understood Ma Vien's aim – to make the weak amongst us believe they could come through alive, if only they gave in now.

'Kim Cuc is down,' Cong shouted, over the furious noise of fighting.

'Can we get to her?'

'Khanh is there already.'

I wanted to fight very badly. My muscles hummed with the patterns of aggression that had been trained into every fibre. I forced my horse past Cong and galloped through, a group of guards swiftly following. We had to fight our way to them, parrying blows from isolated Han Cavalry and defending against more insidious attacks from the small units of Han infantry that instantly turned their attention to me, but we cut a path through to where Khanh had dragged the body of her sister over her own horse and was trying to lead the animal back out of the fray. I cleared space for her, chopping down the Han aggressors that, suddenly, were everywhere. I pulled my own horse sideways on, to shield her as she mounted up behind Kim Cuc's body and turned blackened eyes towards me. I made my decision as I stared into those dark pits.

'Run,' I said. 'Over the river. Tell everyone.'

Khanh nodded and kicked her horse into a gallop.

'Back! Back!' I shouted, and Nhi heard my order and brought her horse around. Cong began shouting the command to retreat also, and it raced like fire through the ranks. I was a long way from General Le Chan. I could not hope to reach her without being brought down – Ma Vien was closer now, a black blur just behind his own lines, pacing about on his horse and shouting commands in the Yellow River tongue. I was fairly sure those commands included capturing *Hai Ba Trung*. I turned to one of the guards.

'Get to General Le Chan and tell her to fall back,' I ordered, 'along with all the other Generals on the way.'

The battle had turned into chaos, and Han troops were now rounding up any isolated bands of Lac they could capture, pulling the exhausted, the injured and the cowardly back to holding areas for prisoners behind their own ranks. We were losing too many people. Our only hope now was to get across the river and regroup. With any luck, Ma Vien's army had taken damage too.

The elephants had been turned back towards the river, and they charged blindly, heedless of the poor people they stamped underfoot. My mother, now on horseback, was making away from the front line, surrounded by Cong's inner guards, though Cong herself was holding the line as best she could with about a quarter of the Me Linh division whilst the rest escaped. Nhi reached me and we rode together, Thao and Chinh close behind. Some Chu Dien units were still fighting, but most had either fled or perished. People swarmed ahead and I urged my horse to gallop faster, wanting to be in front, to curb the retreat once we had crossed the river. My tattered army needed to be gathered back into shape.

★★★★★

When Trac ordered me down from the elephant, I raced to

get to Chinh. I had a bad feel for this battle, even though I was raring to fight. The Han army had flowed out to meet us like spilled blood, their fastidious formation undulating gently and irrevocably across the plain. Ma Vien was almost graceful, his black silhouette resembling a peacock head, a tail of troops fanned out behind him. The arrows flew like feathers through a pale sky. It didn't surprise me when Dat fell. I knew we would count the dead among our own that day.

Still, I raced to retrieve Chinh. She was raging with grief-stained violence, and for a while, I joined her, knowing better than to try and restrain her from the kill. I used the excuse to kill many myself and for a while, I lost track of everything but the red mist out of which the Han soldiers kept appearing. When Chinh slowed up, I felt it, and we shifted back, other warriors crowding in to protect us while I got Chinh back on a horse. She was wincing and I knew her whole body must ache, but she didn't hesitate before taking command again.

Try as we might, we couldn't make progress after that. Kim Cuc and Khanh were surrounded and we couldn't get to them. When the Lien Lau force joined us, they helped to clear the cavalry that had engulfed the Thi Sisters' division, but it was too late. Perhaps some of the Han had mistaken those two sisters for *Hai Ba Trung* in the confusion of the fight, especially when both Trac and I had dismounted from the elephants. That might explain why they came under such persistent attack, or maybe it was just a result of their initial offensive being so successful, that they found themselves cut off. I was driving the Lien Lau units forward when I saw that Trac had gone to help Khanh and then the call to fall back rang out in a cacophony of voices, the first of which I heard clearly from my sister, as if it was personally meant for me.

All across the plain we sped, fending off the last few skirmishes and looking to see that we'd salvaged the important people. I had intended to ride east, to Le Chan, but Trac shouted at me that she had already dispatched a messenger. I could see Le Chan's division still fighting. It looked worse than I imagined the assault on the Chu Dien division had appeared and I knew why she did not retreat even though it must be obvious to her now, that we were running from the front line. She wanted to give us the best chance. She was holding their attention while we escaped, just as her family had distracted Captain Gang, long ago, when she had fled from Hai Phong. It wouldn't matter that Trac had sent a messenger. Le Chan would fight to the end. Another body to count, along with Kim Cuc and Nghiem Dat and hundreds of people from our home district of Me Linh who had come here to fight for us.

Ma Vien did not follow, not then, when he had thousands of prisoners on his hands and his own army to repair. We made it away across the water and into Chu Dien territory, from where we turned west, towards Me Linh.

★★★★★

At the foot of Mount Tan Vien, within the bright, curving arm of the Red River, lies a place that is the heart of the Lac nation; a place where Hung Kings lived, ruled and died; a place we were born to own. Me Linh wrapped our bruised army in soft wings while we healed.

'Cuts and scrapes,' I said to Hung, who watched my wounds being tended. Trac, too, had her share of injuries but neither of us had anything too deep, that a stitch or two would not take care of. Thao had done something to his back and he was having trouble bending down but I hoped that would recover with rest. Chinh, like us, had flesh wounds, but her real pain ran deeper. She didn't speak about Dat at all, and we'd left his body on the battlefield, which was an added hardship for her to bear, but she refused to be pitied or consoled.

We'd lost Khanh along the way – she'd split from us after we crossed the river and was probably deep in Chu Dien by now, following the kingfishers along the marshy tracts that led to the sea. Maybe she'd rejoin us after she'd dealt with Kim Cuc's remains, but I doubted it. I expected her to be resentful and to blame us, just as I expected soon to hear news that Le Chan was dead.

There were countless nights of waiting, thinking and worrying and each day we were faced with the state of our army, reduced to a tiny fraction of its original size. Only Trac's most loyal supporters had remained – the Me Linh division led by Cong, who had managed somehow to get away from Ma Vien, some of the the mountain lords – from Mount Tan Vien and Mount Tam Dao – and Chinh's division, from the districts west of Chu Dien along with the Tay Vu fighters. The few we had originally drawn from further south, the Cuu Chan people, had fled back there and we knew we could expect no more support from them.

'One more battle,' Mother encouraged us. 'All you have to do is take down Ma Vien. I'll go for him myself, girls, my time is nearly done anyway. You fight the battle, I'll take him down. Just clear a way for me.'

Trac used to grin at her, on those evenings; everyone felt hope when Lady Man Thien spoke. I began to believe that it was possible. Mother might be right – one lucky strike was all we needed and we'd send the biggest message back to the empire – Nam Viet won't be tamed. We were on the land of our spiritual ancestors. They wouldn't fail us. Mother talked about the Jade Tiger and I stroked the little, cold replica that was strung on my neck.

We had one day of fear, when our look-outs said a large formation of armed people were making their way towards Me Linh. We knew Ma Vien had started looking for us. Had he finally understood that we would be in Me Linh? He'd split his army to search, but we knew he was concentrating his efforts in the delta around Lien Lau and Chu Dien. He'd taken Lien Lau, without much effort because Ton Vien, I presumed, would be eager to welcome him with his practised blend of negotiation and diplomacy. But I expected that no one, unless the Han were willing to torture them, would explain to Ma Vien that Me Linh was the place they should look, the place we would undoubtedly be. He'd find out soon enough, I was sure, but until then, the surrendered Lac were at least keeping their mouths shut and feigning ignorance. The news of armed units heading our way made us think the time had come, but quickly it was established that these were not Han – they were not in the plated armour and their hair was in the Nam Viet style.

I'm not sure who was more surprised – Trac or I – when we discovered it was Khanh, returning to us with what was left of her Chu Dien force and a goodly amount of stragglers and defectors that she had persuaded into joining her. I rejoiced in the added numbers, of which we were sorely in need. Trac gave one of her rarest smiles, the kind that for so long had been completely absent, and welcomed her as a sister. Khanh re-entered Me Linh, the place of her previous detention, with a broken heart but the ghost of good humour in her eyes.

It was the last of the good news. After that, Ma Vien began travelling up the river and I knew the time had come. I'd been putting it off for as long as possible – I should really have done it as soon as we retreated from Tay Vu, but it was too hard. Now, I was out of time. Thao had rested his back and he was able to ride again. He knew what was coming.

'Now Hung, listen to me,' I said. 'The Han are coming and Mother must fight again, but this time you are going with Father, into the mountains. I want you to stay there until it is safe.'

'Will Diep come too?' He twisted his little hands around his folded up knees.

'Yes, son, Diep will come with you, and Auntie Linh and Uncle Hien too. You'll go to Uncle Nhat's home.'

'I don't know Uncle Nhat.'

'You've never met him, but he's a nice man and will be very

kind to you. He lives a long way away, up in the hills where the Han won't reach you.'

'You come too, Mother.'

'I'll try, but I'll be a very long time. Father will look after you. And Diep will too.'

Thao took over, distracting Hung before he could dissolve into countless questions, reminding Hung that they would have a lot of riding to do and new things to see. I sat back and listened and concentrated on the hard stone in my chest, the one I imagined had grown when Chien died. I imagined it swelling now, taking over all my heart until I became as hard and impenetrable as Hung Mountain itself. Later that day, before they rode away, I squeezed Hung to me until he winced, and pressed his soft cheek to my face. Thao and I bowed to each other, but didn't speak. Many other people were present, Hung needed constant reassurance and it was not possible for Thao to hold me. Our real goodbyes had already been given in the dark of night. Still, as he set off on horseback with Hung nestled in front of his bulky body, I wished I had said something – anything – to sustain him for when I was no longer there.

★★★★★

We waited for the Han in a clearing lined with rhododendron bushes. I was on horseback in the centre, at the front. Nhi was to my left, our mother to my right. The left wing of our army was headed by General Chinh, the right wing by General Cong. Khanh led the rear guard and the lesser Generals flanked us. The clearing was too awkward for Ma Vien to usher in his whole army and his formation would be forced into a tight column. It gave us a chance, a fighting chance. The weather was stark, as if Au Co had painted the sky with her white wing-tips and dripped harsh, chilled light on the grass and the trees. I summoned her, in my head. I called on the Hung Kings and on their father, Lac Long Quan. I called on the rebel King of Tay Vu and on the rebel fighter, Lu Chia, and on Thuc Pan and even on

Trieu Da. I called on my husband Sach and his sister, Kim Cuc and on all the Le family of Hai Phong.

Ma Vien came through the trees, pacing his horse and leading his divisions, spaced perhaps two hundred men wide. They assembled opposite and then he shouted. It was the first time I clearly heard his voice, which was measured and low-pitched.

'Surrender to the Emperor.'

It echoed from the mountain ridges, as if the earth had thrown his order back.

'Never,' I answered. My horse whinnied and snorted steam into the air.

He slid out his sword and levelled it at me. I drew my own and then both sides charged. Crossbows fired from both sides and the clash of steel, iron and flesh began. Nhi and I went in for the kill. Our mother fell in behind us, following the path we created. Ma Vien stayed frustratingly protected as we hacked and chopped. In the clearing, the noise was deafening. They would hear it back in Me Linh. I thought about the old men and women, about the people still wounded and suffering from the last battle, about the babies and children who waited with mothers or with older brothers and sisters for the battle to end, and their future to be determined. I swung my sword time and again, not counting the men who died, but knowing it was not enough. When they tried to encircle us, Nhi and I stayed close and they could not break through. We were making progress; maybe we could not kill them all, but we could do what our mother had instructed - clear a path to Ma Vien. We were close enough to make out his face, lined and serious, with a down-turned mouth and scrutinising eyes. He watched our progress towards him and I felt we were being studied. He was thinking about how he would report this to the Emperor, how he would describe the Trung sisters. I wanted to prevent his words ever reaching the Yellow River. I wanted the tale of this battle to be in our language and to tell of his death, and of the death of Han rule in the land of the Lac. No more missives to the Emperor, no more bowing to these invaders. I spurred on and we were almost there. We were losing many people, but it did not matter, if only we could bring him down and kill the idea of him. If we could do that, it would be worth all the sacrifice.

Then my horse took a blade in the gut and fell screaming to the floor. I hit my side as we went down and had no time to push myself clear. My leg was trapped between horse and ground. I pulled and heaved, and my horse, thrashing in pain, lifted his body enough that I slid free. Our foot soldiers scrambled to cover me from the Han and we were all caught in a mash of horses and swords. My leg was twisted from the horses weight, but not broken, and I did not feel the bruise to my side. I just went on fighting, while Nhi stayed on her horse, trying to get to Ma Vien. Han soldiers were pouring through our front line, driving with determined accuracy into our centre and splitting our formation apart. Through the mess of fighting, I saw a gap where Han soldiers were backing away. The awful howling coming from that direction made me wonder why no one was putting the sufferer out of her pain. Hers was one raised voice amongst many, but the tone was different, primal. My understanding dawned and I squashed it far down, away from conscious acknowledgement

To my left I saw our old neighbour Bao, of all people, grimly thrusting forward with an axe - the head was old, bronze and shaped like a foot, so that it could both chop and thrust. A savage weapon. He spared me the briefest of glances, his face spattered with bloody strings. Then other figures blocked my view of him and he was gone. Two Han were in my path and I caught a slice to my forearm just before I brought up my sword and deflected a second strike. I smashed the blade into plate armour, making one man stagger back, and the other I took down with a thrust under his cuirass, slanting the blade upwards into his abdomen.

I had to throw myself into a ground roll, to avoid a third man, and by then I knew I was being surrounded. Cong tried to get her horse through to me, but it was taking too long and now my side really was hurting and I realised I was limping. Blood was running from the slice to my arm, making my sword hand wet. I went to parry a blow, and my hilt slipped in my hand. The Han, sensing his luck, pushed back and then quickly thrust his sword into my stomach and withdrew it triumphantly.

He died before I felt the pain of the incision. A glittering blade broke through his own chest from behind and as the Han soldier fell forwards, he left a black shadow behind him. In the flickering before I lost consciousness, I saw her, dead-eyed and spattered in blood, killing everything around us before she charged her shoulder into my still-standing body and tipped me upside down, shaking my last fractured scenes of the battle into blackness.

24

It finally occurs to me to ask why she saved me. She could have gone on fighting and left me to die. Nhi looks at me appraisingly and thinks about her answer.

'I failed,' she says, at last. 'His guards were too strong and I couldn't push through. Mother flanked me and then she ordered me back. She told me to get you away. She told me to run, that we had done enough.' She pauses as she sees the effect of those words upon me. 'Why are you crying?'

I can feel the warm roll of tears travelling from the outer edge of my eyes into my hair. Dusk is falling, though it is in the early stages, and the sun is making a brief appearance below the cloud bank. It turns the horizon into ruffled currents of fire as the rest of the sky sparkles like fish-skin, pink and silver. In the rice paddies, the water is golden and the plants shimmer, copper and green. This moment, this peaceful end, is our mother's last embrace.

'You didn't fail,' I say. 'You were right about what matters. You were right to bring me here. It would have done our people no good to see us die on that field.'

I pull myself up to a sitting position and the pain shoots through me, sharp and bracing. I bite into my lip and moan and Nhi grips my arm. My vision is failing again, blackness pricked with stars. I close my eyes and breathe until the world around me steadies. The low thrum of horse hooves beat in the distance.

Chinh comes to my other side and they lift me up. It is no good. My legs buckle and I dangle helplessly between them as they grapple to recover me. Nhi grasps me under the knees and hoists me, her other arm around my back, holding me like a baby. Chinh walks with us to the waterline. I am in danger of passing out again so I force myself to focus on the beating of the hooves, closer now. I will not let my little sister do this alone, not after all that she has sacrificed for me.

General Ma Vien rides at the head of his Company. He slows to a canter, then a trot as he sees us on the bank. He might be smiling, I am not sure. He throws himself from his horse with the nonchalance of a man half his age and walks a few steps towards us.

'It's over,' he says. 'You are my prisoners and Giao Chi will return to the empire. You must face the Emperor.'

'This land is called Van Lang,' I say. 'It was named for the ancient water bird spirit that protected the Hung Kings. It will never belong to the empire.'

He tips his head on one side. General Ma Vien is a thinker. Is he compassionate, like they say Tich Quang was? I hope so.

'I saw a sparrow-hawk at Lang Bac,' he answers, slowly, as if he is reconsidering a previous analysis. 'It flew defiantly through the rain. I saw its wings bow under the effort and I admired and pitied the creature. Then the heavy downpour pressed it into the rushing river where it drowned.' He motions a Colonel to his side. The man comes slowly, but he is coiled, ready to run at us.

'You cannot fight the spirits of this land,' I reply. 'They will consume you. The sparrow-hawk shows your own fate, General, not ours, as you knew when you saw it. From the heavens, I will pour the rains which will drown you.'

His smile is gone.

'Now.' I whisper.

Nhi leaps, clutching me tightly, struggling under my weight. We splash down into the water still holding each other. Chinh jumps from the bank, eyes closed, and our last few remaining guards draw their swords to try to prevent the Han diving in after us.

★★★★★

Trac talks tough, but she is shaking. She couldn't have done this alone and I'm glad I stayed with her. Ma Vien knows that she is dying, but he wants our heads for his emperor, not just our deaths. He is edging close, with his eager Colonel. When she

333

tells me to jump, it's not a moment too soon.

There's a rush of air and then the shocking cold of the water as I take two strides and throw us out, into mid-air and hard into the river. We submerge for a moment, then resurface, gasping for breath. We're already being swept away from the fracas on the river bank. There's no sign of Chinh. She's gone under already, no life left to pull her back above water. Trac would be drowned on the bottom now, if not for me. I'm surprised I have this strength left in me. I have my own wounds, mostly superficial, but leaking life all the same, and I'm exhausted. Darkness is falling and horses hooves follow us along the bank, stirring some ancient, buried memory. I begin to laugh, choking as I swallow water.

'Why are you laughing?' Trac gasps.

'My nightmare. You know the one when I was young, the one that worried Father so much? I dreamed *this*.' It's difficult to talk. The river tries to fill my mouth, my lungs are weakening and I know we can't stay up for much longer. My body is freezing cold and tired, but I'm elated. Trac just looks at me, head lolling from the effort of keeping afloat. 'I'm not afraid,' I tell her, 'it means we got it right. We followed the Way.'

She nods, her eyes closing. I clutch her tighter to me. My skin is going numb, my heart is slowing, but there's no pain now. While my sister and I are together, we are invincible.

AFTER THE DEATH OF THE TRUNG SISTERS, MA VIEN IMPOSED HAN RULE THROUGHOUT NORTHERN VIETNAM. A THOUSAND YEARS LATER, AFTER COUNTLESS INSURRECTIONS, MIDDLE KINGDOM DOMINION FINALLY CAME TO AN END. IN THE 11TH CENTURY, TRAC AND NHI WERE ISSUED WITH POSTHUMOUS IMPERIAL APPOINTMENTS BY THE VIETNAMESE KING AND WERE WORSHIPPED AS RAIN MAIDENS. MODERN VIETNAM HONOURS THE TRUNG SISTERS ANNUALLY, ON THE 6TH DAY OF THE SECOND LUNAR MONTH, AT THE HAI BA TRUNG TEMPLE IN HANOI.

POSTSCRIPT

The Trung Sisters, celebrated across Vietnam as 'Hai Ba Trung,' revolted against the Chinese when the occupying force began to increase taxes and suppress native customs in the early part of the first century CE. Vietnamese accounts refer to the execution of Thi Sach and the punishment of his wife, Trung Trac. Then, Chinese and Vietnamese accounts concur that the Trung Sisters forced the Han occupation out of northern Vietnam, retook sixty-five cities and ruled between 39 and 42CE. The legend of Le Chan has been less easy to uncover but some sources describe her as resisting To Dinh's attempt to marry her, for which her family were executed (I adapted this, in my story). She is described as giving her allegiance to the Trung Sisters and dying in battle or drowning herself afterwards. Phung Thi Chinh appears in many modern accounts as a General in the Trung army who birthed her baby on the battlefield and carried on fighting, newborn strapped to her chest. One copywriter I stumbled across found this amusing. I found it beyond horrific, and whether or not the tale has any truth to it is really less important than the message it sends about the collective Vietnamese memory of the Trung revolt. There exists enormous pride in the women warriors of the time who faced such a horrendously bleak fate.

The Trung Sisters' deaths are remembered very differently in Chinese and Vietnamese texts. Whilst the Chinese account describes Trac and Nhi as having been executed and their heads delivered to the Emperor, the Vietnamese accounts suggest they drowned themselves along with Chinh and her baby, or floated up to the heavens. General Ma Vien is characterised in Chinese texts as of relatively noble attitude – nothing like the greedy and callous representation that surrounds Governor To Dinh whose mismanagement and loss of much of the Giao Chi Circuit must have been an irritating embarrassment to the Han. Ma Vien's fleet difficulties are recorded in the historical texts, along with the reports of his army building a road to secure access into northern Vietnam. It is true that he was an older man, with a distinguished career behind him, and sources suggest that although he executed a large number of Trung followers, and took many more prisoner, he re-established Han rule across northern Vietnam by a war as much of hearts and minds as of the battlefield. Some sources say he simplified Han laws in Giao Chi territory, and that he won the people over by focusing on irrigation and flood defence work – a big issue of the time for the Red River delta. One very encouraging piece of evidence is the finding that bronze drums were still being made in the Giao Chi region well into the post-Trung, Han period of occupation. This suggests that local culture was not entirely suppressed under Chinese influence.

The lack of a writing tradition in Vietnam, both in the period of the Trung Sisters and for many centuries afterwards, severely impacts our understanding of the years 39-43CE. The earliest Vietnamese written account of Trac and Nhi appears in the Dai Viet su ky toan thu (Complete book of the historical records of Great Viet, 1479), a work drawing on some previous Vietnamese sources no longer in existence. This fifteenth century version of the story was undoubtedly influenced by political interests of the time, and such a large chronological gap between the events and the written record means we must acknowledge the importance of the oral tradition in disseminating and undoubtedly distorting the events. Chinese history records the women from a much earlier date and gives us wonderful detail, but as with Tacitus' account of Cartimandua (which is the primary source for my previous novel), this is a historical account written by the victors. My version incorporates aspects from many sources, along with aspects of clear invention. Nhi's relationships, her infant son and her friend Bao are all fictitious, along with Trac's miscarriages. The links between the Trungs and the Le family of Hai Phong are entirely imagined, as was the drum dispute. I invented a

Governor – Vo Xuan – for reasons of plot, theme and practicality. I wanted to separate the golden days (though I am sure they were not so rosy for the general populace) of Tich Quang from the carnage that occurred under To Dinh, and in any case, I encountered a gap between these two governors and was never able to establish for certain who held the post in the period (roughly) 25-36CE. Some websites and texts list Nham Dien as the intervening Governor, but this man was based in Cuu Chan in the 20's, not in Giao Chi (although he left a detailed account of his fervent attempts to change various local customs in that region, and he makes a brief appearance in my story). I had already created Xuan, and he neatly fitted as a caretaker governor, ruling as a kind of deputy for Tich Quang.

The Jade Tiger theme is my invention, but based on a folk tale which describes the sisters as killing a troublesome tiger to win support for their cause. The tale says they wrote a call to arms on the skin, which I re-imagined slightly differently, since they had no written language with which to do this. Trac, as you know, wears the skin instead.

For readers who wish to learn more, I strongly recommend Keith Weller Taylor's superb book, *The Birth of Vietnam* (1983) which provides a comprehensive and very readable account. Also, *Vietnam: A Natural History*, by Sterling, Harley and Minh (2006) provides a beautiful exploration of the flora and fauna of the country, along with an examination of the geological and archaeological history of the region. For a political and socio-economic understanding of the setting, I gained much useful information from *The Cambridge History of Southeast Asia, Volume One* (1992), edited by Nicholas Tarling.

ANCIENT LAC HISTORY

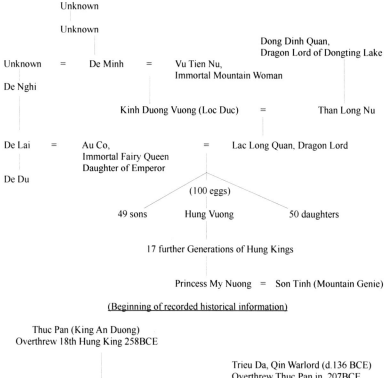

Than Nong, God of Agriculture and August Ruler of Middle Kingdom

Unknown

Unknown

Dong Dinh Quan,
Dragon Lord of Dongting Lake

Unknown = De Minh = Vu Tien Nu,
Immortal Mountain Woman

De Nghi

Kinh Duong Vuong (Loc Duc) = Than Long Nu

De Lai = Au Co,   = Lac Long Quan, Dragon Lord
Immortal Fairy Queen
Daughter of Emperor

De Du

(100 eggs)

49 sons   Hung Vuong   50 daughters

17 further Generations of Hung Kings

Princess My Nuong = Son Tinh (Mountain Genie)

(Beginning of recorded historical information)

Thuc Pan (King An Duong)
Overthrew 18th Hung King 258BCE

Trieu Da, Qin Warlord (d.136 BCE)
Overthrew Thuc Pan in 207BCE

My Chau (d.207BCE) = Trong Thuy (d. 207BCE)

Trieu Van (d.124BCE)

Trieu Anh Te (d.113BCE = Ku Thi (Han - became Queen Regent)

Trieu Hung (child)

(Rebellion, led by Lu Chia against increasing Han power via Regent Ku, was crushed by Lu Po-te
in the name of Emperor Wu Ti in 111BCE)

339

LIST OF CHARACTERS

Characters marked with (★★) are taken from historical sources and/or Vietnamese folk legend.

Trung Trac★★:	Queen
Trung Nhi★★:	Commander
Lady Man Thien★★:	Mother of Trung Sisters and Prefect of Me Linh
General Lac Lanh★★:	Father of Trung Sisters
Bao:	Friend and neighbour
Mrs Chau:	Mother of Bao and prominent trader
General Ma Vien★★:	Han General sent by Emperor in 40CE
Uncle Man Hien:	Brother of Lady Man Thien
Auntie Linh:	Wife of Hien
Sang:	Eldest son of Hien and Linh
Governor Tich Quang★★:	Han Governor of Giao Chi Commandery 1-25CE
Governor Vo Xuan:	Han Governor of Giao Chi Commandery 25CE-36CE
Governor To Dinh★★:	Han Governor of Giao Chi Commandery 36CE-39CE
Administrator Nham Dien★★:	Han Governor of Cuu Chan Commandery during 20s CE
Nguyen Tuan:	Tailor in Lien Lau
Dang Chi:	Tailor in Lien Lau (wife of Nguyen Tuan)
Auntie Pho An:	Cousin of Lady Man Thien; lives in Lien Lau
Giang:	Son of Pho An
Thi Hoc★★:	Prefect of Chu Dien
Thi Sach★★:	Son of Hoc, husband of Trung Trac
Thi Kim Khanh:	Middle daughter of Thi Hoc
Thi Kim Cuc:	Youngest daughter of Thi Hoc
Auntie Ly Nhu:	Maternal aunt of Sach, Khanh and Kim Cuc

Trang Hoa:	Prefect of Khuc Duong
Mai Nhat:	Eldest son of Trang Hoa
Mai Thao:	Youngest son of Trang Hoa
Ton Vien:	Prefect of Lien Lau
Diep:	Servant of Trung family
Tran Thi Chau★★:	Prefect of Hai Phong
Le Dao★★:	Husband of Tran Thi Chau
Le Chan★★:	Eldest daughter of Chau and Dao
Le Chien:	Youngest son of Chau and Dao
Phung Thi Chinh★★:	General of Trung Army
Nghiem Dat:	Husband of Phung Thi Chinh
Cong:	General of Trung Army
Hung:	Son of Thao
Captain Gang:	Han Captain (later to become Corporal)
Tuyen:	Victim of tiger attack
Liu★★:	The name of the leading family of the Han
Emperor Guangwu★★:	Middle Kingdom Emperor (Founder of the Eastern Han Dynasty, from 25CE)
Emperor Wang Mang★★:	Midle Kingdom leader during the Han interregnum (9-23CE)

(Legendary characters prior to Trung period are shown in royal descent tree)

LIST OF PLACENAMES

Me Linh:	District within Giao Chi Commandery - seat of ancient Vietnamese royalty and home of Trungs
Cam Khe:	Natal village of Trung Sisters, within Me Linh district
Chu Dien:	District within Giao Chi Commandery
Lien Lau:	Capital district of Giao Chi Commandery
Giao Chi:	Commandery roughly equivalent to modern-day upper northern Vietnam
Giao Chi:	Circuit of Han rule, covering modern parts of south China and north/central Vietnam

341

Cuu Chan:	Commandery roughly equivalent to modern-day lower northern Vietnam
Nhat Nam:	Commandery roughly equivalent to modern-day central Vietnam
Tay Vu:	District in centre of Giao Chi Commandery providing northbound access towards Middle Kingdom
Co Loa:	Ancient citadel in Tay Vu district
Nam Viet:	Ancient territory of Trieu Da (207-111BCE) – modern day northern Vietnam and southern China
Au Lac:	Ancient territory of Thuc Pan (257-207BCE) – modern day northern Vietnam and southern China
Van Lang:	Ancient territory of the Hung Kings (2524-258BCE) - modern day northern Vietnam and southern China
Xich Quy:	Ancient territory of Hong Bang Dynasty (2879-2524BCE) - modern day northern Vietnam and southern China
Fan Xi Pan:	Largest mountain in modern-day north-west Vietnam
Hai Phong:	(meaning Defensive Coastal Area) on east coast of Giao Chi Commandery
Cat Ba:	Island in the gulf, near Hai Phong
An Dinh:	District within Giao Chi Commandery
Cau Lau:	District within Giao Chi Commandery
Bac Dai:	District within Giao Chi Commandery
Ke Tu:	District within Giao Chi Commandery
Khuc Duong:	District within Giao Chi Commandery
Nam Hai:	Commandery in Giao Chi Circuit (modern central Guangdong)
Hop Pho:	Commandery in Giao Chi Circuit (modern south coastal Guangxi)

Thuong Ngo: Commandery in Giao Chi Circuit
(modern eastern Guangxi)

Chau Nhai: Commandery in Giao Chi Circuit
(modern Hainan Island)

Ha Long Bay: Bay of islands and caves, on eastern coast of
Giao Chi, north of Hai Phong

East Sea: Modern-day Gulf of Tonkin

Hai Van Pass: (meaning Pass of the Mountain Clouds)
near modern-day Hue

Lang Bac: High ground to the north-east of Tay Vu
overlooking (in the Trung era) a lake

Hoang Lien Son: Mountain range in modern-day northern Vietnam
(includes Fan Xi Pan)

Truong Son: Mountain range separating modern-day Vietnam
from modern-day Laos

Cham territory: Modern-day central Vietnam, below the
Hai Van Pass

Phu Nam: Modern-day southern Vietnam – the Mekong delta

Khmer territory: Modern-day Cambodia

Tai territory: Modern-day Laos/Thailand

Nine Dragon River: Mekong River

Ba Shu: Sichuan province in modern-day southern China

Lightning Source UK Ltd.
Milton Keynes UK
UKOW04f2140031214

242626UK00004B/150/P